Daredevil Hearts

*Lost Paradise:
Book Two*

Daredevil Hearts
Lost Paradise:
Book Two

Francine Quesnel

YellowRoseBooks
a Division of
RENAISSANCE ALLIANCE PUBLISHING, INC.
Nederland, Texas

Copyright © 2002 by Francine Quesnel

All rights reserved. No part of this publication may be reproduced, transmitted in any form or by any means, electronic or mechanical, including photocopy, recording, or any information storage and retrieval system, without permission in writing from the publisher. The characters herein are fictional and any resemblance to a real person, living or dead, is purely coincidental.

ISBN 1-930928-28-9

First Printing 2002

9 8 7 6 5 4 3 2 1

Cover art by Carla van Westen
Cover design by Mary D. Brooks

Published by:

Renaissance Alliance Publishing, Inc.
PMB 238, 8691 9th Avenue
Port Arthur, TX 77642

Find us on the World Wide Web at
http://www..rapbooks.biz

Printed in the United States of America

Acknowledgments:

One of the best things about having a second novel published is that you get a second chance to thank all the people you forgot to thank in the first book.

A big thank you goes to Casey for editing not only *Daredevil Hearts* but also *Lost Paradise.* You've done a fantastic job and I'll be forever grateful.

To Cathy, RAP's CEO, for signing my works. Without you and your fantastic team, my dream of seeing my stories printed would never have happened. Thank you so much.

To Trish, Sharon, Dawn, Kodie, Lyn and everybody who took the time to write me and let me know how much they love Kris and Nicole. I really appreciate the positive criticism you've given me.

And finally to Cindy, my best friend. Without you, this story, and my life, wouldn't be as exiting since a lot of the devious ideas came from you! You're the best.

— Fran, a.k.a. WolfDragon

Dedication

Since the first days of filmmaking, all kinds of memorable characters graced the silver screen, from leading men and women, to amazing action heroes. They are memorable because a lot of these characters are exciting to watch, thanks to the unsung movie heroes, the stunt performers. Without these men and women, action films wouldn't be as entertaining as they are. Their names are not widely known outside the business, their faces rarely shown on screen and their work largely unacknowledged through the media.

I dedicate this book to these talented athletes, the stunt performers, who have managed to amaze and entertain us with their daring and imaginative performances.

I hope the following story will help you to better understand the risks these performers take to keep us riveted to our seats.

Chapter 1

It was a beautiful day in the small Austrian village. Only a handful of people were walking along the quiet country roads enjoying the fresh air as they did their early morning shopping on this quaint spring day. It was your typical, ordinary "nothing ever happens around here" place. The only sounds heard were of birds singing, people talking, children laughing, dogs barking, gun shots ringing through the air...gun shots?

People stopped their daily activities and looked in surprise in the direction of the village bank. Men and women were running everywhere, screaming. Two men with nylons over their heads ran out of the building and towards a white sedan. They were halfway into the car when the driver saw the security guard coming out of the bank with his gun ready to shoot. The driver shot him and the car left with its tires screeching. The guard crumpled down on the sidewalk as another car, a black Porsche, raced after the sedan at breakneck speed through the village.

At the height of the chase, a small boy decided to cross the street to get a better view of what was going on. The driver of the Porsche, trying to avoid the boy, spun the car to the right and rolled it three times before finally crashing through the large picture window of the general store and ending upside down. When the flying glass, wood, dirt and broken articles had settled down, the people gathered around what was left of the once beautiful sports car.

"CUT! Perfect! Wonderful! That's a print. Everybody okay?" asked the movie director. Ken Davidson got a few nods from the extra stuntmen around the car who acted as villagers. One of those stuntmen was Franz Von Deering, the stunt coordinator for the movie project. He helped the driver out of the wreck and checked to see if everything was all right. A nod was given as the helmet came off, letting long, black hair fall on broad shoulders.

Kristina Von Deering smiled at her older brother then looked at the director. "You liked?" she asked simply. Ken was a hard man to please. He had often made stuntmen angry by having them repeat the performance over and over when, according to the crew, everything had been exactly as it should have been. Kris always made sure that she and the director understood what was wanted and that it was delivered only once, unless she felt the stunt hadn't gone right. The stuntwoman was one of the rare people that the gray haired American never argued with. Having worked with her on many previous projects and trusting her good judgement, he pretty much left her to her business.

"Perfect. That was a good show. Always available if we need extra shots?" Ken asked from his perch beside the camera. "We're moving the crew to the Glungezer ski resort. The second team is already set up. I'd like it if you'd take a look at the daily and tell me what you think about it. I still wish you'd do it yourself."

"There are many good stuntmen around, Ken," Kris replied. "Give them a break, will you? Even though I created that accident stunt, Franz knows as much about it as I do." She finished taking her driver's jumpsuit off and packed her duffle bag along with her gear.

As Kris walked to her expensive, sporty red Lamborghini Diablo, people passing by couldn't help but notice this wealthy, young Austrian stuntwoman. Stunning was more the word. Six foot tall, dark hair and incredible blue eyes that could shock a person to speechlessness. Though not big on conversations, this remarkable young woman's actions spoke volumes. And action certainly was her middle name. Being a stuntwoman wasn't all rest and relaxation.

The grueling hours of preparation, planning and a very strict regimen of physical activities made for a very impressive lean and muscled body. She put on her leather jacket, threw her duffle bag inside her car and then nestled herself comfortably behind the steering wheel.

"Kris! Hang on a minute," came her brother's voice. "There's a message for you from Michael Norman. He's at the Wildkatze with some friends of his. He wants to see you now."

An eyebrow lifted at the apparent "order" her friend had relayed through her brother. Michael was a first class promoter, also a first class pain in the butt sometimes. He was the one that was responsible for the American movie contracts, finding the Von Deering family more work than they could handle, but they always managed to perform their best. Michael, of course, built himself a very good name in the process.

"Lucky for him I was headed there anyway," she said smugly. Everyone knew no one told Kris what to do, her friend just loved to live dangerously. She waved at her brother and left him standing in the dust.

A short time later, Kris pulled up at the Wildkatze's parking lot and chose a spot near the door. As she got out and slid the door shut, she heard footsteps behind her and turned to see an elderly man examining her from head to toe.

"Guten Abend, Herr Füller. Something wrong?" she asked, suspiciously looking down at black boots, black jeans, white, opened collared shirt and leather jacket. Everything seemed to fit perfectly over her well-defined body, nothing seemed out of place.

He smiled. "Something wrong? Oh, no, no! Can't an old man just enjoy the view?"

"Always the charmer, aren't you?" She smiled at the bar's regular customer and walked to the door.

Upon entering the establishment, Kris was greeted by warm welcomes and appreciative whistles from the racecar drivers, motorcyclists and stunt people who made up most of the bar's clientele. None, however, were foolish enough to touch the respected stuntwoman and risk broken bones. The raven-haired beauty spotted a vacant stool by the bar and headed towards it, where the smiling bartender was polishing a glass.

"Hey Ben, how are things?"

Benny just grinned at her and served her the usual, a Guinness. "Well, no fights since you last came in here," he said with a mischievous grin.

"Whoa, that wasn't my fault," Kris protested as she winked at the German bartender. "Where's Michael?" Ben pointed his thumb over his shoulder, indicating the back of the bar. "Thanks." She grabbed her beer, and made her way through the crowd, stopping periodically for a fan or friend.

Several tables away, Michael Norman, a muscular man in his forties and as tall as Kris, stood up from his table and waved at her. A few people were already sitting with him.

"Hello, Kris. I'm sure you remember Lars Gunnarsson?" Michael asked as he directed her attention to the man who sat next to him.

"Sweden's most famous stuntman." She grinned. "Of course, nice to see you again, Lars." Everyone knew having Kris and Lars in the same place could lead to a very explosive situation. After a drink or two, he loved to see how far he could tease Kris before she would throw him clear across the room. They had the most exciting brawls together. Having lived through the dark woman's wrath and remained in one piece to talk about it was one of the reasons why he was so "famous." Despite their heated exchanges, Kris considered him a good stuntman and friend.

"How's the leg?" she asked innocently as she took a sip from her beer.

"Better than it was three years ago, thanks to you." He grinned at her with dancing blue eyes. Lars was a handsome man, looking very much like a typical Swede with blond hair and blue eyes. His beard and mustache gave him the look of a modern-day Viking. He pointed towards Kris with his bearded chin. "She's the one who broke my bones in the small between friends reunion." He chuckled. "Kris, there's someone I'd like you to meet. My wife, Frida." The woman beside him brought her chair closer to the table.

"Your wife? Well, you finally put that hangman's noose

around your neck, didn't you, Lars?" Kris shook the man's large hand with vigor then turned her attention to the woman. "Frida, I was expecting more from you than this guy." She welcomed her friend with a clap on the back.

"He was the best available, my friend. I couldn't do better," Frida replied as she winked at her husband who laughed.

Kris had met the Swedish woman four years previously at a party, celebrating the end of the filming of an American action film. Frida was what most people thought of as a groupie. They usually walked around movie sets, hoping to meet movie stars and the like. But what made this woman stand out apart from the rest was that she didn't care much for the actors. Her interest was in the technique behind the making of movies, especially the special effects.

At the American party, Frida had worked her way into an argument between Kris and another technician, debating the value of one technique over the other. She had brought up interesting questions and theories to the conversation. She turned out to be an unemployed special effects technician, hoping to grab someone's attention and land a job with a company, any company.

Kris had laughed herself silly after figuring out the woman's game. She had watched Frida closely, and listened to what the Swede had to say. She hadn't had much work experience, but her ideas were good and solid and the projects she had worked on made up for her lack of experience.

After making a few inquiries, Kris had been willing to give Frida a chance to prove herself by offering her some work on a project the Von Deerings were working on. Home sick, Frida left three years later to return to Stockholm.

"What brings you to Austria?" Kris asked her friend.

"Well, since you never call or come our way, we decided to come and see you." Frida smiled with a wink. "Seriously, there's a documentary being produced about stunt performers. They started filming some time ago, stopping in Sweden to catch the guys in action. We decided this documentary wouldn't be complete without talking to the famous Von Deerings. So, here we are."

"Oh, great," Kris grumbled. "Will this one make us look like half witted idiots too?"

Lars laughed. "I must agree with you on this one, Kris. The production StarDash did on that last documentary wasn't that serious."

"They made us look like thrill seekers."

"Aren't we?"

"No." Kris shook her head. "You know better, Lars. Most of us never take unnecessary risks. We're not daredevils." She turned her attention back to Frida. "Who's working on this latest documentary?" she asked as she took another sip of her beer.

"I am," a voice sounded from an approaching figure.

Kris looked up to see a petite woman standing across the table in front of her. Even though she had delicate features, she was far from fragile. Her form fitted jeans showed a slim waist and firm thighs while her red polo shirt gave a clear view to her toned arms. The woman had long blonde hair that brushed against her shoulders but the green eyes studying Kris held a hint of apprehension, not sure of the welcome she would get.

"Kris, meet the person who's filming the documentary," Frida said with a grin. "Nicole McGrail. I think you've met before?"

"Hello, Kristina. It's nice to see you again," the blonde said as she held her hand out.

The stuntwoman was speechless, something people didn't see often. She automatically reached out to shake the offered hand and blinked a few times, wondering if she was dreaming. She then grabbed her beer mug and took a long swallow, wanting to give herself time to regain her composure. So many memories came crashing back to her, some of them painful.

"It's been a long time," Nicole said nervously.

Kris lifted her blue eyes and stared at the woman as she sat down, willing the walls she had built so long ago to surround her protectively. "Twelve years, but who's counting?" Kris replied dryly. *She's almost the same. But she looks much more mature, more confident.* Her heart clenched as she remembered what she had lost. "What do you want from me?"

Nicole softly cleared her throat and gave Frida a brief

glance. The Swede nodded encouragingly. "Um, I'm...hoping to be able to interview and film your family. Do you think it would be possible?" She could feel Kris' icy control as her ex-lover tried her best to look bored. She had hoped for a warmer welcome than this but then again, it was too much to ask for, especially after what happened between them a dozen years ago.

"I can introduce you to Franz. He's the one in charge of public relations." Kris fidgeted with her beer mug as questions raced through her mind. *Why is Nicole here? There were so many stunt people she could interview, why couldn't she choose somebody else than the Von Deerings?*

"I would also like the chance to talk to you," Nicole added uneasily as if reading Kris' thoughts.

"If you want," she said matter-of-factly. "Just tell me when." She didn't like this turn of event. Nothing good would come out of it. Nicole was going to say something, but was cut off by an impatient Michael.

"Can we get down to some business here?" Michael finally spurted out. Kris settled an icy glare on him, making it known that now was not the time. He sheepishly lowered his eyes and mumbled, "or it can wait."

"I knew there was a catch to this meeting," Kris grumbled. "Oh, what is it, Michael? Just spit it out."

Nicole wondered if the biting remark was due to her presence or if it was just because of the insistent promoter.

"As you know, the World Stunt Championship will be held in Stockholm, Sweden this year. I want you there with...wi—" Michael hesitated, at the impatient glare Kris gave him.

"Excuse me? You...*want*...me...there?" she asked dangerously. The look on the promoter's face was priceless.

"Um, I...I know that you don't have any contracts for that time period and...and I would very much appreciate it if...ah, if you could show up," Michael quickly rephrased. "Everybody's asking if you'll be there. I know it's your brothers who'll be performing but think about the publicity your presence will bring. The Swedes are going to be there. So are the Americans, the French, English, everybody." Michael rattled his speech as fast as he could.

"You're worse than an agent, you know that, Michael?" Kris sighed as she brushed her fingers through her raven hair. She looked at Lars. "Are you with the Swedish team?" He nodded with a huge grin on his face. "Well then, I guess I'll have to be there and make sure that the world title doesn't fall in your hands," she said, her sense of humor returning somewhat.

"And why not?" Lars asked. "It's about time someone other than a German gets the title."

"Who's German? Last year it wasn't a German. It was my brother-in-law. He's Austrian, like me." Kris flared as she got up from her chair.

"German, Austrian, same thing," Lars taunted, knowing full well Kris' temper was rising.

"That's enough, Lars." Frida grabbed her husband's hand. She knew that Kris was getting angry and wanted to avoid another major brawl. She was used to her friend's temper and she just didn't like it when Lars was on the receiving end of it.

"Are you going to be there, yes or no?" Michael wanted to know so he could get out of this place. The tall stuntwoman just stared at Lars; her blue eyes almost the color of ice from the anger.

"I'll be there," she growled as Michael stood up and with a nervous smile, left the group.

"Aw, come on, Kris. You can't be that angry because of what I said, can you?"

"You know how I hate being called a German," she snapped and jerked her hand when she felt a soft touch on it. Kris turned in a cold stare at whom that hand belonged to and came face to face with Nicole, who shyly smiled at her, trying to calm her down. And it worked. As soon as their hands touched for a second time, Kris' heart just stopped beating and her breath caught in her chest. Memories of similar gestures and long buried feelings rushed to the surface. The blonde gently gave the bigger hand a squeeze before letting it go.

Kris sat down, calmer but much more confused. She hadn't expected to react this way to Nicole. Anger and frustration were more the emotions she thought she would feel towards this woman, especially after what Nicole had done. But now, she just didn't know what to think.

"Kristina, phone call," the bartender called out, interrupting her thoughts.

"Be right there," she called back. "If you'll excuse me," she said to those seated at her table and finished the last of her beer then headed to the phone. Sighs of relief echoed around the table as the obvious tension eased a bit.

"Ladies, I'll be right back." Lars chuckled as he got to his feet and left to meet a friend of his.

Frida gave him an exasperated sigh before he left. "That wasn't funny, Lars," she called over her shoulder then looked at the silent blonde. "You have a magic touch on her, Nick."

Nicole was lost in her thoughts. She had made a hard decision so many years ago and now she wondered how wise that decision was. She had been madly in love with Kristina, but the pictures her father had shown her had proved that her choice of lover would only bring her heartache.

She still remembered the look on Kris' face when she had broken the news to her. Kris had demanded an explanation, wanting to know why she was doing this. Nicole hadn't been able to answer her and had just left the house they had been sharing, crying and angry. The tall stuntwoman had then left Montreal to go back home to Austria.

Nicole finally settled and married her childhood friend, Neilson, who had become a well-known stuntman himself. Neil was a wonderful man who had cared a great deal for Nicole, as she did for him, but there were no true feelings of love. His love was for his work and hers was for another.

Neither Kris nor Nicole believed that they would ever see the other again, but they briefly did, at Neilson's funeral. Kris had come back to Canada with her brother, Franz, representing the Von Deering family, wanting to show their respect for a fallen comrade. But the women never had the chance to talk as Kris had left soon after the service.

Nicole never did find another lover. The problem was that she never stopped loving Kris, even with all that had happened.

"Nick?" Frida asked, causing Nicole to come out of her reverie with a start.

"I'm sorry, what did you say?"

"I said, maybe you could spend some time with her. I know the two of you used to be close. I'm sure you could use the time to clear a few things." Frida smiled at her. They had met in Sweden a few weeks before and had quickly become friends.

"After the reaction Kris just had? I'm sure she's got other things to do than hang around an ex-lover." Nicole's shoulders slumped slightly. "What about her girlfriend, Natasha Romanoff?"

"Oh, that was over a long time ago. And what do you mean reaction? She was angry. She would've done that no matter who touched her. Don't you realize that she never got over you?" Frida said softly as Nicole slowly cast her eyes down, trying to avoid looking at her friend. "The last time I was at her house, Kris had this long, colorful braid she kept fingering and told me about the day you both had it done. She laughed when she explained the joke you pulled on her with the fluorescent colors you had chosen without her knowing. She was laughing but I could see tears in her eyes as she remembered. She still cares for you." Frida stopped when Nicole glanced up at approaching figures.

"What's up?" Lars asked.

Kris frowned slightly. "I have to go. Franz just called from the Glungezer Resort. The skiing stunt they were doing went wrong."

"Did anybody get injured?" Frida asked, concerned.

The tall woman nodded. "The skier is in the hospital. The planned accident happened too fast. She went out of camera range and into the trees." Kris took her car keys out of her pocket and fingered them absentmindedly. "I'm the only stuntwoman who knows the stunt enough to perform in such short notice."

"Will you be gone for long?" Nicole asked as she got up from her chair.

"Not if everything goes well," Kris replied, forgetting for a moment her anger and surprise at seeing her ex-lover again. "The crew is repairing the damage done to the slope, so everything should be ready for me when I arrive. You guys want to come?"

"We'll be there." Frida nodded. "But we have to stop by the

hotel. We'll meet you at the resort."

"No problem."

"Ah, would it be possible for you to give Nicole a lift?" the Swede asked Kris.

"Why do we have to—" Lars started but stopped when his wife elbowed him in the ribs.

The gesture wasn't lost on Kris but she didn't say anything.

"That is, if you want to go, Nicole," Frida continued.

"Yes, I'd like to come, too," the blonde said softly and looked at Kris, trying to see any signs of hostility. A neutral expression was all she got.

"Alright, but I have to stop by the house first to get my other gear." Kris watched as the Swedish couple left the bar and then held Nicole back for a moment, giving them some kind of privacy. "Listen, you want to talk? That's fine with me because there are a few things I'd like to say too."

"I thought that maybe after such a long time we could talk more calmly. I'd like to know what happened," Nicole said gently.

Kris wanted so much to stay upset with her, but she was finding it hard to do so. She remembered the happy times they had shared together and wanted so much to find out why Nicole had left her. Maybe she would finally be able to put that part of her life away and stop hurting every time she thought about it.

"Yeah, I'd like to know too," she replied then headed towards the door with Nicole following close behind.

"Don't tell me this thing is yours, Kris?" Lars asked as he inspected the red Lamborghini from fender to fender.

"Okay, I won't tell you." Kris switched off the alarm and unlocked the sports car's doors. She slid the passenger's door up to let Nicole in, then walked around the vehicle to take her own seat.

"I guess your taste in toys isn't much different than mine." Lars chuckled.

"It depends on which toys you're talking about, Lars." Kris' blue eyes twinkled as she gunned the engine then noticed the nice blush creeping all over Frida's face. Kris smiled at the Swedish couple and left the parking lot, spitting rocks and dust behind.

They drove on in silence. Nicole, used to stuntpeople, knew that Kris was using the time to go over the routine that needed to be performed soon. She also didn't know what to say or at least, didn't know how to start. She had so many questions she wanted to ask and answers she needed so she could continue with her life and put Kristina out of her mind once and for all. *But is that possible? Even my dreams are filled with her.*

From time to time, she stole a glance at her companion. Kris was more beautiful than ever, but what captured Nicole's attention the most was that look. She always got lost in those blue eyes. A rush of emotions went through her as she remembered how every inch of the dark haired woman's athletic body had felt under her fingers and lips. The faint mix of Kris' perfume and the scent of leather brought back so many memories that Nicole had to close her eyes for a moment and try to push them away. *But do I really want to do that? I haven't been complete since the day she left.*

She opened her eyes and looked at Kris, just in time to see a movement of her eyes, indicating that the taller woman had been watching her. Only the slight chewing of her cheek told Nicole that Kris was nervous and she knew that it wasn't because the stuntwoman was about to perform.

Busted. Kris swore as she shifted her eyes from the blonde woman to the road. It had been years since she had felt this confused. There used to be a time when she knew what Nicole thought but now she had no idea. She spotted the light drumming of her fingers against her thigh and Kris knew that her companion wasn't as calm as her exterior expression suggested.

As much as she wanted to stay indifferent to Nicole's presence, her body obviously decided to react otherwise. Memories of how good it had felt to have the smaller woman in her arms and how soft and gentle those lips had been on hers bombarded Kris from all sides. She could still see how those green eyes had looked at her, so filled with love. She took a deep breath to calm her raging hormones and shifted gears, wanting to arrive at her house as soon as possible.

They traveled on a small country road and Nicole just

leaned back in the black leather seat and enjoyed the ride, having noticed the increase in speed of the sports car. She gave the driver a quick look and saw that she was now smiling and glancing to her left.

A beautiful Palomino ran along the fence, her mane flying loosely in the wind. Kris matched the horse's speed with the car, enjoying the animal's strength and grace.

Both horse and car slowed down as they arrived at a fairly large Tyrolian house where a number of horses could be seen running in the fields. The Palomino made her way to the first stable that was on the left side of the house and joined her companions, most of them quarter horses with a few Appaloosas.

There was still enough snow in the mountains to ski, but most of it around the house and the small lake that lay behind had already melted. Only a few spots littered the grassy landscape. The Alps could be seen in the background in all their beautiful glory. Snow covered peaks stood out above the few clouds that were slowly gathering by the growing wind. At the right side of the house, next to the lake, was the second stable, this one larger and more modern. Most horses behind the fenced-in field were pure Arabians. The breeding program Kris had started so many years ago was going very well and had gained international recognition.

The tall woman parked the car in front of the house in the U-shaped driveway and cut the engine. She took her duffle bag and led Nicole into the house. A large German Shepherd, her tongue hanging out of her mouth and her tail swishing from side to side, happy to have her mistress home, greeted them.

"Hi Fräulein." Kris smiled and played with her dog briefly. "It won't take long," she told Nicole as they entered the main area, then turned left to go to her personal gym at the back of the building.

"Hi there." Nicole kneeled down and scratched the dog behind her ears. Kris called out to someone but Nicole didn't understand any of the German conversation. She lifted her eyes, and took a look at the huge room while she waited.

Even though it was a single level house, the ceilings were high and well aired, supported by strong, wide wooden beams.

Two slowly turning fans hung from the ceiling at both ends of the living room. What took most of the space was a huge stone fireplace right in the middle of the back wall. Piles of wood were neatly stacked at its left, while a well-furnished wet bar, with high legged chairs closed off most of the left side. A nice, wide bay window graced the right side of the fireplace, giving an incredible view of the Alps. An impressive library occupied three quarters of the right wall, and the rest hosted an entertainment unit, the latest on the market.

Nicole got up from playing with the dog and stepped down three stairs to stand in the middle of the room. She could now see the bear skin that rested in front of the fireplace. Three sofas of wood and black leather sat in front of it at different angles, facing it. Everything looked so warm and inviting. She turned around and spotted the trophy wall. Shelves of awards and trophies, pictures of friends and family, shots taken with actors on the different projects Kris had worked on and souvenirs of trips taken around the world. She spotted a long, colorful braid and trailed her finger on it, remembering the day spent in Old Montreal. *So, she kept hers as well,* Nicole thought with a sad smile. A photograph caught her attention and she reached for it.

A picture taken so many years ago, both women much younger looking then they were now. A smiling, just barely over eighteen years old Nicole had Kris' strong arms gently wrapped around her waist, her chin resting on top of the blonde head. They stood on the deck of a beautiful sailboat, wind blowing through their hair, mixing the pale with the dark mane. Both had enjoyed a beautiful day spent on the Caribbean Sea. It seemed like centuries ago, Nicole thought as she put the photograph back on the shelf with a trembling hand. *Why did Kris hold on to that picture?* She heard approaching voices and went back to the main area.

"Got everything done?" Kris asked in English to the man walking beside her as they appeared around the corner.

"Yes, I did," the man replied. "I sharpened your skis and your bindings needed calibrating." He looked so much like Kris. The same dark hair and steel blue eyes.

"Great. I have all my gear ready." She looked at the blonde

woman waiting for her and hesitated briefly before introducing them. "Nicole, I'd like to introduce you to my baby brother, Hans."

"Stop calling me that. I'm twenty-eight years old for God's sake," the young man exclaimed. "Nice meeting you, Nicole," he said pleasantly as he tried to remember where he had seen her before. "Have we met?"

"She's never been to Austria before, at least not here," Kris said as she slung her bag over a shoulder.

"I think he means the photograph," Nicole answered, indicating the picture on the shelf.

"Oh, that Nicole." Hans smiled.

"I'm not sure how to take that," Nicole replied, looking at Kris who was glaring at her brother.

"I meant it in the best possible sense," Hans quickly added. "I always wanted to meet the woman who had captured my sister's heart so easily."

"Huh...I," Nicole cleared her throat softly, not knowing what to say.

"Hans," the tall woman warned dangerously. "Come on, let's go," she mumbled, wanting to get away from her teasing brother. The last thing she wanted was for Nicole to know that even after twelve years, Kris still thought of her.

"Take it easy, Sis." He grinned. "I'm going back home if you need anything. It was nice meeting you, Nicole. Hope we see you again, soon." Hans shook her hand gently, yet firmly.

"It was a pleasure meeting you," Nicole said as she walked out the door with Kris. After putting the equipment into the car, they left for Glungezer resort on another silent drive, each lost in her own thoughts.

Ken Davidson was waiting for the stuntwoman at the main ski lodge. He chewed on a pencil and walked back and forth in front of the crew. "Where can she be? The weather isn't getting any better, the wind is blowing harder and some icy rain was reported already."

Franz was also worried that the conditions would only make the stunt harder to perform. "Will you calm down, you know very well she must have checked the weather and will adapt to whatever will happen," he said, knowing his sister's habits. He was sure that she was somewhere testing the snow. Being a stuntman himself, he knew that it would be the first thing he would do.

"We don't have much light left." Ken, the director, was getting upset. It didn't take much to set him off, and everybody was used to his complaints. He spun around as the door opened and was disappointed to see a blonde walk in instead of the stuntwoman.

"Hey! How was the trip?" Lars leered at Nicole, aware of the history that she and the dark haired woman shared.

She glared at him, silencing his teasing and looked over her shoulder at the tall stuntwoman walking behind her.

"Where the hell have you been?" Ken demanded.

"Be nice," Kris growled at the director, her voice dropping to a dangerous level, which softened when she looked at her older brother. "It's blowing hard on top. The snow is starting to get icy but I can manage."

"Okay people. You heard the lady. It's a go. Everybody out, now! Take your stations. Kris, take your position on top and wait for my signal." The director didn't wait for her answer, already feeling her stare burn through him. After scrambling for his papers, he made his way through the crew filing out of the lodge.

Walking back outside and to the chairlift, Kris listened distractedly as Franz went through the last minute changes due to the weather, but her attention was mostly focused on Nicole. So many conflicting emotions were playing deep within her. She was angry with the younger woman for walking out of her life for no reason, but she was also glad to see Nicole again. She even caught herself hoping for a chance to clear the air and maybe become friends once again.

"Kristina, are you listening to me?" Franz asked in annoyance.

"I'm sorry, what were you saying?" Kris brought her full attention back to her brother.

He turned where Kris was looking and saw a young blonde walking with Frida and Lars. "Kris, I know how you feel, but snap out of it, okay? You need all your concentration on this. The stunt is complicated enough as it is. There will be plenty of time for you to talk things over later."

Franz knew his sister well. He knew that even though the breakup with Nicole had hurt her very much, Kris still had some feeling for the small Canadian. He sighed and went over the changes one more time.

As Franz was leaving, Kris heard footsteps behind her and turned to see Nicole running towards her. She slowed her quick pace down to allow the shorter woman to catch up.

"I heard that the stunt you'll be doing is kind of dangerous." Nicole's voice sounded worried as she looked up at her.

"All stunts can be. But I know the routine well. Everything will be okay."

"You just be careful," Nicole said as she gave the muscular arm a squeeze then let go.

Kris blinked in surprise at the sudden show of concern and gave her a small smile. "I always am."

Nicole watched as the stuntwoman's skis and poles were put into the waiting chairlift by a technician and Kris sat down for the long ride up the mountain. She kept watching until she couldn't see the red racing ski suit anymore and then went to join the waiting Frida and Lars at the bottom of the trail.

Two cameras were placed at different angles on top of the slope looking down and two waited lower down the slope to catch most of the action. Some more were fixed at the very end to film the conclusion of the stunt.

Kris could see everybody getting ready for her planned crash as the medic unit stood ready, which was a necessity every time a stunt was performed. A shiver went down her spine. Was it only the chilly rain that had started to fall or the thought of having an accident? She shook her head to clear her thoughts and took a deep breath to relax as she warmed her muscles.

"Everybody stand by," somebody shouted over the blowing wind.

"Ready, Kristina?" a young man asked her. She nodded and the technician took the parka he had covered Kris with off her shoulders. She warmed her muscles one last time and got ready.

"Ready? In three...two...one...and ACTION!"

Kris started with a surge of power, crouching low in the

straightaway. She then barreled down through the fast, swooping turns on the upper part of the course as all the cameras followed her descent. The slope was faster than when she'd checked it earlier and she found herself low on a gate, slipping lower still and nearly falling as she struggled to hang onto the hill. She had recovered by the time she shot down towards the trees and the left turn above the Corkscrew. She got ready to pre-jump the four-foot high mound, but found she was moving too fast and she started her jump a fraction of a second too late.

Her knees slammed up against her chest and she was in the air for twenty-five feet on the lower side. Kris flew off balance and was aware of the blur of the trees coming at her from below. She fought to get forward over her skis and raised one arm to protect her face from being smashed against the trunks. She missed the trees and crashed into the snow, sliding, spinning and tumbling out of control another fifty feet through the security fence and continuing down the hill. She finally stopped sliding a few feet from the cameras.

"CUT!" yelled the director. "Fabulous! That was great! You okay?" he asked the stuntwoman but she didn't move. "Kris?" No answer. Franz approached his sister as he waved the medics their way and saw her lying on her back, unconscious. People gathered around her inert body.

"Don't move her!" somebody yelled and the medics were quickly by her side.

Nicole pushed her way through the crowd and knelt down in the snow beside her. "Kris." she said in a shaky voice, touching her face gently.

The dark haired woman was bleeding from a nasty cut above her left eye, her skis had been torn away from her boots during the crash and one pole was still locked into her hand. Nicole pushed the snow away from Kris' face when a blue eye opened slowly and tried to focus on the familiar face looking down at her.

"Wh-what happened?" she mumbled as she tried to get up but many hands held her down and a wave of dizziness hit her full force.

"Be still, Tiger," Nicole whispered the pet name given to

Kris so long ago. "You're hurt. Let the medics check you, okay?"

"Can you move your legs? How about your arms?" one of the medics asked.

Slowly, Kris moved her legs but only managed to cause herself more pain. Her jaw clenched as she rode the painful wave. "I can move," she growled as she stubbornly lifted a hand slightly to show she still could.

A sigh of relief could be heard over the waiting crew as they continued to disentangle her from the fence.

Kris felt warm hands on either side of her face as they supported her head and looked up to see Nicole with tears in her eyes.

"Everything will be okay, Tiger."

Kris smiled weakly and lost consciousness.

Chapter 2

Late that evening and several hours after the accident, four very anxious people waited in the small waiting room of the emergency hospital. Sitting in a corner with Lars, Frida played distractedly with Kris' leather jacket as Nicole paced around the room. The shock of the accident had hit everyone hard, especially Nicole. She had stayed with the unconscious stuntwoman the entire time, refusing to leave her side and had even managed to convince the medics to let her ride in the ambulance to the hospital. As Nicole paced about the room, memories of Neilson's death rushed back to her.

She had been there, ready to videotape the show and hoping that he would break the world record. The motorcycle jump that the Canadian daredevil wanted to attempt would carry him over three stationary helicopters sitting side by side, their rotors spinning for an added touch of danger. The previous man won the world's record when he jumped and cleared the copters with only thirty inches to spare. Neilson believed that he could do better.

Nicole could still see in her mind his motorcycle gathering speed as it neared the solid wood ramp. Everything was going perfectly until the motorcycle's rear tire had slipped slightly as it left the ramp. That little slip was all that was needed for precious speed to be lost. His motorcycle sailed over the helicopters effortlessly until the end when the blade ripped through the rear wheel of Neilson's bike. Nicole remembered watching in horror as her friend flew through the air, all semblance of control lost and the motorcycle thrown mercilessly to the ground as it ricocheted off the ramp. The stuntman had died instantly upon impact.

Franz sat by the entrance to the waiting room, looking up expectantly every time there was some movement in the corridor, hoping for a doctor to come in and assuage his fears for his sister. A man dressed in a white lab coat finally approached them. Franz quickly got up from his seat, slipped a backpack over one shoulder and greeted the doctor as he walked into the waiting room.

"The Von Deering family?" he asked as he looked around the room and set his eyes on the dark haired man.

"Franz Von Deering. How is Kristina?" he asked as he shook the doctor's hand.

"I'm Doctor Hoffmann. Kristina is a very lucky woman," the doctor started, looking at the assembling group. "Her helmet absorbed the better part of the impact, leaving her with a mild concussion. To my amazement, nothing is broken. She did sprain her wrist, however, and has some bad bruises and cuts but she should be just fine. I'd like to keep her overnight just to make sure there are no complications." Dr Hoffmann closed the medical file he held.

"Can we see her now?" Nicole asked anxiously.

"You can for a few minutes. She's in room 297." The doctor smiled politely at the group and shook Franz' hand again. "Just remember that she needs her rest."

Taking the lead, Franz walked to the room then slowly pushed the door open and went inside, followed by the others. Kris lay in bed with her eyes closed. The gash above her left eye had been stitched and bandaged. As he glanced over his sister's visible injuries, he noticed that some of the cuts and bruises marred her beautiful features, but nothing serious enough to scar. He also noticed that her left wrist and thumb were wrapped.

Lars and Frida stood at the end of the hospital bed while Franz sat on the chair at Kris' left side. Quietly, he put his sister's backpack on the table beside the leather jacket Frida had brought with her. The only sound in the room was of Kris' regular breathing and Nicole as she went to sit on the edge of the bed.

How she wanted to reach out and hold Kris in her arms and gently run her fingers through the long, silky dark hair. With a sigh, Nicole took the larger hand, and squeezed it gently to let her know that she was there for her.

Kris' eyes fluttered open and saw Nicole smiling down at her. "Hey," she whispered. "Guess I screwed that one up, huh?"

"Accidents happen. The doctor says you'll be fine," Nicole reassured her softly as she unconsciously played with the dark bangs. "You're just like a cat. Always falls back on its feet with plenty of lives to play with."

"Yeah, but this time I landed on my butt. How many lives do you think I've got left?" she asked with a smile then noticed for the first time that they weren't alone.

"Enough lives to keep us worried sick," Frida chipped in.

"It's the creature that wouldn't die," Lars added with a grin, feeling better since Kris was making jokes already. Everyone present could attest to the fact that the stuntwoman wasn't the best patient when she was injured, and this often led to heated conflicts between her and the doctors.

Kris sighed and laughed. "Just shut up, Lars."

"Whaaat?" Lars blinked innocently at her.

Kris turned her head slowly to her left and noticed that her brother was being unusually quiet as he fiddled with his fingers, avoiding her eyes. Franz was usually all too eager to have her out of the hospital and back to work, sharing his sister's dislike for hospitals. Now he just looked beat.

"Hey, what's wrong?" she asked softly.

He looked up at his younger sister, blue eyes so sad it hurt to see him this way. "It could have been you," he said simply.

Kris didn't understand what he meant. He had never reacted to an injury this way. "But I'm fine, I'll be out tomorrow and back to work. What's going on, Franz?"

"The accident. You could have been seriously hurt, just like Sophie was."

She held her breath. Sophie was the stuntwoman Kris had filled in for because of the skiing accident earlier that morning.

"How bad is it?" Her brother's shoulders slumped as he looked out of the window.

"She's paralyzed from the neck down," Franz whispered.

Kris let go of the breath she was holding and closed her eyes. Injuries were always a possibility in this line of work, too many times becoming a reality. But the worst kind of injury one could suffer was to be paralyzed. She often prayed to whatever gods that may be listening, to grant her death rather than to finish the rest of her life unable to move and not capable of taking care of herself.

Aside from the risk of injuries, the other drawback of being a stunt person was that no insurance company would cover you for obvious reasons. It was often taken among the performers to "play at your own risk."

"Franz, I know we're not responsible for her injuries, but I want Sophie's medical bills to be taken care of." Kris' eyes met her brother's and an understanding passed between them. Sophie had a husband and a six-year-old boy. Things were going to be tough for the small family.

"Of course, I'll take care of it." Franz looked up as a nurse opened the door to give the visitors a knowing look as she pointed to her watch.

"I guess our time is up," Lars said as he walked to Kris' side. "Listen, you take care of yourself, my friend. We're heading back to Stockholm early tomorrow morning, so I guess this is good bye for now." He shook her hand while Frida stood beside him.

"We'll see you in a month?" she asked, looking intentionally at both Kris and Nicole.

"I'll be there," the stuntwoman replied, speaking for herself.

Nicole had just smiled at the question, wanting so much to be able to say that she was going to be there too, but she had no idea how things would end up between Kris and her. She looked up at the Swedes as they walked to the door. "Can you wait for me? I'd like to talk to Kris for a minute."

"I'll drive you back, Nicole," Franz said as he stood up. "I'll wait for you in the corridor." He lightly kissed his sister on the cheek. "Use the time to rest, we have lots of work ahead," he whispered in her ear and left the room along with Lars and Frida.

Nicole was still sitting on the edge of the bed and with everybody gone, she suddenly felt very nervous. She glanced at Kris who was looking everywhere but at her. *Somebody better start talking,* Nicole thought and took a deep breath.

"Kris, I'd like to know—"

"Nick, why did you—"

They looked at each other and smiled at the awkwardness of the situation.

"I'm sorry. You start," Nicole said as she looked down at her hands. Her heart was racing so much it hurt. Was it because of the silence that had suddenly fallen in the private hospital room or was it because of the fact that she was sitting so close to Kris? She took long breaths as she tried to calm herself.

"Why did you return my letters?" Kris simply asked, pain evident in her voice. She stared at the quiet woman who had confusion written all over her face.

"What letters?" Nicole asked in a puzzled voice. "I never received anything from you, not even a phone call."

"I called, many times," Kris explained. "But I was always told that you weren't home. I left messages every time but you never called back. Why?" Her anger started to rise and she briefly closed her eyes to stay in control. "Every letter I wrote was returned to me, unopened. Why?" She looked as confused as Nicole did.

"I never got any messages or any letters," Nicole stated. "I got nothing from you after you left, not even an explanation. I thought you loved me, Kris. Instead I saw pictures of you all over another woman." Emerald eyes glistened with unshed tears of anger and hurt as the images of the betrayal came flooding to her mind's eye.

Flashes of Kris laughing and holding hands with another woman painfully cut through her memories. Her lover's beautiful, smiling face as she whispered into the dark haired woman's ear tormented her. She remembered Kris lovingly kissing the top of the other woman's head. She also remembered how her heart and soul fell to pieces that day. Teary eyed, Nicole had torn the pictures apart, leaving her father alone with the shredded pieces of her heart on his living room floor. She only wished it were as easy to tear the memories from her mind.

"What are you talking about, Nicole? What...woman? What pictures?" She shook her head, totally frustrated, confused and getting a little upset over all these misunderstandings.

She tried to remember whom she could have been with that could have given the impression that something else other than friendship could be going on. Kris was not friendly with many people, especially since she was far from being the touchy-feely type of person, unless it was her own family. Her brother Franz was often the recipient of a quick kiss on the cheek, but that was more to tease him than anything else. The only other member of her family that she cared enough to give a heartfelt hug to was her younger sister, Marianne.

"Believe me, you're the only one I have ever loved. There never was another woman," she said softly.

"Then who was it in those pictures? They were taken in Montreal when you were there." Angry, Nicole started to get up only to be held back by Kris.

"What did she look like?"

"What?" The blonde frowned.

"The woman in the pictures, what did she look like?" Kris repeated, watching the younger woman go through the painful memories.

"She...she was a little shorter than you are, dark hair, younger." Nicole blew a breath in frustration. "What game are you playing, Kris? I know what I saw," she exclaimed, her temper out of control.

"You wanted a chance to talk calmly, Nicole, so just relax, okay? Can you give me the bag Franz brought with him?" Kris indicated the bag on the table. "Please?" she added in her most soothing voice.

The small blonde marched over to the bag and brought it back with her, giving it to Kris with a tightened jaw.

Kris quickly went through her belongings and found what she was looking for. A worn photograph from her wallet. "Is this the woman you saw?"

Nicole cautiously took the photograph and looked at it. The

picture had been taken many years ago where a younger Kris stood in front of a wooden fence and smiled at the camera. A beautiful dark horse was behind her, its head almost resting on her shoulder. Sitting behind her on top of the fence and holding Kris in her arms was that same girl. Long, dark hair, blue eyes and a familiar smile. Nicole looked at Kris dumbfounded. Without saying anything, she simply nodded.

"Her name's Marianne and she's my younger sister," Kris explained softly. "The photographs you saw were of her. She was on her way to Los Angeles when I was in Montreal and had decided to drop by and say hello, wanting to surprise me." She sighed. "I don't know who took the pictures or why, but it obviously wasn't what it appeared to be."

Nicole just sat back on the edge of the bed, shaking. She couldn't believe what had just happened. All those years she believed that Kris had found another lover, thinking that she had never loved her. She looked up to see Kris watching her closely.

"But he said that you were lovers. That you didn't care for me and...and that you were just using me for your own pleasure. He lied," she breathed, unable to believe it. "My own father lied to me!" Nicole couldn't hold it anymore. The floodgate of emotions collapsed and she broke down, crying. She leaned against her friend as the taller woman opened her arms and held her tight.

Kris could feel the sobs racking through the smaller woman's body and softly brushed her fingers through the blonde hair. Her anger towards Nicole quickly disappeared only to be redirected towards the younger woman's father. So many years had been wasted, all because of one man.

"Why didn't you call me?" Kris whispered into her hair and gently brushed away a tear with her thumb when Nicole raised her teary, red eyes to her.

"I...tried to...I," she explained. "I wanted to call, but father threatened to...saying that if I did..." She shuddered at the memory, remembering his discipline and temper. "When I came back from spending a week at my aunt's place to think about what had happened, you had already gone back to Austria. Only then, did I finally believe what my father was telling me."

"It's okay, it's over now. Shh," Kris said in a soothing voice as she wiped another tear away. The nurse came back and as she opened the door, Kris caught a glimpse of Franz waiting in the corridor and quietly motioned him in. "Where are you staying?" she asked the smaller woman.

"At the Weisses Kreuz on Herzog-Friedrich Strasse," Nicole said as she sat up and wiped her eyes with her fingers.

"Well, what do you say if Franz drives you to the hotel so you can pick up your stuff then go back to my place? I have plenty of rooms." Kris looked at her brother who silently nodded. "We can continue this conversation at home tomorrow, okay?"

Nicole smiled and nodded at her friend. "We have so much to catch up on, don't we?"

"Yeah, we do." Kris gently squeezed her hand. "See you tomorrow." She smiled reassuringly as Nicole waved goodbye and left. Franz winked at his sister and nodded to the nurse holding the door open for them.

❖❖❖❖❖❖❖

Later the next morning, the doctor visited Kris, examined and probed her bruised but otherwise healthy body. She felt sore and stiff, which was to be expected, but it was something she could handle. The dizziness had subsided and what was left of her headache was just enough to be annoying. The doctor finally signed her release papers, telling her to take a couple of days rest. Kris smiled, knowing that she would be back to her normal routine as soon as she got out of the hospital.

Not having the patience or desire for a nurse to wheel her out, she helped herself out of the bed as soon as she woke up and walked around the room testing her muscles and balance. Everything seemed all right considering. At least her wrist and thumb weren't broken.

There was a soft knock on the door before it opened, and a blonde head peeked in to see if Kris was still asleep. Nicole found her sitting in the corner looking out the window, lost in her thoughts. She quietly walked in and closed the door behind her.

Sensing someone in the room, Kris turned away from the

window to see who it was. Her guarded expression quickly changed to a beautiful smile at seeing her surprise visitor. "Hi." Her blue eyes twinkled at her friend. Nicole looked so young, especially in the faded blue jeans, sneakers and light green pullover.

"Good morning. How are you feeling?" Nicole asked as she walked around the bed and sat on the edge.

"I'll be better once I'm out of here."

The smaller woman dropped her jacket and a backpack on the bed then handed Kris a paper bag and cup. "I remembered your favorite breakfast. Thought you'd be hungry."

"Thanks." She smiled as she took the bag and a few sips of the coffee. "Hospital food isn't exactly something I look forward to." She looked into the bag and broke into a grin. "Apple strudel. Great," Kris exclaimed then hungrily took a bite from her pastry. "The doctor signed the release papers this morning. I'm free to go." She took another sip of coffee and looked at Nicole who was watching her carefully. "You did get something to eat before you left, right?" She knew her friend's insatiable appetite.

"Yes, I did. Your housekeeper did a wonderful job at feeding me this morning." Nicole smiled, trying not to let the nervousness she was feeling show. "Thank you for letting me stay at your house, Kris. I really appreciate it. I...hmm, thanks."

Kris nervously played with her coffee cup. "I figured that after the talk we had, you...probably didn't want to be alone. I...called Oma and told her you were on your way there." She looked up and met with friendly green eyes. She shrugged. "She's a good person to talk to."

Nicole nodded with a smile and looked down at her fidgeting fingers. Even though they had talked a little, she was still unsure of how Kris felt toward her. She could see that the anger in her friend's eyes the day before was now gone. So was hers for that matter. But how did Kris want to proceed from now on? Did she want to just be friends, willing to start all over again? Or did she share the same feelings as she did and hoped to get back what they had together? Nicole knew that it wouldn't be easy. One just couldn't easily forget living for twelve years in hurt and in anger, but she was willing to give it her best effort. She wanted it so much.

The time spent so many years ago with Kris had been a heck of a ride. The joy she had felt in the company of the raven-haired woman was exhilarating. The excitement she felt every time Kris decided to "have fun" by either going on long motorcycle rides, renting a speedboat for a day outing on the lake or just simply going horseback riding was unforgettable. The older woman often liked to surprise her. She fondly remembered an unscheduled trip to Mexico for a few days with Kris, just because she had mentioned she had a craving for Mexican food.

"Are you okay? Kris asked, worried. "You seemed so far away."

Lifting her green eyes to meet Kris' blue, she nodded and smiled at her companion. "Just remembering our trip to Cancun."

"Hmmm, that was fun wasn't it?" She smiled at the memory. "The look on your face when you found out where we were headed was priceless. I still have that picture of you trying to hit that colorful toy...what was the name of it again?" Kris laughed as she remembered Nicole swinging that bat around, blindfolded, hitting everything imaginable except the toy.

"Well, at least I was going after the Piñata, not the waiter." Nicole laughed along with her friend.

"He had his hand on your butt," Kris said in mock outrage.

"He was guiding me. It was nice to see your reaction, though. My savior." Nicole chuckled at the nice blush on the dark haired woman's face.

Kris' jaw muscles tensed up with pain as she gingerly got up from her chair by the window and walked to the bed. Nicole hesitated between going to her friend's aid and staying where she was. She remembered how Kris hated to be fussed over, especially when she was in pain. But she also remembered how her ex-lover had reacted to her gentle touch as it soothed her sore muscles. Nicole thought of wrapping her arms around Kris' slim waist and giving her a hug, but she didn't know how she would react. *Damn, I wish I knew what Kris was thinking.*

The blonde woman softly cleared her throat, wanting to think about something other than having the beauty in her arms once again. "Franz was supposed to come and pick you up this morning but I asked him to let me. He wanted you to know that your car is back home in the garage." She patted the backpack on the bed. "I brought some clothes for you to wear. I think you'll have to forget the racing suit you wore. It was cut to pieces by the hospital staff."

"That's okay. Thanks for the clothes and wanting to drive me back home. I really appreciate it." Kris smiled as she pulled her jeans and shirt out of the bag, looking forward to be out of the hospital gown. Those things never seemed to fit anyone right, especially not her six foot frame.

She dressed slowly, making sure not to stress her muscles more than needed and stole a glance at Nicole while she looked out the window. After all these years, she still had feelings for the younger woman. Even through all the hurt and anger she had felt, deep down within her, she still cared a great deal. The problem now was figuring out if they could pick up the pieces of their lives together and how to tell Nicole that she still loved her.

Nicole turned around as Kris was about to put her shirt on. She was amazed at the unbelievable sight that greeted her. Bruises covered most of Kris' strong muscled back, especially the left shoulder blade and hip, which had taken a serious hit, the colors ranging from greenish-blue to red, yellow and purple.

The sight was too much for Nicole and she stood up, walked to Kris, and gently took the shirt from her hands. "Here, let me help you," she said as her green eyes examined the damage done to Kris' body.

"Hmm...it's okay, I," Kris stammered as she turned around and was surprised by Nicole's close presence.

"Just hold still, will you?" The younger woman smiled as she gently squeezed her arm. She helped Kris put her left arm into the sleeve and as she carefully lifted the shirt over the bruised shoulder, she realized how close she stood to Kris. Nicole could feel her warm breath on her neck, smell her friend's familiar scent that she remembered so well. She briefly closed her eyes and took a deep breath before gently helping the other arm in and lifted the shirt to close it. Going for the buttons were two pairs of hands reaching at the same time, their fingers brushing.

Their eyes met as if for the first time. Kris looked down at the hands she held and slowly lifted them to her lips, kissing each of them. Nervously, she looked at Nicole for any reaction and her heart pounded harder when Nicole smiled and didn't pull her hands away.

"I missed you so much," Kris said simply, not trusting her shaky voice to say more.

"I missed you, too." She hesitated. "Could you...just...hold me?"

Without a word, the tall woman wrapped her arms around Nick, gently brought her closer and rested her cheek against the blonde hair. She smiled as Nicole's arms circled her waist and laid her head against the older woman's chest. *I found my way back home*, they both thought as they held each other.

The moment was interrupted when a nurse came in. Seeing the women in an embrace, the nurse quickly gave the release papers to Kris, before hurrying out of the room with a smile.

"I guess that's our cue to leave, what do you think?" Kris asked as she released Nicole and kissed her on the forehead.

"I won't argue with that." She smiled as Kris finished fastening her shirt, tucked it in her jeans then sat down on the chair to put her boots on. "Oh, I forgot to tell you. I saw some reporters and photographers waiting in the lobby. They might be for someone else, but I did hear some of them mentioning your name. Do you want to get out by another door?" she asked as she took Kris' leather jacket out of the small closet and handed it to her. She then picked up her own from the bed.

"They can be annoying sometimes but I never avoid them," Kris explained as she carefully slipped into her jacket. "But you may want to take that other exit. There's a good chance you'll turn into a target for their gossip columns."

"I'm not going to start hiding, Kris. I know who I am and I don't care what they might say about me. All I want is to be with you," Nicole said before she could stop herself.

Kris smiled at the unguarded comment. "Well, some of them can get nasty, though. They almost ruined someone's career with one of their articles."

Kris never hid or lied about her sexual preference, but she

never talked about it simply because it was no one's business but her own. But the day Sharon was photographed in the presence of the Austrian stuntwoman, everything had gone to hell for the American actress.

The picture by itself had been an ordinary one. Kris' hand was resting on Sharon's shoulder as both women were looking and laughing at each other. What made it worse was the article that followed with the title: "Sharon Peterson Staying With Gay Stuntwoman."

It wasn't a lie, Sharon was spending some time at Kris' estate, but it was only because the actress was preparing for an upcoming movie that dealt with horse breeders. The women had been friends for a long time and Kristina had one of the best-reputed stables in all of Austria. Who better than Kris to teach her about the world of horse breeding?

That article soon found its way to Hollywood. Movie projects previously offered to Sharon were, for one reason or another, withdrawn and given to other actors. Once the news of Kris' preference became public, some people shied away from the Austrian stuntwoman, and gays who lived "in the closet" for fear of their lifestyle being discovered, refused to even be seen in her presence. It also brought a ridiculous side to the story. Kris was soon surrounded by publicity seekers. They didn't care what was being said about them. Like the saying went in Hollywood: any free publicity is good publicity.

Nicole nodded as she remembered reading the gossip column. "I know about that article. It was the first thing I heard concerning you since Neilson's funeral." She looked down at her hands, suddenly feeling sad about the loss of her friend but strong fingers lifted her chin up and she gazed into incredible blue eyes, seeing concern there.

"Neilson was a good man," Kris said softly. "You two were childhood friends, right?"

Nicole smiled. "Yeah. But we used to have the best arguments when we were kids. I remember we used to play warriors and peasants. I wanted to be the warrior but Neil kept saying I couldn't be because I was a girl. We were about seven years old then. He wanted me to be the girl in trouble and he would be the brave warrior coming to my rescue. Of course, I was against the idea especially because I'd have to wear a stupid dress. We ended up shouting at each other so much that our parents came out to see what was going on." Nicole chuckled at the scene playing through her mind.

"What happened after that?" Kris asked, interested in the story.

"We both ended up wearing dresses." She grinned as Kris burst out laughing.

"I would have loved to have seen that." She could picture a younger Nicole, mumbling under her breath as she gave Neilson evil looks. Kris took a deep breath and grabbed her backpack. "So, you ready to face the vultures downstairs?"

Nicole backhanded her lightly on the stomach. "Hey. You forget that I'm in the same line of work. That makes me a vulture too," she replied, sliding her backpack onto her shoulder.

"Ah, but you don't look for garbage like they do," Kris said as she opened the door to let Nicole out.

"No, I don't. I only look for nice healthy subjects and if my memory serves me right, I have a very nice view of one before me." Nicole couldn't believe her eyes. *Since when did Kris start blushing so easily?*

"Come on, let's go," Kris said to her younger companion.

Down in the hospital lobby, the reporters noticed the tall stuntwoman and practically threw themselves on her, fighting to be the first one to get an interview. Chaos erupted as people shouted questions at Kris, thrusting microphones into her face while flashes temporarily blinded both women. Nicole instinctively stepped closer to the taller woman.

"It was announced yesterday that you will be part of the World Stunts Championships. Any chances of you not making it because of the injuries you suffered?" one reporter asked.

"The injuries were minimal. There are no reasons why I shouldn't go," Kris said as she pushed through the photographers.

"Two separate accidents occurred while performing the same stunt. Do you suspect any foul play? Someone wanting you out of the competition, perhaps?" a reporter with a British accent asked.

"No foul play was involved. Both accidents were caused by the weather," Kris stated, pushing her way through the crowd more forcefully while simultaneously trying to guide Nicole with a protective arm around her.

One photographer noticed the gesture and quickly stepped out in front of them and took a picture of the couple. As soon as the camera flashed, Kris reflexively grabbed it with an iron grip and gave the man an icy glare that froze him where he stood. It took all of her control not to shove the camera down his throat. She knew that such a display of aggression would only invite more daring photos and trouble.

"Back off!" she hissed at the photographer as she slammed his camera back into his chest. They continued fighting their way out until some security personnel helped clear the way. Then they entered Nicole's rented BMW and left the hospital's parking lot.

Chapter 3

Living alone was often a good thing, Kris thought as they arrived to a quiet house. She appreciated the solitude it offered. Even with two full staffs working at the stables, they were close enough to the house to make it lively but still far enough to give her the privacy she needed. Her brothers didn't visit often, only showing up when there was work to do on a stunt project, somebody's birthday or for a special occasion.

"I still can't believe the scene at the hospital," Nicole said as Kris closed the front door. "Are they always like that?"

"Not when we really need them," she grumbled. "Then, they're nowhere to be found. But they do react well to juicy stories." Kris hung their jackets in the closet and stepped down the three stairs into the large living room.

"Oh? I'm considered a 'juicy story' then?" Nicole grinned as she followed her tall friend. She sat down on the black leather sofa in front of the fireplace while her sparkling eyes followed Kris to behind the bar.

"Well, let's just say that you're new to them and they'll want to learn everything there is to know about you." She held a jug of apple cider for the smaller woman to see and served two mugs when Nicole nodded. "I'm sure you'll hear interesting stories," she said as she put the drinks in the microwave to heat for a minute.

"Can't imagine what they would find about me, though. I've been kind of quiet lately." Nicole looked around the room. It was such a beautiful place. A little off to the right was a large window that covered from the fireplace to the right wall reaching all the way up to the ceiling. The view was absolutely fantastic. The Alps loomed in the background and the lake and part of the Arabian stable's field were in the foreground. She returned her attention to Kris when the older woman offered her a mug of hot cider. "Thanks."

Kris sat down beside her. She propped her feet on the coffee table as she wrapped strong hands around the hot mug to sip the sweet liquid.

Nicole leaned her head back against the sofa and closed her eyes, feeling a sense of security and peace she hadn't felt in quite some time. "How are you feeling?"

"I'm fine," Kris replied and twisted her left wrist to test it then winced slightly at the pain. Her companion stared knowingly at her. "Well...a little sore, but I'm okay, really." She smiled as the head slumped back to its previous spot, knowing that Nicole didn't believe her.

Farther down the corridor, a door opened and the sound of claws clicking on the wooden floor could be heard. A large German Shepherd barreled around the left corner and down the stairs straight into the living room. The big dog almost yodeled with happiness to see that her mistress was home while her long dark tail wagged vigorously.

"Fräulein, hey girl!" Kris smiled as she gingerly put her legs down and reached for the dog then winced at the sudden movement in her wrist.

Nicole stopped scratching the dog behind the ears, looked sideways at Kris and muttered, "I'm fine my—"

"Kristina! *Wie geht's?*"

Nicole looked up at the elderly woman walking into the living room after the dog. The housekeeper seemed out of breath.

"*Sehr gut, danke,*" Kris replied and switched to speak in English. "Is Fräulein giving you any trouble, Oma?" She tried to hide a grin. The dog was always making the woman run.

Oma clutched her chest and replied in the same, but heavily

accented, language, "Your dear pet decided to go visit the stables again, scaring a few horses on the way I might add." The woman looked up to see a smiling Nicole. "Ah, nice to see you back. Anybody hungry?" The elderly housekeeper looked expectedly at the women.

"I'm sure Nicole here is hungry. She always used to be. A little snack maybe?" Kris teased. A backhand quickly found its way to her stomach.

"I had a wonderful breakfast this morning, thank you, ma'am," Nicole said, giving Kris a half-serious glare.

The housekeeper smiled. "Oh please, call me Oma. Everybody else does."

"I'll show Nicole around for a while. I guess we'll be ready to eat something when we come back." Kris watched the smiling woman leave, knowing that she was happy to have someone else to cook for.

"I thought that Oma meant Granny," Nicole said after the housekeeper had left.

"It does. That woman is more to me than just a housekeeper. She took care of us when we were growing up," Kris explained. "My brothers and I gave her the nickname a long time ago and it stuck ever since. She's a wonderful person." She got up and gave Nicole a hand. "Come on, what do you say if I give you the grand tour?"

"I'd love it."

"Well, the main part of the house is the original family home. I added the left section five years ago, the one that goes all the way back towards the stable."

They stood in the lobby, facing the living room.

"To the right," Kris continued, "at the end of the corridor, you'll find the garage with the work shop. The following rooms are the planning and conference rooms, the main office and two guestrooms with bathrooms available to friends or my family when they work late. Preparing stunts and shows often takes long hours and since the main work shop we have is located here, they often sleep over and continue working without bothering to travel."

"I really like the room that I'm in. Franz says it used to be yours when you were growing up." Nicole grinned, trying to imagine a much smaller Kris, running down the halls.

"Well, at least he gave you the nice one," Kris commented. "The other used to be his room. I'll always remember the time I made a small hole in the wall to be able to spy on him." Kris chuckled at the memory.

"Kris, you didn't!" Nicole exclaimed, laughing.

"It was the best way I could blackmail him into bringing me to shows and performances. He never figured out how I knew so much about his plans."

"You must have been something else when you were growing up," Nicole said as they walked towards the left side of the house.

"*Hölle auf Rader* is what my father used to call me. Hell on wheels."

Kris opened a door and they entered a dark room. As soon as the light came on, Nicole was amazed at what she saw. The four walls were stacked with books, ranging from rare classics to medical books for horses. A worn leather reclining chair was in the corner right beside an old wooden desk where years of use were visible. Nicole looked at the different titles, her eyes wide in fascination as she found treasure after treasure of knowledge.

"This is unbelievable," she exclaimed.

Kris leaned on the doorframe, arms crossed over her chest, smiling as Nicole walked around the room in awe. She knew that the smaller woman loved reading. "This used to be my father's favorite room. I left it exactly as he liked it." She took a deep breath, hoping that Nicole would agree with her idea. "You know, you can come here anytime you want since you'll be staying and working here with us."

Nicole stopped walking and looked back at her, not sure she heard correctly. The tall Austrian smiled at her. She took a few steps towards Kris and stopped in front of her. "You mean you agree to let me film you and your family?" Nicole asked hesitantly, happy to know she might be spending a lot more time with Kris than originally planned.

"I would have agreed to the documentary no matter what. I'm just glad you'll be staying here with me...if you want to that is." She wrapped her long muscular arms around her companion.

"Thank you," Nicole whispered as Kris kissed the top of her head. Still with an arm around each other, they switched the light off, walked out of the room, and closed the door behind them.

The two friends walked past the formal dining room and then the kitchen. From there, they turned right and went down the corridor.

"This is the newest section of the old house. Chances are, this will be the place you can find me if nowhere else. It's about the only place I've got left that's private, away from everything else. This section is built vertical to the main house as a natural separation from the other side for when I have company and have to entertain guests. It's about as long as the original house," Kris explained as she guided Nicole to the end of the corridor and opened the door that was in the middle of it. They entered Kris' bedroom.

The furniture in the spacious bedroom was of a simple elegance. On the left with two nightstands on each side, the king-sized bed with its warm pastel colored comforter dominated the room. Directly in front of the bed were two large, glass French doors. Nicole opened the doors to breathe in the fresh mountain air and the mesmerizing sight of the distant mountains. The small blonde couldn't help but wonder what it must feel like to wake up every morning to such beauty.

The doors led to a private patio, which ran partway along an L-shaped swimming pool complete with diving board. Across the pool were two picnic tables and a few chairs scattered across a second patio. *For the family's use,* Nicole thought.

"Over here to my left," Kris drew Nicole's attention back into the room and toward two oak doors on the same wall as the bed, "is my private office. The room next to it is my bathroom complete with a Jacuzzi and sauna." Kris quirked an eyebrow as an interesting noise came from Nicole's direction.

"Hmm, Jacuzzi."

With a smile, she pointed to the remaining oak door and showed Nicole her private and fully equipped gym.

"It's really a beautiful place you have here, Kris," she said with an appreciative smile and turned back to look through the glass doors.

Two lean arms gently engulfed Nicole's petite body from behind, capturing her in their strong embrace, securely holding her against the tall woman. Her heart pounded inside her chest as Kris rested her cheek against her head and felt her friend's warm breath against her ear. She dreamily leaned back into Kris' chest and closed her eyes, totally absorbed by the moment.

"I missed this so much," Nicole whispered. Silent moments passed before she twisted in the dark haired woman's arms and looked up into those passionate, blue eyes. "Kris, can I ask you a personal question?"

Kris' jaw muscles briefly tightened as she wondered where this question was leading. Just as quickly though, she relaxed and was able to smile, albeit a slightly worried one. "Sure you can ask, what is it?"

"Why isn't there anyone in your life right now? I mean, you're a very beautiful woman. You must have had your share of offers." The arms gently tightened their hold on her.

Kris took a deep breath before answering. Somehow, she knew that this question would come up sooner or later. Lord knows her brothers and sister had asked often enough.

"I did fall madly in love once," Kris started, gazing through the French doors at the spirited horses running through the fields. "As soon as I laid my eyes on you, I knew I had found my soulmate. I gave you my heart, my soul, everything. And then, we went our separate ways. I promised," she stopped as her voice cracked with emotions. "I promised myself that I would never, ever open my heart to another like I did for you. The pain of it all was just too much to bear." Kris took a shaky breath as a single tear rolled down her soft cheek. "Oh, there were women I wanted to be with, but I realized it could never be. None of them were you." Kris turned her misty eyes to a soft, caring face with angel eyes.

Nicole gently wiped away Kris' cheek as silent tears of her own fell. She had never heard her friend speak so openly before. They simply stood there, not saying a word, staring into each other's souls as they watched the mixed emotions of fear, worry and hope dance through the other's eyes.

Finally, Nicole swallowed back her tears and broke the silence. "I wanted to talk to you about the things my father accused you of," she started with a quivering voice. "But I never had the chance because you left several days earlier than planned. I truly believed that I meant nothing to you and that I was just another conquest." Nicole's voice cracked as a fresh flood of tears streamed down her fair face and sobs raked through her body.

Nicole buried her face into Kris' chest while she wrapped her arms around the stuntwoman's body, refusing to give up her anchor and her shelter. In between sobs, she was able to speak. "Neilson was the first to help and talk to me. I told him everything, about you, about us. My heart poured out to him, explaining how I fell in love with you and how happy you made me feel. And then I told him of the hurt and pain I felt at your betrayal."

Nicole wiped away the few stray tears and looked up at Kris. "Even though he saw the pain you had caused me, he never judged you or spoke bad of you. He did everything in his power to make me smile. We were never apart."

"I'm glad that you weren't alone," Kris said softly. "The mistake we made was not talking to each other. If we had, things would have turned out differently."

Nicole shook her head sadly. "The biggest mistake was believing my father. I was so stupid. I should've known better after all that he did to me."

"You weren't stupid, Nicole. You wanted so much to see your father like he used to be that you accepted his change of attitude without question," Kris said as she softly brushed a strand of blonde hair behind Nicole's ear.

She thought back to the threats the man had uttered that day, saying that if she didn't stop trying to find Nicole, he would make sure that horrible things happened to her. "What happened with your father after you came back?"

"After seeing that Neilson and I spent so much time together, he took it upon himself to make a 'proper' woman of me, as he was fond of saying. He convinced me that marrying Neilson was the right thing for a young woman like myself to do." She took another calming breath as she looked out the

French doors, unable to look at Kris. "Neil knew that my father wouldn't leave me alone, so we made a deal...and got married," she finished in a whisper.

Kris' strong, slender fingers brought Nicole's face around to look at her. The soft fingertips glided tenderly across her cheek to be entangled in the blonde hair.

"I never stopped loving you, Kris, although I wanted to hate you for what I thought you did. I'm so sorry I didn't speak to you before I left. All this could have been avoided." Nicole closed her eyes as Kris kissed her head gently.

"I'm so sorry that I didn't try harder to find you. I wanted so much to know why you didn't want to see me anymore but your father threatened to—" Kris stopped, wondering if she should tell her what had happened that day. Taking a deep breath, she chose to tell the whole truth. "He threatened he'd hurt you in unimaginable ways and make your life so miserable that you'd wish you were never born," she said, feeling the anger rising again within her.

Nicole looked up at Kris with startled eyes. She couldn't believe her ears. "He...he wouldn't have...you think that—"

"Maybe he was all talk but I simply couldn't take that chance so I left," Kris explained as she gazed upon her friend's beautiful face. She chewed the inside of her cheek nervously, wondering if what she was about to do was going to be a mistake. "I...hmmm, well, I was wondering that maybe we could...give ourselves a second chance?" The seconds felt like an eternity as Kris nervously searched Nicole's face for some sign of hope.

Nicole's heart skipped a beat as she took in the worried creases marring the dark haired woman's beautiful face. Was it possible for them to start all over again? She couldn't help but smile as hope sprang into her heart as Kris chewed nervously on her lower lip. She took the larger hands, and held them to her pounding chest, noticing how vulnerable Kris now looked.

"There's nothing I would rather have than a second chance with you," Nicole said as a single tear of happiness rolled down her cheek. "I missed you so much."

Kris wiped the tear away with her thumb as she bridged the gap between them to gently brush her lips against Nicole's in a tender kiss. The magic between them flared to life in that single contact.

A soft knock on the door and the sound of Oma calling that lunch was ready broke the spell. Reluctantly, the kiss ended and they pulled back enough to gaze at each other.

"Ah...wha...hmm, what say you, if we...hmm, go finish this tour in the kitchen?" Kris asked a bit nervously, trying to get her body back in control again. "I don't know about you, but I'm famished."

"Hmm, wh...yeah, I...yes, that's a good idea," Nicole stuttered, a bit flushed. As if on cue, her stomach growled in protest and Kris broke down laughing at the young woman's typical reaction at the mention of food. Nicole smiled sheepishly, shrugging her shoulders.

They walked out of the bedroom and Kris twisted around behind Nicole to close the door. She realized her mistake too late when the odd twisting angle of her wrist sent shards of pain through her forearm. An almost imperceptible intake of air escaped her lips.

"Are you okay?" Nicole asked.

"Just a little stiff, I guess. Nothing to worry about. Come on, let's go get something to eat," Kris said, wanting to change the subject quickly, otherwise, she knew that Nicole would never let up. She just wasn't comfortable talking about her aches and pains and had spoken more than enough about her feelings for one day. But she also knew that a simple change of subject wouldn't keep Nicole from trying to pamper her.

"Do you know what would be good for you?" Nicole asked the suspected question, which made Kris laugh. "What's so funny?"

"Always ready to help, aren't you?" Kris smiled to take the edge off of her comment. "You know, you'd make a very fine nurse."

"As long as I'm your nurse, I don't mind." She took Kris' uninjured hand and squeezed it.

"All right, my personal nurse, what would be good for me?" Kris finally asked.

"For starters, I prescribe a nice long soak in the Jacuzzi.

Once you're all nice and pruny, a relaxing massage would do all those tense muscles of yours a world of good," Nicole replied, thinking over the possibilities with a smirk.

"You really are interested in that Jacuzzi, aren't you?" the tall woman teased.

"Hey. Any chance of getting you in that—" Nicole realized too late what she had started to say. A booming laugh tore out of Kris, making her blush even more. She couldn't believe the slip she had made. "What I meant was that it would be nice to see you in—" More laughter came from the dark-haired stuntwoman. "Oh, I give up," Nicole exclaimed, frustrated. She was pulled into a warm embrace, feeling Kris' laughter go through her body and looked up to see a blue eye wink at her.

"Don't you ever change, Nick. I love you just the way you are." Nicole shivered. "Hey, are you cold?" Kris asked as she lightly rubbed the smaller woman's arms.

"A little bit."

Instead of stopping at the kitchen, Kris led Nicole back down through the hallways to the living room. "I need to ask Oma something so why don't you sit down and relax. I'll bring the lunch back and start a nice fire, okay?" She heard the sounds coming from the kitchen. "I'll go see what Oma made for us."

"I can start the fire if it's okay with you." Nicole knelt down to scratch behind the ears of Fräulein, who had just come out of the kitchen.

"Good idea. I won't take long," Kris replied, disappearing down the corridor.

The tall, raven-haired beauty entered the kitchen and found Oma cooking up a storm. A pot of homemade soup simmered on the stove while she prepared two small bowls of tossed salad and bits of cheese. A small tray of sliced ham and turkey lay on the countertop and the smell of freshly baked bread filled the air. Kris reached to sneak a piece of sliced meat off the tray only to have her hand slapped away by the housekeeper.

"Hmm, Oma, why don't you take the rest of the day off. I'm sure we can manage for tonight." Kris grinned at the older woman.

"Ah, you want to be alone with the young woman, *ja*?" The

housekeeper smiled. "She is very nice. It's about time you found someone to be with you, Kristina. Living alone is not healthy. I saw the way she looks at you. She likes you, *ja*?" Oma wiggled her eyebrows, chuckling at the blush creeping up Kris' face.

"Yes, she does and I like her too, very much. We have so much to catch up on," she said as she chewed the stolen meat.

The housekeeper handed the younger woman the tray and put freshly cut pieces of bread on it. "You bring that with you and I'll bring the soup," she said, pushing Kris gently out of the kitchen.

Kris thought fondly of the older woman, who was the closest thing to a grandmother the stuntwoman ever had. Her real grandparents had been killed in a freak accident before she was born. Now that Oma herself was getting older, she rued the day when she would have to say goodbye.

The tall woman entered the living room to a roaring fire in the fireplace while Fräulein stretched out lazily in front of it. She put the tray with their food on the coffee table to join Nicole who was lying on her side on top of the black bear fur staring at the flames.

The blonde woman looked back at the sound of something being put on the table and smiled. "Oh, that looks delicious," she said, hungrily eyeing the full plates of food and stretching up to reach for a piece of meat. She looked up when Kris snickered. "What's so funny?"

"Since the first day I met you, you've been reaching for food. I guess not much changed after all. I just wonder where it all goes," Kris teased, trying to suppress her giggles by munching on a piece of cheese. "You do look real good, Nick."

"Well, thank you." She blushed lightly. "I'm just lucky that I picked up your habit of running."

The housekeeper entered the living room with two big mugs and put them beside the tray. "Everything okay here?" The older woman smiled as the women nodded with their mouths full. "I left a lot of food in the kitchen ready for you. I will be going now. You kids have a nice weekend. See you Monday, *ja*?"

"Thank you, Oma," Kris said, certain that the older woman knew exactly why she was thanking her.

"Have a nice weekend, Oma. Thanks for the lunch." Nicole waved at the housekeeper as she left and then wrapped her hands around a mug of soup to warm them.

"Are you still cold?" Kris asked and pulled the smaller woman against her. Nicole nuzzled into Kris' side.

"Too emotional a day, I guess. Though I have to admit, I wouldn't have missed any of it for the world. Well...we could've gone without the accident." Nicole smiled.

❖ ❖ ❖ ❖ ❖ ❖ ❖

Sunset brought cooler air from the mountains and Nicole, after putting on a warmer sweater, went back to the living room and added another log in the slowly dying fire, creating a nice soft glow to the darkened room. Kris had gone to her office to take care of an insistent phone call, leaving her to play with Fräulein, who was lying on her back enjoying the attention. The food prepared by Oma had been eaten a long time ago and the dishes put away in the kitchen.

Nicole looked up as Kris came back into the living room. She had taken the time to change into more comfortable clothing, leaving her jeans and shirt for a pair of loose fitting jogging pants and a sweater.

Having closed the house for the night, Kris walked over to her smiling friend and looked at her in amusement. The dog lifted her head at her approaching mistress, wagged her tail then dropped her head down again on Nicole's right thigh.

"Somebody's comfortable." Kris chuckled at the Shepherd as she sat and leaned back on the bear rug beside Nicole, adjusting the pillows that had been thrown there some time ago.

"I think she adopted me." She laughed as she scratched the dog behind the ear then looked up at Kris. "Now it's my turn to get comfortable." She grinned as she wrapped her arms around the taller woman's waist and leaned her head on her chest. "Everything okay?" she asked with a sigh of content.

Kris smiled down at the relaxed woman in her arms and nodded to the dog that rested comfortably on her leg. "I'm glad I'm not the only pillow here." It had felt like forever since she had been this comfortable with another, just relaxing this way in front of a nice fire. She gently circled her arm around the smaller woman's shoulder, hugging her closer. "And yeah, everything's okay. It was just Franz calling, wanting to know how I was doing. I told him I was doing fine, now that you were staying here."

Green eyes looked up at this information, watching for any reaction that might indicate how the conversation had gone. "He didn't look too thrilled to see me before you did the stunt at the resort."

"He wasn't upset at you, Nick. I...well, I wasn't concentrating enough on what he was telling me. He kind of figured what I was thinking about when I couldn't keep my eyes off of you."

"Oh! I-I hope that accident wasn't..."

Kris shook her head slowly. "That accident wasn't due to a lack of concentration, Nicole."

"Good. I mean...not that I'm glad you fell. What I mean is I'm glad that I wasn't the cause of it. If I was, I could understand why Franz would be upset with me and—"

"Nicole?" Kris said softly and waited until her companion looked up at her. "Why are you nervous?"

"Nervous? Why do you say that? I'm okay, I just..."

"You're babbling." She smiled as a blush slowly crept up Nicole's cheeks. "Don't worry about Franz, okay? I had a long talk with him, and everything's fine. In fact, he's looking forward to knowing you; they all are," Kris said, a hint of amusement in her voice, and small arms tightened their hold around her as Nicole settled in closer.

"And how many people would that be, three brothers and your sister? Humph! That'll be interesting, facing the whole Von Deering clan," she muttered with a touch of nervousness in her voice.

Kris gave Nicole a light squeeze. "They're a little rowdy but I know you'll like them." She chuckled. "We'll be meeting tomorrow at the stunt school my brother Ludwig owns. You might want to bring your camera and do some shooting there for the documentary. We'll be working on the coming competition."

"Great. I was looking forward to continuing the project. I'm sure it'll be awesome," Nicole replied as she trailed her fingers lightly down on Kris' ribs, feeling the strong muscles under the sweater.

The dark haired woman closed her eyes, enjoying her friend's touch. "Tell me, Nicole, what brought you to Europe?" Kris managed to ask, trying to think of something else besides making love to her beautiful companion. She wanted to so badly, but she also wanted their time together to be special and not only about sex.

Nicole took a deep breath. "After Neilson's death, I had a major argument with my father. I wanted to travel and see the world. Of course, he was against it." She sighed softly as her fingers trailed over Kris' flat stomach and she stared into the flames. "He wanted me to go back to school and finish my studies in Management and get a good, stable job so I wouldn't be hopping around the world like some drifter. But the courses were more his choice than mine so I left home to get away from everything and start my life over. There was really nothing solid holding me back."

She remembered the night she had packed her belongings and got her money out of the bank before her father got home from his weekend trip. She knew that he would never have approved of her decision to leave and would have prevented her from doing so. How she wished her mother were still alive. Things may have turned out differently.

"How did your father take the news?" Kris asked softly, knowing what Nicole's father was capable of.

"I haven't heard from him since. I don't think he's even made an attempt to find me or if he even cares," she said solemnly.

Kris was happy to hear that Nicole had finally taken her own destiny in her hands and decided to live her own life the way she wanted it. "What happened next?"

"Well, I spent four years taking video projects in France for a stunt company, the Armand brothers, by doing publicity work for them. I worked in England, Italy and traveled all the way to Australia with a film crew as second camera. Then one day, I was introduced to an independent filmmaker, Robert Brooks, who was going to produce a documentary on stunt people. It turned out Robert was a friend of Neilson's and when he learned that I was taking project offers, he asked me if I wanted to work for him in Sweden. Of course, I accepted." Nicole smiled at the memory. "I ended up in Stockholm, meeting a friend of his, a stuntman named Lars Gunnarsson." Nicole laughed, remembering the wild staged brawl they had planned for her to videotape.

Kris chuckled at this information. "I just hope you weren't injured by flying pieces. They do get...enthusiastic, sometimes," she said, knowing Lars' habit of overdoing it in front of cameras, especially when beautiful ladies happened to be around.

"Nah, Frida made sure I was at a safe distance. We had a good time together. She's a real nice person." Nicole smiled. "And she kept Lars in line."

"That'd be something to see." Kris chuckled. "By the way, is she the one who convinced you to come here?" she asked with a grin, knowing how insistent her Swedish friend could be.

"Well, Frida and I became good friends and one night she started talking about the work she had done with you and asked me if I had planned on filming the great Kristina Von Deering. I must admit, hearing your name caught me by surprise and I froze at the prospect of seeing you again."

Kris nodded soberly. "That must have been a difficult decision for you to make," she said as she absently played with Nicole's blonde hair. "I just hope she didn't force you to come here."

"Not really." Nicole smiled. "Frida must have noticed my hesitation at the mention of your name because she asked me what was wrong. I told her we had met some years ago and that we once had something special. She obviously knew you because she outright asked me if I had been your lover."

"Direct and to the point. That's Frida all right." Kris chuckled.

"Anyway, I guess my blush must have answered her question because she changed the subject, giving me one of those knowing smiles. The next thing I knew, Lars came to tell us that the very next morning a meeting was arranged with Michael in Innsbruck and that he would make sure you'd be there. I guess the rest is history, as they say," Nicole said as she lightly patted Kris' stomach.

"Were you afraid to meet me?"

She thought about that for a moment, wanting to find the best way to say what she had felt then. "Afraid that you would refuse to talk to me, yes. I didn't know how you would react to my presence. I knew filming you and your family would be great for the project but most of all, I wanted to take the chance to find out what had happened. I wanted to see you one more time."

A long moment passed in silence, both lost in their own thoughts. The only sounds were of the slowly burning wood, the regular breathing of the women and the slight snoring of the dog lying at their feet.

"I'm glad I took the chance," Nicole finally said, her voice softened by sleep as she settled into Kris' warm embrace.

"I'm glad you did too," Kris whispered into her ear as she gently brushed her hand along the smaller woman's back. "Nicole?" Kris looked down when she received no answer and saw that her companion was out like a light. *Not too many things changed.* Kris smiled as she slowly extended her long arm behind them and reached for the blanket lying on the sofa. She brought it back with her then wrapped it over the curled form of her friend.

Lulled by the gentle glow of the fire and the warm body beside her, Kris soon followed her companion into slumber.

Chapter 4

The first rays of sunshine slowly crept up the length of the younger woman's body, finding her still sleeping on the bear rug in the middle of the living room floor, wrapped in her taller companion's embrace.

Kris sleepily opened her eyes to the lovely sight of her golden haired friend, which brought a smile to her lips. Nicole's arms were wrapped comfortably around her waist, her head resting against her shoulder as she slept soundly. She gently kissed the top of Nicole's head and stroked the soft hair causing the younger woman to stir slightly and mumble incoherent words.

"Good morning," Kris whispered in her ear, as Nicole tightened her hold around the waist.

Hearing sounds from the two humans, Fräulein woke up and sat in front of her mistress, licking the hand closest to her.

"All right, all right. Time for you to go out, isn't it?" Kris asked, getting the dog all excited as she trotted off to the kitchen door to wait. Kris tried to wake up her companion again, with only the previous results. A full smile spread across her face as an idea crossed her mind. "Breakfast is ready."

Green eyes quickly fluttered open and Nicole sat up then looked down at her stomach as a low grumble interrupted the morning.

Kris chuckled. "Somehow, I knew that would work."

Nicole winced as she rubbed the stiffness out of her neck. "I can't believe we fell asleep like this." She softly groaned in pleasure as Kris massaged her tense neck. "Oh, that feels sooo good." She smiled, closing her eyes.

"Why don't you relax a while longer. I'll let the dog out into the back yard, go for a quick run and come back for breakfast. Deal?"

"Are you nuts?" Nicole exclaimed as her smiled faded. "You were just let out of the hospital yesterday with a head injury, don't you think you should take it easy?"

"Don't worry, I'll take it easy. I just want to get the soreness out of my limbs." Kris looked into Nicole's pale green eyes that were studying her seriously. "I promise."

"I'll make a deal with you," Nicole bargained. "We'll both go for a *light* run. I need the exercise anyway. How about it?" She got up from the floor and stretched her limbs out.

"Do you need the exercise or do you just want to keep an eye on me?" Kris winked at her and got up then gently brushed her knuckles on Nicole's cheek. "Either way, you have a deal. Meet me in the back yard."

Once changed into her running gear, Nicole found Kris playing fetch with the excited German shepherd. The vision that greeted her left her breathless. Kris wore black spandex running pants that showed every muscle and curve in her lower body, leaving very little to the imagination. Nothing was missed by her attentive eyes from the shapely legs to the taut muscles of her abdomen that was only partially hidden by the half-length gray sweatshirt. Kris' silky, ebony hair was pulled back in a braid giving Nicole an unrestricted view of her strong, beautiful face.

The stuntwoman looked at Nicole and caught her staring. "You ready to go?" she asked and the blonde managed a feeble nod. Kris successfully hid her grin, not wanting to embarrass Nicole more, even if her shy blush only increased her natural beauty. Although, being truthfully honest with herself, Kris secretly enjoyed the attention. "We'll go around the lake, that should be enough for a nice easy run, then come back for breakfast, how about it?"

"I'll be ready to eat a horse by then," Nicole replied, then laughed as she heard one of the animals outside whinny at the offensive comment.

After stretching a good ten minutes longer than usual due to Kris' injuries, the women started down the dirt road around the lake leaving the Tyrolian house and stables behind. They ran side by side at a leisurely pace, Fräulein following happily behind.

When they finished their light run they headed back to the house to grab a refreshing shower. Nicole headed for the guest quarters while Kris hopped into her own private bathroom.

After her shower, Nicole dumped her sweaty clothes for a pair of khaki pants, beige blouse and brown hiking boots. Her stomach soon demanded that she pay a visit to the kitchen.

The petite blonde went through all of the kitchen's cupboards, trying to find what she needed to make breakfast after their rejuvenating jog. For Nicole, it was a real challenge keeping an even pace with Kris' longer strides. She couldn't remember the last time she had such a workout.

Her friend on the other hand barely broke a sweat. Nicole knew Kris' muscles were still a little sore and knotted, but otherwise she didn't show any outward signs of pain. *As if Kris would show any with me around,* Nicole remarked to herself as she cooked breakfast.

With their meal almost ready, she went to find Kris in the labyrinth of rooms that made up her home and found the tall woman in her private office, talking on the phone. Because her German was very limited, Nicole couldn't make out all that was said, but by the tone of her voice, it didn't sound very pleasant.

Kris, on a cordless phone, paced the length of her office, dressed in nothing but her warm, white cotton bathrobe. The stuntwoman passed her hand through her still wet raven hair and uttered a curse. With each passing moment, her voice got deeper in anger.

Kristina turned around and finally noticed Nicole standing in the doorway as she was about to leave. She waved the younger woman in, mouthing the words "Come in." She quickly ended her conversation and laid her cordless phone back on its base.

"You okay?" Nicole asked as she walked in the office and stood in front of her friend.

"Yeah." Kris sighed as she gently scratched behind Nicole's neck. "What smells so good?"

The blonde's face changed as she remembered what she had been doing. "Oh my gosh. I almost forgot." She grabbed Kris' hand and pulled her out of the office and down the hallway towards the kitchen.

"You made breakfast?" She looked at Nicole with appreciation when a plate of eggs and ham was placed on the table as she lowered herself to a chair.

Nicole threw some bread in the toaster. "I wanted to surprise you." She smiled as she put her own plate on the kitchen table and walked back to the counter as the toast popped. "Hope you don't mind."

"Of course I don't. Thank you, that was very nice. You want some coffee?" Kris asked as she picked up the container on the table and poured two mugs of the dark liquid when Nicole nodded.

The smaller woman sat down at the table and hungrily attacked her food. "So, we're headed for the school afterwards?" Nicole asked in-between mouthfuls.

Kris nodded, taking a sip of hot coffee. "I talked to Ludwig this morning and the family's there already. He's got a new group of students starting today, it should be interesting." She gently rubbed her forehead and closed her eyes at the sudden pounding in her head. *Maybe the run was too much.*

A worried look crossed Nicole's face. "Hey, are you okay?"

The older woman looked up from her plate as she chewed a piece of ham. "Just a slight headache, nothing to worry about. How long will it take you to get your equipment ready?" Kris asked, hoping the change of subject would deter the young woman's concern. It did, but not before a loud sigh and her companion shook her head.

"All I have to do is pick up the bags." Nicole toyed with her fork, then looked up at the silent woman. "Kris? What made you so upset on the phone?"

Kris gave her a startled look not having realized that Nicole had heard part of her conversation. "Oh, Franz' choice for a new employee," Kris grumbled as she finished her breakfast. "He wants to add another technician to the team for the competition in Sweden. I agree we could use the added help but the problem is, he wants to hire a woman I really have problems with. Her name is Martina Lauften." She got up and took both emptied plates and put them in the dishwasher. The tall woman just stood there, staring out of the kitchen window, lost in her thoughts.

Nicole got up from the table, walked to the silent woman, and put a small hand on the muscular arm. "I gather you don't like this woman?" she asked, gently rubbing Kris' back, seeing the tension in her friend's posture.

She looked down at her companion. "Not liking her is putting it mildly. Let's just say that there's no love lost between the two of us." She sighed. "Martina was once a very good stuntwoman. She often worked with us on various projects." Kris turned around to lean her long frame against the counter. "There was always a great deal of competitiveness between us and not always of the good kind. A lot of small things, 'accidents' or 'slip-ups' seemed to happen whenever she was around. I could never prove Martina ever had anything to do with these incidents. Franz always said that it was my imagination."

"You said she was once a good stuntwoman, what happened to her?"

"A stunt she was working on failed miserably and put her in the hospital. Both of her legs were amputated at the knees. As much as I hate to admit it, she's also a very good special effects technician. That's why Franz hired her." Kris passed her hand through her still damp hair and looked at the clock on the wall. "Let me get dressed and we'll drive over to see Lou at the school, okay?"

Nicole watched her go, knowing that her friend was still upset at the prospect of having to work with the ex-stuntwoman. She had heard hushed rumors from Lars' people back in Sweden about careless mistakes slipping by the Von Deering tech team; errors that any experienced technicians would never have made. Little things that had cost Kristina a broken leg, keeping her away from work for quite some time. Nicole wondered if Martina had anything to do with it. Now wasn't the time to discuss it she decided as she went back to her room to get her video equipment.

❖❖❖❖❖❖❖

The school grounds were quite impressive. If Nicole didn't know better, she'd think that this was a training camp for the army. As they drove down the paved road that led to the main auditorium, she was able to get a half-decent view of the area. Looking past the tall chain link fence that separated the road and training course, she spied the four high fall towers lining the right side of the fields. Each tower varied in height to give the students an added workout. Close behind the towers was the obstacle course with a climbing and rappelling wall.

A glance to her left revealed a small building with five doors leading to classrooms she guessed. Right next to it was a large western style stable and corral. Nicole noticed that a little farther back, at the ends of the grounds, was what appeared to be a driving track. There seemed to be several different types of circuits but she could only make out one partly made up of asphalt and gravel.

What she found most impressive was the huge building for the auditorium located right in the middle of the stunt school grounds, where they just happened to be going. Many cars were already parked and the red Lamborghini made its way to its reserved parking space by the front entrance doors.

New students, men and women alike, stood outside the building waiting for the lessons to begin. As Kris stepped out of her sports car, a hush fell over the assembled people. Whispers of "It's her" and "wow" traveled through the crowd, reaching the stuntwoman's sensitive ears.

Kris was a sight to behold. Her long, dark hair was tied back in a ponytail while her dark sunglasses gave her an air of mystery. Completing her look, she wore black leather pants and boots, along with a white open collared satin shirt. A long leather trench coat hung about her frame, giving her the appearance of actually being taller than she was. She casually retrieved Nicole's equipment from the trunk and closed it with a slam then walked back around the car to hand Nicole her case.

As the two women went to the main doors, the crowd quickly parted to let them through. Nicole had a hard time not smiling as she overheard a few whispers of awe from the crowd. She looked at the taller woman noticing how much Kris really enjoyed the attention. Only someone who knew her very well would see the almost imperceptible smile.

Kris looked over her sunglasses at her smaller companion, raising an eyebrow at the small snicker she caught coming from Nicole. "What?"

"You like this, don't you?" she mischievously asked once they were past the crowd and in the auditorium building. "All the attention and worship?" Nicole stopped walking as Kris turned and gave her a serious look. Her smile fell from her face, fearing she had poked fun at the wrong subject.

The older woman bent over and whispered suggestively into Nicole's ear, "I'd rather have *your* attention and worship." She gently kissed the ear then stood back and winked at the furiously blushing Nicole. She smiled and continued down the hall ahead of her companion to the instructors' room.

Kris waited at the door to the office until the shorter woman caught up to her. "You ready?" she asked with a grin. A nod and a nervous smile were her only answer. "Relax, they won't eat you." Kris laughed and lightly tapped one long finger on Nicole's nose before opening the door.

"I know that." She sighed. "I just wish you would, though," she mumbled, thinking Kris hadn't heard the comment and walked right into the surprised woman.

All Kris' siblings stopped their conversations to look curiously at their sister as she just stood there staring slack jawed at her shorter companion. The silly grin on her face didn't go unnoticed either.

"I can't believe I said that," Nicole said in a stunned tone as she tried, unsuccessfully, to hide her face with her free hand. She was thankful for the tall frame that hid her embarrassment from the approaching Von Deering clan. A howl of laughter erupted from Kris as Nicole slowly peeked through her fingers to look up at her friend.

"What's so funny?" Franz asked as he approached the two women, smiling at the unknown joke. He was happy to see his sister in such a good mood.

Kris just shook her head, wiping a tear from her eye. "Inside joke," she replied with a smile then looked at her younger brother who had joined the group. "Hey Hans." She ruffled his hair as if he were a boy, knowing that mussing his hair always got on the young man's nerves.

"Kristina!" her brother exclaimed, exasperated, then waved at Nicole. "Nice to see you again."

"Hello Hans." Nicole smiled then looked at a tall muscular man as he made his way towards them. A woman walked beside him and she recognized her from the picture Kris had shown her. It was her younger sister, Marianne. *And he must be the last of Kris' brothers,* Nicole thought. *They all look so much alike.*

"Kristina, so glad you're okay," the man said smiling.

"Guess I just got lucky again, Ludwig." Kris then turned her attention to her sister who waited patiently by her brother. "Marianne!" She smiled, opening her arms to her younger sister who quickly fell into Kris' warm embrace. "It's been such a long time, kiddo. How's life been treating you in America? Your hubby still in Los Angeles?"

"He couldn't leave the project but he'll be at the competition for sure. It's not the same without you, Kris. I miss my big sister." Marianne hugged her again, making her wince at the pressure on her still sore body.

"Easy, Marianne, easy. Remember the bruises." Kris smiled as her sister pulled back. She then turned her attention to the whole group. "There's someone I'd like to introduce to you. Nicole McGrail," she announced as she gently pulled the silent woman next to her. "Nicole will be working close with us while she's doing a documentary on stunts."

"How close will she be working with you, Kris?" Franz whispered mischievously into her ear, startling her.

Kris backhanded him in the stomach as he stepped away, a sly grin on his face. "Why don't you tell them your plans, Nick?" She smiled at the smaller woman, purposely not answering her brother's question, and sat on the corner of the desk.

"Well, first I'd like to thank you all for agreeing to work with me," Nicole started, glancing at Kris for support as a tinge of nervousness crept into her voice. The tall woman urged her on with a wink. "What I'd like to do is get a few tapes of everybody in action; both the instructors and the students. Kris informed me that a new class is starting today. It would be the perfect time to start filming the students, showing their progress as we go." Nicole went to stand beside her friend and smiled when a strong hand found its way to the small of her back, rubbing gently to calm her nerves.

Nicole looked around the small room at the Von Deerings looking back at her, all silent, as they seemed to contemplate her ideas, her, or both. They didn't appear hostile, nor did they appear friendly. She couldn't help but wonder what was going through their minds.

Suddenly, the man Kris had called Ludwig, approached her and stopped directly in front of her, his arms crossed over his muscular chest. His head bent downwards to stare Nicole straight in the eyes in challenge as he remained silent. She couldn't get over the bulging muscles that seemed to pop out of his black, skin tight, T-shirt. She doubted that there was even an ounce of fat on his tanned body.

"Ludwig," Kris growled dangerously.

As Nicole refused to break eye contact with the behemoth of a man, unthinkingly, she found herself reacting to the situation. She stretched her small frame to its maximum on her tiptoes, bringing her face to the level of his well-developed pectoral muscles. Defiantly, she put both fists on her hips and glared into his eyes. "Something wrong?" she questioned, her voice under cool control.

A few long seconds passed as both refused to break the stare. Suddenly, an amused grin spread across Ludwig's face as a hearty laugh broke through. "You've got spunk, girl." Lou smiled at Nicole and winked at Kris. "You sure know how to pick them, Sis." He turned back to the blonde woman and extended a hand. "Welcome. It'll be a pleasure working with you."

Still baffled, Nicole shook Lou's and the other brothers' hands, not exactly sure of what had just happened. She watched them leave and then turned to Kris. "What was that all about?"

"One of his stupid tests." Kris groaned as she shot a menacing glare at her brother's back. She turned to a confused Nicole.

"He respects people who dare to stand up to him, like you did. I guess this means that he approves of you."

"I thought he was going to squash me like a bug."

"Nah, he wouldn't. You're too cute of a bug," Kris whispered as she got up from the table and lightly kissed her cheek.

Nicole turned at the sound of a bell ringing outside the room.

"The students have been called in. Would you like some help with your equipment?" Kris asked as she bent over to grab the video camera, only to have Marianne's hand reach the case first. She looked at her younger sister in surprise, not realizing that anyone else was left in the office.

"You go get ready, Kristina, while I give Nicole a hand. It'll give us a chance to chat." Marianne smiled mischievously at her older sister.

"Marianne," Kris warned. "Enough of that."

Too late. She was already leading Nicole out of the office. "Relax, Sis, your secret is already out of the bag. Don't you read the newspapers?" Marianne shot her sister a wink over her shoulder as she pointed with her chin towards the desk. "Besides, Franz already spilled the beans on you two." She smiled, gently pushing Nicole quickly out the door to avoid any retaliation from her sister.

Kris picked up the paper from the desk. Before reading the headlines, she caught her younger sister stealing a quick glance behind her to see what her reaction would be. She looked back at the paper, noticing that it was one of those gossip papers whose articles were written more for entertainment than factual journalism.

On the front page was a large black and white picture of herself and Nicole leaving the hospital. The picture showed Kris' arm wrapped around the smaller woman for her own protection from the mob of reporters. Of course, the paper read more into it. In large bold print, the headline read: "Stuntwoman Kristina Von Deering caught with new flame!" Kris quickly scanned through the article and sighed in resignation. At the time of the picture there was nothing going on between them. Now, however, Kris would have a hard time denying the title's claim. She threw the paper down on the desk and left to join everyone else in the auditorium.

The students had filtered into the spacious auditorium, taking seats in front of the stage. Nicole had her video camera out and ready as she waited for the instructors to make their appearance on stage. As she waited patiently, she looked around the room, noticing that the place could easily sit a hundred people. A quick movement from the corner of her eye caught her attention and she turned to smile at Marianne approaching her. Some distance behind her, she recognized Kris' sparkling blue eyes and lop-sided grin just before the stuntwoman turned to head backstage.

Nicole couldn't get over how much the stuntwoman's sister looked like a younger, shorter version of Kris. "You're not going on stage?"

Marianne shook her head as she handed Nicole a soda. "Sorry to disappoint but it's just not my game anymore. I was tired of the pain and of the high risks involved. I guess I don't have the fire in me anymore." She looked at Nicole with a sad smile. "I've seen Kristina lay in a coma and my husband injured with severe burns on his body. Every single one of them," Marianne indicated the stage with her can of soda, "have ended up in the hospital at one time or another. Some serious injuries, others not so serious." She looked at the silent woman next to her. "Being a stunt person isn't easy. Neither is loving one."

"Yes, I know," Nicole replied as she thought back to the nervousness she had felt when Neilson did stunts. But she remembered more the nerve wrecking emotions that played on her when she saw Kris perform. It really was different when watching a friend compared to watching someone she really loved. Someone like Kris.

"Do you love her?" Marianne asked, startling Nicole out of her thoughts.

The blonde woman didn't hesitate for one moment. "Yes, I do. Very much." She popped the tab of her soda and took a sip. Her eyes lifted to meet an exact copy of Kris' pale blue eyes. "I don't know how much you know about us but the last thing I want to do is hurt her."

Marianne gently squeezed Nicole's arm, causing her to smile slightly. "And I know that Kris loves you. I've been watching my sister ever since you've arrived. Do you know her eyes stayed on you the entire time? I don't remember seeing Kristina this happy." Marianne gave Nicole's arm a last squeeze before the clapping started and diverted their attention to the stage.

Nicole quickly put her soda aside, grabbed her video camera and hauled it onto her shoulder with practiced ease.

Ludwig stepped onto the stage, up to the edge and looked out over the many men and women gathered before him. He waited until the applause stopped before speaking.

"Ladies and gentlemen, welcome to the Von Deering stunt school. My name is Ludwig Von Deering." He waited with a smile as more applause drowned out his voice. He turned to someone behind the curtains, gave them a quick shrug and a smile. His pale blue eyes looked over at the crowd once again and he lifted a hand to quiet the people.

"We know some of you are here because you want to become a professional stuntman or just to prove to yourself that you can do it. Still, others are here for the adventure and thrills of doing stunts." Several people laughed while others nudged their fellow students. "The reason why you're here doesn't matter. Just know that you will receive the best training in the business and when you have finished this course, you'll have what you need to make it. It's up to you after that to do something with it. So get ready to learn how to play hard without all the added bruises."

The crowd erupted with shouts of excitement and more enthusiastic clapping. Smiling, Ludwig turned and nodded to the waiting instructors just off stage, signaling them to get ready. He returned his attention to the front of the stage and gave a grandiose bow and a sly wink at Nicole's camera.

"Before I introduce you to your instructors, I'd like to ask you to hold off on your applause until after all the introductions are made, thank you." The crowd quieted down. "Now, ladies and gentlemen, I'd like to introduce to you the people who are going to teach you what you need to know and wish you'd stayed in bed.

"The man who'll teach you about unarmed combat, Tony

Sanders." A tall, middle-aged man jogged onto the stage, waving his hands in the air to the crowd.

"Our high fall specialist, Steve Carpenter," Ludwig continued as a shorter man with dark blond hair walked onto the stage and took his place beside Tony.

"And here're two women who really know their stuff. Mai Sung, our martial arts expert, and Monika Hekberg, your climbing and rappelling instructor." The petite Asian woman, Mai Sung, entered the stage flipping gracefully head over heels as she demonstrated an elaborate, but simple kata for the crowd. Seconds later, a rope dropped from above and stretched down to the stage floor as Monika Hekberg rappelled in full gear from the rafters.

"And finally, our fire expert, Gunther Broca." Further back on the stage, behind all the instructors, a wall of flame shot up and out jumped Gunther, unscathed and waving to the audience. Cheers, shouts and applause erupted in the auditorium, echoing off the walls. Ludwig waited a few moments before raising his hands to the crowd, trying to quiet them.

"Even though a good stuntman is—"

"And stuntwoman!" a female voice cried out from off stage, making all the instructors look in the direction of the voice.

"And yes, a good stuntwoman too. Thank you Kristina, I was getting to that." Ludwig smiled at his hidden sister and continued his speech. "Even though stunt people are trained in most disciplines, we all have our specialties. Here, you'll find out what your specialties are. Maybe it's with a form of hand to hand combat or pyrotechnics. Then there are those who will find that they are multi-talented like the next people I'd like to introduce to you, my family."

More applause erupted. "Franz Von Deering, who will be teaching you the art of precision driving." Franz burst onto the stage waving to the crowd.

"Hans Von Deering, the man who'll show you how to handle a horse." Hans sauntered onto the stage, smiling and waving to the crowd, and stood next to his brother, Franz.

"Although she is no longer involved with stuntwork, standing over there in the shadows," Ludwig said, pointing towards

Nicole and her camera, "is our beautiful, younger sister, Marianne." He smiled at her as she lifted her hand in the air and waved to the crowd.

"And last but not least, our very own, tall, dark, *and* dangerous—"

"Hey! Watch it." A warning sounded from left stage, making everybody laugh.

"See, I told you she was dangerous." Ludwig blinked innocently at the students. "The very famous, Kristina Von Deering."

Cheers and whistles resounded throughout the auditorium as Kris walked onto the stage with a bull whip in her hand, waving at the students. Then she headed straight for Ludwig who made a show of hiding behind the diminutive Mai.

"Kristina is our weapons master," Ludwig said as he returned to the front of the stage. "Or should I say Mistress?" He gave her a wink. "She will show you how to handle knives, staves, swords and whips."

Ludwig turned as his sister unfurled her whip and snapped it in his direction, wrapping the tip gently around his neck and giving it a small tug towards her.

"And she says she's not dangerous," he squeaked out a chuckle. "I hope you will be able to learn a lot from us. Just enjoy yourselves, play hard and stay safe." More applause sounded as the instructors left the stage to mix with the students.

Nicole turned the video camera off and put it at her feet. As she took off the battery belt around her waist, she saw a grinning Kris heading her way.

"I think that went well." She smiled at Nicole and Marianne. "We'll be walking the students around the school grounds, that should take the rest of the day. You'll be able to get more footage, Nick."

Nicole leaned on the stage wall, took her soda, and offered it to Kris. "Thirsty?" She smiled as the taller woman nodded vigorously and took a sip of the cool drink. "So, what's the schedule for this week?"

Kris took one last drink before handing the can back to her companion. "Well, the students will be divided into groups. They'll alternate the courses, giving them a chance to experience each specialty. You'll have free access all over the school to tape as much as you want."

"I'd be glad to show you around if you want?" Marianne offered to Nicole.

"That would be nice Marianne, thank you. I'm really looking forward to seeing you all in action." Nicole grinned at her tall friend. "Your brother, Ludwig, can sure be the comedian sometimes. I'm sure it'll look cute on tape." She laughed, thinking back to the wink she received from the school owner.

"He sure can be. Oh," Kris suddenly remembered, "talking about comedians, the boys wanted to know if you'd like to come out to dinner with us tonight. It'll give you a chance to get to know them and gather some incriminating stories about the family." She smiled, looking forward to officially welcoming Nicole into the family.

"I'd love to."

The three women turned as Hans called everybody outside. The tour would be starting soon. Kristina helped Nicole with her equipment as they headed outside the auditorium to follow the group.

Nicole spent the rest of the day filming the different instructors as they explained to the students what was going to be taught to them and what to expect. She succeeded in finishing up a few tapes, ready and waiting to be shipped to her editor, Robert, who would be pleased to see all her progress.

Around seven o'clock, the instructors and the Von Deering family left with Nicole for a late dinner. The evening was spent in ease with jokes and much laughter. They cracked up over some funny goof ups on the set and cheered their successes, purposely avoiding talking about the bad stunts.

All in all, the brothers and Marianne welcomed Nicole into the family with a warm reception. Their friendliness and openness to her was overwhelming. They left her speechless, which rarely happened to the talkative, blonde haired woman. Kris had never been more proud of her family than at that moment.

Several hours later, the red Diablo and its passengers traveled back towards the house along the deserted country road.

"Kris, pull over," Nicole suddenly said.

"What? What's wrong?"

"Pull over. Come on, before the fireworks end," the young blonde said as she pointed to the colorful display before them with the Alps as a background. Nicole laughed gently as she rested her hand over the larger one handling the gear stick. "I'm sorry, didn't mean to scare you."

"It's okay. I just didn't—"

"You remember the ones we saw in Montreal?"

Kris smiled as she pulled the car over by the side of the road and shut the motor off. "You mean the fireworks competition?" she asked and chuckled when her companion nodded with a dreamy expression. "Yeah, I remember. It was more impressive than what we're seeing now, huh?"

"But those fireworks we saw were part of an international competition, nothing much can beat those. I went back twice after," Nicole hesitated. "Well, after you left Montreal. It just wasn't the same without you." She remembered that day spent in the presence of the tall stuntwoman, their new-found friendship growing stronger every day. If she thought back to those early days and the small gestures Kris had made that evening, Nicole now knew how her friend had felt toward her. But she had been too blind then to see that the feelings they shared for each other was more than just friendship.

Kris nodded slightly as she kept her eyes on the pyrotechnic display before them, not sure of what to say. That evening had been interesting on many levels. Memories of that summer day were as clear to her as if it had happened yesterday. She looked at her silent companion, certain that she was also thinking back to their outing together.

"Trust me, Kris. Drive up the ramp to the second level and go all the way to the end of the pier," Nicole shouted to be heard over the roar of the Harley-Davidson.

The tall woman nodded and did as she was instructed. Choosing a fairly quiet corner to park, Kris shut off the motor and took her helmet off then tied it to its assigned hook. "I can't believe all that traffic. Are the fireworks that spectacular to see?"

"Oh yeah." Nicole smiled brightly as she climbed off the bike and removed her helmet. "If you think there's a big crowd here, you should see the one near the clock tower pier closer to the show. It's insane." She tied her helmet beside Kris' and walked towards the railing. "That's why I guided you here. I know how much you hate crowds."

"You're so kind to me," Kris teased with a wink as she followed the younger woman. "So, when's the show supposed to start?"

"Ten o'clock," Nicole answered. "We'll know they're ready when the giant Ferris wheel on the island and the lights on the bridge are shut off."

"They shut off the lights on a major bridge?" Kris asked, surprised.

"Not only that, but traffic's also stopped. The fireworks are very close to it."

As if on cue, the lights from the amusement park to their right were shut off, causing the people surrounding them to clap their hands excitedly. Next was the Jacques-Cartier Bridge, which crossed from the south shore to the island of Montreal, its huge iron skeleton pitched into darkness.

Nicole took a few steps forward to lean against the railing then peered at the calm water below them, trying to imagine a time when Trans-Atlantic ships used to dock at the Montreal Port. Today, only small cruising boats and yachts moored at the marina. She watched as small vessels sailed out and headed for a better spot to watch the pyrotechnic display, their navigational lights bright in the night. A shiver passed through her and she lightly rubbed her hands on her bare arms to warm them a little bit.

A motorcycle ride then an evening by the St-Lawrence River and you expect to be warm? Very intelligent, Nick. Next time, at least bring a sweater. *She silently cursed her lack of foresight. She felt a close presence and Nicole turned her head and smiled when she saw Kristina standing guard behind her.*

"Should've listened to me and worn something warmer, hmm?" Kris chuckled in her ear, causing tingles to shoot down Nicole's spine.

"It's not that bad," she lied.

"Yeah, right. Then why do you have goose bumps all over your arms?" the tall woman asked as she removed her leather jacket and placed it on her friend's shoulders.

"I...hmm, well, because...I'm excited?" She smiled at Kris. Well, that wasn't far from the truth, she thought. I'm excited to see the fireworks but mostly it's because I get to spend some time with Kris. "Thanks for the jacket," she said softly.

As if reading the smaller woman's thoughts, Kris stepped closer and slid her hands around Nicole and grabbed the railing in front of them. "You're welcome," she whispered in the small ear close to her lips and smiled at the satisfied sigh from her companion.

A few people near them switched their radios to the same channel, and the music blared. "What the..." Kris looked at her friend with a grin. "There's only one radio station in Montreal?"

Nicole rolled her eyes in mock exasperation. "No, silly." She laughed. "While we watch the fireworks, the music for them plays on the radio. All we're missing is the ground show located at the site and—" Her explanation was cut short by the first colorful explosions as the competition got underway, with music from the Big Band era playing. Unconsciously, Nicole leaned into Kris' chest and rested her head back against it to watch the display while strong arms wrapped around her slim waist, giving her a gentle squeeze.

The fast-paced segment opened to multi-break shell-of-shells in red, blue and gold comets with green comet candles below. Next came silver comets and crossette candles, with glitter comet shells above. A classic performed by Ella Fitzgerald changed the pace and gold charcoal candles opened the more serene segment, followed by candles in blue and gold, with gold weeping willow shells above, their glittering fronds descending towards the water. The song "What a Wonderful World" continued the soft display as shaped-burst shells produced well-formed red hearts, lighting up the sky.

The pace intensified gradually and the noise became fearsome with enormous volleys of salute candles and shells of the flower-like dense toubillons with double petals. The show was *incredible as the size and number of rockets increased. Then there was a momentary pause, followed by a line of incredibly dazzling silver candles and a final tremendous barrage of enormous salutes. The crowd screamed their delight at this fantastic display of pyrotechnics where an amazing one thousand three hundred roman candles were fired.*

Realizing that she had unconsciously been holding Nicole during the whole show, Kris gave her a final squeeze and let her go. "That was amazing."

"You liked it?" Nicole asked as she turned around to face her friend who nodded at her. "We could come back to see the next performance if you're not busy then," she said hopefully.

"I'd like that very much." Kris smiled and started towards her motorcycle. "You're ready to go?" The dark haired woman stopped when she spotted the disappointed look on Nicole's face. "What's wrong?"

"Nothing, I," she shrugged. "I thought we could walk around the Old Port for a while until the traffic lets up. But if you've got things to do..."

"I don't," Kris replied. "I thought you were tired. You've been yawning all day."

"I'm wide awake now." Nicole grinned. "Maybe we could go and buy a couple of Beaver Tails to eat. I'm starving."

Kris laughed, not surprised that her friend was hungry, again. Remembering the sweet tasting pastries Nicole had introduced her to, she nodded. "Sure, let's go. I'll just bring the Harley closer to the booth so that they can keep an eye on it."

"Great," the blonde exclaimed excitedly and gave her companion's back a gentle tap. "Then we could go back to see the artists in Old Montreal, stop by to hear the musicians and maybe get another one of these done?" she asked with a grin as she playfully dangled the colorful braid both women wore in their hair.

The stuntwoman shook her head with a smile, chuckling softly as she listened to Nicole planning out the rest of their evening.

Coming back to the present, Nicole sighed, more for the

feelings the memory gave her than the small firework display that just ended. "That was very nice."

Kris looked at her friend and frowned. "Nick, that wasn't the best we've seen."

"No." Nicole laughed softly. "I didn't mean the fireworks. I was thinking back to that day we saw the competition in Montreal."

"Oh, yeah. It was a very nice evening indeed." She smiled. "Ready to go? You look tired."

"Hmmm, yes I am. Thanks for stopping."

"My pleasure." Kris winked at her and gunned the engine.

Back at the house, the powerful car slowly entered the garage, the door closing behind it as the two women stepped out. The sound of their laughter carried into the empty house, bringing life back into the quiet home.

Opening the side door and entering the guest area, they were greeted by Fräulein, a worn ball in her mouth. "Hey sweetie." Kris knelt down to scratch the dog behind her ear. "Did Ingrid take good care of you?"

"Who's Ingrid?" Nicole asked as she headed to her room to put her video equipment away for the night.

Kris looked up at Nicole, a grin playing on her lips. "My mystery woman," she teased her young companion. "Ingrid is our resident vet who is rarely seen by anyone other than the horses. She takes care of both stables and also lets Fräulein out whenever I'm not around." She stood in front of a tired looking Nicole and gently brushed her fingers on her friend's cheek. "You look exhausted, why don't you get some sleep, huh? I still have some work to do in the planning room, so I'll be up for a while."

Nicole nodded drowsily, closing her eyes at Kris' soft caress as she leaned into the touch. "I had a beautiful evening. Thank you."

Kris took a step forward. "I'm glad you had a good time." She lowered her head to gently kiss Nicole. "Good night, sleep well."

"Good night," Nicole whispered half in sleep and half in dreams caused by the soft kiss. She watched as Kris headed off to the planning room, then entered her bedroom to go to bed.

Around two in the morning, Kris heard soft plaintive sounds coming from the adjacent room. The whimpers became more agitated until they escalated into full-blown screams. She quickly got up from her work desk, rushed across the corridor and pushed through the bedroom door. Kris looked on in concern as Nicole tossed about the bed, caught up in the throes of a disturbing nightmare.

For Nicole, the violence of her dreamscape was the only thing that was real to her. Her body thrashed about trying to free herself from the strong hands that roughly held her down. She couldn't move. As much as she tried, she couldn't escape. She tried to kick her attacker but did little damage. The sharp sting of a slap across her face and a split lip was her reward for fighting back. The rough hands shook her vigorously and a voice yelled incomprehensible words. The hands just wouldn't let her go.

Nicole woke up with a start as fresh tears fell from her eyes. Through the fog of her remaining nightmare she heard Kris' voice softly reassuring her that everything would be all right. Frightened eyes, almost wild, stared into concerned sapphire ones.

"I've got you now, shhh," Kris whispered into the frightened woman's ear as she cradled her in her arms, gently rocking her. "It's just a nightmare."

"My father." Nicole sobbed into Kris' shoulder. "He trapped me and I couldn't get away from him. He was yelling and screaming at me. I...couldn't stop him from hitting me, I just..." Nicole's voice died away to sobs as the memories of the dream haunted her.

Kris shifted her position on the bed as she tried to make herself more comfortable. Nicole's eyes went wide in terror as she, almost painfully, gripped Kris' waist. "Please, don't go."

"I'm not going anywhere, Nick," Kris assured the frightened woman as she gently lay down on the bed, pulling the smaller woman along with her in her strong embrace. She remembered how this position used to keep Nicole's nightmares at bay and hoped that it would help her now. "You're safe here. I won't let anybody hurt you, I promise."

Calmed by the soft voice whispering in her ear and the warm

body beside her Nicole fell back to sleep, her head still nestled comfortably on Kris' shoulder.

The stuntwoman softly kissed her companion's blonde hair and closed her eyes, feeling Nicole slipping into a dreamless slumber. She was not far behind.

❖❖❖❖❖❖❖❖

A long way from Innsbruck, Austria, a newspaper was being read. Unsteady fingers traced the outline of one of the women in the picture. The uneven rasps of breath broke through the silence of the dark room, which was illuminated only by a single lamplight. "I've got you now," hissed the man through clenched teeth as he distractedly crushed the paper between his hands.

Chapter 5

Nicole slowly woke up as she became aware of the comfortable warmth of a body against hers with strong arms wrapped around her waist. Memories of last night's nightmare came rushing back to her, startling her to full consciousness as she sat up, waking Kris in the process.

A worried expression crossed Kris' face as she looked at the shaken woman through sleep deprived eyes. "It's all right, Nicole. You're safe," she soothed, brushing the blonde hair away from Nicole's eyes. "It was just a bad dream."

Nicole sighed as she passed a trembling hand through her long hair. "Bad memories," she corrected. "It's been such a long time since I've had one of those nightmares." She looked at her friend and smiled shyly. "Thank you." She patted Kris' hand. "I'm sorry you didn't get a better night's sleep. That's twice in a row now."

"Hey, I'm not complaining, am I?" Kris replied softly as she affectionately tightened her grip around the smaller waist. Her expression grew serious as she thought of the damage Nicole's father had done. "Nicole," Kris hesitated, wondering if she really wanted to know the answer to the question she was going to ask. Finally, despite her personal feelings, she decided she needed to know the dreaded answer if she wanted to help her friend heal. "Did your father...well, did he ever...I mean, hmmm, you know, if you don't want to talk about it, it's," Kris sighed. *Damn, I've never been good at sensitive talks. Just ask her.* Kris took a deep breath as she looked into Nicole's green eyes. "Did your father ever...molest you?"

Even though the situation was far from being funny, Nicole let a small sad smile tug at her lips. She took the dark haired woman's hand and gently squeezed her fingers. "No, he never did," she said as she got up from the bed, and wiped the sleep from her eyes. She turned as Kristina got up also and wrapped her arms around the petite woman. "My father was a harsh man, violent and moody but he never tried to rape me."

"Is there anything I can do? Anything to help get rid of your nightmares?" Kris asked sincerely, hoping Nicole would ask her to give McGrail a taste of his own medicine.

She gave Kris a smile. "You already have, Tiger." She smiled as she kissed Kris' lips tenderly. "Thanks for caring so much."

"I'll always be here for you," she said as she gently hugged the smaller woman, breathing in the smell of Nicole's hair. It felt so good to be able to hold her like this, she thought as her hands wandered over Nicole's back. She gently slid her hands down the blonde woman's sides, her thumbs lightly brushing past the edges of her breasts and kissed her lips softly, feeling Nicole respond to her touch.

As the grandfather clock chimed seven they broke their embrace and looked at each other, out of breath. Kris could see the nervousness and the desire in Nicole' eyes as she felt her own need start to rise.

"Hmm, ready for another day at school?" Kris asked as she gently tweaked Nicole's nose, trying to calm her breathing.

"Only if you're the teacher." She smiled feeling a little less flushed now that her heart had calmed its furious pace. That kiss had been more than just a friendly kiss. She felt that Kris was opening up to her again, and maybe was even ready to take another chance at love.

❖❖❖❖❖❖❖

The next day passed with an easy routine. They showed up

at the school in the morning, Kris left to teach her group for the day while Nicole went about recording the material that she needed. Kris was pleased that the students were quick learners and eager to show what they could do. This encouraged her to want to teach them even more.

Wanting to have some fun, Kris and Monika decided on a rappelling demonstration part way through their lesson. The students always loved to see the instructors showing their stuff and it was a good way to see the experts first hand.

Hearing from Kris about the demo, Nicole had brought her camera.

The light banter between the two stuntwomen made the assembled students and instructors laugh as they slipped into their gear, tightening straps and making sure their harnesses were properly installed. Safety mattresses of medium thickness were installed at the bottom of the wall, always playing it safe, especially since the wall was fifty feet high.

The wall had a wide platform on top, where up to five people could rappel down at one time. Each woman grabbed their rappelling cables and climbed the side ladder to the top. They made one last check of their equipment before Kris and Monika got ready to "walk" down the wall.

Not too far away, a lone figure hidden among the trees watched intently as the two women neared the edge of the platform. The eyes were locked on Kristina. The tall stuntwoman was putting her gloves on, laughing at a joke from the assembled crowd below. The figure's breathing became erratic as the women threw the ropes down the tower, fixed them through the safety hooks and stepped on the ledge.

Nicole was having a great time filming. The exchange between the two, and the crowd at the bottom was priceless and she had to bite her lips in order not to laugh for fear of being heard on tape. She settled her camera on the women and waited for them to start their demonstration.

"What they're about to do is called Australian Rappelling," Ludwig announced. "Usually, rappelling is done with the individual facing the wall as they make their descent. This technique is done with the back to the wall facing down at an angle of nearly seventy degrees. It gives it the appearance that you're walking down the wall. Very impressive to look at but also very difficult to master."

Kris looked down at the crowd, seeing attentive eyes following their slightest moves. She spotted Nicole working her camera and waved in her direction. Both women gave Ludwig the thumbs up signal and tightened their hands around the rope as they prepared to go down the wall. They heard, "One, two, three, go!" and the stuntwomen started their descent, easily "running" down the wall.

As the weight of the women stretched the cables to their maximum, the fibers started to break apart on both lines as the carefully braided cords quickly unraveled and became unstable.

Kris felt a strange tug from the rope and suddenly was free falling towards the ground. Half way down, her quick reflexes permitted her to twist her body in mid air, knowing the ground was coming up fast and prepared to land flat on her back on the security mattress.

The impact was tremendous, causing the wind to get knocked out of her. She felt another impact crashing onto the pad, nearly landing on top of her. She closed her eyes and tensed her jaw in pain as it shot through her body.

Nicole was video recording when the ropes broke under the women's weight, sending both of them hurling down towards the ground. The collective gasp from the students was followed by a deafening silence that was broken only by the women's clothing rustling in the wind, which made for a very eerie atmosphere.

The stuntwomen's reflexes were quick enough to avoid a disaster as Nicole saw Kris twist and adopt the normal high fall position to land on her back. Her heart stopped as she watched helplessly as her friend fell out of control. The terror that she had experienced when Neilson was killed was released and filled her with dread. As the tall, dark haired woman hit the mattress with a loud thud, Nicole dropped her camera and sprinted towards her.

Ludwig and Franz were among the first to reach them while the rest of the students crowded around. Monika rolled off the mattress, testing her limbs and shaking her head as she slowly stood up, clearly shaken but otherwise unharmed.

Kris' chest burned as she tried to get the necessary air back into her lungs, trying hard to shake off the panic and confusion of the accident. She slowly checked her limbs to make sure that nothing was broken and winced when she discovered that her newly healed wrist had been re-injured. The ill-fated skiing accident a few days ago made her slow to get to her feet.

"Kris!" Nicole pushed her way through the crowd to the older woman, worry etched across her face, her eyes filled with panic. "Are you okay?"

"What a drop that was," Kris said as she shook her head to clear it. "Kids don't try this at home. The first step is kinda high." She bit her lip as she gingerly got up with Nicole's help. Reassuring her friend that she was indeed okay, she looked at Ludwig who was studying the cables and walked to him. "That accident was no coincidence."

"I think I would have to agree with you. Look at this." Ludwig showed the cable to Kris and Franz. It looked like it had been cut partway, making it weak and ready to pull apart at the slightest amount of weight.

Kris remembered taking her cable from beside the ladder already rolled and easily accessible to anybody who passed by. Suspicious eyes scanned through the gathered crowd as any one of them could have tampered with the ropes. Every face she looked upon had nothing but genuine concern as they passed by her giving her an encouraging pat on the back. They all appeared to be very relieved that both women were all right, and she didn't believe any of them would be foolish enough to cause something like this. A fleeting image of Martina, the ex-stuntwoman, went through her mind causing Kris to wonder where she was at the moment.

Close enough to see the action but too far to be heard, a screech of frustration sounded as the figure cursed and slammed the walking cane repeatedly into the tree. Another plan of revenge had failed. Eyes full of rage and hate stared at the tall stuntwoman as Kris looked at the assembled crowd around her. A creepy sense washed over the fuming figure as Kris' steel eyes seemingly looked beyond the students and straight towards the tree line. Just as quickly, the Austrian's eyes looked away and the lone figure limped away from the scene, the beginnings of another plan already forming.

❖❖❖❖❖❖❖

With Marianne's help and guidance, Nicole had much of the school's installations and instructors on tape by the end of the morning. She had already sent many tapes to Robert, the independent filmmaker she worked for. With all the work she had done so far, the documentary was progressing quite well.

The late afternoon break found Nicole sitting on the grass under a big tree, cleaning her camera lens. She had just finished filming a particularly messy session involving cars racing and performing side rolls on varying types of tracks. Nicole looked up from her cleaning and a big smile spread across her features as she saw the tall stuntwoman approaching her with a broad smile plastered across her face.

"What happened to you?" Kris asked, chuckling, as she sat down on the grass beside the younger woman.

Nicole was covered from head to toe in dirt and mud. The baseball cap she wore had kept her hair from suffering the same fate as the rest of her body, though the pony tail that stuck out of the back of her hat sported a few specks of mud.

"I got a little too close to some of the action this morning," she answered with a grin. "But I got great shots from the driving circuit." She smiled as Kris, lost in thought, absently brushed away a fleck of mud from her cheek. Nicole put her camera beside her and gently reached for Kris' hand. "What's wrong?"

Kris slowly took a look around the school grounds, watching the students talk among themselves, reliving their exploits, exchanging stories. She squeezed the smaller woman's hand gently and stared at their entwined fingers. "I have to go to Los Angeles for a TV interview."

"Oh, when are you leaving?" Nicole asked, disappointed in not being able to spend as much time as she would like with her friend.

"I'm leaving Friday night to give me enough time for all the traveling. We're taping the show on Monday," Kris said, lightly rubbing her thumb on Nicole's fingers. She looked up to see a sad smile playing on the blonde woman's lips.

"I'll miss you," Nicole said in a small voice. She took a deep breath and asked in a more chipper voice, trying to lighten the mood, "Will you be gone for long?"

"A few days, maybe a week, depending," Kris replied, letting the statement linger as she watched her companion intensely.

A small frown played on Nicole's face. "Depending on what?"

"Depending on if you come with me or not," Kris said with a grin. She watched as her statement registered in Nicole's mind.

The reaction she received was the last one she expected. Nicole joyously threw herself on Kris, hugging her tightly, making the tall stuntwoman lose her balance. Before either one knew what was happening, they crashed down into the soft grass with an audible "ouf" coming from Kris.

"Yes! Of course I'd love to come with you." Nicole laughed, looking down at the sparkling blue eyes inches away from her own. Strong arms encircled the slim waist, hugging Nicole close as they just lay there staring into one another's eyes.

The moment was disturbed when somebody discreetly cleared their throat to get the women's attention. They looked up in the direction of the sound and saw Franz standing a few paces away, his arms crossed over his chest, with a silly grin on his face. "I hope I'm not interrupting anything," he said as he winked at his younger sister.

Nicole had started to sit back on the grass, slightly embarrassed that they had been caught in one another's embrace only to be held solidly against the tall woman's chest. "Not yet anyway," came Kris' sly remark as her hands affectionately roamed over Nicole's back and she flashed her brother a mischievous smile.

Franz chuckled and shook his head. He liked seeing his sister this way: relaxed, happy and obviously in love. He was also glad that everything had been worked out between the two friends. As he looked at the two women still in their embrace on the ground, he really started to feel like he was intruding on a private moment.

"Ah, Ludwig wants you to know that we'll be working all the students at the high towers for the rest of the day." He winked at his sister before turning and heading towards the towers, giving them some privacy. "See you guys tomorrow," he called over his shoulder waving good-bye.

"Well," Kris looked at her companion lying comfortably on her chest, "we've got the rest of the day off. What do you say we go for a nice dinner complete with a walking tour around Old Innsbruck?"

'Just the two of us?" Nicole asked, a seductive smile on her lips as her fingers played lazily with Kris' hair.

"Just the two of us," she affirmed with a twinkle in her eyes.

"Dinner sounds wonderful," Nicole said as she started to get up off of Kris.

They looked down at one another and started laughing at the dirt that covered both of them.

"We're not going anywhere without taking a shower first." Nicole laughed as she wiped some of her mud off Kris' cheek. "Yep, we definitely need a good shower."

Nicole brushed off her jeans as best as she could, then reached for her camera. Kris jumped to her feet, beating her to her equipment as she flashed the young camerawoman a playful smile. With her free hand, she snatched up Nicole's hand and guided her towards the Lamborghini.

It was early evening by the time the women arrived home, took their showers and dressed for their night out. The setting sun splashed a myriad of colors over the Alps and surrounding countryside.

Kris finished fastening the last of her blouse and tucked the ends into her khaki pants, topping the ensemble off with a beige cashmere sweater. Looking at herself in the mirror for the fourth time, she couldn't help but feel nervous. *Damn,* she thought as she brushed her long, dark hair for the third time, *I feel like a schoolgirl on my first date.* She mentally reviewed all the things she had to do, making sure she hadn't forgotten anything. She wanted this evening to be something Nicole would never forget.

She picked up her cell phone, hesitated, then put it back on the desk, not wanting to be disturbed on this special night.

She slipped her low heel boots on and checked herself one last time in the mirror. *Will you relax, girl,* she chastised herself, taking a deep breath to calm her nerves before leaving her room to go find Nicole. She remembered the evenings were still slightly chilly this time of the year and reminded herself to tell Nicole to bring a warm sweater.

The smaller woman wasn't much calmer. She wasted twenty minutes trying to figure out what to wear. The fact that the last few months were spent living out of a suitcase didn't give her a wide variety of choices. All she had were comfortable clothes, nice enough to wear at casual parties and outings, some jeans and T-shirts and one very nice ensemble. She slipped into her black dress pants and picked up her favorite light green blouse, the one that brought out the color of her eyes in a stunning fashion. She hesitated at wearing high heel shoes, wanting to give herself a little more height to Kris' tall frame but opted for a pair of comfortable shoes, guessing that her friend would probably have them walking half the night.

As she picked up her jacket, she looked at the small velvet box on the bed. She had gone shopping with Marianne for a few hours while Kris was busy with the students. Not particularly interested in buying anything, only browsing through the different items at a local artisan's shop, Nicole's eyes came to rest upon the most beautiful piece she'd ever seen. Right away she knew that Kris would love it. Even though she knew how much of a fuss Kris would probably make over her getting such an item, she just had to buy it.

She slipped her black jacket on, untucked her blonde hair from under it and tugged her blouse collar up and over the lapels. She stared down at the buttons trying to figure out how many she should leave undone. "Should I leave two or three? Hmmm, better not push it." She chuckled nervously and decided on two then looked again at the small box. She grabbed her long coat and slipped the velvet case into the inner jacket pocket then left the guest bedroom.

As she came into the main area, Nicole saw Kris quickly

close the front door and act like she had been caught with something she shouldn't be doing. "What's going on?"

"Nothing much," Kris replied innocently as she slowly approached and looked at her younger companion with appreciative eyes. "You look wonderful." She gently lifted Nicole's hand to her lips and kissed it lightly.

"Thank you," she smiled shyly, "so do you."

The housekeeper walked towards the women, hands behind her back and a devilish smile on her face. "So, you two kids ready for a nice evening, *ja*?" Oma asked as she winked at Kris, making the taller woman smile.

Seeing that her companion was slipping into her long leather trench coat, Nicole smiled at the older woman. "I guess we are," she answered as Kris took Nicole's coat and held it open for her. "Thank you."

"Are you sure you're going to be warm enough with this? It can get chilly in the evening."

"I'll have you to keep me warm." The smaller woman winked at her friend.

Kris chuckled softly as she walked to the door and opened it. "Have a pleasant evening, Oma. See you tomorrow." She guided Nicole out of the door and quickly took an item from Oma and hid it behind her back. Kris almost walked right into her companion who had stopped dead in her tracks, as a small gasp escaped her lips.

Waiting in front of the house was a black stretch limousine with the chauffeur patiently holding the door open for the two women.

Nicole looked up at Kris, speechless, her eyes wide in surprise. "You...this...we," she stuttered, looking from Kris to the waiting limo and back to her friend.

With a smile, Kris brought out a bouquet of red roses from behind her back and handed them to a stunned Nicole. "I wanted this evening to be special, Nick," she said as she played with a rose petal, looking shyly at her companion.

Nicole brought the flowers up and breathed in the sweet scent then looked at Kris with tears in her eyes. "You make me feel so special. Thank you," she said as she lightly kissed Kris on the lips.

Standing in the doorway of the house was one very happy Oma. She quietly went back into the house after watching the two women climb into the limousine and leave. "Yes!" the older woman exclaimed with a smile, clapping her hands together once she was behind closed doors and got ready to return to her own home for the night.

The limousine stopped in front of the restaurant where the valet opened the door, letting the tall, dark haired woman exit the vehicle. Kris turned and offered her hand to help Nicole out and smiled as the blonde left her bouquet of flowers behind but took a single rose with her.

A young couple walking along the sidewalk spotted the famous stuntwoman and shyly approached her holding out a piece of paper and pen. They spoke in German while she kindly signed her autograph for them.

Unable to understand the conversation, Nicole took the time to look around. The old section of Innsbruck held a variety of attractive old buildings as well as ancient monuments. She noticed that the Nordkette, lit by the full moon, made an imposing background with its rocky crown rising to more than seven thousand feet, the foreground punctuated by the bulbous towers of the Spitalskirche and the Belfry.

A gentle hand squeezed her shoulder and she turned to see Kris looking at her. *I wonder if she's as nervous as I am?* Nicole thought as she saw the calm and peaceful expression on her friend's face.

"Beautiful sight isn't it?" Kris asked as she looked out at the mountains.

"Yes, beautiful," Nicole replied dreamily.

Kris glanced down at the smaller woman and saw that she was looking at her with a seductive smile on her lips, causing Kris to blush slightly. "Shall we go in?" She smiled as she wrapped her arm around Nicole's slim waist and they entered the restaurant.

A tall, brown haired woman greeted the couple, her hazel eyes sparkling as she recognized the stuntwoman who was a regular customer. The smile never faltered as she greeted Kris' dinner partner but Nicole thought she noticed a hint of disappointment as the hostess spied the strong arm around her.

"Kristina, how nice to see you again," the hostess said then turned to the other woman, also giving her an easy smile. "Welcome to Innsbruck, Nicole isn't it?" she asked as she invited them to follow her.

"Yes, it is," Nicole replied as she gave Kris a puzzled look.

"The newspaper article Marianne talked about," she whispered in Nicole's ear as they walked towards the more private section of the restaurant. Kris hadn't missed the looks Nicole gave between her and the hostess and she chuckled at the question written on her friend's face. "I used to come here often," she explained then whispered in her ear, "Joan was interested in having me become more than just another customer." She smiled as understanding flashed across Nicole's features.

The establishment was modest in size and offered a very relaxed atmosphere as soft music played in the background. They were guided to their reserved table, with only another couple talking quietly a few tables away as neighbors. The hostess graciously offered and took the women's coats and left with a smile.

Kris sat down after she gallantly pulled Nicole's chair out for her to sit in and accepted the menus the waiter handed them. "Do you trust me to order the meal?" Kris asked with a grin as Nicole nodded vigorously, then ordered dinner in German.

The waiter smiled as he picked up both menus and left.

Kris played with the empty wineglass and saw that her hand was shaking slightly. She quickly set the glass back on the table and smiled shyly when she realized that Nicole had been watching her. "I guess I'm more nervous than I thought."

Nicole smiled along with her. "Then that makes two of us," she said as she reached for Kris' hand and squeezed it gently, needing the contact to calm her nerves but also to reassure the older woman.

As the evening went pleasantly by, they relaxed considerably as they talked and laughed, catching up with one another's lives.

Dinner was very pleasant. Good food and wine plus the good company helped make the evening a memorable one. They left the restaurant and walked the old Innsbruck streets, with Kris showing Nicole the sights as they passed the old buildings that were so full of history.

Nicole had both of her hands wrapped around Kris' arm, listening with interest to the story the tall woman was telling her.

"And so the story goes that the Duke of the Tyrol, who, wishing to put an end to the jokes about his poverty, had the little roof of the structure, in full view of passers-by, covered with golden coins." Kris ended her story and looked at Nicole, who seemed impressed by the legend. Not sure that the story was exactly true but remembered hearing the story before.

"What was the name of the house again?" Nicole asked. Sometimes legends and real history were hard to separate.

"Its called *Goldenes Dachl*, Little Golden Roof."

They walked past the old town hall and Kris gently guided Nicole left. "Here we are," she said as they climbed the few steps leading to the Belfry. The tower sat on a square base from which rose an octagonal renaissance structure, bristling with turrets and crowned with a dome.

The security guard, recognizing the tall woman from an earlier talk, opened the locked door and gave Kris a small lantern. He let the women in with a smile and a tip of his hat and closed the door behind them.

"Kristina, where are we going?" Nicole asked, amused at the mischievous look on Kris' face. Her tall companion was clearly enjoying herself and Nicole admitted that even though the evening had been one surprise after the other and that she had no control over what was going to happen, she was having the time of her life.

"Come on, you'll love it," Kris said excitedly.

The staircase was dark and Nicole instinctively held Kris' hand tighter as they climbed the stairs, the small lantern barely lighting their way. Right before the last step, Kris stopped.

"Close your eyes," she instructed as she took Nicole's hand in hers and lead her up the last step then walked up to the half wall. "You can open your eyes now," Kris whispered in her ear.

Nicole slowly opened her eyes and gasped at the sight. They were standing on a terrace lit by the full moon, where they could see the whole city. She put her rose on the edge and leaned over the wall and was met by the thousands of lights that looked like diamonds on black velvet. In the background were the majestic peaks of the Serles and Nockspitze, which marked the entrance to the tranquil Stubaital to the south.

Two strong arms surrounded Nicole from behind. Instinctively, she leaned back into Kris' comforting embrace. "This view is absolutely breathtaking!" the younger woman exclaimed as she looked at the beautiful panoramic view in front of them.

"It's you who's breathtaking," Kris whispered in her ear as she gently kissed her temple and slowly made her way down Nicole's neck.

The blonde woman turned in Kris' arms, passion filling her eyes as her hands sensually slid into Kris' long, opened coat.

Her body burned where Nicole's soft, gentle hands slowly blazed a trail up her torso suggestively over her firm breasts and finally entangling themselves behind Kris' head. Dazzling emerald eyes looked up into crystal blue ones with a burning desire. Nicole's eyes closed in heated anticipation, her lips parted slightly as she leaned up into Kris' soft lips. They met in soft passion, then their kiss deepened with a hunger neither could deny.

Both women became sensitive to the way the other's body felt by their breathing, which had become labored, and of the beating of their raging hearts. Their skin tingled at a touch, their nipples erect with desire.

As the security guard called from below, they regretfully broke their embrace, looking into each other's eyes as Kris called back down in German, then brushed Nicole's hair away from her face. "It's time to go," she said, smiling at her young companion.

Nicole was still trying to get her breathing under control. How she wished they were at Kris' house right now but on the other hand, she wanted this magical evening to go on forever. "This has been the best date I've ever had," she said, smiling at her flushed friend. Nicole tightened her arms around the woman as she contently nestled her head against Kris' chest and smiled inwardly as she listened to the furiously beating heart. "Thank you."

"The evening isn't over yet," Kris said softly as Nicole reached for the rose left on the wall's edge. "I remember an evening spent in old Montreal a long time ago." She smiled at Nicole's furrowed brows as she thought back to their many evenings spent together twelve years ago. "You'll see what I mean." Kris chuckled at the curious woman. She took Nicole's hand and grabbed the small lantern, then started down the path to exit the tower.

They were met by the smiling security guard as he took the lantern from Kris and indicated the latest arrival. By the side of the road was a beautiful horse-drawn carriage, the black Oldenburg and the driver waiting patiently for the riders to come aboard.

Nicole looked up at the tall woman with a tear in her eye and squeezed Kris' hand. "You remembered." After all these years, Kris had kept her promise. It was on a summer night that they had taken a ride like this through the streets of old Montreal. Nicole had been showing the Austrian the local sights when Kris had told her young companion that she would do the same for her when she came to visit Austria. Neither knew then that certain future events would put a hold on that promise.

Kris handed the guard an envelope. "Danke." She smiled at him and walked to the carriage with Nicole still holding on to her hand. "I was looking for the right time ever since we talked. I wanted this evening to be special and I also remembered how you loved riding in carriages, so..."

Two arms were suddenly wrapped around Kris' waist as Nicole buried her face in her chest. She could feel small sobs coming from the smaller woman and she lifted Nicole's chin to look at her with worried eyes. "What's wrong?" Kris asked as she wiped a tear off of her cheek.

"Nothing's wrong, everything's perfect." She smiled at Kris, the mix of tears and laughter confusing the tall woman even more. "It's just that I never thought we'd be doing this again, never thought that I'd be this happy once more, especially with you."

Kris held the blonde close to her and looked into Nicole's

eyes. "Life is full of surprises," she said softly. "I don't intend to let anything, or anyone, come between us again." She gently cupped Nicole's face with her strong hands and kissed her inviting lips.

Her eyes closed as the dark haired woman's soft lips pressed firmly against her own, their kiss becoming passionate once more.

"You mean everything to me, Nicole," Kris whispered in her ear between kisses.

The smaller woman looked at her friend, not knowing what to say. She was so different from the brash, young stuntwoman she had met so many years ago. Different in a pleasant way, Nicole quickly added to herself as a small smile lazily formed on her soft lips. She found that this new Kris was more willing and more open to talk about her emotions. That smile of hers that could melt hearts adorned her beautiful face more these days as her silky laughter rang through the air frequently. She also noticed how her tall, stoic companion had become a hopeless romantic.

Nicole tried to suppress a growing grin. "I love the new and improved Kristina Von Deering," she said as she sensually traced the outline of the strong jaw with her finger.

"I just thought you'd appreciate all this mushy stuff," Kris teased, indicating their surroundings with her hand then offered it to help her companion up into the carriage.

Nicole still wore a bright smile as Kris settled in comfortably next to her on the leather-cushioned seats. "Come on, Kristina, admit it. You like this as much as I do." She chuckled accusingly as their eyes locked.

Kris raised an eyebrow at the small woman, trying to be very serious but only half-succeeded before she broke down and smiled. "All right, I admit it. Just don't go spreading it around, okay?"

Nicole nodded. "I promise."

Kris kissed the tip of Nicole's cute button nose before bending down to open a wooden box at their feet. The blonde watched curiously as a bottle was taken out of the ice filled box then as two glasses were pulled out of a side pocket.

"Champagne?" Kris asked as she handed Nicole the fluted glasses, then opened the bottle and poured the bubbly liquid.

Nicole couldn't believe the changes in Kris. She really liked the playful side of her friend. She had fallen in love with her once before, and now she was doing it all over again.

"Did I ever tell you how beautiful you are, Kris?" she asked as she accepted the glass.

That caught Kris completely off guard. She just sat there, not knowing what to say and blushed all of a sudden. "Huh...thank you," she mumbled, playing with her untouched champagne. It was amazing. Kris thought how such a simple phrase set her heart racing and rendered her speechless when it had been said so many times to her by other people, but never really affecting her emotionally.

Nicole smiled as she snuggled into Kris, careful not to spill their drinks and sighed in contentment as the taller woman wrapped her free arm around her shoulder. "You're so cute when you blush," Nicole teased and lifted her glass. "To us." She touched her glass against Kris' producing a gentle ring.

"To us," Kris repeated as they took a sip of champagne. The driver took this as his cue and started the horse into a trot, heading back to the waiting limousine a few miles away.

Chapter 6

The limo pulled away as the women entered the house and Kris locked the door behind them. She reached for Nicole's long coat and opened the closet with her other hand. A sharp pain shot up her arm as the weight of the coat settled, reminding her of her re-injured wrist. A small wince momentarily marred Kris' relaxed face.

The pained look didn't go unnoticed by Nicole's watchful eyes. Without saying a word, she gave Kris a scolding look as she casually took over hanging her coat in the closet. Her face softened as she slipped behind Kris, helped her out of her long leather coat and hung it as well.

"It's not that bad," Kris said defensively to Nicole's unspoken words. She knew that if she had said anything previously, Nicole would have insisted on coming back earlier than planned. "It was just a bad move, that's all." Kris couldn't help but smile at the determined look on her friend's face as she unfastened Kris' pants and hauled her arms through her sweater just before they reached her bathroom.

"Don't move," Nicole ordered as she prepared the Jacuzzi.

She smiled. "Wouldn't dream of it."

"I want you in there relaxing those muscles," she said with a sly grin and a twinkle in her eye as she returned to Kris, who hadn't moved. Nicole stepped up close to the taller woman and slid her hands under Kris' sweater, gliding them up the sides of the firm torso and over her head, removing the sweater. She suddenly stopped as she looked at Kris with wide eyes as she stood before her in her blouse. Nicole blushed furiously, realizing what she was doing.

The raven-haired beauty only smiled as she took a step closer and cupped the cherub face in her hands and kissed her softly then slowly slid her long fingers down Nicole's neck and chest.

"I'll agree to go in there," Kris said as she sensually undid Nicole's blouse, her lips quickly capturing those of her beautiful companion again, "if you join me."

It took all the control Nicole had for her knees not to buckle as Kris' warm hands slipped her blouse off of her shoulders, letting it fall to her feet. Kris' soft lips trailed down Nicole's sensitive neck as her nimble fingers expertly undid her bra, sending it to join the rest of their clothes on the floor.

Kris' heart pounded with desire as she looked at the beautiful woman in front of her. Nicole's strawberry blonde hair hung loosely on her naked shoulders and the feel of the soft, fair skin beneath her strong fingers as she slid them down the toned arms was stimulating. Her mouth watered as her pale blue eyes settled on Nicole's perfect, erect nipples. Kris' fingers softly brushed up against her breasts as she kissed her way down. *They look so inviting,* she thought seconds before her lips gently kissed Nicole's hardened nipples and heard a soft moan coming from her partner.

Kris trailed a teasing tongue over the sensitive flesh while her hands continued their sensual descent over the young woman's belly and down to the top of Nicole's pants. Kris' agile fingers wasted no time in undoing them. Her hands slid inside as she slowly took them off, kneeling in her descent, her mouth blazing a trail of desire down Nicole's abdomen. Her mouth stopped just below the navel as she pried the smooth, shapely legs out of the restrictive pant legs.

Kris' lips continued their ministrations as she worked her way back up Nicole's delicious torso. Her lips captured the smaller woman's neglected breast, giving it the same sensual attention. Nicole's breathing became labored as Kris' wet mouth sucked gently on her breast. As the young blonde's passion took over, her hands unconsciously worked their way through Kris' silky hair, holding her to her breast.

Kris smiled against the soft flesh as she extricated herself from it, kissing her way back up to Nicole's sweet lips. Hungrily, she captured the small woman's lips, locking them in a passionate frenzy. Nicole's wandering hands sought out the buttons of Kris' blouse and swiftly undid all the bothersome fasteners.

As the blouse slid off of Kris' shoulders, a low moan escaped Nicole's lips as her green eyes were treated to the sight of firm, bra-less breasts. She lovingly caressed the soft flesh, teasing the hardened buds with her fingers, then, desire overtaking her, she leaned in to taste Kris' soft flesh. Her tongue flicked and nibbled at the erect nipples while her hands played over the muscular abdomen, tracing curious fingers over taut muscles.

As Kris captured the younger woman's mouth with her own, Nicole's fingers deftly unbuckled Kris' belt and unzipped her pants, loosening them around her hips.

"You are so beautiful," Kris murmured, her voice heavy with desire as she slid her hands back up on the smaller woman's breasts. She could hear her own heart beating in her ears. She was on fire and she knew she was going to go up in flames if she didn't do something about it.

Kris stepped out of her clothes and, not wanting to break contact, glided her hand around Nicole's waist and bent down to put the other under her knees. She lifted her young lover in her arms then slowly climbed into the Jacuzzi.

A surprised gasp escaped Nicole's lips as she was lifted and carried towards the tub and wrapped her arms around the tall woman's neck.

Kris looked into Nicole's green eyes full of desire as her young lover leaned down and met her lips in a passionate kiss. Lowering into the warm, bubbling water, Kris sat and stretched her legs then guided the smaller woman to straddle her thighs, facing her.

Two strong hands gently wrapped around the slim waist, snuck up Nicole's back and ever so slowly crept up and around to caress the smooth breasts, causing the younger woman to moan in pleasure. "I love you, Nicole," Kris whispered into her ear, gently nibbling on it.

"Oh Kris," she murmured, her speech refusing to cooperate as Kris' wandering hands played all over her body and ended up stroking her buttocks slowly. "Kris...we...I," Nicole stammered incoherently as shivers of pleasure traveled down her spine as soft lips kissed their way down her neck and shoulder. A low, throaty moan escaped her lips as Kris gently sucked and tugged on the hardened nipples with her teeth.

A small hand captured the larger one and guided it up front under the bubbling water, pressing it firmly to Nicole's center. A surprised gasp escaped Kris at the boldness of the smaller woman's act, her body shuddering in excitement at the gesture that was so out of character for Nicole.

Strong yet gentle fingers made their way into the younger woman's folds, slowly stroking and exploring, causing Nicole to groan in pleasure. Kris held her breath and watched with rapt attention as her young lover seductively licked her lips and snapped her head back with a moan, breathing heavily, her hips moving against Kris' hand.

Feeling the pressure building inside her lover, Kris slowed her movements to finally stop, leaving Nicole wanting.

"No!" she pleaded, her voice full of lust. "Please, don't stop."

The desire Kris saw in those green eyes stirred her to the core. "Not yet." She smiled as she whispered seductively into Nicole's ear. Strong arms gently wrapped around Nicole as the tall woman stood up, carrying her lover in her arms and out of the tub, the light weight of her partner making it an easy feat for the muscular woman.

After Kris set her down on her feet, the dark haired woman grabbed a large white bath towel and wrapped it gently around Nicole. The young woman's body shivered with need as Kris slowly dried off her wet body, their eyes never breaking contact. Soon, she finished her task and grabbed a similar towel for herself and started to wrap it around her body.

"Come here." Nicole smiled. She stole the ends of the soft

cloth and tugged it towards her, bringing Kris into her arms then capturing her luscious lips as she tied the towel over the tall woman's chest.

Nicole opened her eyes from the kiss to see Kris' lopsided grin as her eyes danced mischievously in front of her. "Wha—" Before she could ask what the look was for, Kris swept Nicole off her feet and carried her over to the bed in the next room.

"You know, I could get used to this." Nicole smiled seductively at her partner as she was set back down on her feet. "You make me feel like nothing else in the world exists."

"And you make me feel so alive." Kris kissed her softly and bent down to pull the covers off the bed and looked back as Nicole let her bath towel slowly drop to the floor.

The blonde woman reached for Kris' towel and tugged it off the muscular body, pulling the taller woman towards her. "I've waited such a long time for this," Nicole whispered huskily as she kissed her way along the strong jaw.

Kris gently, but firmly, held Nicole as the stuntwoman lowered onto the bed. She wasted no time in capturing Nicole's lips once more in a long sultry kiss. Moving down her young lover's body, Kris trailed her tongue around Nicole's aureoles with avid craving, switching between her tongue and fingers, flicking and pinching the erect nipples.

Nicole's body was already intensely aroused by the time Kris laid her on the bed. As Kris gently sucked her breasts, Nicole's hand glided down her own taut abdomen, and on down between her legs as she softly ran her other hand through Kris' silky, black hair. Nicole's fingers entered her wet folds and thrust them in and out, matching the rhythm Kris had started with her tongue on her breasts.

The passionate stuntwoman reclaimed her lover's mouth in a carnal kiss as she covered Nicole's hand, expertly replacing the small fingers with her own, thrusting them into her young lover's wetness, taking up the set rhythm.

Kris broke the kiss to crawl a bit up Nicole's body and allow the smaller woman to suck on the offered breast. The young blonde's fingers glistening with her own juices found their way into Kris' mouth and her tongue swirled over and sucked each and every finger as she savored the delicious taste of her lover.

The movement of Kris' fingers inside her and the sight of the dark haired beauty sucking on hers became too much. The smaller woman moaned breathlessly and then screamed her lover's name as her body shuddered in an intense spasm, signaling the onset of an incredible orgasm. Kris slowed her movement and then ceased until Nicole's body stopped its spasms. She gently removed her soaked fingers from Nicole's throbbing center as her young lover's heavy breathing tried to return to normal.

Kris lay down beside her partner, and cradled her tightly in her arms as Nicole's breathing and heartbeat slowed down to its normal beat.

"Wha—" Kris exclaimed when she found herself flat on her back, tipped over by the surprisingly strong Nicole who wore a mischievous grin on her small, innocent face. She positioned herself between her lover's legs and laid her body on top of Kris'.

"Now, you just relax and enjoy," Nicole said as she took Kris' right nipple into her hungry mouth while watching the intense, blue eyes close in pleasure. She reached for the lonely breast, and teased a painfully erect nipple, gently pinching and tugging the soft bud.

Nicole could hear Kris' ragged breathing as she captured the stuntwoman's mouth for a long, slow kiss, exploring and tasting her lover. She pulled reluctantly back to descend on the older woman's neck, gently sucking and nipping her way down, trailing her tongue down the woman's well-worked abdomen muscles, leaving a wet path leading towards Kris' burning center.

Kris moaned in anticipation as she reached for Nicole's blonde hair and gently brushed through the soft locks, opening her legs to give her lover full access. Her back arched passionately as Nicole's warm tongue worked its way around and inside her. The soft tongue flicked the swollen button several times before a softly sucking mouth claimed it again.

Gods, I think I'm going to die! Kris thought as a moan escaped her lips. "Please...Nick," she breathed, her voice heavy with desire. "I want to feel you inside me." Her body froze as her young lover's fingers eased into her wet entrance, the muscles sealing tight around the welcomed digits as Nicole slowly thrust. "Yesss."

Nicole leaned down to give her lover an intimate, lingering kiss, slowly lapping at the juices. As Kris' orgasm built, she increased the rhythm of her tongue and the thrusts of her fingers. The tall woman's body tensed.

"Nicole!" Kris called out as she soared high, riding the wave of passion until she climaxed in a mind-shattering explosion of pleasure.

Nicole crawled over Kris and snuggled into the woman's warm embrace, brushing her fingers over her lover's overheated skin and listening to the furiously beating heart slow down. "I never want to be apart from you again, Kris."

Kris closed her eyes at the admission and smiled, hugging the smaller woman even closer. "You won't be able to get rid of me, Nick," she said as she gently scratched Nicole's back, causing the younger woman to close her eyes in contentment as she fell asleep, completely spent.

Trying not to move too much and risk waking Nicole, Kris reached for the discarded blankets and covered themselves, then reached for the light and shut it off for the night. She planted a small kiss on the blonde head under her chin.

"Good night, my love."

❖❖❖❖❖❖❖

The next morning, the shrill ringing of the phone woke Kris from her peaceful sleep. "What now?" Kris groaned still half asleep as she stirred to stop the annoying ringing. Without disturbing the beautiful young woman beside her, her hand shot out and clumsily knocked the phone off the hook. Satisfied, she returned her hand to its resting spot around Nicole. Feeling her in bed next to her brought a smile to her face.

Kris' eyes cracked open once again as the insistent ringing continued. Had it been her regular phone, the answering service would have picked up by now. As she listened, she recognized the irritating ring of her cell phone. No one called that number except for important business.

She quietly extracted herself away from Nicole's sprawled-out limbs and gently moved her head from its resting spot on her shoulder to the pillow as she got out of bed and hustled over to the desk. Kris mumbled a few curses in German as she picked up the infernal machine.

"What?" she answered the phone irritably, causing Nicole to stir and wake.

"Kristina, where the hell are you?" Franz barked.

"Well, good morning to you too," Kris said sarcastically. "What is it?" She smiled at Nicole who listened to the conversation, her disheveled blonde hair glistening in the morning sun.

An exasperated sigh met Kris' ear. "What do you mean 'what is it'? Do you have any idea what time it is?" her brother asked. "We had a meeting at the school this morning for the competition."

Kris quickly looked the clock on the nightstand on Nicole's side of the bed, which read 9:30 a.m. "Oh shit!" she exclaimed and headed towards her bathroom to start her shower. "I'm sorry Franz, I'll be right over."

"Don't bother. We rescheduled the meeting for late afternoon. Maybe you can show up then, if you're not too busy that is?" Franz chided, anger still in his voice.

The tall woman stopped walking and stared at her phone, not believing the unusual sarcasm coming from her brother. She could feel the heat in her face as her temper rose. "Now you listen to me," Kris started, her voice at a dangerously low level. "I've never been late for anything, so don't you dare put this crap down on me."

Kris sensed a presence near her and turned to see Nicole waiting patiently for the older woman to notice her. If there was one thing to be learned around the dark haired stuntwoman it was to never touch her from behind, especially when she was in this kind of mood. A small smile appeared on Kris' lips as she looked at Nicole who was dressed in a bathrobe.

With the way her hands disappeared inside the sleeves and how the robe collected at her feet, it wasn't hard to tell that Nicole had on Kris' bathrobe as she flapped the arms when she waved "hello." At her smile, Nicole walked up to the tall woman and wrapped her arms around Kris' still naked body.

A long pause on the phone was followed by an exhausted sigh. "I'm sorry, Kristina, I shouldn't have snapped at you that way."

Kris gave the smaller woman a squeeze with her free arm and kissed the top of Nicole's head, smiling at the bright green eyes looking back at her. "What's wrong Franz?" Kris knew her brother didn't get angry easily. He sounded so tired.

"The computer simulations for the motorcycle stunt aren't working out right. I've been working all night on it with no success. I guess I just wanted you here this morning to help me out. I'm just so damned frustrated."

"E-mail me what you have so far and I'll take a look at it, okay? I'll see what I can do."

"Thanks, Kris." He sighed gratefully.

"And Franz?" she added. "Get some sleep." Kris heard a low chuckle at the other end of the line and smiled.

"What would I do without ya, Sis?" he said, his voice much calmer.

"See you later, Franz," Kris said softly and shut off the cell phone then looked at the small woman still in her arms. "Good morning." She threw the phone on the bed and gently kissed Nicole. "That wasn't how I planned to wake you up this morning." Kris nodded towards the phone lying on the bed.

Nicole chuckled at the apparent disappointment in Kris' voice. "Maybe not the wake up call you intended, but I'm not complaining. I still have you standing naked in front of me." Nicole glided her hands over Kris' chest, and gently sucked a hardened nipple then the other.

"Nicole," Kris warned half heartedly, "we're already late. Don't get me started." She kissed the teasing woman.

"Tell you what," Nicole started between kisses, refusing to let the naked beauty in front of her go. "We both go into that shower," a kiss between the tall woman's breasts, "then you can look at Franz's problem," another on her stomach, "while I go get us some breakfast." Nicole was now at Kris' belly button and working her way down.

The bathrobe was suddenly stripped off of Nicole and she

was in Kris' arms, heading back to the bed.

"Breakfast can wait." Kris smiled, her eyes dancing with passion.

❖ ❖ ❖ ❖ ❖ ❖ ❖

The rest of the week was a blur for Kris and Nicole. When they weren't at the stunt school with Kris teaching and Nicole videotaping, they were either sightseeing and eating at great restaurants or just plain relaxing at Kris' house letting Oma pamper them, who was more than happy to do so. She was ecstatic to see both women so happy with one another.

Graduation day had finally come and gone for the hopeful students at the stunt school. The graduates each performed a small stunt before walking on a nicely constructed outdoor stage where none other than Kristina Von Deering handed them their hard-earned diplomas.

Kris still smiled at the memory of one student who had staged a mock fight scene on the ground in front of the stage then rolled out of the fight to jump up onto the stage next to Kris. The young red-haired student had reached out a shaky hand to receive her diploma from her mentor. The enthusiastic student was always so excited when she was around Kris, that the stuntwoman hadn't been sure if the shaking was the result of the exertion of the stunt or just plain hero worship.

After diplomas were handed out, she had agreed to pose with the students in a group photo. Kris, along with the other instructors, had been heaved up by the students and held in the air above their shoulders as the picture was taken. The afternoon finally drew to a close after Kris and the other instructors agreed to pose for individual pictures. The students went to the local pub, dragging their less than resistant teachers along and celebrated until the next day.

Morning's light found both women packing their bags for the trip to Los Angeles. They knew it would be a long trip. Leaving Innsbruck for Chicago and staying overnight at the hotel, using their time there to do short interviews for entertainment shows and then finally catching another plane to L.A.

Kris didn't mind all the traveling, as long as she had Nicole with her, she thought with a smile as she left the last of the luggage by the front door for the limousine chauffeur to pick up later. They would be leaving to catch their flight as soon as the short meeting in the planning room was over.

Waiting for Kris' brothers and some of the technicians to arrive, the stuntwoman grabbed the planning room cordless phone, walked back to her bedroom and found Nicole looking out the glass doors at the Alps.

Kris wrapped her arms around the smaller woman and gently kissed Nicole's neck. "Everybody should be here soon. Do you think I would be missed if we stay here and play for awhile?" she whispered conspiratorially into Nicole's ear, making the young woman smile.

"What do you think I've been thinking of all this time?" Nicole responded as she turned around in Kris' arms and wrapped her arms around the tall woman's neck. "After days of preparations for the graduation and then the unscheduled party afterwards, I can hardly wait to be in California," she said kissing the older woman's lips. "At least then I'll have a couple of days with sandy beaches, sunshine and a beautiful woman in a bathing suit all at my disposal. What else could I ask for?"

Kris looked at her young lover with a mischievous grin. "How about a naked woman in your bed?"

Nicole laughed. "Well, that's a given. As long as that woman is you, I'm all for it."

The phone in Kris' hand rang, making the smaller woman jump. "Sorry about that." Kris kissed Nicole on the lips, then answered the call.

Nicole wrapped her arms around Kris' waist, giving the tall woman a gentle hug. She looked up to see her lover smile at her. Nicole couldn't understand what was being said, but she loved the sound of Kris' voice when she spoke German. She also loved laying her head on her chest, feeling her voice rumble. She looked up again as Kris finished her conversation on the phone.

"Everything okay?"

"Oh yeah. The horses are back from shooting the commercial. I'd like to go and make sure they're okay. Wanna come?"

"Sure, I'd love to." Nicole loved horses, but she'd always been a little nervous around the big animals. She remembered the first time they had gone horseback riding and they ended up walking back to the stables with Kris unwilling to let her ride on the big mare after a near fall.

They had gone once more after the incident so Nicole wouldn't be afraid to ride horses. She remembered with a smile the feeling that had run through her body as the older woman had climbed on behind her. The sense of being protected was soothing as Kris wrapped an arm around her slim waist and she leaned back into the woman's chest, feeling the taller woman's hot breath brushing her neck.

Nicole mentally shook herself. This was no time to think about that. Especially since they had no time to do anything about it.

They walked out of Kris' bedroom and exited the house by the door beside the kitchen, which was adjacent to the path leading to the stable. The modern and well-kept building had a section to the right loaded with horse healthcare products where most minor wounds could be treated if need be. Beside it was the tack room with a workshop.

"Most times, we can take care of the horses' injuries ourselves." Kris nodded hello to the employees in the stable. "We have a vet working here full time, mostly at the Arabian stable on the other side of the house," she explained as they walked down the aisle, looking at the horses in the stalls.

"I noticed you have all kinds of breeds. How come you have the Arabians separate from those here?" Nicole stopped to pat an Appaloosa that was having her shoe fixed.

"The other stable is reserved for the breeding program," Kris explained, scratching the horse behind her ear. "These here are mainly show horses. Not in the sense of competition, but they're trained for stunts."

"Oh," Nicole was intrigued, "what kind of stunts can they do?" When she thought about stunts, she always thought of high falls, cars crashing or motorcycle jumps, but never thought about horses.

"Well, all the horses we have here have their own specialties. Some are fast runners, some will easily take falls and others will handle fires. Nushka here is a jumper. We'll use her when we have to jump over a deep area or over high objects. She's also very good at jumping off small cliffs and into water."

They continued down the stable, with Kris checking the horses once in a while as they were brought inside. Nothing seemed out of the ordinary as she watched the vet examine the animals. Kris noticed that Nicole was lost in thought, mumbling silently to herself. "What are you thinking about?" Kris asked, amused.

"Oh. Well, I was thinking that it would have looked good in the documentary to tape a few moves, you know, some tricks they can do," Nicole replied, smiling at Kris.

Kris gently pulled Nicole out of the way to let another horse come into the stable, smiling at the handler, then at her companion. "I'm sure we can arrange something on our way back from the States." She then guided her lover to the fenced field, where horses were free to roam. They stopped and Nicole climbed the fence, to sit on top of it as she watched the different breeds run across the field while the sunrays shimmered on their strong backs. Kris stood behind Nicole and wrapped her arm around the younger woman, holding her in place so she wouldn't fall.

"I talked to Robert today," Nicole said as she watched the horses being put back in the corral.

Kris looked up at her lover, a slight frown on her face. "And what did your boss have to say?"

Nicole smiled as she glanced at Kris then turned back to the horses. "Well, he's not my permanent boss anyway. Robert says he's very thrilled with the tapes I've been sending him. He says he's got enough to finish the documentary."

"That's good, isn't it?" Kris asked, not sure why Nicole looked so lost in her thoughts.

"He's offered me another project," Nicole replied, looking at Kris for any reaction. The tall woman's emotions were hard to read sometimes.

"Oh?" Kris said as the implications registered. "Where would that take you?"

"On a movie set in Argentina. I was offered a job as main

camera." The stuntwoman chewed on her lip as she fought with her emotions. Nicole turned on the fence, brushed her hand through Kris' black hair, and gently tilted her head up so she could see Kris' eyes.

"That's a great step for you." Kris tried to smile, happy to see that her friend was making her mark in this business. "I'm sure the money will be good too."

"Money, lots of traveling, making a name for myself, sure that's great. But what's the use of taking a job if I won't be happy doing it?" Nicole asked as she jumped down from the fence to stand in front of Kris.

"What do you mean, not happy doing it? You love your work. You told me you always wanted to travel and see the world."

"I told Robert I'm not taking it," Nicole stated in a voice that bore no arguments. "I just found what I really wanted, Kris, and that's to be with you. No job, no matter how much I like doing it, will make me feel the way you do." She gently wrapped her arms around the tall woman, waiting for Kris to say something.

"But what about your work? It's always been so important to you. Are you sure you're doing the right thing by refusing the job?"

Nicole let go of Kris as if she had been burned. She looked at the older woman, confused by her reaction. "Are you saying you want me to go?"

Kris quickly reached for Nicole and pulled her back to her. "Oh Gods no, that's not what I meant." Kris brushed her fingers through the golden hair. "I don't want you to go," she blurted out, stepping back from Nicole so she could look at her lover. "I just wanted to make sure that this is what you really want. I don't want to lose you again, Nick, I'm thrilled that you want to stay with me."

Kris knew she was babbling. How could she say how much she wanted Nicole to stay and live with her? She was overjoyed at knowing that after the competition, Nicole would still be there. She tried to speak but her voice refused to cooperate.

Nicole put a gentle finger on Kris' lips, and smiled at her

friend. "I understand. You wanted to make sure I knew what I was doing and I appreciate that. I'm also thankful that you didn't try to influence my decision, when you could have done it so easily."

"I didn't want you to base your decision on some old stuntwoman's wishful thinking."

Nicole kissed Kris, letting all her emotions go through that single contact. "To be with you is my one and only desire, Kris. I love you more than words can say."

A lone tear fell down Kris' cheek as she kissed the woman that meant so much to her.

The phone in Kris' hand rang. Not wanting to let go of the moment but having to, Kris took a step away from Nicole and answered the phone. "*Ja?*" She turned around to look at the road leading to the house, seeing cars coming their way. "Danke," she said as she ended the communication. "It's show time." Kris smiled at her younger companion and kissed her one more time. "Do you want to come to the meeting or would you rather stay here?"

"It's okay, I wouldn't understand a word you said anyway." Nicole laughed. "But thanks for asking. I think I'll stay here and chat with Ingrid. She was nice to talk to before."

"Oh, really? How nice was she?" Kris teased as they walked back to the house.

"Wouldn't you like to know?" Nicole replied as she lightly kissed Kris before they parted company.

As Kris went back to her house, her smile quickly faded when she noticed the woman getting out of Franz's truck. Her brother hadn't mentioned that Martina would be present. Even though this small meeting was to be a short one, Kris had the gut feeling that it was going to be a very stressful one.

❖❖❖❖❖❖❖

Nicole looked at her watch and noticed an hour had gone by since Kris left for the meeting. *They must be done by now,* she thought as she went to the planning room and saw that the door had been left opened. She poked her head through the door and noticed Kris sitting at the head of the table, rubbing her temples while she examined some papers in front of her. She looked extremely stressed.

Around the table sat Kris' brothers, Franz, Hans and Ludwig. Two other men were also present, Gunther Broca and Steve Carpenter, instructors from the stunt school. Also at the table was a very intense looking redhead. The woman had eyes only for Kris who was doing her best to ignore her. The look wasn't of admiration or respect but rather one of pure hatred. What bothered her more was how the look seemed to intensify when nobody was watching.

Catching a movement by the door from the corner of her eyes, Kris lifted her head and saw Nicole. The tension drained away from her body as her lover smiled and winked.

Switching from German to English, Kris looked at her older brother and stood up. "Is there anything else I should know about before we leave? We're already late for the airport." She picked up her folder and slipped it into her briefcase.

"No, not really. Like I said, the trucks will be leaving tomorrow morning for Sweden with all the equipment. By the time you come back from the States, everything will be set up. We'll meet you there," Franz said as he stood up and gathered his papers, the other men doing likewise.

While Kris made last minute preparations with her older brother, the red haired woman got up with the help of a cane and walked towards the door to leave the room. The woman's rough walk, caused by the two artificial legs, clued Nicole in that this was the infamous Martina. The woman had a nice smile, Nicole thought. Too bad her expression looked like a cat's right before it pounced on its prey. Nicole took a deep breath to calm her rising nerves. She had no intention of being that prey.

"Well, I finally meet Kris' new little friend. She speaks very highly of you, you know," Martina said, her eyes cutting a hole into Nicole's soul.

"She spoke to you about me?" Nicole asked in disbelief.

The smile faded slightly on Martina's face, her eyes never wavering from the petite blonde. "Not really. Your relationship is all over the news. You really don't know what you're getting yourself into, do you?"

"I don't know what you're talking about," Nicole said, wanting nothing more than to just be away from this woman. She looked around and found Kris talking on the phone, Franz still with her. She felt uncomfortable under Martina's icy glare.

"Of course you don't. You're just another plaything to her," Martina spat as she nodded her chin in Kris' direction. "She'll use you and once she's had enough of you, she'll spit you out like a bad seed."

"Is that what you think happened to you?" Nicole asked. A humorless snort was her only answer. "If you despise Kris so much, why do you work for her?"

"Ah, but that's the beauty of it, little girl, I don't. Her brother hired me and she's got nothing to say about it," Martina explained with a cruel smile. *She ruined my reputation, my career and my life. I'm going to make sure she understands the meaning of being ruined. And then we'll see how she likes it.*

As Nicole turned to leave, Martina's hand shot out, and grabbed hold of her arm in a vice-like grip.

"Take my advice and leave. You'll only end up getting hurt by her," Martina hissed into Nicole's ear.

"You're crazy. Let me go," Nicole said as she tried to pull away from the hateful woman, who only tightened her grip to a more painful level.

A hand shot out of nowhere and grabbed Martina's throat. The redhead found herself facing a furious Kris whose eyes held a dangerous spark. "You take your hand off of her, right now," Kris growled at the surprised woman.

"Easy, Kris, I was just saying hello. What's your problem?" Martina lied as she let go of Nicole and held both hands up in front of her in a sign of surrender.

Franz quickly came between the two women, looking from Nicole who was rubbing her arm, to Kris and Martina. "What's going on here? Kris, let her go." His voice was a touch nervous. Kris all but ignored her brother as she tightened her grip around Martina's throat.

"Don't you *ever* touch her again, or I promise, it'll be the last thing you do," she hissed through clenched teeth. Martina's face turned red as Kris squeezed her fingers around Martina's throat for emphasis before pushing her away. She had known something was going to happen with Martina around. Then she spun around to her brother, giving him a warning glare. "Obviously my word isn't good enough for you when I told you she couldn't be trusted. You hired her, Franz. You handle her. I don't ever want that woman anywhere near my equipment or us. You better make sure you keep her under a tight leash. Is that clear, Franz?"

"Kristina, you're over reacting. You keep blaming her for accidents that happened, but nothing was ever proven that she deliberately had anything to do with them."

Martina stood back and watched the two siblings arguing over her, enjoying this little scene tremendously. It was so easy to make Kris lose control. As long as she played her cards right with Franz, acting like the little victim, Martina could succeed in putting a damaging wedge between the Von Deerings, especially with this latest player. The redhead looked at Nicole and smiled. Things were going to get very interesting.

"I remembered her around the car before that stunt, Franz, even though she was not allowed access to it. That accident almost cost me my life!"

"All I wanted to do was help," Martina chimed in, innocently looking at Franz. "I don't know why you hate me so much, Kristina." The redhead smiled shyly at her.

Kris was about to lunge at her again, but felt a soft hand on her arm and looked at her young lover who stood between the women. "Kris, I need fresh air. Please come with me?"

She sighed and nodded to the smaller woman. She looked up at her brother and then addressed the remaining people in the room. "We're leaving in half an hour. I want everybody gone before then." She turned a heart-stopping glare on Martina. "And I want that woman off my property, right now." Kris left the room with Nicole beside her.

Franz just shook his head. This was so extreme, even for Kris. Maybe she was just nervous about the TV interview in Los Angeles, he thought. He knew how much she hated those kind of public events.

He picked up his papers and sneaked a look at Martina, catching her with a sly smile playing at the corner of her lips and a devilish glint in her eye. *Maybe Kris was right about her. There's more going on here than meets the eye.* "Come on, let's go," he told the stunt technician in a neutral voice as he led the way out.

❖❖❖❖❖❖❖

Back at the stable, Kris leaned on the fence softly brushing Morrigan's nose, her favorite horse. The Golden Saddlebred came closer to her mistress with big brown eyes watching her and pushed her nose into Kris' chest then laid her head on the tall woman's shoulder. Kris' dog, Fräulein, was doing her best to drive the horses crazy. She could see Oma on the other side of the corral trying to coax the dog out of it.

Kris shut off the cordless phone and looked at her companion. "The limo will be here soon." She gave a tired sigh. No sooner did she utter those words than Nicole's fingers kneaded Kris' tense shoulder and neck muscles. "Ooh, that feels so good." She smiled as some of the pent up tension left her body.

Nicole smiled at Fräulein's antics as she massaged her lover. She couldn't believe how knotted up Kris' muscles were. "You're so tense. How 'bout I give you a good massage once we're in the limo and on our way?"

"A full body massage?" she teased the smaller woman who playfully slapped her arm. Kris gave Morrigan a final scratch behind the ear as the Saddlebred nudged her one last time and turned to join the other horses.

"That," Nicole kissed Kris on the cheek, "will have to wait until Chicago." She smiled as she continued to rub the tall woman's shoulders. Kris relaxed even more when she caught sight of everyone leaving in their vehicles. "You okay?" she asked as Franz's truck left with its two passengers aboard. They were close enough to see Martina looking straight at them, a wicked smile adorning her malicious face.

"I am now," Kris said as the vehicles departed. Then, without warning, she turned to her lover, playfully grabbed her ribs and found the ticklish spot she knew was there and tickled until Nicole squirmed and squealed in a fit of laughter.

I'll get to you through the things you love the most, Martina promised herself as she watching the playful women grow smaller and smaller as the truck rolled on down the road.

Minutes later, the limousine arrived ready to drive them to the airport and towards a few days of rest and relaxation in sunny California.

Chapter 7

Kris woke up and stretched her shapely legs, thankful that they were in first class where the space was much more adequate for her long frame. She looked down at her traveling companion and smiled. Sleeping peacefully on her shoulder just under her chin, Nicole had a tiny smile on her lips and her arm draped lazily across Kris' stomach.

They had been on long, uneventful flights. Leaving Innsbruck on a late Friday evening and spending the next night in Chicago. After an interview the next morning, they grabbed another flight and were now almost to Los Angeles.

Kris gently glided her hand down the sleeping woman's back and brought it up to lightly scratch Nicole's neck, as her young lover woke up with grunts of satisfaction as the stuntwoman's fingers gently brushed the sensitive skin.

"I swear if you were a cat, you'd be purring right now," she whispered.

"Who says I'm not purring?" Nicole's voice was heavy with sleep as she wiped away the tiredness from her eyes. She reluctantly sat up when the Captain announced their descent into Los Angeles. "With all this traveling and waiting, I'm lost."

"We're in California," Kris simply said and smiled at her friend's reaction, getting swatted in the process.

"I know that." Nicole laughed.

"Oh. You mean...I'm sorry. It's Sunday," Kris replied innocently, biting back a smile as Nicole did her best to look annoyed. "It's eleven thirty."

"Thank you. Talk about taking the long road to China," she exclaimed in mock exasperation, then looked at her lover as Kris took her hand. "So, what's on the schedule for today?"

"Somebody from the talk show will be meeting us at the airport and driving us to the hotel. I thought maybe some lunch and a walk on the beach for the rest of the day?" Kris smiled at the young woman, not sure if Nicole's grin was for the mention of food or the beach. "I could make a phone call and rent a car for the time we're here. That way we can go anywhere we want without the attention a limousine attracts."

"You don't have anybody like an agent or assistant to take care of those things for you?" Nicole asked, surprised.

"Most stunt people don't have agents. We usually deal with our contracts ourselves. Franz is our public relations man, he also sees about our salaries for the jobs we do like the documentary you did for Robert."

"But what about Michael Norman? I thought he was your agent," Nicole said, remembering the forty-three year old man who seemed to have an endless supply of tales about Kris while they waited for her to arrive at the bar that fateful day.

"Michael's a promoter. He does find us lots of work, but he's not an agent or assistant."

Slowly, an idea formed in Nicole's brain. *This could be a nice challenge,* she thought. "You know, ever since I left home and started to travel the world, I had to look for jobs, find places to sleep and eat, find ways to get to the work," she said, looking at Kris seriously. "Sometimes I didn't have enough money between jobs and I had to use a lot of imagination. I'm sure that's what assistants are for right?"

The tall woman looked down at Nicole with an amused look, having already figured out where she was heading with this idea. "Yes, that and a lot more like taking and making appointments, making sure her 'boss' isn't late for those very same appointments. She also has to make sure her 'boss' is well fed, relaxed and gets to wake her up every morning."

Busted, Nicole told herself and laughed. "Where does one apply for this job? Is there any audition I need to go through?" she asked as she gently ran her fingers on Kris' chest.

"Are you serious about wanting to be my assistant?" Kris asked, putting her hand on the smaller one.

"Oh, I'm very serious, Kris. I know I can be valuable to you."

"You don't need to work for me to be valuable, Nicole. But if you really want the job, it sure would help me a lot." Kris smiled at the beaming woman. "Congratulations, you are now my personal assistant with full benefits."

"Oooh. And would those benefits be the ones you mentioned before, including your famous massages and Jacuzzi?" Nicole smiled seductively.

"That and a lot more." Kris bent to kiss her lightly on the lips. "Including an interesting salary."

The plane touched ground and taxied to the gate.

At the airport, a young woman nervously stood outside the arrivals doors, waiting for a specific passenger to come out. She looked at the clipboard she held tightly and studied the publicity photograph her boss had given her.

The picture was of a dark-haired woman with stunning crystal blue eyes, the likes of which she had never seen before. *She's beautiful,* the brunette thought. *Her high cheekbones and those lips...* She quickly looked up from the photo as passengers started to appear with their bags.

This was her first assignment as assistant and she didn't want to screw it up. She remembered the scene her boss had made when his prior assistant hadn't performed to his satisfaction. She didn't want to end up in the same humiliating situation the other girl had found herself in.

Two women walked out the doors, one of which looked exactly like the photograph but much taller than her picture suggested. Her companion was a petite woman, who was younger and shorter than the dark haired beauty. She watched as the blonde talked, gesturing a lot with her hands while the stuntwoman listened and finally broke out with laughter at something her petite companion had said.

The woman took a deep breath, clutched her clipboard even tighter to herself and walked with determination towards the women. "Ms Kristina Von Deering? My name is Sarah, Mr. Duncan's assistant."

"Yep, that would be me." Kris smiled at the brown haired woman who appeared more nervous than she would have them think.

"Welcome to Los Angeles." Sarah smiled shyly, shaking both Kris' and Nicole's hands. "I'm sure you're both exhausted from your lengthy flight. If you'll follow me, we'll be on our way. I have a limousine waiting for you."

Walking through the busy airport to the exit, Nicole watched as their young escort fidgeted with everything from her cell phone to her hair and the pen on her clipboard, all the while anxiously scanning the area. Finally, she found what she was looking for and went into a march towards her destination with the guests in tow.

Nicole looked up at Kris. "She looks so nervous."

"Maybe she's having a bad day?" Kris volunteered as they neared a chauffeur standing next to a black stretch limo.

The man quickly opened the door and politely took the two women's luggage, which he put in the trunk.

Kris let Nicole climb into the plush vehicle first and then followed behind, taking a seat next to her lover. The fidgety brunette climbed into the limo after her and seated herself in the leather seat across from them. Kris looked at the younger woman who nervously fingered her clipboard. "Are you okay?" she asked as the limo pulled away from the curb.

The assistant jumped slightly. "Oh. Yes, I am, I'm fine. Thank you."

Nicole looked at her companion then turned her attention to the younger woman. "That's a nice necklace you have there, Sarah," she said with a warm smile.

The girl looked surprised at the compliment from the petite blonde. She reflexively touched her necklace. "Thank you," she replied shyly. "My mother gave it to me when I moved here."

"Where are you originally from?" Nicole asked, trying to get the assistant to relax a bit.

"I'm from Vancouver, Canada," the girl answered, feeling less stressed. *This woman's nice,* she thought as a smile worked its way onto her face.

"Really? I was born in Montreal. How do you like it here?" she asked as she settled herself comfortably beside her friend.

Kris smiled. That was so like Nicole to try and help people around her feel better and more comfortable. She could see the young assistant relax visibly as the women chatted about everything and nothing. She knew how lucky she was to have Nicole back in her life. Before Nicole, business was great, money was certainly no problem and she had a couple of friends. But there always seemed to be something missing in her life. Even though she smiled, she wasn't happy. How did she succeed in living without the love she felt right now, without the human contact? To have someone love her for who she was.

Kris looked down at her lover who slowly stroked her thigh, sending shivers through her body with the simple touch. *I can't live without this anymore,* she decided, smiling at the squeeze she received from the smaller woman.

The limousine went up the drive and stopped in front of the Sheraton Grande. The driver opened the door for the women and took the bags out of the trunk and handed them to the bellhop.

The assistant, looking calmer after the light chat with Nicole, smiled at the women and shook their hands again. "Well, I wish you a very nice day and I'll be seeing you tomorrow at seven a.m."

Nicole looked up at Kris and mouthed, "Seven in the morning?" She stuck her tongue out as she scrunched up her face into a sour expression, making her companion laugh. They headed for the desk to sign in and get settled.

The hotel was considered among the finest in Los Angeles, the suite magnificent with wall-to-wall windows and a superb city view. By the time they took a quick shower and changed, room service arrived with their lunch.

Kris looked up from the cart in pleasant surprise. "When did you call for this? I was going to do it after our shower," she said, still drying her long, ebony hair with a towel.

Nicole grinned at her lover. "Well, as your personal assistant, it's my job to keep you well fed, right?" she asked innocently as she wrapped her arms around the tall woman. "Also, knowing how much you love driving 4x4's, I rented a Jeep Cherokee for us to use this week."

"You've been a busy bee, haven't you?" Kris asked and gently kissed Nicole's lips. "Thank you. I really appreciate it."

"Anything to please you, oh boss of mine." She smiled. "Besides, I was hungry too."

"Well, I'll be your boss tomorrow," Kris said as she put her finger on Nicole's nose. "But today, I want you to do nothing else but relax and just enjoy yourself, okay?" Nicole nodded and they sat down to eat their club sandwiches.

"As long as we hit the beach, I'm happy. I've never seen the Pacific Ocean," Nicole said as she munched on a French fry.

Surprised, Kris looked up. "What do you mean you've never seen it? You've been to L.A. before, haven't you?"

"Yeah, I've been here twice before but it was always all work and no play. Spent half a day in Pasadena videotaping and then we were gone."

"Well I guess it's settled then. We're heading for the beach and going to have some fun."

They parked the Jeep at the Santa Monica Pier and headed straight for the golden sand. Nicole tried to get her running shoes and socks off while walking and nearly tripped herself a couple of times in the process, causing Kris to shake her head in amusement. She eventually stopped, stripped off her remaining sock, rolled her jeans up to just below her knees and walked into the water, letting the waves crash upon her legs.

"That's it! I've made it!" Nicole exclaimed, throwing her arms into the air triumphantly. "Now I can say I've been in the Pacific."

Kris removed her shoes and socks and walked to Nicole who looked out at the ocean. The tall stuntwoman bent down behind her and lifted her up in her arms.

"Whoa!" Nicole quickly wrapped her arms around Kris' neck and looked at her in surprise.

"Actually, you can only say you've stepped into the ocean. Don't you really want to be able to say you've been in it?" Kris teased, bending closer to the water and lifting her friend only when a wave came past them.

"Kris," she warned, tightening her hold around her lover's neck, "you wouldn't dare!"

The muscular woman stopped moving, holding Nicole just barely above the water. "Wouldn't I?" she asked with a devilish glint in her eyes as a lopsided grin played across her face. Kris straightened and walked deeper into the ocean.

"I warn you! I don't have anything else to wear if I get wet." Nicole looked down and saw that Kris was already in up to her waist. She quickly looked up at the grinning woman and realized what was going to happen. "Oh no! You're not going to—"

The stuntwoman fell into the salty water, taking the shrieking Nicole in along with her.

The small woman surfaced, spurting water out of her mouth and glared at her laughing friend. Just as she was about to say something, another wave hit her and she stumbled into Kris' arms.

"Oh, you're gonna pay for this," Nicole said as she brushed her wet hair back and away from her face.

Kris chuckled and floated with the waves, an evil grin on her face. "And what are you gonna do about it? Make me wet? I might like that."

"Kris!" Nicole was getting a little bit exasperated. "I didn't bring any clothes. We're far from the hotel and..."

"I brought us each a set of clothes," she said casually, talking at the same time as her upset friend.

"What are we going to do if we decide to—" Nicole stopped. "You brought clothes?"

Kris nodded, dove under the water, and surfaced behind Nicole with her arms wrapped around her slim waist. "Yep, that's the bag I threw in the Jeep," she said into her ear and gently nipped the lobe.

Nicole turned to her friend. "You had this all planned out didn't you?"

"Well, you did say that you've never been in the Pacific Ocean. I didn't want to deprive you of a memorable experience." Kris grinned then slowly stepped back as a dangerously mischievous look crossed her lover's face.

"Memorable?" she asked as she pushed through the water, closing the gap between her and the dark haired woman. "You want memorable? Remember this!" She grinned from ear to ear as she threw herself onto the tall woman, sending them backwards under the water. Nicole surfaced seconds before Kris, her arm pulled back and ready to bombard her with armfuls of splashing water. The water fight was on.

Several hours passed with the couple rotating between swimming, floating and just relaxing on the beach. It made little difference that they were still wearing all their clothes. They eventually tired of being loaded down with wet, heavy jeans and headed back to the Jeep to get their dry clothes and changed in the public restrooms. A quick stop back at the 4 x 4 to drop off their wet clothes in exchange for their light jackets and they were ready.

They strolled along Ocean Front Walk towards Venice, stopping once in a while to look at the different items for sale at the numerous stalls lining the way. This was the most entertaining beach community Nicole had ever seen. A throwback to the psychedelic sixties combined with the narcissism of Muscle Beach. A non-stop parade of scantily clad men and women on roller blades, body builders, singers and musicians made the stroll a very interesting one.

Kris and Nicole stopped at the beachfront Sidewalk Café for a meal, enjoying the warm sun and participating in what seemed like the favorite pass time on the beachfront, people watching. They made their way back towards Santa Monica then walked along the pier's weathered boardwalk, stopping at the old-fashioned amusement park to admire its giant Ferris wheel and roller coaster. Beautiful shades of red, yellow, and orange from the setting sun splashed across the surface of the ocean making the view breathtaking from where they stood near the end of the pier.

Nicole slipped her windbreaker over her head and Kris' arms surrounded her from behind, the tall woman's breath on her neck as she lightly kissed it.

"How did you like your day?" Kris asked, looking out over the magnificently colored ocean.

Nicole covered the larger hands with her own and gave them a squeeze, then she leaned into the warm body and rested her head back, sharing the view of the beautiful sunset with her lover. "I had a wonderful time." Nicole smiled dreamily as she tilted her head sideways letting Kris nibble her ear. "A little tired, but a day I wouldn't trade for the world."

Suddenly, Nicole remembered something she had brought with her. She reached into her jacket pocket but the feel of Kris' lips along her jaw line made thoughts difficult to keep coherent. "Kris, there's...um, I'd like to...ah, can you, I mean..." Kris turned her around and softly kissed her lips, sending shivers through her body.

The dark haired woman had maneuvered them into a corner where there were fewer people and the ones present didn't seem to notice or care about the two of them. "Thank you," she said.

Nicole gave Kris a confused look. She wrapped her arms around Kris' neck and looked into blue eyes. "What are you thanking me for?"

"For being here with me." Kris kissed her lips again.

"Thanks for inviting me." She took a long breath. "There's something I wanted to do back in Innsbruck."

"You mean there's something we haven't done yet?" Kris teased, then smiled even more when her companion looked down at her feet, guessing that a blush crept over her face.

"Well yes...no! Um, I mean I'm sure there's a lot we haven't done yet." Nicole looked back up and smiled seductively at her. "Some of those I'd like to try tonight." Kris' full lips formed into a gentle smile as her eyes softened. How she loved seeing Kris' love for her shine on her beautiful face. She could never get enough of it or of her touches that set her skin on fire. And the way she tasted when they kissed...umm.

She mentally shook her mind free of the erotic memories of their previous lovemaking and cleared her throat. "What I'm trying to say is the evening you planned in Innsbruck was such a surprise, so overwhelming that I couldn't find the right time to do this."

Kris studied Nicole's face, curious at what she was trying to say. She glanced down as Nicole handed her a small velvet box.

"I saw this when Marianne and I went shopping. I thought it would look nice on you."

She looked up at Nicole with a raised eyebrow and opened the box. A silver wrist bracelet with intricate carvings twinkled back at her. Kris, unable to say anything, just stared at the beautiful piece of craftsmanship.

Encouraged that her friend didn't utter any protest, Nicole took the bracelet from Kris' fingers and attached it around her lover's left wrist, the short length making it a nice snug fit.

"Nicole, I don't know what to say...it's beautiful. But—" Nicole's soft lips brushed against hers, silencing anything else she may have wanted to say.

"You've always given me things to remember you by," Nicole said, running a finger over the silver bracelet. "When I saw this, I knew it belonged to you." She lifted her eyes in time to see Kris' clear blue eyes mist up. "Please, accept this." She closed her eyes as Kris' hand glided through her blonde hair and she leaned into the touch.

Kris gently hugged Nicole tight. "Nobody ever gave me anything quite like this before," she said, her voice heavy with emotions. "You don't know what this means to me." She smiled as green eyes looked up at her. "Thank you."

Nicole lifted Kris' wrist and pointed at the bracelet. "See, there are little pieces of jade in there. When you look at them, you'll think of me, they match my eyes."

Kris laughed. "I'm always thinking of you, no matter what." This earned her a smile and a long, loving embrace.

The sun had completely set and the wind had picked up, causing Nicole to shiver a little bit.

"It's been a long day," Kris said as they turned back and looked at the multi-colored lights on the boardwalk. "What do you say if we call it a day and head straight for our room?"

Nicole nodded as she wrapped her arm around the taller woman. "A nice shower to take this ocean salt out of my hair will feel soooo nice."

"How about if I give you a nice massage to soothe those aching muscles?" Kris asked as they walked to their Jeep, putting her arm across her partner's shoulders.

"What aching muscles? Not that I mind receiving a massage from you." Nicole grinned mischievously.

"The muscles you kept stretching when you thought I wasn't looking?"

Nicole smiled sheepishly. "Oh. Those muscles. I didn't think you'd notice."

Kris laughed, hugging the small woman tighter against her. "Come on, let's go."

❖❖❖❖❖❖❖

"Are you ready?" Kris asked her young companion as she came out of the bathroom, fixing her jet black hair in a pony tail. She went to the bed and checked her pieces of equipment one last time, making sure everything was in good working order and that she hadn't forgotten to pack anything.

A soft sigh was all Kris heard before she looked up to see Nicole staring out of the hotel suite's window. She left her gear on the bed, half packed and joined her young lover by the window. She wrapped her arms around the slim waist and softly kissed Nicole's neck. "Are you okay?" she asked, a little worried.

Nicole took a deep breath before turning around in Kris' arms. A small smile tugged at her lips. "I'm okay, just a bit nervous about the stunt you'll be doing."

Kris gently rubbed Nicole's back. "Hey, that's a very basic stunt, I've done it hundreds of times." She lifted Nicole's chin with a finger so she could look into her lover's green eyes. "I know you're nervous, but everything will be okay. Trust me."

A nod and a small smile answered the tall woman. Kris gave her a quick kiss as a knock sounded on the door. She let go of the small woman and went to answer the door.

The same woman who had picked them up at the airport stood in the corridor, once again nervously playing with the clipboard in her hands. "I'm terribly sorry we're late. The traffic was awful and there was an accident and—" She stopped when Kris waved her hand for her to slow down.

"Relax, it's okay." Kris motioned for the small woman to

enter and closed the door behind her. "Don't worry, I won't bite."

"Not unless you ask her to!" The assistant heard a voice coming from the other side of the suite.

Kris turned around and Nicole winked at her as she approached them. She was glad to see that her young companion was making jokes. She gave her lover a small squeeze on the shoulder, winked at her and left to finish packing her gear.

"So, how do you like working for Alan Duncan?" Nicole asked the young assistant, who was still fidgeting with her clipboard.

"It's wild!" The brunette blurted out, not sure if she meant it in an excited way or a petrified one. "Most of the guests are not as nice or as patient as you are though," she said before she could stop herself. She looked up thinking she may have insulted them in some way, only to find Nicole smiling at her, patting her shoulder in understanding.

"You won't get the star attitude from this one." Nicole giggled, pointing her thumb over her shoulder. "She's very easy to talk to, don't worry."

"But she's so tall and muscular," Sarah whispered. "I've heard about other stunt people being wild and crazy, I didn't know what to expect from her." The brown eyes grew larger as Kris swung her bag on a shoulder and approached them.

"Oh, she can be wild and crazy if you give her half the chance." Nicole turned to Kris. "Right, wild thing?" she added, grinning mischievously at her lover.

"Oh, I can show you wild, all right." Kris voice rumbled in Nicole's ear as she kissed the blonde woman soundly on the lips, leaving the assistant staring at them with her mouth hanging open. "I'm ready whenever you are." Kris winked at Nicole as she straightened up.

Nicole laughed at the double meaning and squeezed Kris' hand. "I'm ready too."

They turned to the assistant, her mouth moving but no sound coming out. "I thought you were her assistant," she finally said to Nicole. "I didn't know you were...that she...oh, I've really done it this time." A blush crept over her face.

"She *is* my assistant." Kris winked again at Nicole, not adding that the title was only twenty-four hours old.

Nicole gently reached for Sarah's shoulder, and gave it a friendly squeeze. "Don't worry about it." She smiled at the young woman. "Shall we go?"

Sarah quickly nodded, opened the door and walked out of the suite with Nicole and Kris on her heels.

The limousine waited for the group at the hotel's entrance. The driver opened the door for them when the women walked out of the hotel.

❖❖❖❖❖❖❖

The drive was spent in pleasant conversation between the young assistant and Nicole. Kris chose to close her eyes and relax, going over the stunt in her mind, once in a while throwing in a witty comment to make both women laugh.

"Well, I'd like to thank the both of you for being so nice to me." Kris heard the assistant say as she opened her eyes and noticed that they were on the studio grounds.

"It was nice chatting with you," Nicole said. "Just relax a bit, you'll survive better in this business."

The limousine stopped in front of the hangar doors where a big sign proudly advertised, "The Alan Duncan Show." The three women exited the vehicle, with Kris being the last one out. She grabbed her gear from the driver and offered her hand to the assistant who hesitantly shook it. "It was a pleasure meeting you too." Kris smiled at the beaming woman. "I'll make sure your boss knows how well we were treated."

Nicole bit her bottom lip, trying not to smile at the look of pure adoration on the young brunette's face as she looked at Kris.

"Thank you," she whispered shyly, realizing she was staring. "If you'll follow me." She walked through the huge doors, entered the studio and the middle of all the bustling activities.

"This place is incredible," Nicole exclaimed, taking in the technicians moving big pieces of equipment, cameras being settled for the coming show, make-up people passing by and numerous others. "It's so much bigger than the studios I worked in before." She looked up at Kris who smiled down at her, took her hand and gently gave it a squeeze. "You look so at ease here." Nicole looked about in awe and back to Kris' calm face.

"After a while, you don't notice all the activities around you anymore," Kris explained as they walked into the main section of the studio and stopped to let Nicole look around. "Being in front of cameras, either in the studio or outside, loses its magic when you have to repeat a scene twenty times over. It's sad to say, but you become blasé about the whole scene."

Nicole looked around at the hundreds of seats facing the soundstage that, in a couple of hours, would be filled with an admiring audience. She turned back to the set, recognizing the decor from watching the late night TV show, gaping at everything with child-like eyes.

"Kristina!" a voice boomed from nowhere causing Nicole to jump. She turned as a burly man in his late forties headed their way. A big grin played across his lips as he grabbed Kris' hand and pumped it enthusiastically.

"Well, I see that your technician is here." The assistant smiled at the women. "Good luck with the show." She waved good bye and left.

"God it's good to see you again," the man said.

Kris smiled. "Kyle, long time no see."

"And who do we have here?" the bald technician asked with a grin.

The stuntwoman's eyebrow lifted at the look Kyle gave her lover. "Hands off, boy," she said and laughed at the big show of disappointment the muscular man made. "This is my partner, Nicole. Nick, I'd like to introduce you to Kyle Middleton, one of the best in his field."

"Well, thank you Kristina. I didn't know you considered me a great rigger." He beamed at the tall Austrian's compliment.

"I never said you were, Kyle." She laughed at the confused look on his face. "I said you were the best in your field which happens to be the field of shameless flirting." Kris turned to Nicole. "Just be careful of him, he's got fast hands." She winked at the smaller woman and turned to see Kyle clutching his heart in mock agony.

"Oh, that hurts, Sprout." His anguished look turned into a smile. "Well, at least you're admitting that I'm the best at something."

Kris noticed Nicole reacting to the nickname. "Don't go there," she warned as she put a finger on the smaller woman's nose. Nicole smirked at her then kissed her finger.

"Ahhh, that's so cute," Kyle said. "Now I understand the 'hands off.' Your taste in women has improved, my friend." He winked at the blushing Nicole as he grabbed Kris' gear bag and motioned for them to follow him. "Come on, Sprout, let's get the show on the road."

"Kyle," Kris warned as they fell into step behind him. Nicole walked next to Kris, her giggles barely suppressed. "Come on." She sighed, knowing Nicole will never let this one go.

"Right with ya...Sprout." Nicole laughed harder as Kris threw her hands into the air in exasperation. Kyle couldn't help but join the young blonde in her laughter.

As they were led through the corridors, they came upon the host of the show, Alan Duncan. The man was surprisingly small, barely taller than Nicole, with short sandy brown hair.

He was talking with the show's director, looking at notes and nodding at one thing or another when they noticed Kris walking their way. An artificial smile automatically plastered itself onto Alan's face, flashing straight, pearly white teeth as he approached the small group.

Nicole watched the man strut towards Kris with an air of superiority and decided right there that she didn't care for him at all.

"Kristina dear, how was your trip? Good I hope. Well, since we're in a rush why don't you get ready and we'll start shooting, okay? Good. See you later," he said condescendingly, brushing them off quickly.

Both Kris and Nicole looked at the departing man then at each other and shook their heads. "Jerk!" they exclaimed together, making them laugh.

Kris noticed that the director stood next to them and she looked at him, daring him to say anything.

"Oh believe me, you haven't seen anything yet," the director said with a humorless smile as he turned and motioned them to follow him to the dressing rooms for the guests.

Kyle, having heard the exchange, agreed with a vigorous nod. "On screen, he's America's number one talk show host, the new and improved Johnny Carson, he says. What a laugh. He's just another spoiled Hollywood brat." Kyle stopped at a door with Kristina's name written on masking tape and opened it, letting the women enter the small room first.

"So, what's the schedule?" Kris asked the director as Kyle dropped her equipment bag on the desk. She sat on the edge of the table and crossed her arms over her chest while Nicole sat on the small couch in the corner of the room and listened.

"Whenever you're ready, we'll start filming as you get dressed, while you explain each stage of preparation." The director studied the notes on his clipboard then looked back up, remembering something. "Oh, and I hope you don't mind, but two of our guests today have insisted on being present at the taping. They wanted to see you perform live."

"As long as they stay at a safe distance from me, I see no problems," the stuntwoman replied and looked at Kyle.

"We have a full security staff that will cordon the area off, three firefighters ready and a medical unit on site," the technician said as he counted the safety procedures off his fingers.

Kris nodded as Nicole silently approached her. She smiled at her young lover and wrapped an arm around the small waist.

"Who are those two guests?" Nicole asked, curiosity taking over.

"Meg Reeves and Donald Holden," the director answered and smiled at the excited expression on her face.

"Oh cool. She's the one who does the ugly alien on *Scavengers*," she said, squeezing Kris' arm.

A laugh escaped Kris as she watched the excited blonde. "It's nice to know you're having a great time, Squirt." The small woman playfully slapped Kris' arm and halfheartedly glared at her.

"Then," the director continued, "once we've filmed you getting ready, you'll do the stunt. The tape will be shown later after

Alan has introduced you. Kyle here has volunteered to be your tech for today. Whatever you need, just ask him. Let us know whenever you're ready."

When the director left, Kris' gaze fell on Kyle who was suddenly very interested in his fingers. "You volunteered?" she asked suspiciously. "Why do I have the feeling that you're up to something?"

A small smile played across his lips as he looked up at her. "Well, it's the only chance I get to feel you up, Kristina." He winked at the dumfounded Nicole. "I'm the one who will be helping her get dressed," he explained with a huge grin as he traced the female outline with his hands.

"If you value those fingers of yours, dear friend," Kris started as she slowly stood up and walked towards the burly technician, "you better behave. No tricks like last time." Kris stared Kyle in the eyes, making sure he understood her point, then reached into her bag and handed him three sets of clothes.

Kyle took them and opened the door. "You know, I had no idea that gel would be so hard to take off." He laughed, unable to stay serious any longer. "I still remember that look on your face as you tried to scrape the goo away from your body. That was too much." He laughed even harder when a disgusted look crossed Kris' face as she remembered the incident.

As he was about to leave the room, Kris called out innocently to him, "Oh, Kyle? Did you ever find out who put that gelatin in your pool?"

Kyle turned back to the Austrian. "No, I never did. I only had the tanker guy there to suck everything out of—no!" He stared at the smiling woman as realization hit him. "You're responsible for that, aren't you?"

"Let's just say I had plenty of help from people willing to see the prankster get what was coming to him." Now it was Kris' turn to laugh. "I think we can consider each other even then, right?"

Kyle shook his head and laughed. "That was one of the best jokes I had ever seen. I only wish I had come up with it."

"What happened?" Nicole asked.

"I woke up one day and went to the pool for my daily morning swim—" Kyle started.

"He's usually blind when he wakes up, he doesn't notice anything," Kris added with a chuckle.

"Obviously. Anyway, I went for my daily morning swim and ended up diving into a pool full of Jell-O. I just about freaked when I realized what was going on." He looked from Nicole back to Kris. "How did you ever do it? I mean I was there all evening, went to bed and in the morning, everything was done? I never heard a thing."

"Oh believe me, we had so much fun doing it. I'll make sure you have a copy of the tape we made." Kris smiled at the man who was staring at her, very impressed.

"You taped the whole thing?"

"Yep. From the time we sucked the water out of the pool to replace it with a tanker full of Jell-O, and that's including your shocked reaction when you dived into it."

Nicole was having too much fun with this. The thought of Kris sneaking around, playing a huge practical joke on somebody was too much to hold in as a fit of giggles overtook her calm exterior.

"But, how did you do it?" Kyle asked.

"Well, we went to see your neighbor who lived right behind your place and asked him if we could use his yard for a couple of hours. He agreed right away. I believe he told us he owed you one?" Kris said with a smile. "So we snuck a fire hose down into the pool and sucked the water out. In the meantime, we had a whole tanker filled with gelatin ready and waiting. By the time the sun came up, everything was finished and we were all hiding and waiting for the guest of honor."

"You worked all night just for a practical joke?" Nicole asked, wishing she had been there to witness it.

"We were dead on our feet, but we enjoyed every minute of it." Kris laughed.

"Congratulations Kristina, that was a masterpiece." Kyle smiled proudly at his friend as he clapped his hands. "But you do know how sweet revenge can be, don't you?" He turned and walked out of the room with the clothes. "See you later," he said innocently over his shoulder.

Chapter 8

The crew was making last minute preparations when Kris walked onto the set in a bathrobe with Nicole following close behind. They stopped where the grinning technician waited for them and Kris bent down to inspect the mixture in the small tub in front of him, running the gel through her fingers.

"Ahh, Kris. It wounds me to see that you don't trust me." The man chuckled. Then more seriously, he asked, "Are you ready?"

Kris nodded and turned to Nicole who was nervously chewing her lip. "Everything will be all right, you'll see," she said as she brushed her hand against her lover's cheek. "Fifteen seconds and it'll be over." She looked at her wrist and took off the bracelet Nicole had given her the day before. "Here, you hold onto that until I'm done, okay?"

Nicole took the piece of jewelry and looked up at her partner. "I know you'll be careful. I just worry about you. At least it shows that I care," she said and stood on her tiptoes to kiss Kris lightly on the lips, not caring who saw. "I'll be waiting for you with a nice shower after the stunt."

"Good, because I'll need some help to take this goo off of me," Kris whispered suggestively into Nicole's ear and kissed her again. The stuntwoman winked at her friend then turned to walk towards the waiting camera crew with Kyle beside them.

The director greeted her with a nod. The show's host approached the group with a makeup technician fussing over his hair and the two guests following close behind. "All right people, we're ready to start taping. Alan, you'll be asking Kris the questions on the cue cards as she gets dressed and ready for the stunt. Meg and Donald, I'm sure you want a good look at what's going to happen, but stay close to Alan. I don't want any accidents." He turned to the stunt technician. "Kyle, are your people ready?"

"The firefighters are ready, medic unit on standby," Kyle answered, professionally.

The director turned and nodded to Kris. "It's your show. Whenever you're ready." The tall stuntwoman took off the bathrobe and handed it to Kyle. "Quiet on the set! Ready! Roll cameras."

Kris was dressed in a black body suit cut low below muscled thighs. The tight fitting suit left little to the imagination as it appeared to be painted on her taut body. She watched with private disgust as Alan looked her up and down while he smiled that artificial grin of his.

"Well Kris, I thought we would have a chance to tape you while you were getting dressed," Alan commented in a velvety voice.

"Sorry to disappoint, but unless you want your show to be like Jerry Springer's, I needed to get something on first," Kris quipped, catching a few smiles and snickers on the faces around them.

"Yes...well, um...what stunt will you be performing for us today?" he asked, trying to swallow a reply that wouldn't have been appropriate for his show. He was bumped aside as Kyle brought the small tub filled with a gelatinous substance to where Kris would be performing the stunt.

"What I'll be doing today is a very basic stunt, but extremely popular in movies. I'll be setting myself on fire," she stated as she reached into the tub, picked up a handful of gel, and generously applied it to her body. She tightened her jaw in reflex as the freezing cold gel shocked her to full wakefulness. "First, I should warn people to not try this at home. We're trained professionals and have been doing this for years."

"What are you doing now?" Alan asked, looking very interested as Kris spread the gel over her arms and torso, with Kyle working on her legs.

"The first thing you have to do is smear your body with a gel and be very generous about it. It saves your skin from burning."

"Would any gel do? How about hair gel?" The host laughed at his own joke. No one else laughed.

"I wouldn't recommend that Alan, unless you want to make your own version of the musical *Grease*." More chuckles from the crew answered her. "This is a Stunt Gel, especially made for this kind of gig."

"It looks so uncomfortable to wear," Meg said as she picked up a bit of the gel from the tub and squished it through her fingers as she tucked a long lock of her wavy red hair behind her ear with her other hand.

"It's also very cold when it's applied onto the body," Kris added. She bent down over the tub and completely soaked her long hair in the goo, dunking several times making sure her whole head was covered liberally with the gel. When she straightened, the stunt technician handed her a pair of socks that dripped with the substance, then smeared her back with more gel.

"What type of material are those socks made of?" Alan continued with his questions, having difficulty making the tall woman laugh. *Damn professionals.*

"These and all the other pieces I'll be wearing are made of Nomex. They're fire-protective clothing. In total, I'll have three layers already soaked in the gel." She put her socks on making a slight face as the cold gel oozed between her toes, followed by the underpants, which weren't much better.

Kyle handed her a miniaturized air-tank that she affixed to her chest, and passed her arms through the straps. The technician made sure that everything was securely attached before handing her the turtleneck undergarment that she would wear over the air-tank, leaving her long, black hair inside the sweater.

"This gel reminds me of something," Donald said as he

examined it, speaking to the sexy, red haired actress who stood next to him.

"The only other use for Stunt Gel is in hamburger commercials," Kris replied very seriously. Meg and Alan looked up at her in surprise. Donald nodded in recognition. "They smear it on the undersides of the meat so that the burgers don't burn to a crisp while they film them going over the grill for the twentieth time."

"You must be joking, right?" Alan asked the stuntwoman who simply continued getting dressed with Kyle's help, putting the costume pants on and slipping into boots that the technician helped lace up.

After putting more gel on her face and into her ears, Kris fixed her breathing apparatus over her face and took the offered soaked Nomex hoods and pulled them over her head and airmask.

With the safety crew working on Kris by tucking the hoods into the turtleneck, Kyle smeared more gelatin on her.

"How do you feel?" Alan asked. "It must be a very sensual feeling to be smeared with this stuff."

Already breathing through the mask, Kris wiggled a finger at Alan to make him come closer. "It feels like being wrapped in an enormous used Kleenex," she said to the shocked host. The crew nearest to them burst out laughing.

"We'll have to work quickly now, she's on a limited air supply," Kyle said as he helped her get the costume on. "The pants and jacket are from natural fibers. We can't use nylon 'cause it would melt and cause problems." Kyle added more gel to her hands and eyelids, knowing that she would have to perform the rehearsed steps blind.

Kyle motioned everybody to step back as the firefighters got into position with extinguishers. The crew painted the stuntwoman with fuel and pulled back as the technician put a torch to Kris' costume, lighting it.

The scene was incredible. Her whole back was ablaze with flames running up and down her arms and legs. Kris walked the predetermined path along with the rehearsed steps and gestures all while blinded by the gel covering her eyes.

The camera crew followed her all the way through the stunt, staying clear of the flames as she turned back and crashed down onto her knees. With arms stretched away from her body, she fell flat on the ground.

Nicole had a hard time stifling a cry as her lover collapsed to the ground and it took everything she had not to run to Kris' side, desperate to know if she was okay.

The young woman watched as the firefighters sprayed the immobile figure on the hard ground, the safety crew dousing the flames with blankets. The cloud of powder caused by the fire extinguishers made it hard to see what was going on.

Through the crowd surrounding Kris, Nicole saw her friend slowly get up and pull off the three hoods from her head. Kyle talked to her as he removed the air-mask, letting it dangle from out of her turtleneck.

Slowly, Nicole made her way towards Kris, nervously watching for any signs that the tall stuntwoman had been injured. As the burnt costume was peeled off she still smoldered from the flames. The firefighters acted quickly.

The only thing Kris wanted to do was to clear the gel from her eyes and look for Nicole who, she knew, must be worried sick. "Get me a towel," she said to no one in particular. "Damn, I'm still burning!" She felt the heat of the flames still on her body. The firemen quickly worked over her, making sure that everything was okay.

The three layers of Nomex clothing were quickly taken off of Kris as a towel was slapped into her hands and she anxiously wiped away the gel from her eyes. She looked through the crowd and spotted Nicole who had both hands covering her mouth, her face tense with worry.

Blue eyes looked into green ones as a slow grin played over Kris' lips and she winked at her young lover, making her laugh with relief.

A bathrobe was quickly wrapped around the stuntwoman, her body shivering from going to the freezing feel of the gel to the extreme heat of the flames, then back to the uncomfortable coldness of the gel again.

"That was incredible, ladies and gentlemen," Alan said,

looking at the camera, remembering the job he had to do. "Give a great round of applause for Kristina Von Deering."

Kyle leaned in closer to Kris to say something, but the clapping from the crew, loud whistles and shouts drowned out his words. Somehow though, Kris managed to understand what he was trying to say and she nodded. She walked away from the overly excited talk show host and stood in front of Nicole, opening her arms.

The young woman didn't wait to be asked twice and threw her arms around Kris, hugging her tight.

"How about that help you promised?" she asked with a smile and they walked to the dressing room and a long, hot shower.

❖ ❖ ❖ ❖ ❖ ❖ ❖

The taping of the show was about to start. Kris sat in a chair while the makeup artist worked on the finishing touches. She knew there was no way around it, without some makeup, the studio lights could make you look so sickly. That didn't mean she had to like it.

With a satisfied nod from the makeup man, Kris got up from the chair and walked back to the guest room to wait for her turn with Alan.

Nicole had stayed in the dressing room waiting for Kris after their shower together. That had been an event all by itself, Nicole smiled. What started out as a normal shower ended up in a wild session of lovemaking until a knock on the door interrupted their passion.

She remembered looking into Kris' blue eyes in surprise as they heard Kyle's loud voice calling after the stuntwoman. They smiled as the tech had to shout to be heard over the shower noise, letting her know that her equipment was cleaned and back in her bag. Kris had shouted back her thanks and smiled as the burly technician wished them a pleasant time in the shower.

Nicole looked up from the magazine she was reading as the dressing room door opened and Kris walk in. She caught her breath at the sight of her lover. What a change from the old jeans and shirt Kris had worn when she left the dressing room earlier.

Now, she wore a pair of black pants, a blue silk blouse that accentuated the blueness of her eyes and the first three buttons of her blouse left undone. Her raven hair was loose around her shoulders, her bangs framing her angular face. The makeup made her look even more beautiful, if that was possible, Nicole thought as she remembered to breathe.

She stood up and walked to her lover as Kris put her jeans and shirt on top of her equipment bag. Nicole had a huge grin on her face as she looked at her partner from head to toe. "Very nice," she drawled, touching the diamond earrings Kris sported. "You look gorgeous."

The tall woman smiled and wrapped her arms around Nicole. "Thanks. But I think they used too much makeup."

"It's because you're not used to wearing any at all." She laughed at Kris' grimace.

"I hate it. Especially studio makeup, I feel like a clown," she complained halfheartedly.

"Yeah, but you're *my* clown," Nicole piped in, kissing Kris lightly on the lips.

A knock sounded and the stuntwoman let go of Nicole to open the door. A young woman wearing a headset smiled at Kris and entered the room.

"You're next," she announced as she put her clipboard between her knees and fixed a miniature microphone on Kris. "I'll need you to pass this wire under your blouse so I can exit it behind you and plug it in this pack here." She motioned to a small box she clipped to Kris' belt near the small of her back.

Kris did as she was asked without comment. The tech looked at Nicole. "Ms. Von Deering asked that you may be allowed near the set. I'll show you where you can stand and watch the show from the monitors." She smiled when the blonde nodded then turned her attention back to the tall woman. "Then I'll show you where you're to wait behind the curtains. When you hear the music start, I'll give you a go and you walk onto the set. Any question?"

Kris shook her head no as the woman lifted her hand to her headset, and listened to somebody speak. "Okay, let's go."

They walked out of the dressing room and through cluttered

corridors. The tech showed Nicole where she could watch the show and then continued towards the curtains with Kris trailing silently behind her.

Nicole watched as Kris chewed her lip nervously, waiting for her cue and smiled as the stuntwoman played with the silver bracelet she had given her.

Kris closed her eyes, took a deep breath, and let it go slowly. *Oh God, how I hate those interviews. I'd rather fall off a building than sit in front of an audience, answering stupid questions.* She felt somebody watching her and opened her eyes to see Nicole smiling at her. Feeling calmer, she smiled back as she heard the host's voice.

"Our next guest is a very special woman. She has been working for over twenty-five years in one of the lesser-known jobs in show business and also the most dangerous. Ladies and gentlemen, please welcome stuntwoman, Kristina Von Deering."

As the music started, Kris looked up at the technician who had guided her there and the woman signaled with two fingers for her to go on stage. Kris looked one last time at Nicole.

The first thing she noticed when she got on stage was the blinding lights. It took a couple of seconds for her eyes to adjust to them and she took this opportunity to wave and smile at the crowd before heading to the host's desk and sofa for the guests.

The applause was deafening. Kris tried to look out at the cheering fans, only succeeding in seeing the first two rows and waved again in their general direction, still wearing a sincere smile on her face.

The actress, Meg Reeves, and singer, Donald Holden, were already sitting there, smiling warmly at Kris as she shook their hands and passed them to sit at the head of the sofa nearest Alan's desk. She reached out over the desk and shook the host's hand then sat down beside Meg. Kristina crossed her leg over her knee as the band stopped playing, then looked at the Alan expectantly.

"Welcome Kristina, it's a pleasure to have you here," he said pleasantly, the same artificial smile plastered on his face.

"It's nice to be here," she replied and looked up with a smile as somebody screamed Kris' name, saying she loved her.

"I see you have some fans up there," Meg said as she pointed to a section.

"It's nice to know that," Kris said as more cheering started. "Thank you." She turned her attention back to the host.

Alan reviewed the notes on his desk, then looked up at the waiting woman. "You've been in the stunt business for twenty-five years. That's amazing. At what age did you start?"

"I did my first gag when I was ten years old. It was in a commercial for an insurance company in Germany," Kris said as she heard a few exclamations of surprise from the audience.

"A gag? I'm sure you're not talking about a joke here."

Kris shook her head no. "A gag is what we call a stunt."

"I don't know if this is the gag you're mentioning, but we do have a clip here. Let's look at a very young Kristina in action."

A silence fell over the crowd as the monitors in the studio played the short scene. The clip showed a young child playing with a ball in a park, accidentally kicking it out onto the rural street. The young girl bolted after the ball between two parked cars and onto the road. A speeding car appeared, heading straight for the child. At the very last second, the car careened to a stop, narrowly missing the young, dark haired girl. A close up of the frightened child's face revealed Kris' unmistakable blue eyes and shoulder length hair. The young girl stared at the car in shocked horror as she stood in the middle of the road, completely forgetting about her ball, as a German phrase appeared at the bottom of the screen followed by a narration in German.

Gasps were heard from the audience, then a deafening applause erupted as the monitors were shut off. "Of course the car skidded to a stop not too far away from me." Kris smiled as if it were no big deal. "Where did you get that? I haven't seen that in years."

"Your brother Franz was kind enough to give us a copy. How did your parents react to your wanting to do stunt work?" the host asked as he shuffled his cards, looking for interesting questions to ask her.

"My whole family, at one point or another, were stunt people so it wasn't a big shock to them. The gag we just saw had my dad driving the speeding car." It always amused Kris to hear people's reaction to that tidbit of information and smiled as she casually reached for the glass of water beside her and took a sip.

"In your long career, you must have had some bad accidents, right?"

Kris toyed with the glass before putting it back on the table. "That's one of the risks, yes. One of them nearly cost me my life. But that's something we don't like to talk about, it has something to do with bad luck," she lied. She just didn't want to make Nicole uncomfortable with the details, knowing that she was listening.

"But what I'd like to know about is the last stunt you did in Austria that could have turned into a nightmare for you. Do you think somebody tried to deliberately sabotage the stunt and movie you were working on? After all, the stuntwoman who performed the stunt previous to you was paralyzed, and you yourself were hospitalized. This doesn't seem at all suspicious to you?" Alan asked with a mock look of concern on his face as he sat back in his black leather chair, quite pleased with his unexpected line of questions.

Kris glared at Alan. This question wasn't on the pre-approved list. *What else will he be asking?* she wondered.

Nicole, watching the show from a monitor, noticed Kris lightly brush her fingers over her silver bracelet, her posture a little more stiff than usual. She wished that she had a way to calm her lover.

Kris took a deep breath. "Those two accidents were just that, accidents. No foul play was involved, the weather was a large factor in the accidents, that's all." She gave the host a warning look to drop the subject.

Alan quickly looked down at his cards and chose another question, a safer one. "You will be attending the world stunt championship in Sweden in two weeks, right?" he looked up at Kris as she nodded yes. "Your family has been participating every year but not you. Why is that?"

"The reason is simple. I was never available for it until this year due to the fact that most of my work is for movies, leaving me little time for much else. My brothers live for the competition however and they work year round just to get ready with preparing new stunts."

Alan put his cards aside and smiled. He knew he was going to get into trouble for this one, especially if he succeeded in making Kris lose her temper. The publicity ratings alone would be worth it. "I don't know if you read the entertainment magazines in Europe, but over here, you've made the front page on a few of them several times and not because of your stunt work," he said to the silent woman. "It seems that you have somebody special in your life right now, correct? Somebody you met a long time ago?"

Kris' jaw muscles tensed. Everybody knew she hated to talk about her private life and Alan was no exception. She also realized that he wanted her to lose control. Why? She had no idea. She remembered the questions he had asked an actor about his drug problem, something that hadn't been made public. The news had ruined the actor's career.

Well, let's ruin your fun. "Everybody has somebody special in their lives, I'm no exception. I'm sure even you do, don't you?" she asked, creating a hush over the crowd as they waited for Alan's reply.

"Yes, of course I do, but she's not a beautiful young lady like your girlfriend, who I wouldn't mind having for myself," he said, not wanting to be shown up on his own show, but realizing too late what he just said.

Kris kept a straight face as the host's condescending smile dropped. "Oh, I'm sure your wife will be very happy to hear that."

"What I mean is that your lover is a very attractive young woman and there are a lot of people out there who find homosexuality hard to accept. How do you deal with these kinds of attitudes?" Alan was trying hard to salvage his control of the show as his carefully laid out plans unraveled.

Kris leaned towards the host who backed away reflexively. "First of all, if you really read those entertainment magazines, you would know that I've never hidden my preference. Second, who I sleep with is none of your business."

People applauded Kris, happy that someone finally beat Alan at his own game.

Before he could ask the question that was forming on his lips, Kris continued her speech. "Also, I don't see how this influences the quality of the work I do. I can't change people's opinion about how they feel. Either they accept it or they don't, I don't really care because this is who I am and I'm proud of it."

A loud cheering from the audience startled the host. He looked around for some support from his crew but found none, only seeing the sign given to him to pause for a commercial. Even the two guests were applauding Kris' reply. He cleared his throat, put his plastic smile back on his face and looked into the camera. "When we come back, we'll show you why Kristina is the spectacular stuntwoman that she is. Stay tuned."

More applause and cheering sounded as the band played the show's theme. Once the red light on the cameras shut off, Kris seized Alan's wrist with lightning speed, and pulled him towards her. She made sure the microphone boom was off the host and then covered her own microphone with her hand and whispered, "That was a dirty trick. My partner and I may not care what people think of our relationship, but we like our lives to stay private. You back off from this line of questioning or I promise, people will hear about some interesting little secrets you have hidden."

Alan tried to take his hand away from the glaring woman, but only managed to have her squeeze his wrist harder. "I don't know what you're talking about," he said, getting nervous about what she could possibly know.

"Oh, really? Then maybe your wife would be interested in learning about *your* little friend?" Kris watched as the man squirmed on his seat.

"I'm a happily married man," Alan stated.

"I never said you weren't. I was just mentioning...what's your friend's name again? Ah yes, Peter." She put a humorless smile on her face.

People around them couldn't hear what was being said, but judging by the look on the host's face, it wasn't pleasant. Everyone steered clear of both of them.

"That's blackmail!" he exclaimed a little louder than he intended and nervously looked about to see if anybody had heard.

"Stick to the planned questions, Alan and it'll be our little secret." She let go of his wrist and leaned back in her chair. Kris calmly picked up her glass of water and took another sip.

Nicole let out a breath she didn't know she was holding as Kris smiled at the two guests sitting next to her and started chatting amicably with them. A shaken Alan had gotten up from his desk after Kris let him go and had disappeared behind stage.

Nicole watched as the makeup artist fixed the guests' makeup, quickly passing over Kris when she glared at the poor man, making Nicole smile. *She really does hate makeup,* she thought as she quietly walked up to the curtains and looked at Kris, hoping to get her attention. She was rewarded when her lover looked up and spotted her standing not too far away.

Kris smiled when her friend mouthed, "I love you." She lightly brushed her fingers on the silver bracelet and mouthed, "Me too."

A stand-up comic entertained the audience until Alan came back to his desk. Kris felt a hand on her arm and looked sideways at Meg who was smiling at her.

"Is that your friend?" she whispered in Kris' ear, nodding in Nicole's direction. "I wish I had somebody as nice as her in my life."

Kris silently assessed the actress. Meg seemed to be honest in her declaration and the stuntwoman turned to see where she was looking and smiled at Nicole. "Yes, she's my girlfriend," Kris proudly said then turned to Meg. "What do you mean, wish you had. I thought Stephen was your boyfriend."

Meg gave a long sigh, looked around them and smiled sadly at Kris. "Stephen is a good friend, but there's nothing going on between us. We go to premieres and are seen in public together for publicity's sake," she said, her voice low so people wouldn't hear their conversation. Meg looked around and noticed that the other guest, Donald, was busy talking to a tech and wasn't paying any attention to them. She looked back at Kris. "I wish I had the guts to come out like you did."

The dark haired woman looked up as the host came back to his desk. Alan was looking everywhere but at Kris, which was fine with her. She turned her attention back to Meg, as they waited for the show to continue. "I know it's a hard decision Meg. I've seen careers go belly up because people came out. But I also know of a lot of careers that are still going strong, even though the whole world knows about their sexual preferences, which, in my own opinion, is nobody's business." Kris gave a quick smile to the actress as she saw everybody ready to continue. "You'll know when the time is right."

The band started playing as Alan put his host smile on, looking straight into the camera, acting like nothing had happened. "Welcome back. We're talking with stuntwoman Kristina Von Deering. Earlier this morning, we taped a very impressive and potentially dangerous stunt that Kristina did for us." He then turned to her. "Is this one of the most asked for stunts that you do?"

She was glad to see that Alan had gone back to the planned questions. Hopefully he would stay on this track for the remaining minutes left in the interview. "No it's not, but it's always very spectacular," she replied and smiled as somebody screamed a "Yeah!" from the audience. "This kind of stunt is called a burn. There are partial burns which means an arm, leg, hand or even the head is on fire. You have submerged burns which can be a flaming car going over a cliff into the ocean, and then you have the full burns or full engulfs where the stunt performer's entire body is on fire."

"Isn't this kind of stunt dangerous?" Donald asked from his seat on the couch, remembering the scene he had witnessed earlier.

"Burns are the least forgiving of all the stunts," Kris answered. "Broken bones can heal but you have to live with your face or body scarred for the rest of your life."

"Well, if you look at the monitors," Alan told the audience, "you'll see what we're talking about." The three guests and Alan turned towards the monitors as the video started.

It showed Kris getting dressed, explaining what was being done. There were a couple of shots showing Meg and Donald watching the stuntwoman with rapt attention and Alan doing a good imitation of being interested too. People in the studio chuckled at the few witty comments and answers Kris threw back at the host.

Silence fell over the studio as everybody watched a burly man approach the stuntwoman and light the fuel that had just been put on her clothes, causing her to burst into flames. The audience responded with gasps to screams as they watched the woman walk blindly, flail her arms, turn back to face the camera then finally fall to her knees and lay down on the concrete floor.

The last shots were of the security team rushing to Kris, fire extinguishers in hand and checking to see if she was all right. Loud cheers erupted from the spectators as she got up and winked, nobody knowing the wink had been for her friend.

As the tape ended, Alan looked back at Kris with his award-winning smile. "That was very impressive, wasn't it ladies and gentlemen?" he asked as more clapping and cheers sounded. "Tell us more about the gel I saw you covered with."

"For a little bit of history, fire stunts have been done the same way for forty years. The stunters had these big asbestos suits making them look like gorillas coming out on fire," Kris explained. "Sometime ago in Australia, they developed a liquid actually preventing things from burning. A factory burned down there and the only thing that wasn't reduced to ashes was a carpet that a drum of this liquid had spilled over. The carpet was okay even though the factory burned to the ground."

"So is this the same liquid that you use now?" Alan asked, in his host mode.

"There are a few differences from the original but basically, it's still the same."

A technician indicated five minutes remaining. Seeing that the interview was almost over, Alan asked one last question. "How much trust do you have in this gel?"

"I have a lot of faith in that stuff. You can take the chemical and put it on your face and through your hair and actually stick your head directly into flames without burning your face or singeing your hair. But you can only do that for a very short period of time because the evaporation will make you susceptible to injury," Kris answered, glad to see that the show was almost finished.

"Very interesting, Kristina." Alan turned towards the camera with a smile. "Well, that's about it for this show. I'd like to thank Meg Reeves, Kristina Von Deering and Donald Holden for being with us today. Be sure to join us tomorrow as we welcome Kate Spencer, Claudia Ryan, and Jeffrey Huntington. Good night everybody."

The band played the theme song and all the guests stood up and shook hands with the host. Once the music stopped and the cameras were off line, Alan quickly lost his smile and left the stage, leaving the guests alone. A technician walked up to them with an embarrassed smile.

"I'm sorry about Alan. Nobody knows what's up with him," a dark haired man apologized to Kris and the other guests. "Everything's done here, so you're free to go." He took the microphone away from Donald's sweater. A female tech quickly did the same with the intimidating stuntwoman. "Thanks again for being here and thank you for that incredible stunt, Ms. Von Deering. That was great."

"Always glad to see it's still a crowd pleaser," Kris said with a forced smile, not wanting to let on how much she wanted to get away from this place. As much as she loved working with TV and movie crews, she hated the Hollywood lifestyle. She couldn't deal with all the hypocrisy that seemed to be the way of doing things here.

She smiled as Nicole walked up to her. "Hey." She gave the small woman a squeeze on her shoulder then noticed Nicole's expression change and turned to see Meg approaching them.

"I'm sorry to interrupt but I was wondering if we could continue our conversation sometime. Will you be in town for awhile?"

"We're here for a few days," Kris said and if she judged by the smile on her lover's face, she knew that Nicole wouldn't mind one bit. "But we could go out to eat. Are you hungry?" she asked her companion and was answered by a huge grin.

"What do you think?" she replied, happy to be able to spend some time talking with an actress that she liked.

"How about if we meet at St. Claire's in one hour?" Kris asked Meg.

"That would be great, thank you so much, Kristina." Meg

smiled at the both of them.

"My friends call me Kris."

"Kris it is. Thank you." Meg nodded with a smile and left.

"This is so exciting," Nicole exclaimed as they headed back to the dressing room to get Kris' equipment. A note had been left on the bag and the tall woman read it then chuckled. "Who's it from?" Nicole curiously stood beside Kris to peek at the paper.

"It's from Kyle," she said as she handed the note to her lover and watched Nicole's reaction to it.

She took the offered paper.

Hi there Sprout!

Sorry I couldn't hang around any longer, but I had a commitment to keep, the blue eye, blonde hair type!!

Talking about blonde haired women, you sure have a nice one there, kiddo. Don't let her go!!

Give Nicole a hug and a kiss for me. I'm sure you will do a better job at it than me!!

I'll see the both of you in Sweden. I'll be with the American team.

Take care my friend and stay safe!

Kyle

Nicole couldn't help the blush crawling all the way up to the root of her hair as she handed the paper back to Kris. "He's such a flirt," she managed to say before laughing.

"Well, he really likes you, otherwise he wouldn't have bothered to mention you." She took the small woman in her arms and kissed her. "Thanks for being here today. Not too long ago, I would have strangled that idiot Alan. Now, I have you to keep me in line. I just didn't want to play his game."

"It was incredible the way you reacted. People around here couldn't believe how calm you were. You should have heard how sorry the crew was at seeing Alan act that way towards you." Nicole reached up again for another kiss. "But I knew you were about to slap him silly. All the signs were there."

"What do you mean by all the signs?" Kris asked, confused.

"Well, when you're upset, your jaw muscles twitch, then

your eyes get smaller and you clench and unclench your hands into fists."

"I do not clench my fists. I chew the inside of my cheek," Kris stated as she put her jeans and shirt into the bag then picked it up.

"Yes you do," Nicole teased. "You chew your cheek when you're nervous and you clench your hands into fists when you're mad. But I do like your new way of calming down, though." She followed the taller woman out of the dressing room.

"Oh? And what would that be?" Kris asked, intrigued.

"You gently rub your fingers on that silver bracelet," Nicole said as she wrapped her hands around Kris' arm.

She smiled as she realized that she did indeed develop that habit. "Well, it does make me think of you." Kris gave her lover one last kiss as they approached the waiting limousine and headed for the restaurant where Meg was waiting for them.

Chapter 9

They took the next few days after the TV interview to relax and really enjoy their trip to L.A. as well as each other's company. Having been in California several times before, Kris automatically went into tour guide mode to make sure Nicole saw all the sights worth seeing in Los Angeles and to make sure she had the best time of her life.

Their first official stop was a visit to Universal Studios. They went early in the morning conveniently missing some of the long line-ups for the rides. They toured the entire grounds first hitting the Backlot Tour ride, giving them an up close and personal look of King Kong and the great white shark from *Jaws* as it snapped its way around Amity Harbor. They continued on to the ground-trembling *Earthquake* and to the classic locations from Alfred Hitchcock's eerie *Psycho* home and to the Little Europe Streetscape.

Kris knew Nicole would simply love The Stars Tour and very easily persuaded her fun loving companion to take the tour. She smiled with open amusement at Nicole's excited enthusiasm as she strained to take in every detail of the celebrities' houses all at once.

A visit to the Hollywood Walk of Fame and a stop at Mann's Chinese Theater brought about a few surprises as Nicole noticed that many of the celebrities' hand and footprints in the cement easily matched those of her own. By this time, a certain someone's complaining stomach reminded them that they had missed lunch during all the excitement of the day and so they stopped at one of the many little restaurants that could be found on the premises. Soon they were back to their sight seeing.

A beautiful, sunny drive back along the Pacific Coast Highway coming back from Malibu, finished off the perfect day. The sun and light wind of the day gave Nicole's fair skin a nice, light shade in contrast to Kris' already perfectly golden skin.

As they walked in front of the hotel's main desk, an employee ran up to Kris when he recognized the unforgettable stuntwoman and handed her a neatly folded piece of stationary from the hotel. Kris thanked the young man, giving him a generous tip. As he turned and walked in the opposite direction, Kris stood for a moment and unfolded the piece of paper. A frown crossed her carefree features when she recognized the name and phone number written on the white stationary.

Nicole noticed the worried frown and jumping jaw muscles beneath the golden skin. "Everything okay?" she asked as she put her hand on Kris' arm for reassurance.

Kris gently led Nicole inside the elevator to go back to their room. "I don't know," she said. "The message's from Ingrid back home. She wants me to call as soon as possible."

"Your veterinarian?" Nicole asked puzzled as her mind thought about the dozens of prized horses Kris owned.

She nodded. "Yeah." Having a full time trusted vet working there and taking care of the horses made her feel at ease when she couldn't be there herself to watch over them. But to have that very same vet call with an urgent message all the way from Austria unnerved the raven haired horse breeder. As soon as they were through the doors of their spacious suite, Kris made a beeline for the phone and called home.

Nicole sat beside her on the bed as they waited for somebody to answer the call. Kris went from tense to rigid when someone finally picked up on the other end. The young blonde quickly lost track of the conversation when Kris talked in her native tongue, so she just sat there watching the stoic neutral expression dominate her face. But Nicole was very good at reading her lover's body language.

She watched as Kris' shoulders slumped slightly, indicating a problem. And even though she couldn't understand a single word being said, she could tell by the monotone voice that Kris was sad about something. Calm but sharp intonations indicating that something was upsetting her replaced the monotone. Then it sounded as if she was taking charge of the situation, spewing forth a list of orders as she ran a shaky hand through her midnight colored hair, another sure sign of agitation.

The tall woman hung up the phone and walked out onto the balcony of their room, absently looking over the darkening city the view offered her. She stretched her arms out to grab hold of the railing, locking her elbows as she leaned forward, releasing a frustrated sigh. Kris looked down as soft, caring fingers brushed against her arm. Her eyes came to rest on Nicole's concerned face.

"What happened?" Nicole asked with concern.

Another smaller sigh escaped Kris' lips as she tore her hands away from the railing and enveloped Nicole in a hug. "Three horses were down with colic. Ingrid didn't catch it in time and we lost two of them, Nushka and Conan. Morrigan is the third one."

Nicole looked up at the names of the horses. She remembered seeing the gentle Appaloosa, Nushka, being shod while Kris had given her the tour of the stables. She heard mention of Conan, but had never actually had a chance to see him. But the worst blow was hearing that Kris' most cherished and loved horse, Morrigan, was one of the suffering animals. Carefully, Nicole asked, "How did it happen?"

"Ingrid believes that the horses were fed an abnormal amount of food," she explained, looking down at her young lover. "What I don't understand is how. Everything from the horses' water to their feed is carefully measured and strictly taken care of. I ordered a closer inspection of the horses, I want to know what happened."

"How's Morrigan doing?"

"She needed surgery to fix her twisted intestines because of all the rolling she did. Ingrid says she's got Morrigan under a twenty-four hour vigil. She has my most trusted staff members taking care of her." Kris took a long breath and rubbed her strained eyes, releasing some tension from her face. "Nushka and Conan were two of my best stunt horses," she added sadly as almost an afterthought.

"But, isn't colic a common problem with horses?" Nicole asked.

"Yeah, but this situation is just too damn bizarre to be a mere coincidence," Kris answered, frustrated. Horses could suffer with colic in many different ways, but the stables were well monitored, the crews working there were professionals and very loyal to her. She just couldn't believe her workers were that negligent in their duties. Then she remembered something Ingrid had told her. "They were outside, not in the stables," she mumbled.

Nicole gently turned Kris' face to look at her. "We're going back to Austria," she announced.

The dark haired woman looked at her friend in surprise. "Don't you want to spend more time here?"

"Kris, listen to me. If I'm getting worried about what happened, I can imagine what it must be doing to you." Nicole kissed the beauty lightly on the lips. "We've already had a great time here. It's time to go home."

Kris couldn't help but smile at Nicole's words. She looked deep into the green eyes and smiled. "Go home. You really mean that, Nicole?"

"Home is where you are, Kris, and where you go, I go," she said as she was engulfed in an incredible bear hug and passionate kiss.

❖❖❖❖❖❖❖

As they headed out of the Innsbruck airport and towards their waiting limousine neither were aware of the silent figure following them. Had anyone cared to look at this person, the pure hatred on the face would have sent them scurrying home.

Though they had taken connecting flights to get back as soon as possible, it had still turned out to be an excruciatingly long trip home. Once back at the house, Nicole knew Kris was very worried for Morrigan and the rest of her horses and so she sent her on to the stables to check things out while she and Oma brought in their traveling bags. With a smile and a quick peck, Kris sprinted off towards the stables.

She reached the stables in minutes, not even breathing hard from the quick sprint. After Kris found Ingrid, inquired about Morrigan's health and checked out the other horses, she saddled up a gelding to go and inspect the fields. It seemed only the stunt horses that were out to pasture had been affected. Thankfully none of the Arabians who were stabled had suffered colic or any other apparent health problem.

Kris galloped through the fields where the colic horses had been grazing, not exactly sure of what she was searching for. Only the persistent gut feeling that had been nagging at her ever since she received the vet's phone call in L.A. led her further into the field. As she scanned the area, she caught a glimpse of a parked car with four people standing by the fence, which bordered the road, looking at the grazing horses.

Kris spurred her black gelding in their direction. As she drew closer, she saw a man, a woman and two laughing children regarding the horses.

"I hope you don't mind us looking," the man said. "They're beautiful animals."

Sensing no danger from the small family, Kris quickly smiled and shook her head. "I don't mind," she said and walked her horse along the fence to continue her investigation. She looked back at the family and realized that anyone could have had access to the horses while they were in the field. Kris trotted along the fence, away from the stables and noticed something irregular in the grass not too far away.

The determined stuntwoman dismounted and knelt beside the curious patch of grass. She scooped up a large amount of grain that had been dumped there within easy reach of the horses. Kris pulled her cell phone off her belt, called the stable and asked to talk to the vet.

"Ingrid, what were the results of the horses' necropsies?" Kris asked, as the remaining grain trickled through her fingers.

"An excessive amount of sugar beet and oats were found. I don't know where the beet came from as we seldom use it here," the vet said a bit perplexed. "Did you find something?"

"I think I did. Send a crew near the main gate. I found the remains of a grain deposit near the road." She pushed the "end" button on her cell phone and hauled out a small plastic bag from the saddlebag to place a sample of the grains in it. Kris waited for the workers to arrive and instructed them to clear the area and to make sure there were no more deposits like this anywhere else. She then ordered the construction of a better fence that bordered the road.

❖❖❖❖❖❖❖

Once the luggage was in the house, Nicole went to the stable, wanting to check up on Morrigan. Not knowing who this woman was, the employee watching over the horse was unwilling to let the young blonde approach the mare. Luckily for her, Ingrid happened to pass by the scene, recognized Nicole and okayed her to see Morrigan.

"How is she doing?" Nicole asked the vet as she gently scratched behind Morrigan's ear and glided her hand along the animal's nose.

"She's a tough little girl, just like her mistress," Ingrid said with a grin. "But don't tell Kris I said that, okay?"

"You're on your own with that one, Doc. Kris really loves this horse, doesn't she?" The small woman smiled as the mare weakly nudged her, the small whiskers tickling Nicole's neck.

"Yes, she does. Kris was there when she was born and took to training her herself. I remember some years ago when I found Kris sleeping in the hay not too far away from Morrigan when the mare was sick. Kris wouldn't leave her side."

"But she's going to be okay now, right?" Nicole asked, giving the horse a small kiss on the nose, missing Kris' stealthy entrance behind her.

The sight of her lover being so gentle with Morrigan went straight to Kris' heart. She silently watched as Nicole scratched the horse behind the ear and leaned her forehead on the horse's muzzle, whispering softly.

"It'll take some time, but she'll make it," the vet answered and looked up to see Kris smiling in their direction. Ingrid went to her employer and friend, then looked back at the smaller woman still patting the mare. "Now, that's one nice lady you have there, boss," the vet said in their native tongue.

Kris looked down in surprise at the usually quiet veterinarian. "Yes, she is." She nodded as Nicole spotted her and headed their way. "And I'm one lucky woman to have her in my life." She gently wrapped her arms around Nicole, and gave the smaller woman a hug.

"What was that for?" Nicole asked, enjoying the sudden show of affection.

"Just because I love you." Kris smiled at the blushing woman then handed the vet the bag of grain she had found in the field.

"It's sugar beet all right, but it's dry, like it hasn't been properly soaked," the vet said as she inspected the grains. "There's also oats in there and..." She dipped her wet finger into the mix and tasted it, then spit it out when she realized what else was in there. "Salt. They must have drank a large amount of water."

"Why would you soak grains?" Nicole asked, intrigued.

"Sugar beet must be adequately soaked. If it isn't, it'll swell up in the horse's stomach with potentially fatal results," Ingrid explained. "Either the person that did this didn't know what they were doing or..."

"Or they knew exactly what they were doing," Kris finished. "There was too much grain there to be just a treat. I think I'm going to have a talk with my brother." She walked to Morrigan and scratched the mare's jaw.

"You don't think any of them had anything to do with this, do you?" Ingrid asked in surprise.

"No, not my brothers, but somebody Franz hired," Kris spat, as her temper rose at the thought of the red-haired antagonizer, Martina. *If that woman is responsible for this, she will pay dearly.*

Nicole slowly approached her friend and gently tugged at

her arm. "Kris, there's not much we can do now. Why don't we go back to the house and rest," she said, biting off a yawn. They had been unable to sleep during their trip because of their worries about the horses.

Kris gave the mare one last scratch before agreeing to Nicole's plan. She was tired too and everything seemed to be back to normal. *Minus two horses,* she thought sadly.

They headed back to the house and entered by the kitchen door with Fräulein greeting them warmly. Seeing the time on the clock on the wall, Kris knew that Oma had already left for the evening. The two of them were alone and she figured that Nicole's offer of a nap wouldn't hurt after all.

"I'll make two quick phone calls and be right with you." Kris winked at her lover and walked into her private office. She looked for the phone number of the hotel in Sweden where the team was staying and dialed the number. The receptionist picked up the call and Kris asked to speak to Franz. After a couple of rings her brother picked up. "Hi Franz, how are things?"

"Kristina. Where are you?" he asked, confused. His sister wasn't due to be in Sweden for a couple of days yet. "Is everything all right?"

"No, it's not," Kris said and then proceeded to explain the events of the last few days. "Franz, can I ask you something?"

"Sure, what is it?"

"When did Martina join the team in Sweden?"

"Kristina, she doesn't have anything to do with this. Everybody left at the same time. We all checked in together."

Damn. "Thanks Franz. We should be in Sweden in a couple of days. See you then." She hung up the phone and after hesitating, picked it up again and dialed another number.

"Becker Investigation. How may I help you?" the deep voice asked on the other end of the line.

"Klaus, it's Kristina. How are you my friend?" She had to pull the phone away from her ear at the loud whoop.

"Hey! If it isn't my favorite stuntwoman!" the man exclaimed with laughter in his voice.

"I'm the only stuntperson you know, Klaus," she replied with a chuckle.

"Doesn't matter, you're still my favorite. What can I do for you?"

"How about taking a trip to Stockholm? I've got a job for you," Kris said, suddenly serious.

❖ ❖ ❖ ❖ ❖ ❖ ❖

Nicole changed for the night and pulled the blankets away from the bed as she waited for Kris to join her. She had already taken one of her favorite nightshirts out of the drawer and laid it on the bed.

Kris walked barefoot out of her office, took her jeans and underwear off and put them on the chair. She headed towards Nicole as she started to undo her black shirt.

Nicole replaced Kris' hands with her own, continuing the job the tall woman had started. "Everything okay with Franz?" Nicole asked as she slid the shirt off of the broad shoulders.

"Hmm, yeah, everything is fine," Kris said with great difficulty as Nicole's soft hands glided over her body. A grin appeared on Kris' face at the intense look on her small lover's face. "I thought you were tired," she teased as Nicole planted soft kisses on her breasts, making the tall woman's knees feel like mush.

"I'm never too tired for you," Nicole replied slyly as her nightshirt was pulled over her head, leaving her naked in front of the older woman. "While you were on the phone, I locked up for the night. We can relax now."

Kris took the smaller woman in her arms and kissed her gently at first, then more passionately as she slowly lowered the blonde down on the bed. She rolled over, bringing Nicole to rest fully on her body as she wrapped her arms around the slim waist.

Nicole couldn't help but lose herself in the incredibly blue eyes. *God this woman is beautiful,* she thought as she kissed her lover along the jaw and down her neck.

Kris closed her eyes as the passion commanded her body. This was going to be another sleepless night, she thought with a smile as she kissed her partner again.

❖ ❖ ❖ ❖ ❖ ❖ ❖

Nicole easily slid into her new job as Kris' personal assistant and by taking care of her business calls, it gave her more time to take care of her Arabian horse breeding program. What Nicole lacked in the German language, she more than made it up with her knowledge of English, French and Spanish.

The tall stuntwoman had settled into the routine of checking the horses herself, then taking one of them out to inspect the fences, fearing another attempt on the animals. Fräulein frequently followed her on her inspections enjoying the extra free time and runs with her mistress. Kris felt a little guilty at spending so much time alone lately and relaxing, knowing that Nicole was hard at work back in the house. But it had all been her young lover's idea for Kris to spend the days this way.

She remembered with a smile the morning after they had arrived from California, how Nicole had pulled her out of her office to take over answering the many calls coming in. The persistent blonde had insisted the office near the front door of the house was now hers to handle Kris' business and schedules.

As Kris was about finished with her inspection of the land, she noticed a car that was parked beside the road, the driver still seated in it. She took her binoculars out from the saddlebag and turned them towards the vehicle, adjusting the focus.

Before she could properly focus her binoculars, the car was thrown into gear and squealed off down the road out of sight. Kris' keen eyes however were able to catch the license plate of the vehicle and commit the numbers to memory. She looped the binocular straps around the saddlehorn and grabbed her cell phone from her belt and dialed a number. *Why do I have a bad feeling about this?* Kris thought as she waited for someone to pick up the line.

"*Ja?*" answered a deep masculine voice.

"Klaus, it's me again. Before you leave for Stockholm, could you run a check on a license plate number for me?"

"Anything for you, Kristina," came the private investigator's reply.

She recited the numbers then asked him if he could fax his

findings to her private office number. He agreed and they hung up the line. Kris spurred the chestnut gelding she'd been riding back towards the house.

Nicole was about to call Kris into dinner when the tall stuntwoman walked through the kitchen door, Fräulein happily trailing at her mistress' heels with her pink tongue hanging out the side of her mouth. It didn't take the panting dog long before she headed for her water bowl.

"Hi there, did you have a nice ride?" Nicole asked as she lightly kissed her partner as she went to sit at the kitchen table.

"Oh yeah, nice weather for it too." Kris smiled. Not wanting to worry her friend before anything had been confirmed, she chose not to tell her about the strange car she came across earlier. "It's been a long time since I've ridden like that. I just wished you were with me though," she said as she walked to the sink to wash her hands. "I didn't find any more grain deposits, so that looks good."

Nicole smiled as the housekeeper put the plates of food on the table. "You sure I can't help, Oma? I'm not used to being served like this."

"Well, dear, you'd better get used to it," Oma said with a wink. "Especially since I have a feeling that you're going to be spending a lot of time here."

Nicole looked up at Kris who looked at Oma in surprise.

"Oh? And who told you this, Oma?" the dark haired woman asked with a grin.

"Listen dear, I may be old but I'm not blind. It's wonderful to see you in love, Kristina, and it's about time," Oma stated as she gave Kris a basket full of slices of freshly baked bread. "And sweetie," she gave Nicole a roguish grin, "I'm very happy to know that you can make that grouch feel human again."

"Grouch? Me? What's that suppose to mean?" Kris asked trying to hide a knowing smirk.

Nicole turned her face away, to hide the grin on her face and the building laughter.

"And I thought I was the only one you called 'sweetie,' Oma," the tall raven haired woman said incredulously. She sat down beside Nicole and whispered into her ear, "You should feel fortunate, there's not many people she'll call sweetie. I think she likes you." She leaned over to give Nicole a quick kiss on the cheek before Oma came back with her plate.

"Let's face it, Kristina, ever since Nicole has been staying with you, you are not the same woman. It's been years since I've seen you smile and laugh the way you have been lately. If this young lady is important to you, she's important to me. Makes her part of the family." Taking one last look to make sure everything was on the table, Oma smiled at them and left to finish the chores.

"If you ever want to know the honest truth, just ask Oma." Kris grinned at the blushing Nicole and started on her meal. "How was your day?"

"I didn't realize that you had so many fans calling you here," Nicole said as she took a bite of her chicken. "I noted all of the requests for interviews and work offers then double checked to see if they were legit. Turned out only three callers were the real thing." She smiled, proud of herself.

Kris looked up, impressed. "Good work. I'm sorry I forgot to tell you about those fan calls. They'll try just about anything to get a chance to talk to me."

"Oh, don't worry. I thought it was fun. All the requests are on your desk for you to look over." Nicole laughed at Kris' expression. The older woman had stopped eating and was looking at her with a silly grin.

"I'm glad you're enjoying your new job." Kris smiled as they continued their meal with a light banter.

The sun had set long ago and Kris decided to go back to her office to try to catch up on some paper work. Nicole had offered to deliver some papers Ingrid had requested since she was heading that way to take a look in on Morrigan.

The fax machine suddenly hummed to life and remembering the job she had asked Klaus to do earlier, Kris got up to check the results of his findings. She read that the car spotted near the stable had been rented at the Innsbruck airport around the time they had returned from L.A. A cold sweat ran over her body as she looked at the name of the driver. Kris dropped the piece of paper as a feeling of terror took hold of her and without a second thought she sprinted out of her office and ran full tilt towards the stable.

Nicole chatted amicably with Ingrid as the vet went from horse to horse taking care of the daily inspections. As the fatigue from her day's work finally caught up to her during this quiet time, she decided to call it a day and politely excused herself to head back towards the house. As she walked, visions of a relaxing Jacuzzi with a radiantly beautiful dark haired woman waiting for her filled her mind.

Walking along in her daydream, Nicole failed to notice a dark figure in the shadows of the night following her. Before she knew what was happening, the figure threw itself on top of her. The weight of her attacker quickly overpowered her as they crashed solidly to the ground, knocking the wind out of Nicole and leaving her slightly dazed. She was about to smile as she thought it was Kris playing a trick on her, rough housing it a little. But the weight was all wrong and the painful jab to her side told her that whoever this was, they meant business.

Her senses were all screaming danger as she struggled to throw off her attacker. A strangled cry escaped her lips before a powerful, rough-gloved hand smothered any further sound. She thrashed about on the ground trying to catch a glimpse of her attacker, but the heavy body straddling her torso was dressed in black clothing and wore a dark ski mask. A quick flash of steel caught her eye as a terrifyingly sharp blade was held firmly against her throat.

"Keep your filthy, lying mouth shut!" the man hissed through clenched teeth, his voice dripping with hatred.

Nicole's terrified eyes widened in recognition of her attacker's voice as she strained to look into the man's eyes. A violent, open handed slap across her face forced her eyes away from the maniacal eyes of her attacker.

"That's right," he said with a growling sneer, "Daddy's home."

She fought to keep her fear down and stop her body from trembling as the sharp edge of the knife sliced the surface of her tender flesh.

"Just give me one reason and I'll slit your throat from ear to ear," he spat in rage, his face only inches away from her own.

Nicole looked up in horror at the man as her frantic mind desperately searched for an escape route. Without warning, a solid body rushed out of the darkness slamming into her father, effectively throwing him completely off of her. Two bodies tumbled through the grass only a few feet away as Nicole quickly rolled away from the struggle. She turned back in time to see Kris tearing off the ski mask as she struggled with Nicole's attacker. Both combatants quickly leapt to their feet and came face to face.

"Kris! He's got a knife!" Nicole screamed as she scrambled to her feet and turned towards the stables and yelled frantically for help from the workers she knew were still inside.

Every muscle in Kris' body tensed as they paced in a circle, their eyes locked, each waiting for the other to make the first move. Kris' face was expressionless contrary to the maniacal smile and crazed look in McGrail's eyes as he held his knife out in front of him. His free hand reached behind his back and another silver flash of steel caught her eye. Kris knew Nicole's father was over the edge as she stared into his eyes and saw the insanity boiling there.

Kris and McGrail feinted in and out in the age-old dance of death. She cautiously kept the insane man at arm's length, making certain to stay away from the slashing blades. He lunged as she side stepped, opening an opportunity for her to deliver a painful elbow crashing down on the back of his neck between his shoulder blades. The unexpected blow sent McGrail sprawling to the ground. His rage, however, gave him the strength to ignore the pain and spring back on his feet.

This time, seeing only red, McGrail charged Kris like a bull, thrusting and slashing his knives towards her midsection. She brought her leg up in time to deflect McGrail's attack causing him to lose one of his weapons. Kris was thrown slightly off balance by the surprising strength behind the initial attack, leaving her vulnerable to the second blade. The slashing knife tore through her shirt and grazed the soft flesh that lay beneath, drawing first blood. He followed up the successful attack with an untrained sidekick, which was easily blocked by Kris. Without hesitation, her strong leg shot out delivering a powerful knee attack to McGrail's sternum. All the air left the man's lungs as he doubled over in pain. As he struggled for air, Kris' booted foot connected just under his chin, lifting him up off his feet and crashing backwards onto the hard ground, causing him to lose the second knife and leaving him temporarily stunned.

"That's for attacking Nicole you bastard," Kris spat out in disgust as her whole body shook with unbridled rage towards the man. Yells could be heard approaching as several young men rushed to their aid, but were still too far away to be of much help at the moment. The furious woman grabbed McGrail by his shirt and pulled him to his feet.

"And this is for breaking us up," she growled as she hauled back her arm to punch him with the force of all her weight behind. Before her fist connected with its target, she was taken by surprise by dirt thrown into her eyes by the devious man. Her eyes stinging and blinded by the underhanded attack, she was left wide open for a surprise lunge. McGrail's knee quickly came up, mirroring Kris' earlier blow to the abdomen. The pain was intensified as it struck the knife wound she had suffered earlier bringing her to her knees while clutching her stomach. She then unsteadily got back on her feet.

"How do you like your own medicine, bitch?" he hissed as Kris, trying to ignore the pain, stumbled away from him to put some distance between them and to give her vision a chance to clear up. Still blinded, Kris didn't notice McGrail retrieving one of his lost knives.

"He's got a knife again, Kris!" Nicole cried out with a heart wrenching fear in her voice just as she started towards the two fighters. Ingrid, ahead of the young men, reached Nicole just in time to stop her from running foolishly into the middle of a dangerous fight which would only succeed in getting the young blonde hurt.

One of Kris' eyes finally cleared enough for her to see McGrail's meaty fist swinging towards her head. Instinctively, she brought her arm up in front of her face to block the attack. Halfway through the swing, McGrail switched his approach, attacking instead with the knife. Kris' eyes were still watering, making her miss the switch until the last instant, unable to avoid the knife's painful bite into her arm with its piercing swiftness.

She grabbed her injured arm and tucked it securely against her chest, filled with rage as the sneering man came at her again. This time, she faked and caught him in the face with her elbow. The crack of his nose and the scream of pain made her smile as she turned and effortlessly kicked the knife out of McGrail's hand. Before she had a chance to grab him, he looked over her shoulder at the young men who were almost on top of them and laughed maniacally as he turned and ran off into the night with the stable employees in pursuit.

Nicole shook out of Ingrid's hold and ran to Kris. "Oh my god. You're hurt."

"I'm okay," she said through clenched teeth, staring into the darkness where McGrail had escaped then turned her attention back to her friend. "Are you injured?"

The young blonde shook her head and put a shaking hand on Kris' arm. "But you're bleeding a lot."

"Let me see," Ingrid said as she tried to pull Nicole away from Kris so that she could get a look at the wounds. The vet finally gave up trying to separate the two and instead steered them towards the stable. Once inside, Ingrid ordered Kris up on a table as she took out the tools of her trade.

"It's no big deal, really," Kris reassured them as she gave her young lover a kiss.

"Yeah right. I'll be the judge of that. Now sit." Ingrid scoffed as she took Kris' injured arm and pulled it away from the stuntwoman's body. Her white shirt was completely stained with blood.

Nicole quietly stood beside her partner, holding the tall woman's hand in hers. "How does it look?" she asked as the vet wiped the blood away from the wound on Kris' abdomen.

"I can't believe I'm being treated by a vet," Kris growled.

"Well believe it. Your pig headedness makes you act like an ass sometimes, so I'd say it's fitting," Ingrid growled back. As she continued cleaning the wound, it was clear that it required stitches but was not as serious as all the blood suggested.

Kris just glared at the vet but otherwise kept her mouth shut.

Chapter 10

After receiving a phone call from Kris after the attack, the private investigator quickly made his way to the stuntwoman's house. Kristina had been a friend of his for a long time and knowing that somebody had tried to kill her made him angrier than words could properly describe.

Klaus arrived at the house, which was so abuzz with activity that he thought he was walking into a carnival. Carrying his laptop computer in his hand, he walked on through the grounds accompanied by a security guard and recognized some of the patrolling people as friends that he and Kris had in common.

"Marianne!" Klaus called out when he spotted Kris' sister walking towards the house.

"Hey, Klaus. I'm glad to see you here."

"Is Kris all right?" he asked, concern catching up with her.

Marianne nodded to the security guard and he left the private investigator in her care. She passed her fingers through her long, dark hair and sighed. "Her injuries aren't life threatening." She looked up at the man. "But she's damn angry, though. It's been years since I've seen her this way." She thought back to the furious reception she had received when she had called Kris earlier, oblivious to what had happened to her sister and friend. Marianne had then quickly rushed to the house and took over the security details so Kris could rest.

"I remember what she can do when she's angry," Klaus said as they entered the kitchen. "Hope she calmed down somewhat."

"You've got nothing to fear," Marianne said as she pulled a chair out for him to sit on. "I'll tell her you're here."

❖❖❖❖❖❖❖

Kris brushed Nicole's silky hair with her fingers as she watched the woman in a fitful sleep in her arms. It took forever it seemed to get Nicole to agree to a mild sedative to calm her frayed nerves. She had insisted that she wanted to stay alert in case her father decided to come back and finish what he had started. Kris glanced down at her sleeping lover, recalling their conversation a few minutes earlier.

"Why?" Nicole asked, her voice cracking with emotion as tears ran down her cheeks. "What did I do wrong?"

Kris slowly lifted her chin to look into her eyes. "Nicole, listen to me. You did nothing wrong. Whatever caused him to act this way was not your fault." She gave her a loving hug, trying to reassure the woman as Nicole took a deep breath, wanting to calm herself and get her emotions under control. "How are you doing?" Kris asked as she wiped Nicole's tears with her thumb.

"The nightmares I keep having, they were of that night when my mother died. Now I remember," Nicole realized tiredly and leaned her head against Kris' chest. "He came home one day, dinner wasn't completely finished. I was still putting the plates on the table when he came in. He got upset and started hitting me." She stopped to take another shaky breath. "Mother tried to make him stop so she put herself between us and he started to hit her instead. I ran outside." Nicole wiped her eyes with her sleeve. Kris' presence was reassuring, giving her the strength to keep talking. "I remember hearing my father yell and my mother crying, things breaking in the house. Then she came running out the door to escape and while crossing the road, a car hit her, killing her instantly." Nicole shook her head from the memories and lifted pained eyes to look into worried blue ones. "Why can't he leave us alone?"

Kris gently took her lover's hands in hers. "I don't know,"

she answered softly, chewing the inside of her cheek. "Are you gonna be okay?"

The blonde woman shrugged her shoulders. "I'm scared, Kris," she replied honestly, her eyes filling with tears again.

"You're not alone. We'll get through this together, you'll see," she said as she gently brushed the smaller woman's back, causing her to get sleepy, aided with the mild sedative taken earlier. In no time at all, Nicole had fallen asleep in Kris' arms.

Kris gently stood up from the bed and covered Nicole's small body with a thick blanket then sat back on the edge of the bed, looking at her lover, feeling the rage in her blood boiling in her veins for McGrail.

The dark haired woman lifted her eyes as she noticed some movement by the bedroom door and saw Marianne standing there. Her young sister quietly walked through the door to stand by her side and lay a comforting hand on her shoulder and looked down at Nicole.

"How's she doing?" Marianne asked in a whisper.

"She's finally sleeping," Kris replied, not taking her eyes off of her friend.

"There's someone here to talk to you. Don't worry, Wilhelm will stay with Nicole while you're away," Marianne explained, gently squeezing her sister's shoulder.

"Who is it?" she asked wearily.

"Klaus."

Kris gently brushed some blonde hair away from the small woman's face and bent down to kiss her gently on the cheek. She stood up and walked to the door, looked back at the sleeping form of her lover then nodded briefly at a friend of the family who was standing by the door before the two women left the room.

In the corridor, Marianne took Kris' arm. "How are you doing?" She took in the drawn features and the weariness that seemed to fill her sister's haunted eyes. Before the tall woman could answer, Marianne threw her arms around her sibling and held her close.

Kris warmed up to the embrace as all her fear, rage and fatigue momentarily melted away. Marianne's body seemed to slump into the embrace as Kris threw her arms around her younger sister. The two stood like that for some time before Kris took a long ragged breath, breaking off the moment.

"I feel better. Thanks, Mari, for being here." She smiled wanly as they started down the corridor, their arms lazily draped across each other's waists.

"Anytime. It's nice to be able to help you out for a change."

"What do you mean?" Kris quizzed.

"Well, seems like you're always bailing my butt out of one situation or another."

"That's what big sisters are for."

Klaus was sitting at the table, drinking coffee when Kris and Marianne walked into the kitchen. He looked up from his laptop's screen to his friend. She looked beat. He noticed her bloodied white shirt and frowned at her.

"I'm fine, Klaus," she answered his unasked question then nodded at Marianne who walked out of the house to check on the security for the night. Kris turned her attention back to the private investigator. "The reason I asked you here is that I don't believe the police will move fast enough." She fell solidly into the chair across from him. "I want that bastard found. I don't care what it takes. He's not going to get away that easily."

"I did a second check on the car you spotted here. The address he gave the airport was his Canadian residence. I did another search of the rented car's license plate with all of the major hotels around Innsbruck and so far, I haven't found a match. The search program is still looking." Klaus started to reach for Kris' hand but stopped halfway, remembering how she hated to be touched and gave his friend a smile instead. "Who's the guy anyway? You know him?"

Kris wearily rubbed her eyes, trying to wake herself up. "He's my partner's father."

"Your business partner's father?" the investigator asked, finding the idea of somebody sharing her horse breeding business hard to believe.

She stopped rubbing her eyes and looked at her old friend. Obviously, he hadn't heard about Nicole yet. "My lover's father."

"Oh," Klaus said, understanding dawning on him.

Kris got up and walked to the counter, and poured herself a cup of coffee. "Nicole's father gave us a lot of trouble twelve years ago. Now that we're back together, he surfaces again," she explained as she sat back down at the table.

A beep sounded from the laptop as a match was made. Klaus quickly scanned the data and looked up at Kris who got up and walked around behind him to check the information herself.

"We found him. You want me to call the police?" Klaus asked.

"And what are you going to tell them? That you found where he's staying by using an illegal program and hacked into hotel computers?" Kris asked over her shoulder as she walked towards the front door.

Klaus quickly shut down his computer and ran after the tall woman. "What are you planning to do?"

The dark haired woman put a black sweatshirt over her blood stained shirt, not bothering to change and grabbed her leather jacket.

"I'm going there to find him."

Marianne arrived in time to see her sister pulling on her jacket. "Where do you think you're going? Kristina, you should get some sleep," she stated as she grabbed her sister's arm, stopping her.

"Don't ask, Marianne. The less you know, the better," Kris replied, anger and determination in her eyes. "I'd like you to keep an eye on Nick for me, okay? I'll be back as soon as possible." Kris started walking down the corridor towards the garage and the Lamborghini.

Marianne refused to release her hold on Kris' arm until she had her say. "Kris, I know you feel like this is something you have to do so I won't try to stop you. Just don't forget about the woman in your room. She loves you and needs you very much right now and I know you need her just as badly. Please Kris, don't do anything foolish and screw up the good thing you have going." She stroked Kris' cheek. "I like the idea of having her for my sister-in-law. Be careful...Sprout." She smiled.

The look of rage on Kris' face softened slightly. "Nicole

told you about the nickname, didn't she?" Marianne only smiled. "Okay mother hen, for the two of you, I'll be careful." Kris kissed her sister on the forehead and left.

Taking a deep breath, Klaus ran after the tall woman. "Wait for me."

"No, Klaus, I'm doing this alone. You could lose your license for this," she said as she walked into the four-car garage and unlocked her Italian sports car's door.

"And you can go to jail, Kris. At least let me watch your back for you. Think of Nicole." Klaus had never met Kris' lover, but he knew that plea would work on his friend. He held his breath as the dark haired woman glared at him, then seemed to cave in to the idea.

"All right, let's go."

Kris and the private investigator went to the hotel's inner phones and dialed McGrail's room number. Getting no answer, they quickly went to the third floor and found the door to his room. Taking a deep breath and giving Klaus a quick look, Kris knocked on the door and waited, listening for movement from inside the room. No sounds or words answered her.

She looked at her watch and saw that it was almost three o'clock in the morning. At this hour, Kris knew there shouldn't be any guests or hotel employees roaming the hallways. She nodded her head to Klaus who then hauled out a pair of gloves and a set of lock picks. After quickly putting the gloves on, Klaus knelt down to eye level with the lock and unlocked the door, thankful that the hotel hadn't gone modern on them by changing the old fashioned key locks for electronic ones.

Hearing the faint click inside the locking mechanism give way, Klaus slowly turned the knob and cautiously pushed the door open. The bright light of the room filtered through the opening causing Klaus to look worriedly at Kris. She returned the worried look but nodded for him to continue when nothing happened.

Before entering the room, Kris followed Klaus' example and put on a pair of gloves so that she left no fingerprints behind. They carefully entered and closed the door behind them.

The room was in perfect disarray. The furniture had been

tossed upside down while half-eaten food lay on the floor amidst mounds of ripped clothing strewn about. Mixed in with the piles of clothing and food were torn up pictures. Kris' heart froze when she recognized whom the mutilated photographs were of that littered the floor.

Kris bent down to pick up one of the less damaged photos and stared at it. It was a picture of a much younger Nicole, the cap and gown she was wearing indicating that it had been taken on her graduation day. She carefully rummaged through other photographs and realized that these weren't only old pictures of Nicole, but also more recent photos of them in L.A. and here in Austria. Kris tore her eyes away from the photographs as Klaus called her over.

The investigator stood in front of a blown up photo of the smiling faces of Kris and Nicole. A large hunting knife had been plunged through the center of the picture, holding it firmly against the wall. Red paint had been sprayed on it, making a big bulls-eye, turning the innocent photo into a target.

"Man, this dude is one fucked up individual," the investigator whispered under his breath and looked up to see that Kris had heard him and remembered that this was her lover's father. He shrugged his apology. "Kris we'd better go. The police need to see this." Klaus pulled the tall woman out of the room and made sure to lock the door before closing it.

Kris' body shook with rage over the scene she had just witnessed. *I'm going to find you, bastard, and make you pay. You'll wish you hadn't messed with Nicole and me.* She felt her arm being tugged and focused her eyes on Klaus who was saying something. Mentally shaking her head, she brought her attention back to the investigator. "What?"

"I said, I'll have an associate of mine inform the police of this. He'll call from a public phone so the cops won't be able to trace it," he whispered. They stealthily made their way down and out of the hotel, sticking to the darker areas to remain inconspicuous to the night desk clerk who was busy watching a movie.

They headed towards the car which was parked a few streets away from the hotel and slid onto the leather seats, closing the doors after them. Kris started the motor and shifted the car into gear as she guided it to a better line of sight of the hotel.

After the phone call was placed, they waited for confirmation that the police had been notified and stayed there, wanting to make sure that Nicole's father wouldn't sneak back into his room before the police arrived. Once the police showed up, Kris drove back to her house, wanting to make sure that Nicole was all right and to be back in her lover's arms.

❖ ❖ ❖ ❖ ❖ ❖ ❖

Oma arrived at the house at six a.m. as usual. The only difference from any other day were the numerous cars parked out front of the yard and all the various people milling about the house. Uneasiness gripped the housekeeper as she tried to remember a scheduled meeting that she might have forgotten then realized that most of the family was in Sweden already except for Kristina and Marianne.

In a panic, she went to the side door and got stopped by a security officer. After explaining that she was the housekeeper, he escorted her to the kitchen area where three men sat at the table along with Marianne who quickly stood up to meet the older woman.

"Mein Gott! Something happened," Oma cried out in distress as she started shaking, fear in her eyes. She looked around for Kris or Nicole but neither were there. The housekeeper grabbed the young woman's arms in a painful grip. "Marianne, what's going on? Something's happened to Kristina and Nicole?"

"Calm down, Oma, they're both okay." Marianne waited until the housekeeper's breathing slowed down to a more normal rhythm.

"But you're sure they're okay?" Oma asked for the third time. The poor woman was still shaking, trying to put up a brave front but failing miserably.

"They're both sleeping," Marianne reassured her.

The older woman nodded again and decided to start breakfast, wanting it ready for when Kris and Nicole woke up.

The doorbell sounded as the sun crested over the mountains some time later and Oma went to answer the door.

"Kristina Von Deering bitte," the man requested politely as he showed his police identification. The housekeeper nodded and let the detective enter, then unhooked the house phone and dialed Kris' extension.

"*Ja?*" the sleepy voice answered.

Oma looked at the man who was waiting patiently. "I'm really sorry to disturb you, Kristina, but there's a detective here to see you."

"I'll be right there. Have him wait for me in the front office." Kris hung up the phone and grunted as she got out of bed. The wounds on her abdomen and arm weren't serious but painful enough to be annoying.

She quickly dressed being careful not to wake Nicole and lightly kissed her forehead. Not bothering to put anything on her feet, she quickly left the room to meet the detective.

Nicole awoke and only caught a glimpse of her lover as she exited the room. Already missing Kris' presence beside her and needing not to be alone, she got up herself and dressed, still a little groggy from the medication.

Kris emerged blurry eyed to the main part of the house and as she neared her housekeeper, she could see the worry etched into her face. "What is it, Oma?"

"Nothing, I'm just glad you're all right." The older woman turned away, but not before Kris saw the tears filling her hazel eyes. She squeezed her shoulder and headed off towards the front office.

The police officer looked up as the tall, dark haired woman entered the room. He got up from his chair, shook her hand and sat back down at the same time as she did.

"I'm sorry to have awaken you this early Frau Von Deering," the detective said, "but I thought you'd like to know that we found where the attacker has been staying."

Kris rubbed her hands vigorously on her face, trying to wake herself up. She'd had only a few hours of sleep. "Yes, thank you. I appreciate that. What did you find?" she asked, knowing exactly what they had found but played the innocent.

"You say this man is," he looked down at his notes and back up at the woman, coughing slightly, a little uncomfortable at what he had just read, "your...lover's father, correct?"

"Yes, he is." Kris gave Oma a small smile as the housekeeper gave her the morning coffee then handed a mug to the detective and left.

"Well, what we found in his hotel room was quite disturbing. We—" The detective stopped when he saw the look on the dark haired woman's face change. He turned to see a smaller woman standing in the doorway behind him. She then walked in quietly and sat on the remaining chair.

"Nick, maybe you shouldn't listen to this," Kris suggested.

"This concerns me as well. I want to know." The determination in Nicole's eyes told Kris that her mind was made up.

She nodded quietly as she motioned Nicole to bring her chair closer to her. Taking the small hand and sliding her strong fingers through hers, Kris nodded to the policeman to continue.

The detective was surprised when Kris had spoken in English. Looking at the woman beside her, there was no doubt that this blonde was the same as in the pictures. He looked at his notes for the name and found it. "And you must be Nicole McGrail," he said in English with a thick accent.

"Yes, I am." She gave Kris a small smile as the older woman squeezed her fingers.

"Well, like I was saying, following an, how do you say...anonymous," His words were hesitant as he searched for the correct English words. "Excuse me. *Mein* English is not very *gute*." Speaking to Kris in German he asked, "Would you mind translating the information I have for her?"

Kris reluctantly nodded her head, not pleased that Nicole would know the disturbing details about her father.

"You said in the police report that he is a violent man. Do you have any idea if he suffers from any mental illness, drug or alcohol problems?" the detective inquired in German.

After hearing the translation, Nicole shook her head no. "My father never drank, not even socially and he had a pure hatred of drugs. As for your other question, if you don't call beating your wife and child repeatedly a mental illness, I don't know what it is then. Why do you ask?"

"After receiving a search warrant, we entered the hotel room where he's staying and found pictures of both you and Frau Von Deering all over the floor and walls. There must have been hundreds of them, many had been cut or ripped into pieces." He watched as the small woman took a deep breath, her eyes tearing up and nodding at something Kristina whispered in her ear.

"We also found letters," the detective continued. "Detailed in the ways he was going to..." He looked at the pale eyes glaring at him then cleared his throat. "Hmm, make you suffer."

Tears freely glided down Nicole's cheeks now. Wanting to get this over with, the detective continued in a faster mode.

"He can't get out of the country. We found his passport, identifications and his wallet, which was still full of money. We have our men out looking for him as we speak. We will do our best to apprehend him." The man stood up and left a business card on Kris' desk. "Contact us if you have any information."

Kris had taken Nicole in her arms and was gently brushing her fingers through her hair. "Thank you, Detective." She nodded as the police officer left the office and turned her attention to her silent friend. "Let it go, Nicole, don't keep everything bottled up inside."

"That man is a stranger to me, he's not my father. I don't care what happens to him," Nicole replied angrily, refusing to shed another tear for him and wiped her eyes with the back of her hand. She stood up and looked down as her lover gently squeezed her hand.

"I don't either. All I care about is you," Kris said softly as she stood up as well and wrapped her arms around the petite blonde who hugged her fiercely. "But you can relax here. With the extra security we have at the house, I don't think he'll try anything again."

"But he's crazy," Nicole said, her anger slowly ebbing. "I don't think he'll stop until he gets what he wants, whatever that is."

"Then I won't let him hurt you," Kris replied softly as she cupped her lover's face in her hands. "Ever again." She kissed Nicole gently.

"My hero." Nicole smiled as she rested her head against Kris' chest, hearing her partner's soft chuckle and lightly scratched her back.

Kris sniffed the air appreciatively. "Hmmm, I smell something good from the kitchen. Wanna join me in raiding it?" she asked with a grin, succeeding in making Nicole laugh slightly.

"I'd love to." She followed the tall woman out of the office and headed towards breakfast.

❖ ❖ ❖ ❖ ❖ ❖ ❖

Kristina hung up the phone and got up from her desk. An important part needed for one of the stunts in Sweden had broken down and Franz had called her to drop by the specialized manufacturer in Innsbruck and pick up a replacement.

Nicole was hard at work in her own office, keeping busy, trying to put the past event as far away from her mind as possible, which was hard to do when a quarter of the phone calls received were crank calls. She wondered if they were made by an ordinary loony, or if it was her father trying to unnerve them. She shook her head as she continued working on the computer.

"Hey," Kris said with a smile as she walked into Nicole's office. Her smile quickly wavered when the small woman jumped in fright. "Sorry. I didn't mean to startle you."

"No, I'm sorry. It's just those phone calls I keep getting, nobody talks, not even a sound." She ran her fingers through her hair a little frustrated then smiled up at Kris. "Guess they're affecting me more than I thought."

"Listen, how about we forget about the calls and you join me for a drive downtown?" Kris asked, wanting to give Nicole a change of scenery. "Franz asked me to pick up a piece for the RTS. We'll take it with us when we leave for Stockholm tomorrow."

"Sure. I'd love to." She shut down the computer and followed Kris out of the office.

"Marianne will be meeting us there."

Nicole's smile brightened. "Oh. She's so nice. She was so worried about me last night. I still can't get over how much you two are alike." She grinned at her lover. "When does she leave for Stockholm?"

"Her husband's flying in from L.A. late tonight. They'll be at the competition in two days."

"Can't wait to meet him," she said as they walked out of the house and got into the Lamborghini. "What's the piece we have to pick up? An RTS?"

"That's a Rampless Turnover System," Kris explained as she got the sports car underway. "It's used instead of a ramp when the scene calls for an explosion and the car needs to be flipped. It's very useful when ramps can't be seen or installed." Kris looked at her lover with a smile. "You know, we could use the time after for a nice walk, what do you think?"

"That would be great," Nicole exclaimed and started to chat like her old self again.

❖❖❖❖❖❖❖

Knowing that it was impossible to approach the stuntwoman's house without being detected, McGrail had parked the car some distance away, carefully hidden among other cars in the store's parking lot. He had replaced the license plates on his rented car with stolen ones and waited for the red Lamborghini, knowing that sooner or later they would drive by, being the only main road in the area leading in the direction of Innsbruck.

Finally spotting the sports car, McGrail tried to follow it, with little success. He decided to put some distance between himself and the Lamborghini, knowing the Italian car could easily be spotted anywhere. He had plenty of time, he thought and he would do this the right way, no foul-ups this time.

❖❖❖❖❖❖❖

Kris and Nicole were coming out of the factory when they spotted Marianne, wearing a big grin on her face, leaning on her Audi which was parked in front of the building, her arms crossed over her chest.

"Hey, Sis. Where have you been?" Kris greeted her sister with a bear hug and whispered in her ear, "Thanks for last night. You've been a great help." She smiled when Marianne winked at her and turned to give Nicole a hug.

"Waiting for you guys. Can't you just go in there, grab what you need and get out? I've been waiting for twenty minutes." Marianne laughed.

"Why didn't you come in?" Nicole asked the younger woman.

"And get stuck in there like you guys were? No thanks." Kris opened the trunk and put the heavy piece of equipment in then closed the trunk. "Besides, I know how Hunter gets when he starts talking about the good old days."

"His memories of his daredevil days are the only thing he's got left, Mari. It doesn't hurt to listen to him once in a while," Kris said half seriously. "Even if we heard the same stories at least a dozen times before."

"Well, I found them very interesting," Nicole chipped in.

"Oh, I'm sure that he enjoyed having a new ear to listen to his stories." Marianne chuckled and rubbed her hands together. "I don't know about you guys but I'm hungry. How about you Nicole?"

Kris couldn't help keeping the smirk off her face. "Need you ask, Marianne? She's a bottomless pit." That remark earned her a playful slap on the butt from Nicole, giving everybody a good laugh as they walked towards a little restaurant on the corner.

Unknown to the trio, they were being watched. McGrail stealthily followed the women, making sure to keep at a safe distance so as not to be spotted. He let them enter an establishment and enjoy themselves for the moment. He waited this long, why not a little longer? He crossed the street and sat on the park bench, safely hidden by a tree that allowed him keep an eye on their movements.

As he sat on the bench, unbidden images surfaced in his mind. He remembered a little girl smile at him, felt his hand slapping a woman's face violently, heard a child's laughter at Christmas, saw a young girl cry in pain and sorrow as she struggled up off the floor only to be slapped back down. So many images, so much pain. He grabbed his head with his hands, shaking it back and forth trying to remove the unwanted memories. The look of terror in his little girl's eyes continued their assault on his mind. *Please...Daddy!* came the desperate plea.

"Stop it!" he screamed to no one in particular. He looked up just in time to see the three women walk out of the restaurant. His hands clenched in fury when the tall, dark haired woman embraced the smaller blonde. *Please...Daddy!* The words still echoed in his mind refusing to let him be. He got up and followed the women as they walked down the street.

"You know, it's great to see the both of you together," Marianne said, looking at her older sister who still had her arm across Nicole's shoulders. "It's about time you found someone who could put you in your place," she added with a smile.

"Are you all ganging up on me? First Oma, now you?" Kris asked laughing. "Was I so miserable that everyone around me knew it but me?"

Marianne grinned at Nicole as she poked her in the ribs. "Well, if Oma said it also, it must be true."

Kris was enjoying herself, especially since Nicole had relaxed a bit and was laughing and joking. She lightly scratched her lover's neck, earning a small contented sigh in the process. Suddenly, for no reason, Kris got the weird feeling that somebody was watching them. She slowly glanced around them as Nicole and Marianne continued chatting, being careful not to alarm whoever may be watching. She spotted Nicole's father right across the street, shadowing their path.

"Nicole, I want you to stay with Marianne," Kris said calmly then turned to face the man who was smirking at her. She was about to take a step forward when McGrail reached into his jacket and she saw the first hint of a gun being pulled out. She threw herself at Nicole and Marianne as he aimed and fired the first shots, the bullets striking just above Kris' head to smash the business' window, raining glass down on them.

"Kris! Wha—" Nicole exclaimed as they were pushed down on the sidewalk, with the tall woman's body over them. Fear took a solid hold on her at the gun being fired followed by the sound of breaking glass. She ducked her head even lower as two more shots were heard, these hitting the parked car they hid behind.

People screamed and ran, wanting to get away from the madman. McGrail turned his attention to a car that headed his way, then jumped out of its path as the vehicle continued on its way, horns blaring.

Still hiding, Kris got up and looked over the damaged car's trunk to see where Nicole's father was, just in time to see somebody almost running him over. "Stay here! Don't move!" Kris ordered as she sprinted towards the gunman.

Finding himself on the opposite sidewalk and seeing the dark haired woman running in his direction, he aimed the gun at Kris and tried to fire. Nothing happened, the gun was jammed. Still holding onto the weapon, McGrail fled away from Kris.

When she saw him leveling the gun at her, Kris quickly tucked and rolled in the middle of the street, expecting a shot. She winced at the surprising pain as a few stitches from the wound in her abdomen popped. Determined, she ground her teeth as she got up again and continued running after the man.

McGrail ran over people lying on the sidewalk and pushed aside anyone in his way, hoping the obstacle of their bodies on the ground would slow up the dark haired she-devil enough for him to get away.

Not wanting to risk hurting any of the people the crazed man pushed away, Kris decided to run in the street between the parked cars and the traffic heading her way. Not caring about the cars honking at her, she concentrated all her strength and speed on catching up to McGrail. Slowly the gap between herself and the madman closed. *There's no way I'm going to let you get away this time, McGrail.*

Marianne and Nicole got up and the blonde started to run after Kris but was firmly held back by Marianne. "Let me go!" Nicole yelled as she tried to free herself from the tight grip on her arm.

"Wait. Let's get my car," Marianne said as she pulled at Nicole's sleeve and ran towards the car that was parked a block away. She took a last quick look to make sure she knew which direction her sister had taken and they were off.

Seeing that the stuntwoman was still following him, McGrail put a little more speed into his already exhausted legs. Wanting to try his gun again, he stopped, took aim and fired a second time. He cursed when he saw that he once again missed his target and had yet to hit her. Without delay, he turned and headed left down into an alley.

Ducking instinctively as McGrail fired wildly at her, she got up in time to see the new direction the gunman had taken, slipping between two buildings. Kris skidded to a halt in the street, made her way between the parked cars and slowed down when she entered the narrow corridor. She was counting how many shots had been fired so far, and knew that he had one more bullet remaining in his revolver. She just hoped he didn't have a fresh supply with him to reload.

McGrail hid behind a garbage can, waiting for Kris. *This time you're dead, bitch!* he snarled to himself as the woman carefully made her way into the alley, sticking close to the wall and hunched down. He slowly lifted the revolver and aimed, not wanting to ruin this shot. Taking a deep breath, he held it as he pulled the trigger.

As Kris was about to take another step, a beige tomcat jumped out of its hiding spot, scaring Kris, causing her to drop down in a crouch. At the same time, a shot rang through the air as a bullet ricocheted off the stone wall behind her at about where her head would have been if she were still standing.

McGrail screamed in frustration as he threw the useless gun at the woman.

Ducking away from the handgun flying at her, Kris picked up her pace to try to catch the man.

McGrail got up from his hiding place and ran down the alley, as the tall woman followed him. Reaching the end of the corridor, he quickly picked up an empty garbage can and threw it at her.

The tall woman parried the object with her uninjured arm to protect her face and let the can bounce off it. When Kris opened her eyes, McGrail was gone. She ran to the end of the alley and looked to her left and saw nothing, then the sound of someone climbing over a chain link fence sounded on her right and she pushed herself even more to try to catch up.

McGrail was breathing hard now. His muscles burned from the exertion as he tried to get away from that infernal woman whom he couldn't shake. He started climbing the fence and looked to see if she was still following. He glimpsed his nemesis as she headed straight for him at an incredible speed. He jumped down, catching his jacket in the spikes at the top of the fence. A mixture of fear and anger ran through him and he managed to rip free his jacket and sprint towards the street.

Marianne and Nicole drove around the block in the general direction Kris had gone in the hopes that they would find her in one piece and unharmed. When the sound of two shots met their ears, Marianne quickly looked at Nicole who worriedly chewed her nails.

Nicole kept looking everywhere trying to see Kris, the fear of finding her lover shot bringing her close to panic. One more gun blast was heard and the pedestrians looked to their right towards where the shots sounded. She held on as Marianne shifted gears and floored the car in that direction.

When Kris saw McGrail was hung up on the top of the chain-linked fence, she gave herself that final push, sensing that he was now within her grasp. Almost on top of him, McGrail managed to free himself at the last moment and scurried towards the open area and a chance to escape. "Shit," she growled and quickly climbed the fence also and closed in on him again.

The bitch almost got me but she's gonna lose me now! McGrail told himself as he exited onto the sidewalk and looked over his shoulder to see where the woman was. Seeing her running faster, he sprinted between two parked cars and started to cross the road.

Tires screeched to a stop as the driver tried to avoid the man that had appeared in front of his car from out of nowhere. There was no way to stop the vehicle in time as it skidded forward, heading straight for the man.

McGrail, hearing the sound of a car's tires screeching, looked to his left and saw to his horror a car racing his way. Paralyzed by fear, the only thing McGrail could do was stare at the speeding vehicle. The thought of his wife being hit and killed in a similar way was the only thing running through his mind as the car hit him with a crunching thud, sending him flying up into the air and over the hood.

Kris saw the man freeze at the same time as she heard the

noise of tires breaking and watched as Nicole's father was hit, his body lifting off the ground, his head crashing through the windshield and bouncing off to slump in the middle of the street. People started to gather around the body, the driver in a state of shock. Kris couldn't bring herself to approach the scene as she tried to get her breathing back under control from the chase.

❖❖❖❖❖❖❖

Marianne and Nicole were waiting at the street corner for the traffic light to change when a commotion off to their right caught their attention. A sense of foreboding took hold of Nicole and she opened the car door and started running down the sidewalk.

"Nicole! Wait!" Marianne yelled and slapped her steering wheel in frustration as the traffic light refused to change. She checked for oncoming cars and seeing none, floored the pedal with a screeching sound of spinning tires.

Nicole could see people assembling in the middle of the street and ran faster when she realized that somebody had gotten hit. She was trying to push her way through when somebody grabbed her arm and pulled her away.

"Let me," she said from between clenched teeth, fighting to pull her arm free, "go!" She turned and saw that it was Kris holding on to her. "Oh God!" She wrapped her arms around the tall woman's neck, holding her tight as she cried into Kris' chest, relieved to see her lover. "Are you all right?" she asked, refusing to let her go.

Kris tightly wrapped her arms around the small woman's waist and held her close, trying to calm her friend. "I'm okay, it's over now," she said as she made soothing noises in Nicole's ear, gently stroking her back. She quietly moved deeper into the alley, away from the crowd that was growing bigger by the moment. Sirens could be heard in the background.

"Did he shoot you?" Nicole asked worriedly as she started to check her partner for injuries.

"I'm fine," Kris repeated as she wiped the tears from Nicole's eyes.

Nicole ran her hand against her companion's black shirt and pulled it back to look at it curiously. "Kris?" She looked at her bloodied hand then back at her friend, her panic resurfacing. Seeing a glistening patch on the shirt, Nicole started to open it to look at the wound. "I thought you said..."

"It's okay, don't worry. Some of the stitches were pulled apart when I was running," Kris explained, brushing her hand on Nicole's cheek. "I'm okay, really."

They looked up as they heard their names being called and walked back to the sidewalk to find a frantic Marianne searching everywhere. The younger woman found them and quickly rushed over. "Are you all right?" Marianne asked, then spotted Nicole's bloodied hand. "He shot you?"

"Pulled stitches," Kris and Nicole answered at the same time.

"Is that him?" Marianne asked, calming down and looking at the crowd and the police trying to make their way through to the scene of the accident. Her sister nodded, as she hugged Nicole closer to her.

"Is he dead?" Nicole asked in a small voice, not sure exactly how she felt.

"I think so. The car hit him pretty hard." Kris watched Nicole carefully. The tears had stopped falling and she looked at the scene before her with a detached air. No sadness or anger was on her face.

"He died like Mama did." Nicole looked up at a worried Kris and smiled tiredly. "Poetic justice I guess," she said as Kris squeezed her hand.

"How are you feeling?" Kris looked into green eyes that seemed so far away.

"I don't know," Nicole replied honestly. "All I know is that he can't hurt us anymore." She tugged on Kris' hand and pulled her towards Marianne's car. "Let's get out of here so we can take care of you."

Chapter 11

Kris and Nicole's first day in Stockholm was spent in the company of Lars and Frida, ever since the two Swedes met them at the airport. Once they checked into their hotel and dropped off their bags, the four went to visit the stunt competition grounds.

The huge empty field just outside of Stockholm now resembled a small village. Fifteen stunt teams from all over the world were getting ready for the championship. A multitude of semi-trucks and trailers lined the way, as well as equipment built especially for the competition such as jump ramps of all sizes and shapes and assorted towers covered much of the field.

Mechanics and technicians worked frantically to get cars and motorcycles ready for their big day. Everywhere was a flurry of activity.

The four friends walked towards the Austrian's area as Lars talked Kris' ears off about the coming championship. Frida and Nicole walked several paces behind them and Frida worked on the blonde to get the up-to-date news about the two women.

"I'm really sorry about what happened with your father," Frida said genuinely concerned after being told the story a few minutes ago. "Are you okay?" Frida had noticed Nicole's expressionless face as she told the story.

Nicole took a deep breath. "If it wasn't for Kris, I don't know what I would have done. I'd be lost without her," Nicole said with a smile.

"So I take it things are going well between you two?" Frida asked with a growing grin.

A shy smile played on Nicole's lips as she looked at the Swede. "Yeah, things are good. She asked me to work as her personal assistant...well, I sort of convinced her that she needed a personal assistant. But she agreed whole-heartedly."

"Really? That's great. Does that mean you'll be staying longer in Austria?"

Nicole cleared her throat as she lightly scratched her jaw. "Well, Kris asked me to live with her," she replied simply as Frida grabbed her arm, dragging her to a halt.

"You little devil. 'Things are good,' she says. They're more than good. You're not telling me the whole story here. Spill it, girl. Don't hold back on me now." Frida refused to budge until Nicole told her what was going on between her and Kris.

Nicole watched as her lover and Lars slowly moved away from them, deep in another argument. She turned her attention back to the waiting Frida. "After we realized that our breakup had been planned by my father, we talked and found out that we were both still deeply in love with one another. Well, one thing led to another and as they say in the movie business, the rest is history." A blush crept up her face and she knew there was nothing she could do to hide it except just go with it. The huge grin on Frida's face showed that she was enjoying this news and probably her blushing too.

The special effects technician wrapped her arms around Nicole and gave her a big hug. "I'm so happy for you both."

"Hey. I hope we're not disturbing you?" Kris called with a smile as she walked back towards the embracing women with Lars in tow. She switched the heavy RTS piece she brought for Franz to her left hand and gently stroked Nicole's cheek with her right.

"Somebody I know is having a hot romance and they didn't tell me about it?" Frida said jokingly as she looked accusingly at the tall woman just as Nicole slid an arm around Kris' waist.

"Really? Who?" Lars asked confused. When the three women started laughing, he just ended up more confused.

"What?"

"Our very independent friend here has found somebody special." Frida grinned at Kris who was doing her best to stay serious and keep the growing smirk away from her face.

Lars looked from his wife to Kris to Nicole and finally noticed the women with their arms around each other's waists. "Oh...Oh!" Lars exclaimed. "Really? That's great," he said, happy that Kris had finally found someone. Then he smiled. "Do you feel that noose tightening around your neck yet, Kris?" He slapped her on the back, remembering the same phrase the Austrian had uttered when she heard that he and Frida had gotten married.

"Lars, they're not getting married you silly thing." Frida slapped her husband playfully as they walked again. She whispered in Kris' ear so Nicole wouldn't hear, "Are you?"

Silence was her only answer but Frida saw the little smile playing at the corner of Kris' mouth. Before Frida had a chance to comment on the silent smile, they were greeted by Franz as they arrived at their camp.

"Hey you guys." The oldest of the Von Deerings smiled warmly at the group, wiping the grease from his hands. "Did you have a nice flight?" he asked Kris and Nicole, taking the needed part away from his sister's hand.

"Not too bad. How are things here?" Kris asked, looking around to see the technical team hard at work. They headed back to where Franz had been working, noticing the car for his stunt was lifted up to allow the mechanics to work under it.

He handed the mechanical part to one of the technicians and indicated the mobile garage with his hand. The big black semi-truck had been converted into a complete workshop. All the equipment needed was there, including spare parts. A long Recreational Vehicle was parked not too far away, giving the tech team a place to eat and rest while away from their hotel rooms.

"We did a lot of work on the car already," Franz said as he absently toyed with the oily rag. "Um, Kris? I know you're not performing with us but do you think you can give us a hand? We really could use your expertise."

"I was going to offer my help anyway, Franz." Kris smiled

at her brother, clapping him on his back.

"What about Nicole?" Franz looked at the blonde woman who was talking with Frida. "How is she doing?" he asked lowering his voice so she wouldn't hear them. Having heard about the two attacks caused by Nicole's father, he regretted that he hadn't been there to help, but was thankful for Marianne's presence and comfort for the two women.

"It'll take some time, but she's strong." Kris looked at the small group and heard Lars and Frida laughing at something Nicole said, describing it with animated gestures. She heard enough words to know that her young friend was talking about the TV interview in Los Angeles. She turned her attention back to her brother. "I gave Nicole a job to do while we're here. I asked her to videotape the competition. I thought it'd be nice to have a montage of the gags that will be performed. It'll also keep her mind off of everything that's happened lately."

"That's a great idea, Kris." Franz nodded his approval as they walked towards the car and the small group of people.

Further off from the group, the young tech headed towards the garage with the spare part when he looked up at somebody calling his name.

"You're Johan, aren't you?" the woman asked him with a disarming smile. Before he had a chance to answer, the woman continued, "Hans wants to see you over there." She indicated the wooden tower that was currently being built not too far away. As he nodded and started in the direction the woman indicated, she reached for the metal part the tech held as he passed her. "Go, I'll take care of this for you."

Johan hesitated momentarily, but seeing the technician's pass with photo around her neck, he complied and set the piece of equipment on the small workbench. "Thanks," he said and then headed off at a quick pace towards the construction site.

Martina looked down at the mechanical device, her smile changing into a snarl as her plan was set into motion. She glanced at the small group some distance away, her eyes darkened into loathing as they fell upon the tall, dark haired woman. She gave a final, silent snarl before she started off with some difficulty towards the garage as she leaned heavily onto her walking cane.

"Listen Kris, we have a meeting in the RV in," Franz looked down at his watch then at the wooden tower that was being built near the lake, "about one hour. We could bring you up to date to what's going on then."

Kris looked at Nicole, Frida and Hans, who were still chatting, and nodded to her brother as she walked toward them. "I'll be there," she said over her shoulder.

The young blonde looked up from the competition layout map Frida was showing her and smiled at Kris. "Hey."

The tall woman gently wrapped her arms around Nicole and leaned her chin on her shoulder. "What's that?" Kris asked, looking down at the paper her friend held stretched out between her hands in front of her.

"I wanted to see where everybody was located in relation to our position." Nicole showed the older woman the map and leaned into the muscular body behind her. "Lars is right here," she indicated a spot on the left, "and the Americans are here." She continued trailing her finger to another spot on the right. "Do you think Kyle's here yet?"

"I'm sure he is. He'd hate to miss being the first one to 'officially greet' all the single women milling about. You wanna go see if he can spare a minute?" Kris asked Nicole then looked at the Swedes.

"You think we can? I mean, do you think he would, what with the competition and all? Especially with everybody wanting to keep their show a secret?" Nicole asked with a playful grin.

"It takes so long to get ready, I don't think a few days is enough to steal and try out a new idea." Kris smiled as she kissed Nicole lightly on the head. "Besides, he's probably already greeted every woman that even thought of setting foot on the competition grounds," she added with a wink.

"I wish we could go, but we've got to get back to our camp and get ready," Lars said apologetically. "But I promise you that the next time we see one another, you'll owe me a beer." He grinned.

"What do you mean, I'll owe you?" Kris frowned at Lars.

"Because we'll be celebrating *my* victory," he answered, his grin quickly turning into a confidant smile.

"In your dreams, boy," Kris retorted as everybody laughed. "Thanks for the drive from the airport, guys."

"You sure you're gonna be okay without a rental car?" Frida asked.

"Oh yeah." A mischievous grin played on Kris' lips. "Franz brought Ares with him."

Nicole looked up at her friend. "Ares?" she asked confused, looking back at Frida for an explanation.

The Swede walked up to Nicole, gently laid a hand on her shoulder and nodded gravely. "It was very nice to have known you, Nicole," Frida said seriously as Kris ran towards one of the trailers and entered it.

"What do you mean? Who's Ares?" she asked, getting worried by Frida and Lars' serious faces.

"He's the Greek god of war," Lars replied, desperately fighting down the laugh building in the back of his throat.

Nicole slapped the stuntman on his arm, giving him an annoyed look. "I know who that *Ares* is, Lars. What I want to know is what in the world does Kris own that she would call—"

The rest of her question was drowned out by the sound of a motor starting up and revving several times. She turned around to see Kris exiting the trailer on a beautiful black and gold motorcycle.

"*That* is Ares," Frida shouted over the noise and smiled as the tall stuntwoman drove up to the group, the sound of the motor rumbling through the air and into their bodies.

"Is that a Harley?" Nicole asked, unable to take her eyes off the motorcycle as Kris rolled the custom bike next to her. The taller woman laughed.

"No, it's not," Kris said in a loud voice to be heard over the sound of the motor. She shut it off and handed Nicole a helmet. "This is a Titan Gecko. It's custom designed, built to my own specifications, and nearly 1600cc. I also had a custom paint job done on it." She proudly indicated the gas tank with the silver wolf howling at a reddish moon. She smiled at the look of awe on Nicole's face as she soaked in every little detail on the motorcycle.

"It's beautiful," Nicole said as she tenderly glided her finger over the smooth surface of the painting. "But why do you call it Ares?" she asked curiously as her eyes met Kris'.

"Wait until we're on the road, then you'll know why. It's got as much attitude as Ares himself was reputed to have." Kris laughed. "Let's go find Kyle," she suggested with a sly grin as she put her black, wrap around sunglasses and helmet on, tying the leather strap under her chin.

Nicole nodded as she tied the offered helmet on, quickly climbed behind Kris, and wrapped her arms around the tall woman's waist. *I almost forgot what it felt like to ride like this,* she thought, remembering the long rides they took back in Montreal so many years ago. She tightened her hold on her lover and gave her a small pat on the stomach. "Ready!"

Kris started the roaring motor, the vibrations of renewed life rushed through the two women as the steady pulse of the powerful motor thrummed through them. Kris and Nicole waved at the Swedes as they rolled away for a ride around the competition grounds.

Franz and Steve were already sitting inside the RV when they heard Kris' unmistakable motorcycle approach and shut down not too far away. The men looked at each other and smiled as his sister and Nicole's conversation floated to their ears.

"What do you mean it's my fault?" Kris asked.

"You didn't have to scare Kyle half to death." Nicole laughed.

"I wasn't planning to," Kris replied defensively as she opened the door to the Winnebago and let Nicole go through first.

The petite woman wiped the tears of laughter from her eyes. "You shoved a garden hose up his pant leg!" Nicole exclaimed as another fit of giggles hit her.

"How was I supposed to know that he was terrified of snakes?" Kris gave her a lopsided grin as she put both helmets in a top compartment.

"Are you sure he's going to be all right? He did slam his head pretty hard under the car," Nicole said as she sat at the table and slid down the bench. She put Kris' cell phone on the table and smiled warmly at Franz sitting in front of her. "Hi."

"Don't worry. He's got a hard head. He'll live," Kris replied, going to the refrigerator and taking out two bottles of water.

"How's my favorite sister-in-law doing?" Franz smiled at the young woman, winking as he spied a blush creep up her neck. He grinned at his sister who looked surprised at the way he addressed her lover. "You know Kris, you're right. She *is* cute when she blushes."

"I'm doing great. Thanks for asking," Nicole replied looking at Franz then at Kris who sat down beside her. They were grinning at each other like kids. "Thanks for making me feel so at home." She smiled as she took the offered bottle of water from her partner just as Gunther and Hans walked in.

"Well, like we told you when you first met everybody, you're part of the family now," Kris said as she gently squeezed the smaller woman's thigh.

"That's right, with all the ups and downs that this bunch can get themselves into," Hans interjected with a grin as he waved "hello" to everyone. He leaned closer to Nicole and whispered loud enough for Kris and Franz to hear, "She hasn't driven you nuts yet?" He nodded at his older sister.

"No, not yet anyway. She must like how I make her feel too much to want to drive me away with insanity," Nicole replied with a wink and a grin of her own.

Everyone howled with laughter at Nicole's suggestive answer as Kris covered her mouth to keep from spewing out the water she was choking on. The bold response from her lover caught her completely by surprise.

"Hey Steve, you almost got showered by Kris, buddy." Franz slapped his seat neighbor on the back, still laughing himself.

"Oh, that's the image dreams are made of." Gunther laughed as he imagined the scene. "Kristina Von Deering giving you a shower."

"That gives a new meaning to getting wet, right Nicole?" Hans teased, hoping to earn another blush from the cute blonde.

"Wouldn't you like to know?" she teased back, waggling her

eyebrows. This cracked everybody up again and earned her a long and very passionate kiss from Kris, creating a roar of more laughter and whistles she was sure the other teams on the other side of the competition grounds could hear.

The laughter was interrupted when the door opened, revealing Martina and Ludwig as they walked into the RV and sat at the other table across the aisle.

"Did we miss anything?" Martina asked, a pleasant smile plastered on her face.

"No, not really. Just the same old acting up bit is all," Gunther volunteered.

Kris leaned in closer to Nicole's ear. "She must be one of the downs Hans was mentioning earlier," she mumbled low enough so that only Nicole could hear as she took her lover's hand and held it under the table.

Nicole gently squeezed Kris' hand as she felt the stuntwoman's body tense. "Easy, Tiger" she whispered, getting a smile from the dark haired woman upon hearing her pet name.

"Well, since everybody's here," Franz said, "we can start this meeting so that we can all go back to our hotel rooms as soon as possible and get some sleep. Tomorrow's gonna be a long one." Franz shuffled through his papers and took out the one he needed. "First, I'd like to thank Kris again for offering to give us a hand this week. God knows how valuable that extra pair of hands will be, especially in prepping my car for the stunt. And being the generous guy that I am, I'll even lend her out to anyone else who might need her expertise."

"Kris," Ludwig started, "we've changed a couple of things with my stunt. Do you think you could go over some of the specifics and give me your opinion?" He didn't notice the dangerous look Martina was giving him.

"Why do you want to change anything?" Martina asked very agitated. "I thought everything was settled already. What makes you think it needs to be improved by her?" She was the technician responsible to gather all the data and she did not like having her work "changed," especially by the likes of Kristina Von Deering. The very thought taxed her temper to the maximum and it took all the control she had to keep her rage from boiling over.

"I didn't say I wanted to change anything Martina," Ludwig explained patiently as if he were talking to a temperamental child. "I just want to know what Kris thought about the last minute changes we've already made."

"Knowing her feelings towards me, she'll probably scrap the whole thing just because I worked on it." The technician sneered as the pencil she was fumbling with broke in two.

"I honestly don't think that Ludwig would be so careless, but if I feel we should scrap the whole thing, then that means somebody hasn't done their job properly." Kris watched calmly as Martina seethed, a vein in her temple throbbing violently. "You have a problem with that?" The tension was thick.

"You know Kristina, you don't have the answers for every problem," Martina spat, throwing the halves of the broken pencil down onto the table. "It wasn't too long ago that you scrapped a perfect simulation that I worked out."

"That simulation was flawed. Franz had spent the whole night trying to fix it. Why do you think he asked for my help?" Kris growled, slowly getting up from her seat. Nicole's hand quickly reached for her and gently stroked the small of her back, calming her.

"You'll say anything, won't you. You always find something to accuse me of. Either something goes wrong or something disappears and you say, 'well it must have been Martina.' I'm getting tired of this real fast Kristina," the technician said as she got up, hobbled the door, and stood just beneath the frame.

"Nobody accused you of anything, Martina. I just wanted to get an extra opinion," Ludwig said, looking at the paranoid woman. The looks she shot at Kris made his blood run cold. She had some serious, unresolved issues, which started to worry him. *She carries so much hate and anger within her...why?*

Nicole continued to rub Kris' back until the tall woman took a deep breath to calm her temper and finally sat back down.

"All right, enough is enough. Let's go back to the matter at hand. I don't want to spend the whole night here," Franz intervened before a repeat of their last meeting happened. "Just so that you are up-to-date on what's been going on so far, Kris, the draw for the order in which we'll perform the stunts was done this morning. Hans will be going first tomorrow afternoon, followed by Ludwig Wednesday afternoon, and then Friday morning I'll do my stunt. Hans, why don't you bring us up to speed and tell us the status of your site."

The younger of the Von Deerings kept looking nervously from his sister to Martina, expecting a fight to break out any second. The technician wasn't helping at all with the dangerous, cold stares she kept giving his sister. He didn't know about Kris, but those looks were enough to make his skin crawl. He quickly turned his attention back to his older brother and the rest of the small group at the mention of his name. "Oh. Uh, well, the ramp for the motorcycle has been completed. We have maybe another hour or two of work left on the tower. There will be one last check on the bike tomorrow morning and after that, we'll be all set and ready to go. Gunther?"

"All I can add is that late tomorrow morning, we'll start soaking the wood on the tower with accelerators and before we're ready to go, we'll dump the rest of the fuel in the tower proper. The fuel is under lock and key and everything's under control." Gunther looked at the paper Hans had been looking over and nodded at the data on it.

"How about the lake floor? Is it deep enough where the tower is?" Kris asked, knowing the height and speed her brother will be hitting the water.

"Those are the results of the inspection," Hans said as Gunther handed the paper to Kris. "We had the diving team check out the lake area near the tower and they didn't find anything dangerous at the bottom, no big rocks or debris. It's also deep enough."

Franz nodded as Hans finished his summary. "How about you, Ludwig, how's it going?"

"Well, not as good as I'd thought. I'm still trying out different scenarios that I hope will work and—" He was interrupted by the sound of the door slamming shut and noticed that Martina had stormed out of the RV.

"What's her problem?" Steve asked, surprised by the sudden departure.

"I told you it was a mistake to hire her," Kris told Franz who was shaking his head. She reached for her cell phone on the table. "She's a time bomb waiting to blow up."

"She's in a bad mood, so what?" Franz said. "Don't tell me you've never stormed out of a meeting before, Kristina." Kris just toyed with the phone.

"I'll talk to her," Ludwig offered. "As I was saying, we've made many jump simulations on the computer but the wind here keeps shifting. We'll have to run one last simulation before the stunt so that we have the speed of both the bike and the plane right. Talking about planes, when is Tiny due to arrive?"

"They're flying in tonight. He'll be with us tomorrow morning," Franz replied then continued discussing the computer results.

Seeing that her brothers were busy arguing among themselves, Kris dialed a number on the cell phone and waited till it was answered. "It's Kris," she said, turning her back slightly away from everyone and lowering her voice. "I want that surveillance done from the time she wakes up until she goes to sleep. Don't let her out of your sight." She listened to the other person and shook her head. "I don't care how many tapes it'll take. Do it." She pressed the "end" button and put the phone back on the table.

Nicole had watched her lover talk on the phone, wishing she understood a little bit more German. She had caught a few words, enough to know that Kris had been talking to the private investigator hired to follow Martina. Knowing that this was not the place to ask any questions about that, she opted to try and get the dark haired woman out of her brooding mood.

Kris looked down as the blonde patted her thigh. "Hmm?" She leaned towards her lover.

"Who's Tiny?" she whispered in Kris' ear, not wanting to interrupt Ludwig and Franz as they discussed the stunt simulations.

"It's Tomas, Marianne's husband. We've always called him that." Kris smiled as she caught Nicole stifling a yawn. "We're about finished here. It won't be long." She patted the hand that was still lying on her thigh then reached for her water bottle.

Nicole looked around and noticed that everybody was listening to the older brothers. She gently tugged on Kris' arm, causing her to lean over once more. "I hope so. I just can't wait to be alone with you," she whispered in Kris' ear, inconspicuously nibbled it and then sat back.

The water bottle froze halfway to Kris' lips as she felt Nicole's soft lips and tongue caress her earlobe. Just as quickly, her lover was sitting back comfortably in her seat, leaving Kris speechless and surprised at the unexpected, but not unwanted action.

Nicole just looked at her with an innocent grin on her face. "What?" she mouthed with a twinkle in her eye.

"How about it, Kris?" Franz asked, looking straight at his sister.

She didn't know what to do. Her attention was split between Franz' question, which she obviously hadn't heard, and Nicole's hand under the table that wandered ever so cunningly onto her lap and slowly made it's way towards the inside of her thigh. Her grip on the plastic bottle tightened as she attempted to act as normal as possible for the people waiting for her answer, even though Nicole wasn't helping much.

"I'm sorry, can you repeat the question?" she asked, taking a deep breath as her face flushed with her rising arousal. She supposed she could always tell Nicole to stop, but did she really want to do that?

"I asked if you could be on the chrono for Hans' stunt. Kristina, are you feeling all right?" Franz asked, worried. "You look a little flushed."

"Yeah...hmm, I'm...I'm fine, yeah. I'm okay, just a little hot in here. I...hmm." Kris closed her eyes to try to regain her composure.

Nicole was having a great time seeing her lover this way. What a rush it was to know that she had this effect on the older woman. A faint smile crossed the blonde's lips as she felt a tremor pass through Kris' body. She lifted the water bottle to her lips and took a sip, acting like nothing was going on while she continued her exploration with her left hand under the table.

"Maybe you should go out and get some fresh air or something," Ludwig suggested.

"I'm fine, really." She turned to look at Nicole who gave her a charming smile. 'I'll get you for that,' she mouthed, a smile tugging at the corner of her lips.

"Promises, promises." Nicole chuckled.

"Anyway, most of the work needed to be done are on the two cars for my stunt," Franz continued. "As soon as everybody is done with their primary jobs, they come back to help there." He started gathering his papers on the table.

"You still want both cars to be ready?" Ludwig asked, surprised. "I thought Kris had picked up the part needed for the RTS."

"She did, but something went wrong twice so far and I don't want to take any chances," Franz explained. "We'll use the second Malibu with the pipe ramp if we can't fix the RTS. So I need two teams to work on those two cars. Any questions? Well then, good night and Hans? See you here tomorrow morning, early," he teased his younger brother, knowing he liked to party.

After everybody walked out of the RV, Kris turned to her lover, shaking her head. "You are in so much trouble." She laughed as she gently glided her hand under Nicole's hair and lightly tickled her neck.

"Tell me you didn't enjoy it," Nicole teased, leaning into Kris' touch.

"Oh, believe me, I did." She smiled bringing Nicole closer to her and leaning down to kiss the teaser passionately.

The door suddenly opened and Gunther walked in and stopped, seeing the women as they ignored his intrusion and continued on about their business. "Oh, sorry. I just...I forgot...bag, I forgot my bag," he stuttered as he blindly searched for his backpack, unable to take his eyes off of the kissing women. "I'm out...see you later...sorry about...that..." He walked backwards, almost tripping on his own feet, still watching.

Not breaking the contact with her lover's lips, Nicole waved Gunther goodbye then glided both of her hands on Kris' back and under her shirt, the gesture causing Gunther to trip this time and exit the RV, falling down on his butt.

"You," Kris laughed as she kissed Nicole's lips, "are," then a kiss on her neck, "so," down her throat, "bad," and worked her way down.

"Yeah, but I'm soooo good at it." Nicole grinned and both looked up to see Franz walking back into the Winnebago.

"Sorry you guys, didn't want to interrupt," he said with a smile.

"It's okay, we were on our way out anyway," Kris said as she got up from the bench and tucked her shirt back into her jeans. She grabbed the two motorcycle helmets from the compartment and handed one to Nicole.

"Thanks for the help, Kristina, I really do appreciate it." He walked towards his sister and whispered in her ear, "I have no idea what happened to Gunther, but you'll have to tell me one day." His mouth formed into a grin as he winked.

"I had nothing to do with it. Well, almost nothing. The imp here is the one who caused him to trip out of here." Kris laughed nodding at Nicole. A sly look crossed the blonde's face at the accusation. "You ready?"

"I'm more than ready," Nicole said, looking seductively at Kris, wetting her lips with her tongue when Franz wasn't looking, causing her partner to swallow hard.

"Let's go...now," she said as she grabbed Nicole's hand and walked quickly out of the RV.

Chapter 12

"I can't believe they put your motorcycle in that room," Nicole said as she put the helmet down on the desk, got out of her jacket, and dropped it on the chair. She walked to the bed and fell on her back enjoying the peace and quiet of the room.

"At least it'll be safe there." Kris chuckled. All she had wanted was a safe place to put her bike, somewhere in full view of the indoor garage's personnel. She hadn't expected the employees to offer a small storage room on the garage level.

Kris closed the door behind her and locked it. She put her helmet beside Nicole's and shrugged out of her black leather jacket.

"I feel like a truck just ran over me," Nicole said as she stretched her neck and made it pop. "My muscles are all bunched together. I wonder why."

Kris chuckled as she went to the bed and gently turned Nicole over onto her belly and straddled her lover's thighs to massage the blonde's neck and shoulders. "And you wonder why you're tense." Kris smiled as she heard a moan coming out of her companion. "You realize how tight you were holding on to me on the ride over here?" she asked as Nicole relaxed under her strong hands.

"You realize how fast you were driving?" Nicole mumbled her retort into the bed cover. She reached for her long, blonde hair and moved it out of the way.

Kris bent down and kissed the uncovered neck. "I don't know," she answered, gently nibbling the soft flesh, "I wasn't looking."

Nicole turned over on her back and wrapped her arms around the beauty's waist, looking into sparkling blue eyes. "What made you hurry that much?" she teased, slowly working her hands under the stuntwoman's shirt.

"A certain blonde that couldn't keep her hands to herself," Kris replied with a grin, which quickly faded as Nicole pulled her hands out from under her shirt and tried to get up from the bed.

"Well, if you didn't like the attention that blonde was giving you," Nicole said in mock anger, "she'll just have to focus it...ugh! Elsewhere." She grunted, still trying to get out from under the tall woman's weight straddling her.

No matter how much Nicole tried to free herself, Kris easily held her in place, grinning at the struggling woman, glad to see that she wasn't really upset.

"Uh-huh, and where would she focus that attention?" Kris asked, looking down at the smaller woman. "Here?" She reached for Nicole's ribs and tickled her, making her squeal with laughter.

"Whaa!" Nicole laughed. Kris' roving hands found another area, creating a different but still very pleasant reaction from the young woman. "You wouldn't be trying to take advantage of me would you?" Nicole smiled as Kris' warm hands glided over her stomach and continued up to her breasts.

"You bet." Kris grinned as she kissed her lover.

❖❖❖❖❖❖❖

The morning went by in a mad rush to get everything finished and ready for Hans' stunt. They had only two more hours before the judges and TV crew arrived on the site.

Nicole spent most of her time video taping the crew and the Von Deering siblings as they went about their individual tasks. She wandered around the site and spotted Kris perched atop the ramp that was going to be used, busy going through final checks and inspection of the padded barrier that would be stopping the motorcycle from going through the tower.

Putting down her camera and a bag stuffed with food by a tree, Nicole was about to call Kris to lunch when she felt a presence behind her. She turned around suspiciously, coming face to face with somebody's stomach. She slowly lifted her eyes up the length of the huge body and looked at the biggest man she'd ever seen in her life.

The man was at least one head taller than Kris who was six feet tall, his sandy brown hair cut very short, his neatly trimmed mustache going down his square jaw, past full lips. The man weighed at least three hundred pounds, Nicole thought as she swallowed nervously straining to look up into his eyes.

The muscular man looked down at the petite blonde in front of him, a grin slowly tugging at his lips. The sound of somebody clearing a throat caught his attention and he looked up the ramp and smiled even more. "Hey Kristina! Long time no see." The man laughed as the stuntwoman climbed down from her perch and walked towards them.

"Are you trying to scare my girl, Tiny?" Kris laughed as she shook the man's outstretched hand.

"This is Tiny?" Nicole asked incredulously as she took in the monstrous man and then looked back at a grinning Kris.

"Yep. That's me. I'm the smallest in my family," he said in a deep baritone voice as he smiled at the young woman. "And you must be Nicole. Marianne's told me so much already, it's nice to finally meet you." He shook Nicole's hand.

She looked down at her hand as it disappeared completely in the massive hands. "It's nice to meet you too." Nicole smiled, finally relaxing at the gentleness in the man's touch and eyes.

"Hi you guys." Marianne waved as she approached the small group and gave Nicole a hug. "Everything okay here, Kris?"

"We're about done. Just waiting for the judges to arrive." Kris smiled at her sister.

"Are you guys hungry? I brought food for everybody," Nicole said.

"Are you sure there's enough, Nicole?" Marianne asked as

she looked at the single bag near the tree and grabbed a blanket to spread on the grass.

"Believe me, there's enough for everybody," Steve said with a grin as he walked up to the group with Franz following behind, each man carrying two bags of food. "Nicole wanted to make sure that everybody was well fed." Steve gave Nicole a wink, sat down on the grass, and grabbed a can of Coke.

"I'll go get everybody else," Tiny said as he lumbered off towards the still working crew.

Kris tugged at her friend's sleeve and gave her a gentle kiss. "That was thoughtful of you, thanks. I was getting hungry. And if I am, then you must be famished," she teased as she rubbed Nicole's firm abdomen.

"Oh, I'm hungry all right." Nicole smiled, her eyes twinkling with mischief as she locked her hands behind Kris' neck. "But what I'd like to eat right now isn't on the menu." She laughed, as the blue eyes grew wider.

"You are such a tease do you know that?" Kris laughed as she gave her lover another kiss. "I only wish we could lock ourselves into the RV for an hour or so and see what kind of desserts are on that menu you're so fond of."

"Well, the RV isn't available so I guess you'll just have to wait," Nicole sang playfully and gently tapped her friend's nose. Before Kris could do anything, she knelt down beside Marianne and helped her retrieve all the food from the bags and spread them out on the blanket.

The dark haired woman shook her head with a look of disbelief and smiled as she sat down against the trunk of the large tree. Kris grabbed a can of soft drink, opened it, and took a long gulp.

Nicole and Marianne chitchatted casually about nothing, occasionally laughing and teasing each other. Franz and Steve were already making themselves some sandwiches as they discussed the coming stunt performance and approaching from the distance were Tiny with Gunther and Hans in tow.

Your typical family picnic, how...normal, Kris thought as she reached for some ham and a piece of cheese. She languidly stretched out her long legs, relaxing in the warm heat of the sun as she enjoyed listening to the different conversations going on all around her. Nicole left Marianne's side with a plate full of food and headed her way with a smile on her lips. Kris stayed where she was as Nicole casually sat between her outstretched legs and leaned against her chest.

"Comfortable?" Kris asked the contented woman who nodded vigorously while she took a bite out of the sandwich then offered it to her lover. Accepting it, Kris glided her free hand around the small woman's waist and rested it on her hip as she ate.

"Some spectators have already started to arrive," Hans remarked to no one in particular as he looked beyond the fence and towards the gathering crowd. The fences were some distance from the area where the stunt would be done, keeping the spectators away for security reasons, but close enough to get a good look at the performance.

Franz looked at his watch and saw that they still had half an hour left before show time. "Where's Martina?" he asked Ludwig.

"She didn't say much, only that she was going out to eat. I saw her getting into a Jetta with some guy. I wasn't paying much attention," he said between mouthfuls.

Nicole looked back up at Kris who only shrugged her shoulders.

"She's doing her job properly, that's all I care. That woman gives me the creeps though," Ludwig continued.

"Why would you say that?" Marianne asked curiously.

"It's not that she's done anything wrong, it's the way she reacts every time we mention you, Kris," he said as all eyes turned towards her. "What happened between you two that makes her hate you so much?" Everybody stopped talking and listened.

Kris took a deep breath. Nicole's small hand gently stroked her thigh, calming her more than she realized. *Where to start? How can I explain something I don't even know myself?*

"All I know is that she holds you responsible for her accident," Tiny said, speaking for the first time since sitting down for lunch.

"What?" Kris exclaimed, looking at Marianne's husband to

see if he was serious. "I had left by the time she did her stunt. How can I be responsible for that?"

"She said that you had an argument before her performance." Tiny thought back to a conversation he once had with the temperamental redhead. "Maybe it was enough to break her concentration and she was careless?" the big man offered. "What was it all about anyway?"

Kris sighed. "Some explosives needed for a stunt we were working on disappeared. Only three people had access to them: Franz, Martina and myself. I asked her if she had seen anybody near the secured area or if she had taken some of it to use on another project. Next thing I know, she starts screaming at me, saying that I'm accusing her of stealing." Kris shook her head at the memory. "She ranted and raved like some lunatic, so I just left."

"But that was so many years ago. She can't still hold a grudge for something like that, can she?" Marianne asked.

"It would make sense," Gunther started. "Martina and Kris have an argument, she gets upset and Kris leaves her fuming all by herself. She goes off to do her gag, still angry over the accusation, her concentration's torn between the stunt and the argument causing her to make a mistake, which cost her legs."

"Come on, Gunther. She can't really hold Kris responsible for her accident. That's just absurd," Franz argued.

"She's unstable, Franz. I've told you that, many times," Kris said, exasperation in her voice.

"What has she done wrong since working on this project besides giving Kris the evil eye? What?" Franz asked the whole group that had gone silent. "As far as I know, it's only a personality problem between Kris and Martina. If she ever does something intentional that might be dangerous, then you say something. Otherwise, I don't want to hear anymore about it." Frustrated, Franz got up and headed towards the tower that was now ready for the stunt.

Silence hung thick in the air at Franz' abrupt departure. Everyone glanced at one another before getting up, knowing that the picnic was over and it was time to get back to work.

Nicole felt Kris' thigh tense under her touch as she gently

rubbed her hand along the strong muscle, trying to calm her angry lover. She stopped her ministrations as she turned around and knelt in front of Kris.

"I know she's up to something, I can feel it," Kris said between clenched teeth. She calmed a little bit as Nicole softly brushed her cheek and smiled.

"Maybe Klaus will find something?"

"I hope he does, or else they'll start thinking that *I'm* the raving lunatic." Kris smiled tiredly.

"Not to me you're not," she said as she kissed Kris and stood up. "Come on, the TV crew is already here."

Kris nodded as she got up and gave Nicole a heartfelt hug. When they broke the embrace, Kris dusted herself off and then they headed towards the stunt site.

After a partly cloudy morning, the sun had hesitantly shown itself for awhile before finally deciding to stay for the afternoon. A good-sized crowd was gathered near the site, a chain linked fence holding them back. For security reasons, the spectators were kept under tight control and were very limited in their access to the stunt sites.

Camera crews were following the judges from point A to point B, taping the entire event, which would then be produced into a TV special to be shown at a later date.

Hans' stunt was located near the lake. A small fleet of boats of all sizes and shapes patrolled not too far away, creating a barrier to keep all non approved boats away. Medical units, both on the lake and on the land were on stand-by, while divers with scuba gear patiently waited for the stunt to begin.

On land, Hans got into his fire retardant racing suit, the Austrian eagle from the Tyrolian province embroidered on his back with "Von Deering" written above it. Most of the crew and siblings wore the same but on a black leather jacket.

Hans kicked started his Suzuki and ran through a last minute check run. He drove around the ramp and tower, watching as the various crew members poured the last of the fuel onto the already soaked wood.

Nicole's video camera was once again hoisted onto her shoulder and taping the footage of Hans getting ready and the crew making their last minute checks. She aimed the camera towards the anxiously waiting crowd and then to the waiting Von Deering siblings.

Kris wore a headset with microphone, keeping in touch with Franz who stood near the tower beside the lakeshore. Ludwig wasn't much farther away where he had taken up his position near the beginning of the ramp. With nothing to do but wait until Hans was ready to go, Kris fidgeted with her silver bracelet, unaware of the easy smile on Nicole's face as she video taped her.

The rest of the crew was assembled at a safe distance, somewhere between the family RV and the tower. Tiny kept a watchful eye on his nervous wife, Marianne. The young woman was unable to stay put as she paced from one side of the group to the other, nervously chewing on her fingernails; a habit formed early on in her previous career as a stuntwoman.

Kris looked up as the judges approached her and took their positions to evaluate the performance. She recognized a few of them as retired stuntmen, while others were somehow connected to the stunt world, qualifying them to judge these events.

The way the competition was won was decided by the level of difficulty and risk and the possibility of a world record to be broken. Each participating team had to submit their stunt plans to the judges and were to follow it precisely. Any deviation from the original plans meant points off their total.

Talking through his headset, the Swedish judge standing beside Kris nodded to her, giving the stuntwoman the "Okay" to start the performance.

Kris took a deep breath and brought the microphone closer to her mouth. "All right people, I just received a 'Go' from the head judge. Whenever Hans is ready." She looked to her right at Ludwig who stood beside Hans, leaning his head near the red and white helmet to talk to his brother. The youngest of the Von Deerings nodded his understanding as he revved the motorcycle. Ludwig clapped him on the back seconds before the young stuntman took off in a cloud of dust.

Kris watched as Hans made one last round with the bike, circling the ramp and tower and passing in front of the tall stuntwoman, giving her a thumbs up gesture. Kris knew that her younger brother wore a huge grin, his body charged with adrenaline. She gave him a warm smile and returned the gesture, watching him take his position some distance away. He stayed where he was for a moment and just waited. Finally, he raised his right arm above his head and made a circular motion in the air with his fist.

"I've got a go to light the tower," Kris said into her microphone. She heard Franz confirming the go and watched as the crew members approached the wooden tower that had been previously soaked with fuel. She took her stopwatch in her hand and waited until a technician threw a lighted torch up into the main part of the tower, simultaneously starting the chrono, counting the seconds allowing enough time for the fire to do its job. The fire rapidly engulfed the whole tower, creating a huge ball of smoke and fire.

"Go! Go! Go!" Kris yelled into her headset when the seconds were up. Ludwig received the go from Kris and signaled Hans to start his performance.

The small but powerful motorcycle quickly gathered speed as it made its way towards the ramp that would lead him straight into the heart of the inferno of the tower.

Nicole anxiously followed the action with her video camera, desperately trying not to lose the rapidly moving motorcycle as Hans drove up the inclined ramp at seventy-five miles per hour and headed straight for the burning tower.

From his unique vantage point, Hans saw the flames approaching at a frightening speed. He could feel the incredible heat as the small motorcycle neared the end of the ramp. He loosened his grip on the handlebars and let his whole body go limp as he prepared for the shock that was about to happen.

Franz watched as Hans made his final approach. The small motorcycle came to a crashing halt against the padded barrier, preventing the bike from going through the burning tower. The ripping and crushing sound of metal tore through the air as the motorcycle's front end crashed into the barrier, catapulting the youngest Von Deering up and over the handlebars. Franz saw Hans' helmet and shoulders crash through the burning tower, sending pulverized pieces of flaming wood all over the place.

Kris held her breath as her brother flew through the air, hoping that the fire had weakened the wood enough so that Hans wasn't injured as he crashed through. He descended and splashed into the calm water.

From her vantage point, Nicole had a clear shot of Hans falling into the lake and continued taping as the divers dove in after the stuntman to bring him back safely to the surface if he was incapable of doing it himself. All Nicole could do was keep the camera trained on the spot where Hans had splashed in and wait, her nervousness rising with every second that the young stuntman spent under water.

As soon as he hit the water, Kris made a mad dash towards the lake and came to a skidding halt next to Nicole as she anxiously scanned the area for any signs of her brother. Ludwig joined them shortly after, worry etched on his features, knowing that his younger sibling had been under for too long.

Excited exclamations sounded from the security boats and Kris looked in their direction in time to see two divers breaking the surface, towing Hans behind them towards the waiting medics on the shore. She and Ludwig quickly joined Franz who was in the water up to his waist.

With wide eyes, Hans looked around him at all the unknown faces looking down at him and then caught Kris' worried face and let a silly grin spread across his lips. She found the smile contagious as she smiled back at her brother who was obviously okay.

He was a little shaken and his knee hurt a bit but otherwise, he was all right. After coughing up some water he had swallowed, he stood up on his uninjured leg and waved at the crowd who erupted into loud cheers.

Everybody stepped out of the water, letting the medics do their job as they examined the young stuntman. Nicole had stopped video taping and stood beside Kris, her left hand lightly patting the tall woman's back. She gave her lover a light squeeze, feeling Kris relax under her touch.

"Did the stunt go as planned?"

Kris looked down at Nicole, put her right arm across her

shoulders and smiled. "It was perfect." She gave the small woman a light kiss on her forehead and looked up to see Steve running towards them barely able to contain his excitement.

"One hundred and fifty feet!" Steve exclaimed excitedly. "That's how far Hans was cannon-balled. If it's not a world record, it's damn close." Before Kris could open her mouth to say something, Steve was already sprinting to the next person to share the exciting news.

"Let's go check out Hans." She chuckled as they walked towards her younger brother who sat inside the ambulance arguing with the medic.

Franz smiled as he saw Nicole and Kris approach. "He's okay," he informed them. "He banged his knee on the handlebars when he took off and got the wind knocked out of him, but otherwise he's back to his usual annoying self."

"He's giving the medics a hard time?" Kris asked with a grin.

"He's just like you," Franz teased his sister and laughed as she gave him the evil eye but quickly smiled.

"You're not much better, dear brother," Kris shot back then looked up as the whole crew clapped and whistled as Hans got out of the medic unit.

"It's party time!" Hans yelled over the shouts as he lead everyone back to the RV to the waiting beers and soft drinks.

The celebration party went on full tilt for a while. Kris and Nicole returned to their spot beside the tree and enjoyed watching the crew relax and share the success of the first stunt for the team at this competition.

Leaning back against Kris' chest with the tall woman's arms around her, Nicole thought there was no better place than where she was at right now. From her comfortable spot, she curiously watched as Marianne got out of the RV, carrying a big box and stopped next to her older brother.

"Can I have everybody's attention for a minute?" Franz asked the noisy group as he motioned with his hands for everybody to quiet down. "Thank you. I just wanted to thank the crew for a performance well done." The group cheered. "But I also want to take this opportunity to officially welcome a brand new crew member. Nicole, can you come here for a moment?"

Nicole looked at her friend in surprise. "Kristina, what's going on?" she asked as she slowly rose.

"I had nothing to do with this." Kris chuckled and winked at her lover, motioning her to go up front.

Nicole made her way through the crew who easily parted for her. Ludwig and Hans were already there, standing with Marianne and Franz.

"Kristina, get your butt over here too!" Franz called after his sister.

"And what a nice butt that is," Steve said, making everybody laugh.

"And it's not yours to play with, Steve," Nicole shot back with a grin, causing more laughter.

Franz waited until his sister arrived and then turned to Nicole who looked at each of the Von Deerings with a frown. "Nicole, we've already welcomed you as a member of our family, but by video taping this event today, we officially declare you a member of the Von Deering stunt crew." Everybody cheered, making the petite blonde suddenly very shy.

Nicole turned to Kris who had opened the box and taken out an exact copy of her own black leather jacket and turned it around to show the embroidered Tyrolian eagle with "Von Deering" above it and "Stunt Crew" at the bottom.

Nicole didn't know what to say. *I'm speechless. Now that's a first.* Kris smiled as she approached her with the jacket and helped her into it. "You knew about this, didn't you?" Nicole asked the grinning stuntwoman.

"I didn't lie. I had nothing to do with this but yep, I knew."

The blonde woman looked around her and was greeted by smiling faces. Marianne and her brothers, Steve and Gunther, even Tiny was grinning from ear to ear, clapping his huge hands together. She looked down at her left arm and noticed that her name had been embroidered there then looked up at Kris with tears in her eyes. "Thank you." She looked at the assembled Von Deerings. "You have no idea how much this means to me, thank you so much."

Seeing the tears form in the green eyes and the lower lip

softly tremble, Kris gently took her lover into her arms and gave her a hug. "Glad to have you with us, Nicole." She gently wiped a lone tear that was making its way down the soft cheek and added in her ear before she kissed it, "and I'm so happy that you're with me."

"All right people, let's get on with the party. Tomorrow's another busy day," Franz told the assembled group.

As everyone returned to the celebration, near the back of the crowd, standing amid the growing shadows of the coming night was Martina. She purposely kept herself separated from the celebrating crew as she looked on with glowering eyes, concentrating on one person in particular. Her free hand tightened into a balled up fist as she saw Kris laughing and joking with the technicians. *This time my plan for revenge will work. I'm tired of playing games with you, Kristina. This time, your luck will finally run out*, she vowed to herself as she secretly went over her well thought out plan of revenge.

The redhead reviewed, in her mind, the time spent with her associate at lunch that afternoon as he gave her explicit details of the success of his task that she had assigned to him earlier that morning. They knew a section of the competition grounds had been reserved for the stunt teams and their families, making the area look like a little village. Tent trailers and RVs of all kinds were set everywhere, the smell of food cooking and firepits helped to give the impression of a huge fair. Children played in an area reserved just for that purpose, safely out of the way of the traffic, right beside the tree line of the forest.

One of those children was an eight-year-old girl, playing mostly by herself, her mother not too far away working in their trailer.

The figure in the shadows waited for the right moment to act. Moving stealthily, he had approached the child, still staying at a safe distance. He waited until the mother went inside the trailer. Quickly he jumped out of his hiding place, grabbed the young girl and put a gloved hand over her mouth to keep the child from crying out for help. Within seconds he dragged her into the forest, leaving a note with instructions on it for the parents to find and follow.

Martina and her associate knew they had their unwilling "partner's" complete cooperation, and was now utterly under their control. The evil smile that had become Martina's trademark easily found its way onto her face as her plan got off the ground. It had been so easy, almost too easy.

❖ ❖ ❖ ❖ ❖ ❖ ❖

Kris rubbed her tired eyes for the third time since they arrived at the camp, trying to wake up. Getting up and out of bed was the last thing she wanted to do this morning. Usually, she was the first one up and working on a project and the last one to go home. Not this time. It seemed all she ever wanted to do these days was to lie in bed snuggled up with her lover, finding it difficult to leave her side.

Kris was now lying on the cold grass under the car dressed in blue coveralls, stifling a yawn as she tried to get the RTS functioning properly. She had been working for almost two hours on Franz' stunt car, the coolness of the morning air chilling her to the bones. She adjusted the old baseball cap that she wore to keep any oil from falling into her hair and continued working. A lazy smile played at the corner of her lips as she thought about how Nicole's gentle face held such peace in slumber. A gentle tug on her boot broke her reverie and Kris slid from under the car to see who would interrupt her.

Nicole's angelic face smiled down at her.

"Hi," Kris greeted as she sat up and wiped her greasy hands on a cloth to give them some semblance of being clean.

Nicole handed her a mug of coffee. "Hi. I thought you might need this to warm up. It's kind of chilly this morning." She laughed when she noticed a grease smear on Kris' face and reached into her own pocket to haul out a tissue and wiped the grease off of the strong cheekbone. "My little grease monkey," the blonde teased.

"Thanks for the coffee, Nick." Kris took a sip and put the mug beside her on the grass then grabbed the small woman around the waist and turned her slightly, causing Nicole to fall down with a thump between Kris' outstretched legs. "I needed that too," she whispered in the blonde's ear as she nibbled at it. "I've been thinking about you all morning."

"Have you now?" Nicole smiled and leaned into the warm body and took hold of the arms surrounding her, drawing them tighter around her waist. "Well, I've been thinking about you too. Visions of a hot tub, a massage and—"

"Well, well, well. Isn't this just the prettiest picture I've ever seen." Martina snickered from where she stood, leaning on her cane.

They looked up at the smirking redhead. "What do you want?" Kris asked, annoyed at the interruption.

"I want a cup of coffee. I didn't know I needed your permission to get some," Martina replied, not moving. She calmly watched as Kris slowly stood and helped Nicole up. "And very gallant on top of it all. Really, Kristina, you impress me."

Taking a deep breath, Kris gently tugged on Nicole's hand and they started walking away from the obnoxious woman. "Come on, let's go," she softly said.

"Ooh! And your pet obeys your every command. You've got her well trained. What kind of tricks did you show her, Kristina?" The technician laughed when Kris stopped dead in her tracks and watched in glee as the stuntwoman's back stiffened.

"Don't listen to her, she's trying to get you to lose control. Don't give her the satisfaction," Nicole softly whispered, squeezing her lover's hand.

"Well, now I'm really confused," Martina said as she limped towards them. "It looks like Goldilocks here has you wrapped around her little finger, how interesting. And here I thought you were the big bad butch in command here. Guess I was wrong." She chuckled.

Kris slowly turned to face the redhead, her temper close to the breaking point. "You have an issue with me, fine. But you leave Nicole out of this. You want to say something intelligent, say it now. Otherwise, I don't have time to waste with you."

"Of course I have something to say, but not to you, it's to your little friend here," Martina said as she smiled sweetly to Nicole. "I heard about your father's death. I'm so sorry. I guess that makes you an orphan now, right? No mommy or daddy around, no siblings to speak of. You're all alone in this big, mean world."

Kris' eyes blazed with hatred as she took a menacing step towards Martina, her hands gathered into fists. As soon as she started to move, Nicole quickly put herself between the two women, desperately trying to keep Kris from hitting the smirking technician. "No Kris. That's what she wants." Nicole looked into blazing blue eyes and could feel the fury shaking the tall woman's body. "She's not worth the trouble, love. Let her be. Come on, let's go." She put her hands on Kris' chest and gently pushed her away from the redhead, then halfway turned to the technician as they walked away. "Get a life, Martina."

"What's going on here?" Franz asked as he looked at Nicole leading his sister away, then at Martina who smiled at him.

"Hi Franz, I'm getting a cup of coffee. Want one?" she asked sweetly as if nothing had happened. Not getting an answer, she shrugged as she turned and walked towards the RV, quietly whistling to herself.

"Kristina, you've got to control your temper better. You're giving her exactly what she wants," Nicole gently told her pacing lover. "She's going to try and push your limits so that you'll end up hitting her and she'll be able to play the innocent victim."

"She can do whatever she wants to me, but I won't stand for her attacks on you, Nicole." Kris wanted so much to kick something, anything, just to be able to let some of the pent-up frustration out of her system. She held back because she knew that Nicole had grown up with a violent father and didn't want her to have to deal with that kind of behavior anymore.

"They're just words, love. I can deal with that. I just don't want to see you get into trouble because of her." Nicole carefully stepped in front of the tall woman and seeing that Kris had somewhat calmed down, gently brushed her hand against her cheek.

"You're right, I'm sorry," Kris said, much to Nicole's relief. "She was right about one thing though." She looked at her confused lover.

"About what?" Nicole frowned as they walked back to Franz' stunt car.

"You do have me wrapped around your little finger." Kris

winked at the smiling Nicole and bent down to kiss her lips lightly. "And I wouldn't change a thing."

Chapter 13

The rest of the day passed without any further "incidents" as Martina went back to working with Ludwig and Tiny for the coming stunt that would be performed tomorrow afternoon.

Nicole found Kris still working with Franz and a young man on the car. The technician was halfway into the motor space as Kris crawled under the car holding the piece in place from below for him to install while Franz held it from above.

"How about now, Johan?" Kris called out.

"Move it up just a little bit." Johan grunted as he reached his arms deeper to align the piece. "Now left." He cursed as he tried to use his tool without success. "I said left!"

"I did move it left, Johan. Chill will ya!" Kris ground her teeth as she tried to hold the piece in place. She frowned at the unusually tense technician.

"Come on guys, we're all tired, stay calm. Now's not the time to start snapping at one another," Franz said as he shifted his grip on the mechanical part to give Johan better access to it. "We'll call it a day after this. All I want is a hot shower."

Johan took a deep breath and tried to calm his shaking hands. "I'm sorry, Kris. Didn't mean to blow up at you." He succeeded in getting the screw in and then tightened it.

"That's okay. We still have enough time to get the car ready, relax. Everything is almost done." Seeing that the part was solidly attached, Kris let go and shook her arms loose, trying to circulate some blood back into her numb hands.

With the broken part from the RTS replaced, the system's calibration was next in line for things left to do. Franz was glad to see that they were ahead of schedule, thanks to Kris' help. He stood up and wiped his hands on a rag, then noticed Nicole silently sitting on a crate, video taping them. He put on the silliest grin he could muster and waved for the camera.

Nicole smiled at Franz' antics and was about to stop taping when he silently signaled her to continue on. "Hey Kris, get out from under there," he said in English, banging his hand on the fender to get her attention.

"I'm sleeping! Don't bug me," Kris shot back humorously. *A few minutes of rest wouldn't hurt.* She closed her eyes again and took a deep breath, enjoying the momentary peace and quiet.

Nicole's eyes grew big when Franz silenced her with a finger to his lips as he headed over to a lone bucket of water. He picked it up and walked back to the car, trying to suppress a snicker. He looked down into the empty space of the motor block and saw Kris directly below it. Quick as a whip, he heaved the bucket up and through the space, emptying the contents directly onto his sister.

A surprised scream came out from under the car as Kris' legs kicked up and her head banged against something hard, causing her to lose her baseball cap. She immediately shot out from under the car, her dark hair plastered to her face with water dripping down her chin and onto her soaked coveralls. "You're gonna pay for that, Franz," she said with an unnaturally pleasant smile on her face. He recognized the look in his sister's eyes and promptly made a mad dash for a safe haven before the words left her lips. Kris was up and on her feet in a flash and took off after her foolhardy brother.

Nicole continued filming as much as she could before a fit of giggles shook the camera too much to film. After wiping the tears from her eyes, she shut the camera off and stood up. She noticed the young technician named Johan, still working and walked up to him. "Hi," she said pleasantly.

Johan dropped the tool that was in his hand as he jumped in

surprise. "Wha...uh, hi!" He knelt and reached for the wrench as he stood up. "I thought everybody was gone."

"Well, it looks like everybody's getting ready to go eat." Nicole looked at the nervous tech as he fidgeted with his wrench looking everywhere but at her. "Are you okay?"

"Yeah, I'm fine. I just want this finished before I leave," Johan said as he went back to work.

"Maybe you should rest a little bit, you really look tired," she offered.

"I said I'm fine!" he snapped, causing Nicole to take a step back from him.

"All right, I'm sorry I disturbed you," she said as she turned back and walked towards the RV. She tried to figure out if she had said something to make the tech angry but couldn't find anything. She eventually came to the assumption that he was tired and just anxious about the coming competition.

Johan watched the blonde woman leave and let out the breath he had been holding. He took the folded paper that his wife had found yesterday out of his pocket and reread the note.

We have your daughter. Do not contact anybody or she dies. Show up at the bar called Akkurat outside the competition grounds at 3pm.

He looked towards the assembling crew near the RV, watching as they laughed and teased each other. His shoulders slumped in defeat as he put the note from the kidnapers' back into his pocket and continued on with his task.

Nicole arrived at the RV just in time to see the wicked smile on Kris' face. The tall woman calmly brushed her fingers through her still wet hair. She took a quick scan of the area and noticed that Franz was nowhere in sight. "What did you do to Franz?" Nicole asked suspiciously when she noticed that Kris was a lot wetter than before. "What happened to you?"

"What makes you think I did anything?" Kris asked innocently as she threw the drenched coveralls she held in her hands onto the table, took her wet sweater off and looked into green eyes.

"Where is he?" Nicole asked, tugging at the tall woman's soaked clothes. Her eyes lingered on the body in front of her as the wet T-shirt Kris wore beneath her sweater clung tightly to her well-defined body. She handed her friend a towel that had been tossed to her by Marianne.

Kris chuckled as she turned around to look in the direction of the lake. Nicole shifted her glance and spotted Franz, soaked from head to toe, sloshing his way back towards them as he rung out what seemed like buckets of water from his clothes. His dark hair was matted to his head as he brushed away water droplets that fell into his eyes.

As the soaked stuntman got closer, Nicole found it hard to suppress a tiny giggle at water squishing out of his shoes with every step he took. The drowned cat look Franz was sporting didn't help her hold back her giggles, but she did and followed the example of the rest of the crew's silent smirking. No one really knew what mood they would find Franz in.

Nicole brought her hand to her mouth to try and help reinforce her resolve to not laugh out loud when she caught the sour look on the man's face. Everyone else also remained quiet, but still smirked as Kris handed the towel she had been using to her silently fuming brother.

He tore the towel from Kris' hand as he passed by and wiped his face. "You always have to go one step further, don't you?"

"You wrestled with me, and you lost," she stated matter-of-factly with only a hint of a smile as she crossed her arms over her wet chest triumphantly.

"Kristina, you didn't have to pick me up and throw me into the lake," her brother exclaimed as most everyone present lost what little control they had and exploded into a fit of laughter. "Is it safe for me to wear something dry now?"

Kris shrugged as her small smile became more apparent. "Only if you don't wrestle with me, that's up to you." Her older brother climbed up the few steps of the RV then laughed himself as he shook his head. Kris looked down at the serious expression on Nicole's face. "What?"

"Do you plan on spending the rest of the day in wet clothes and catching a cold?" Nicole asked as she pointed her index finger towards the RV. "There's another sweater in there."

"But I thought you liked me in a wet T-shirt," Kris said with a hint of mischief in her voice.

"Not if it's going to make you sick. Now go." Nicole successfully kept her face serious but had to bite her lip in order not to laugh. Of course the puppy dog look Kris gave almost broke her.

Kris sighed as she went to the trailer then looked at Ludwig as he smiled mischievously at her.

"So, we finally found somebody who dares tell the great Kristina what to do." Her brother chuckled, ignoring the glare his sister gave him.

"Oh shut up!" she told him with half a smile before she entered the RV.

❖❖❖❖❖❖❖

Wednesday afternoon arrived quickly. Ludwig was ready to do his stunt performance and was checking the latest data with Martina and Tiny. They went over the flight simulation once more, including the latest wind speeds and directions, just to make sure they hadn't missed anything.

The stunt was simple enough to the spectator. Simple, but one wrong move and everything could turn into a disaster for the stuntman and the pilot.

By now, most of the crew had moved to watch Ludwig's performance and to show their support. The TV cameras were already setup at the different points along the runway to catch every angle of the stunt. The helicopter that was going to film the whole flight was already in the air, while the medic unit was positioned to deal with any accidents. Only a small portion of spectators had been allowed along the runway behind a fence and a line of security guards.

This stunt, unlike the others, needed very little help from the technical crew. They were able to do most of their work through computer calculations and simulations, Martina being the main person to supply the plane and motorcycle's speeds in order to succeed. The rest of the preparation had been between

Tiny, who flew his Stearman biplane many times at a frighteningly low altitude and Ludwig driving his motorcycle close to the plane.

Kris stood along with the rest of the crew, wishing for something to do. The fact that Martina had worked on the more crucial details made her terribly uncomfortable. She had voiced her concerns on numerous occasions to Franz who had assured his sister that both Ludwig and Tiny had gone over the data themselves and agreed with the specs. All that was left to do now was wait until the judges gave the signal to start.

Nicole had taken a position half way along the route so that she could get better angles while she filmed both the plane and motorcycle as they came together. From there, she could then move a little to the left and still get great footage of the stunt as it was carried through to the end.

Tiny and Ludwig nodded and shook hands as they turned to get to their respective vehicles. Tiny got into the antique biplane and started its engine with a puff of smoke. He slowly taxied the plane then took off to fly and wait.

Walking back to his motorcycle, Ludwig looked at the judges who gave the "okay" to start the stunt. He kick started the bike and drove to the end of the runway. He brought the motorcycle to a stop beside Steve as he gave him a thumbs up and waited.

"Alpha to Bravo, do you read, over," Steve said into his radio.

"This is Bravo. I read you Alpha, over," Tiny replied over the sound of the plane's motor and the wind.

"Alpha to Bravo, we have a go. I repeat, we have a go, over."

"Bravo to Alpha, we have a go, understood, over and out," Tiny said as he dropped the nose of his plane into a small dive, bringing it into position along the runway in the pre-arranged flight plan.

Taking a deep breath, Ludwig started down in a straight line, towards the concrete wall that had been built at the end of the runway. He consciously kept an eye on the speedometer, making sure to keep the motorcycle at the precise speed.

Nicole had started filming as soon as she saw Steve give the ready signal. As she followed Ludwig with the camera, Tiny's plane soon found its way into Nicole's view. She took a deep breath as she filmed both men and their vehicles as they came dangerously close to one another.

Kris watched as the Stearman biplane approached the motorcycle from behind, flying a foot or so off the ground. She remembered that only a few feet would separate the tip of the propeller blades from the motorcycle's rear wheel.

Coming closer to the stuntman, the only thing Tiny could see was Ludwig's back. He cautiously flew the plane closer and slightly above the motorcycle, hoping it was close enough for Ludwig to catch but not too close where he could bump the motorcycle and cause the stuntman to crash. Tiny brought the plane's left wing and N-strut down in front and near Ludwig's outstretched hand and waited for the stuntman to make the grab, seeing the concrete wall approaching at an incredible speed.

The plane was so close that Ludwig could almost smell the unburned fuel. The sound from the motorcycle, airplane motor and the wind rushing past was almost deafening. Ludwig turned slightly sideways as he saw the Stearman approaching, the plane's wing within his reach. He reached out and grabbed the struts with his right hand and held on firmly as he let go of the motorcycle and finally reached for the other strut with his left hand.

As soon as Ludwig grabbed onto the plane, causing it to tilt one way, Tiny successfully compensated for the extra one hundred and eighty pounds and all the drag caused by the hanging body, by correcting his flight.

Kris held her breath as her brother grabbed the plane's wing and let go of the motorcycle as it continued on for a short moment until it crashed into the cement wall in a ball of fire caused by the explosives installed on the bike.

Nicole continued to film as the plane with its new passenger veered off and climbed in altitude, helping Ludwig to swing onto the wing and make his way towards the empty passenger seat and into the open cockpit.

"Bravo to Alpha, green flag, I repeat green flag, over," Tiny yelled into his microphone as he fought to be heard over the rushing wind.

"Alpha to Bravo, green flag understood, over and out." Steve grinned as he received confirmation that everything had gone well.

Ludwig let out a heartfelt scream as he sat and buckled his seat belt. He then grabbed Tiny's outstretched hand and pumped it enthusiastically. Feeling the plane dive at a steep angle, the stuntman could see the ground approaching at a frightening speed then got the surprise of his life when Tiny pulled the plane into a roll, causing them to fly over the crowd hanging upside down.

Loud cheering was heard as Steve waved the green flag signaling that Ludwig was safely aboard the plane. The whole crew ran towards the midfield where the plane would stop and waited for the men to land.

Kris quietly made her way to Nicole who hadn't stopped taping, stealthily walking behind the blonde woman, keeping out of her line of sight. She followed Nicole around like this as the younger woman walked around, filming the excited crew just before the plane landed.

As she heard the plane approaching, Nicole trained her camera towards it and waited until the Stearman taxied and finally stopped not too far away. She smiled as Ludwig got out of the plane and jumped up and down, arms raised in victory. Marianne rushed to the two stuntmen and threw herself into her brother's arms for a big hug and then into her husband's. Nicole filmed everyone for a few more minutes before deciding to stop and shut the camera off.

She looked around her, seemingly looking for something or someone. Kris gently tapped her on the shoulder from behind, causing the young woman to jump slightly. "Looking for me?" Kris grinned.

"You scared the hell out of me," Nicole exclaimed as she put the heavy camera down on the ground. "Where were you? I tried to spot you with the camera." She wrapped her hands behind Kris' neck and leaned against her.

"I was behind you the whole time." Kris smiled as she hugged her partner.

"You seem to be in a good mood. The stunt went well I assume?" Nicole enjoyed the sudden show of affection from her lover.

"More than that, no accident happened," Kris said as she watched Martina smile and shake people's hands. "I really thought that she was up to something. I'm glad I was wrong." Kris looked down into Nicole's smiling face. "Come on, let's go join the crew."

Everybody moved to the closest local bar, the *Akkurat*, and continued the party there. Kris looked around the room and smiled at the celebrating crew knowing that most of them would be hung over the next morning. She brought her attention back to their own table as Franz and Ludwig relived the triumphant stunt, going over it detail by detail with Tiny. Marianne kept Nicole entertained with conversation and the occasional embarrassing family story since they arrived at the bar.

Kris reached for her Guinness and spotted a familiar figure next to the bar, waving her over. She swallowed the rest of her beer and leaned against Nicole to talk into her ear, making sure she would hear her over the sound of the music and people talking. "Klaus is here. I'm going to go talk with him outside for a moment." She kissed Nicole's blonde hair and stood up, taking her leather jacket with her.

"All right." Nicole smiled at the tall woman. "Do you want me to order you another beer?" she asked as she noticed the empty glass.

"Sure, thanks." Kris winked at her lover and left to join the private investigator outside the bar.

It was getting late in the evening and the weather had grown colder since the late afternoon. Kris slipped her motorcycle jacket on, pulled her long, dark hair free, and walked towards the waiting investigator. "Enjoying Stockholm?" Kris asked as she shook her friend's hand.

Klaus shook his head and laughed. "She's got us running all over the damn place," the investigator said as he leaned against his rented car. "I've got two other people taping her also. So far, we haven't seen anything out of the ordinary."

"What have you got on Martina so far?" Kris asked with

mixed emotions. The stuntwoman was glad that her worse fears hadn't come true during Ludwig's stunt. She was so sure that the red haired technician was up to something. Now, Kris was beginning to worry that she was the one being paranoid like Franz had suggested.

"Well, what we have so far is a lot of tapes of her working with Ludwig, lunches and talking with the crew." Klaus thought back to his meetings with his associates and looked into his pocket-sized notebook for any additional information he might have forgotten. "She did meet with a man a couple of times in the last two days. He doesn't seem to be part of any crew. Do you want me to check him out?"

"No, stay with her. He might just be a boyfriend or something." Kris looked up at the brilliant moon shining through the few clouds. She still couldn't shake the feeling that Martina was planning something. "I know that she was at the bar earlier. Where is she now?"

"They reported her with that man again. She's been with him since seven." Klaus rubbed his tired eyes and stifled a yawn.

Looking back at him, Kris smiled and clapped his shoulder. "Go get some sleep my friend. We still have four days to go before we're back in Austria."

"Yeah, back into my own bed." He smiled tiredly at Kris and nodded. "I'll keep you posted if anything special happens." He walked to the car's door and opened it. "Oh. Thanks for the crew passes, Kris. It makes our job a lot easier." He slumped into his seat and started the engine.

"Take care, Klaus," Kris said as she closed the car's door and watched the private investigator leave the parking lot then turned to walk back to the bar and to Nicole.

The tall stuntwoman made her way through the crowd, stopping once in a while to chat with a crew member or a fellow stuntman relaxing at the bar. She finally made it to the table, pulled out her chair and sat down then took a sip of the cold beer. Looking at Nicole, she noticed her friend's red eyes and frowned. "Everything okay?" she asked worriedly.

"Oh yeah. I'm just tired." Nicole smiled as she patted Kris' thigh and left her hand there. "Franz was telling me that since the preparation on the stunt car is almost finished, everybody can sleep in tomorrow morning." Nicole wiggled her eyebrows, gently squeezing the muscled thigh under her hand.

"Something wrong with your eyebrow?" Kris asked, trying to stay serious as she reached for it with a finger and got swatted in the process.

Marianne laughed at her sister's grin. How she loved to see those two teasing each other. Nicole was probably the only one who could get away with so much where Kris was concerned. Even she didn't dare tease her older sister that much—not with Kris' well-known temper. It had been amazing to see the changes in her in the last month or so. "Talk about killing a mood, Kris." Marianne chuckled.

"We'll just have to revive it once we're back in our room, now won't we?" Kris teased her young lover, gently tapping the tip of Nicole's nose.

"I don't know about that," Nicole said trying to look upset. "Marianne's right, you kind of put a damper on the mood." The blonde woman picked up her glass of Coke and took a swallow, almost spitting it out when a strong hand slowly slid between her legs. She looked at Kris who wore a smirk on her face, toying with her beer glass in her left hand.

"Something wrong?" Kris asked innocently. "Maybe a sense of déjà vu?"

Nicole tightly held her glass, trying to look as normal as possible. She was aware of Marianne looking at her and of Franz saying something, but the rush of blood to her ears caused by Kris' slowly wandering hand made it difficult to concentrate. Her heart thumped furiously and her breathing became irregular. "You're bad." Nicole smiled at Kris then whispered in her ear, "Just wait until we're alone."

The dark haired woman lifted an eyebrow and whispered back, "Looking forward to it." She grinned.

"Well you guys, we wish you a very good evening," Tiny said as he and Marianne stood up. "It's been a long day."

"We'll see you around noon tomorrow then." Franz nodded at the big man and kissed his younger sister on the cheek.

"Good night everybody," Marianne said and smiled at

Nicole. "I know you will." Even though the lights in the bar were dimmed, Marianne knew that Nicole was blushing. She gently squeezed the small woman's shoulder and winked at her smiling sister.

"See you tomorrow." Nicole waved at husband and wife as they left.

"I think we should head back too. What do you think?" Kris asked Nicole as she laid her arm across the small woman's shoulders.

"I wonder why you want to head back," Nicole teased.

"So Kris, I guess your fears didn't come true," Franz broke in, a smug look on his face. "Martina didn't cause a major disaster like you thought she would. Told ya."

"Franz, the competition isn't over yet and she's still with us. I won't relax until she's out of my sight for good," Kris said as she got up and took Nicole's brand new leather jacket and held it opened for the blonde woman to slip into.

"She was hired for Ludwig's stunt and that's over. She's not working on the car so why worry? You're getting too paranoid, Kris," he said as he munched on some pretzels.

"I'd rather be paranoid and have nothing happen, than be careless and someone get hurt. I don't trust her Franz and even though she did a good job today, that will never change." Kris drank the rest of her beer and handed Nicole her motorcycle helmet.

"Whatever," Franz said as he shook his head. "Once your mind is made up, I don't even try to change it. About tomorrow, we'll do a test drive with the car. I need that piece of junk to go over one hundred miles an hour. I want to make sure the motor's in shape for it."

"We've had so many problems with that car Franz, why don't we just use the back up Malibu with a pipe ramp?" Kris asked. "That car's almost as good as the original one, minus a few gadgets."

"Because the original plan we gave the judges calls for a Rampless Turnover System, not a pipe ramp. We're going to be penalized in points if we do that. We're already leading in overall points, Kris, this stunt will give us a win, I know it." Franz grinned at his sister as he stood up and walked along with her and Nicole towards the door.

"All right, it's your stunt anyway. We'll do the dry run tomorrow. Will Johan do the calibrating on the system?" Kris asked as she pushed the bar's door open, letting Nicole exit first and then walked to her motorcycle. She put her helmet on and tightened the strap under her chin, as Nicole did the same.

"He was working on it when we left this afternoon. I don't know what's going on with him, though. He's not his usual self. He would never miss a party like this." His sister straddled the Titan and started the motor, letting Nicole sit behind her and wrap her arms around the tall woman's waist.

"I know, I noticed it too. He blew his top at Nicole earlier too. He said he was just tired," Kris said over the sound of the motor. "Maybe it would be good to give him a day off. I'll talk with him after the test run."

"All right. You guys be careful driving back, okay?" Franz tapped Kris' shoulder affectionately and brushed his knuckle on Nicole's cheek. "Get some sleep my sister-in-law, you look dead tired."

"We will, eventually." Nicole grinned at the chuckling Franz and waved.

The oldest Von Deering watched as the motorcycle with its two riders made its way through the darkness, then turned back to join the rest of the crew.

❖❖❖❖❖❖❖

In a motel room some distance away, a meeting was taking place. Slender fingers caressed the device, lovingly tracing every detail. "Are you sure this will be enough?" a voice asked from the corner of the room.

The man lying lazily on the bed nodded, his smile showing crooked, yellow teeth. "It doesn't look like much but that little baby packs a punch," he said as he gulped down the last of his beer and threw the empty can across the room, missing the trash bin and watching it as it rolled on the floor.

"You're such a pig," the voice said disgustingly, glaring at the belching man.

"Hey honey, you didn't hire me for my good manners." The man snorted. The woman approached him like a panther stalking her prey and his laughter died in his throat at the look of pure madness in the redhead's eyes.

"And you better make sure that you live up to your bragging or else I'll make you regret the day you ever agreed to work for me," Martina spat as she turned her glare from the man to the device in her hands. "I don't want any mistakes this time. I'm sure our 'associate' will give us his full cooperation?"

The man released a breath, glad that the mad woman had changed the subject. *As soon as this job is finished, I'm outta here.* "Oh yeah. He's been very helpful so far," the henchman replied. "The fact that we have his little girl helps a lot too."

"When are you giving Johan the device?" Martina asked as she cradled the explosives. She tilted her head and smiled evilly. "I want to have a front row seat for the event."

"I told the technician I'll be meeting with him at six o'clock tomorrow morning," the henchman said as he got up from the bed and took the device from Martina. "The whole Austrian team is still celebrating as we speak. Nobody will show up before noon. It'll give him plenty of time to install this little toy." He bounced the apparatus in his large hands. "This is so much more fun than getting a bunch of stupid horses sick."

Martina walked with the help of her cane towards her partner, a wicked smile on her lips. "You better be more successful than that mission." She glared at him. "I wanted Kristina's favorite horse killed and it's still alive." Martina grabbed her jacket and slipped into it. "Just make sure that Johan understands what's going to happen to his daughter if he doesn't succeed." Martina exited the motel room with her henchman following close behind.

❖ ❖ ❖ ❖ ❖ ❖ ❖

The motorcycle and riders made their way towards the Austrians' camp, the late morning sun and clear skies promising another beautiful day for the competition. The crew had started to arrive slowly, some of them sporting major hangovers from last night's partying as Kris spotted them sitting quietly at the picnic table, holding their heads in misery.

The tall stuntwoman smiled mischievously as she spied her younger brother among the technicians. She guided the Titan close to Hans and revved the motorcycle's engine to its maximum, causing some of the men to howl in pain from the incredible noise.

"Will you cut that out!" Hans exclaimed, giving his sister a dirty look.

"Good morning to you too." She chuckled as Nicole slapped her on the back. Shutting off the motor, Kris waited until her friend got off the bike and stood up, took her helmet off and put it on the motorcycle beside Nicole's. "Fun party last night, huh?" She smiled at the grumbling technicians.

"You left a little early. Where were you?" Hans said as he took a sip of his black coffee.

"We had a party of our own." Kris winked as she wrapped her arm around Nicole's shoulders and walked off towards Franz and Johan who were already working on the car.

"That was a little mean, Kris." Nicole giggled as she squeezed the tall woman slightly. "Did you have to make that much noise with the bike?"

"You can't expect to drink that much and not pay for it." Kris chuckled. "Besides, I owed him one. Last time I had a hangover, he woke me up with four speakers installed in the room and heavy metal music playing full blast."

"Oooh, that must have hurt." Nicole laughed, trying to imagine a hung over Kris waking up with a start to the music blasting at her.

"I think he hurt more than I did when I finally caught up to him." Kris smiled at the memories. Remembering something, Kris stopped walking and looked down at her lover. "Oh, I forgot to tell you that I talked to Frida yesterday and she wanted to know if we wanted to join her and Lars for dinner tonight and maybe for a tour of Stockholm. I hope you don't mind that I agreed already?"

"Of course I don't mind silly," Nicole said, poking Kris

slightly in the stomach. "We did visit the city a little bit, but it will be fun to get a tour from the natives. Get to see the interesting sights, though I must admit that I much prefer what I saw last night." Nicole smiled seductively at Kris, slowly running her hands over the tall woman's chest.

"Hmmm, was it the ride back to the hotel?" Kris asked, teasing her young lover. She smiled as Nicole shook her head no. "Was it the pond with the huge fish and the multicolored lights?" Another shake from the blonde woman. "Hmm. Oh. I know. It was that big chocolate cake at the restaurant."

Nicole slapped Kris on the arm, causing the tall woman to laugh. "You just love to tease me, don't you?" She wrapped her arms around Kris' waist.

"Hey, you guys," a voice called from behind Kris and she turned to see Kyle walking their way. The big American technician was grinning from ear to ear. "How are my two favorite women doing?"

"Kyle," Nicole exclaimed as she hugged the big man. "We didn't expect to see you before the end of the competition. What a nice surprise."

"Always nice to see you too, Nick. Any garden hose I should beware of?" he asked as he hugged the small woman again and winked at Kris. "You nearly scared me half to death!" He chuckled.

"We didn't know you were scared of snakes." Nicole smiled at the tech.

"What brings you here? Some time off from your crew?" Kris asked as she shook the big man's hand, and the three of them walked towards Franz.

"Just wanted to drop by and say hi." The American smiled and shook Franz' outstretched hand. "Nice to see you again, Franz. I hear you guys are leading in the competition, congratulations."

"Hey buddy. Thanks, but it's not over yet." Franz put the last of his tools back into the toolbox and dropped it inside the car. "Kris, since you're here, would you mind helping us calibrate the car one last time before my test drive?"

"No problem. Where will you be doing it?" she asked as she

took her leather jacket off and gave it to Nicole.

"Great. We have access to the runway where Ludwig did his stunt. I'll drive the car over there," he said as he got into the Malibu and started the motor and drove off.

"I'll go get the video camera and drop the jackets off. I'll meet you there," Nicole said as she gave Kris a quick kiss and took off in a light jog.

"Hey, Sprout, I hope you realize that you have a real jewel in Nick," Kyle said as they walked towards the runway.

"Oh believe me Kyle, I know it." Kris smiled as she looked back to watch her lover run off towards the RV. "She's the best thing that's ever happened to me."

Johan watched the interaction between the three people, his nervousness growing by the minute. How could he do it? So many people might be injured or worst, killed. Why didn't he just go to the authorities as soon as he heard that his daughter had been kidnapped? He sighed heavily as he walked to the runway and one step closer to do the awful deed.

Back at the site, Nicole found Kris working on calibrating the motor while Franz sat inside the car, revving the engine. She noticed that Johan stood some distance away, looking around him in a nervous fashion. He kept passing a trembling hand through his hair and swallowing convulsively. Nicole walked up to where Kyle sat on the grass and put her video camera down beside him then looked again at the young technician as he made his way towards Kris and reached inside the motor compartment.

"All right, Franz, that's enough. I think it'll do," Kris said as Franz climbed out of the car and walked to her.

Johan took a shaky breath as he reached in and pressed the button on the device that would start the countdown, then walked away from the car, closing his eyes as he cursed his weakness for getting himself involved in such a hideous act.

"Hey Franz," Kyle called as he stood up and walked towards him. "Did you hear about the stunt the French team did yesterday?" He related the extravagant gag he had witnessed.

Nicole watched Johan walk away. "Kris, can I talk to you for a moment?" she asked as she walked to her lover.

"Sure." The dark haired woman took a cloth from the toolbox and started wiping the grease from her hands and walked to meet Nicole halfway.

Johan opened his eyes as he heard the blonde call after Kris and saw her approaching. The big man had gotten up and he too was heading towards the car. Panic took over his body as he fully realized the gravity of the act he was about to do. He couldn't live with himself knowing that he had caused the death of four people.

Having been told there was no way to stop the device, Johan ran towards Franz who was closest to the car and pushed him as hard as he could, trying to get him away from the impending explosion. "Get away from the car! It's going to explode!" Johan frantically yelled as loud as he could.

Hearing the scream, Kris turned and looked over her shoulder to see Johan brusquely push Franz, his warnings cut short by the violent explosion that sounded, blowing up the stunt car in a ball of fire.

The force of the blast sent pieces of twisted metal raining down everywhere. Kris was thrown to the ground by the wind the explosion had caused and felt something hit her full force as she tried to get up, sending her crashing back to the ground. The last thing she saw was Nicole being thrown back and land solidly on the ground before darkness took a hold of her.

Feeling somebody beside her, Nicole opened her eyes and gingerly sat up on the grass still hearing the sound of the blast in her ears. She looked around with startled eyes as she saw Kyle getting up slowly himself. "Wha-what happened?" she asked shakily. "Kris?"

All Nicole could see was the burning stunt car and pieces of twisted metal lying everywhere, the smell of melting plastic and rubber filling the air. Looking for Kris, she spotted Johan's immobile body close to the wreck and Franz's some distance away. In a panic, Nicole got up when she saw her lover lying on her stomach, the car's twisted hood on top of her. "Kris!" she screamed as she stumbled towards the downed stuntwoman.

As he was testing his limbs for any damage, Kyle heard Nicole's cry and ran to help check on the unmoving victims. Franz was unconscious and one of his legs was twisted at a weird angle with a bone protruding through the skin, a puddle of blood already forming on the ground under the wound. Looking around for any piece of cloth to stop the bleeding and finding none, Kyle took his sweater off and tried his best to minimize the damage already done. He saw many people running their way as the distinct sirens of a medical unit permeated the air.

With shaking hands, Nicole dragged the hood off of Kris and pushed it aside, cutting her hands on the jagged edges. "Kris?" she called, her voice cracking with emotions. "Kris, can you hear me?" she bent closer and noticed blood running on the ground under her friend's head. Panic took over as she looked around them, realizing exactly what had happened. "We need help here!" Nicole screamed, tears running down her cheek as she lightly stroked the side of Kris' face.

Chapter 14

As the medical unit came to a screeching halt near the scene of the explosion, several medics quickly jumped out of the back of the vehicle carrying a stretcher and their kits towards the injured. They yelled to the gathered crowd to clear the way as they carefully pushed their way through. One medic veered off towards Franz who lay motionless on the ground, while another made his way towards Johan.

Kris slowly woke up when she recognized Nicole's shaky voice calling over a nearby medic. She cracked open one eye and saw that the small woman was holding her hand. Kris gently squeezed it, causing Nicole to spin back towards her and bend down to whisper into her ear.

"Don't move, Kris. The medics are here," she said as more tears fell down her cheeks. She softly kissed the dark haired woman's cheek, and lightly brushed back bloody hair from Kris' face. "God I'm so glad to see you awake."

"Nick?" she mumbled as she looked into watery green eyes, still dazed from the blast. "Wha' happened?" A wave of nausea threatened to overtake her and she took a steadying breath.

"Franz' car exploded and you got hit by the hood." Nicole saw Kris suddenly shut her eyes closed. "Take it easy, Tiger." She gently rubbed Kris' back.

Kris cautiously tested her body for injuries and slowly stretched out her legs one at a time and then her arms. She was relieved to find that everything responded without any sharp pain. She gingerly twisted, testing her ribs and found no unusual pain. Encouraged by the positive results of her probing, she slowly turned herself to come to a sitting position on the ground next to Nicole.

"Kris, you shouldn't be moving around so much," Nicole said trying to sound strong. She tentatively reached for her left eyebrow, which sported a nasty gash with a trail of blood leading from it down the side of her face and her jaw.

"Ugh." Kris sighed as she placed her hand over Nicole's against her head and focused intense blue eyes onto her lover. "Are you hurt?"

"Oh, love, I'm fine but you're not. Please, wait for the medics to check you over," she almost pleaded, not wanting her friend to suffer any needless pain.

A medic rushed over and knelt beside them. He spoke in Swedish as he started to take care of Kris' cut. Seeing the confused expression on both women, he inquired again in English with a heavy accent. "Are you hurt?" He quickly scanned the petite blonde for injuries.

"I'm okay," Nicole answered, not taking her eyes off Kris.

"Your hands are cut." He looked at the woman's bloodied hands.

She looked down as if seeing them for the first time. "They're not deep cuts. I can handle it." Her concern was for Kris, who was more quiet than usual, which worried her. "Kris, are you feeling all right?"

The stuntwoman winced painfully when she brushed back some errand strands of hair from her face and her hand went unknowingly over her wound. She pulled her hand back and saw her fingers stained with blood. "Dizzy," was her curt reply to Nicole's question. Kris gently took the smaller hands in her own, turned them over and inspected the bloody cuts. She looked up into Nicole's eyes, concern etched in her features. "You sure you're okay?" A silent nod and a smile answered her.

Relief spread across Kris' face, grateful that her partner

wasn't seriously injured. Now that she knew her lover was all right, Kris tried to take in as much of the scene as she could see without interfering with the medic trying to patch her up. Her roaming eyes noted the remains of the car that still smoldered as firemen worked on the wreck. Not too far off, she caught sight of another medic working on someone else.

She stretched her neck to see around her own medic to find out who it was, but was unable to due to the crowd looming above and around them. She managed to spot Kyle helping with the injured and continued looking around for Franz. She caught sight of two medics some distance away from the burned out car, carrying away a heavy, black body bag between them. Panic gripped her heart as she shot up onto unsteady legs. She pushed away the surprised medic and started towards the body bag, fighting her vertigo with every shaky step she took. Nicole quickly jumped to her feet, as she and the medic tending to Kris quickly caught up to her.

"Franz!" Kris screamed as she pushed her way into the crowd like a drunkard and looked at the stretcher. She reached out a fearful hand, hoping against hope that this couldn't be happening as a single tear fell from her eye. Her head pounded more fiercely as the dizziness started to claim her, making her stomach churn.

"Kris!" Nicole shouted in panic as she quickly caught the tall woman just as she began falling forward.

Kris' large frame slowly dragged Nicole down with her, forcing her to her knees as Kris slumped in her arms.

"Relax." Nicole caressed her lover's cheek while cradling her with her other arm. "That's not Franz, love," she said in soft, reassuring tones hoping to calm the panicked woman. "I just saw him, he's alive." With a little effort along with the medic, she helped the muscular woman get back to her feet. Nicole wanted her to get away from everything and decided that she would tell Kris later that it was Johan who hadn't made it, not wanting to add to the stressed situation.

"Where's—" Kris started to ask as they made their way towards the other medic and let out a small cry when she saw Franz lying on the ground in a bloody, awkward position.

Upon seeing the compound fracture of the leg, the dislocated shoulder and numerous cuts on her brother, Kris managed to push away from the medic and Nicole once again and moved quickly towards him. She soon realized that her sudden movement was a mistake as the sharp, stabbing pain ripped through her head.

Again, Nicole caught her as the dizziness reclaimed the dark haired stuntwoman. Kyle quickly jumped in and caught Kris around the waist to help Nicole keep her from crashing to the ground.

"You can be so pig headed sometimes, you know that?" Kyle scolded. "Are you trying to make Nicole worry more than she already is?"

Kris blinked several times trying to get her bearings as everything that Kyle was saying sank in and she looked into Nicole's pain filled eyes, knowing it was because she was concerned for her. She let herself be slowly lowered to the ground near her brother.

"I'm so sorry. I didn't mean to worry you." Kris took a deep breath as she sank into Nicole's protective arms.

The petite woman knelt down beside her lover and gently rocked her in her arms as she held her close. "I know you didn't mean it love, but listen to the medics, okay? For me?" Nicole smiled as the older woman looked sheepishly into her compassionate eyes, finding nothing but love there and slowly nodded.

Upon hearing the explosion from their camp, the whole Austrian team finally arrived on the scene and quickly cleared the area of all the curious onlookers. In the midst of it all, Nicole and Kris watched with concern as the medics carefully put Franz on a stretcher and into the ambulance. Within moments, they came back for Kris, who willingly went along with them while a medic took care of Nicole's cuts on her hands.

Now that she knew that Kris was safe and on her way to get treated, the tight control Nicole had over her emotions collapsed as her body was taken over by uncontrollable sobs.

Marianne had kept an eye on her new friend afraid that this very thing may happen and wanted to make sure she was there for Nicole. She quickly wrapped her arms in a comforting embrace and guided her away from the crowd with Kyle and Ludwig close behind.

"Why did he do it?" Nicole sobbed into Marianne's shoulder. "I noticed that he was acting strange, but..." The distraught woman couldn't help but glance at all the debris that littered the ground where they had been standing not so long ago. She kept going over Johan's peculiar mood swings of the last day, searching for an answer to her question but found none.

"Who did what?" Marianne asked softly, giving Ludwig a questioning look.

"Johan," she answered, shaking her head, still unable to believe what had just happened. "I knew he was tired and a little edgy, maybe even a little nervous. But to do something like this?" Nicole took the offered tissue from Marianne and wiped the tears from her eyes and cheeks as she took a steadying breath.

"All I know is if Johan hadn't warned us—" Kyle sighed, cutting off his own sentence not wanting to upset Nicole anymore than she already was. He laid a strong, comforting hand on her back, gently rubbing it.

Ludwig brushed his hand through his short hair and sighed. "I'm going to get that wreck inspected and go see Johan's wife to tell her what happened," he said as they neared his rented car. "Are you going to be all right, Nicole?" He smiled at her nod and gave her a quick kiss on the cheek. "Glad you're okay."

"I just want to be with Kris right now," Nicole said.

"I'll drive you to the hospital. I want to be there too," Marianne said as she took the offered keys from Ludwig. "The medics told me what hospital they were taking them to."

"Let me know how Franz and Kris are doing," Ludwig said, deeply concerned for his siblings but knew that there was nothing he could do about it. But finding out why the explosion happened was something he could do. He planned on heading straight for the competition organizers to ask for an inspection of the car to see if there was any foul play involved. *Jesus, maybe Kris was right all along about Martina,* he thought as he turned to join the rest of the crew that was looking at the demolished stunt car.

"Hey, you don't think you're leaving me behind do you?" Kyle chipped in. "Somebody's got to protect the hospital staff from Kris," he added with a smirk, causing Nicole to smile slightly. "That's my girl." He hugged the small woman.

"Come on, let's go," Marianne said as she got into the driver's seat and waited for everybody to get in and then drove off of the competition grounds in the direction of the hospital.

Some distance away, Martina's henchman had been watching the whole scene develop. *That idiot technician ruined the whole thing,* he grumbled to himself, *Not only is Kristina still alive, she's barely injured. The boss won't like that one bit.* He scratched the stubble on his chin, wondering what to do next. "I better get the hell out of here before—"

"Before what?" a voice said close to his ear, causing him to jump. He turned to see Martina standing there, a calm look on her face. "You said that nobody would survive." She casually looked at the firemen and crew checking out the wreck. "Surprise. No one died," she commented with a dead calm. "Well, no one except poor, dear Johan that is."

Her outwardly calm demeanor was in stark contrast to the screaming and cursing he had expected from the fiery redhead. A shiver passed through him none the less. *The calm before the storm.* He waited nervously as the silence wore on, not really knowing what to say next.

Martina calmly checked her fingernails one by one. "You still didn't provide the service I paid for. I specified that I wanted at least one of the Von Deerings dead." She looked up from her fingers. "As far as I can tell, they're still alive, especially the bitch."

"Look, you paid for an explosion, you got one. It's not my fault that that asshole Johan warned everybody. Now I want the rest of my money and then I'm outta here. The cops will be crawling all over the place when they find out it was a bomb," he hissed in a low voice and then turned to leave. He felt piercing fingernails dig into his arm, forcing him to stop.

An evil smile played on Martina's blood red lips as she glared at the henchman. "There's one more thing we have to do. Johan didn't live up to his part of the bargain. I certainly don't want to do the same. Let's go to where his kid's stashed."

"You go there yourself. I don't want anything to do with this anymore." The man looked into the crazed eyes glaring back at him and he swallowed hard.

"You want your money? You drive me there." She walked even closer to him then smiled sweetly. "Besides, how am I supposed to get myself there?" She indicated her artificial legs.

A frustrated sigh escaped the man's lips. *You could take a cab*, he thought but didn't dare say anything for fear of making her angrier. Seeing no other way, he headed off towards his car, Martina following close behind as her sweet face was slowly replaced by the look of a madwoman.

❖❖❖❖❖❖❖

The private investigator had been following Martina since she left her hotel room, video taping her every move. He followed her, eventually ending up in this field, away from any ongoing competitions. He had been curious about why she wasn't with the Austrian crew. He looked to see what had caught the woman's interest. Down below, on the runway, Klaus spotted Franz working on the car with Kris, Nicole and another man nearby.

Nothing seemed out of the ordinary until Klaus heard the explosion. His attention had been divided between doing his job by keeping the camera on the subject and his wanting to go and help the injured people that were also his friends.

Still keeping the camera on the subject, he saw from the corner of his eye Kris get up from the ground and had been amazed by the redhead's violent reaction to it. The woman had a fit. Even without any sound, Klaus could see her scream in rage. She had then left as fast as her prosthetics would allow and ended up talking with the same man his team had taped earlier on several separate occasions.

Seeing that Martina was about to leave, Klaus pulled his cell phone out of his jacket and called his second team. "It's Klaus, where are you?" he asked the other investigator.

"We have the subject in sight near the parking lot," the

voice replied.

"I want the both of you to follow her. I think we've got something here. Don't lose her," Klaus ordered as he pushed the "end" button and put the cell phone back into his jacket. *Now, all I have to do is find out where Kris has gone to,* the investigator thought as he ran towards the Austrian crew.

Everybody had heard the explosion, but since so many stunts for the competition used explosives, it wasn't given much attention. Word quickly spread through the competitors and the crowd that the explosion hadn't been planned and that some members of the Austrian crew had been seriously injured. As soon as word reached Lars' and Frida's ears, they were in their vehicle rushing to the hospital they were told the injured were taken to.

The Swedes ran through the hospital's emergency doors and quickly found Nicole sitting in the waiting room resting her head in her bandaged hands. Frida went to her side and sat down next to her. She could tell the blonde woman was so caught up in her own thoughts that she barely noticed their presence.

"Hey," Frida said softly as she gently placed a steadying hand on the shaking woman. Slowly, sad green eyes looked up at her and recognized the Swedish woman.

"Nearly a month ago, we were all sitting in a room similar to this," Nicole said in a small voice to no one in particular as she remembered Kris' skiing accident. "We really must find another place to meet. I'm starting to hate hospitals."

Frida gave the blonde woman's arm a squeeze. "Now you understand how Kris feels about them," she said with a hesitant smile. "How is she doing?" Before Nicole had a chance to answer, steps came towards them and they looked up to see Marianne walk into the waiting room.

"Franz is awake," Marianne announced, letting out a sigh of relief, flashing both Frida and Lars an appreciative smile as she sat down on the other side of Nicole. "His leg's badly broken and his shoulder's dislocated. But otherwise he's doing okay and so is Kris," she said, answering everyone's unspoken question.

Kyle walked into the waiting room shaking his head and chuckling under his breath. "Kris has that 'look' down to a science doesn't she?" He smiled as he sat down opposite Nicole and winked at her.

"What do you mean?" She frowned at the big man.

"They wanted her to stay here overnight." Kyle laughed as he remembered hearing Kris' voice through the closed doors. "To make a long story short, she explained with a few choice words that she was *not* going to stay here overnight. I was at the nurses' station right across from her room when I saw the nurses nearly run out of it. Just as the door was closing, I caught the 'look' she gave the doctor."

"So she's okay?" Nicole asked.

"Oh yeah. She's back to her big, bad self," Kyle said as he leaned towards Nicole. "She asked me about a dozen times if you were really okay. Between you and me, I think she likes you." He smiled with a wink, earning himself a tiny smile from Nicole. "She's with Franz right now. You want to go and see her?"

Nicole's eyes lit up as she nodded and smiled at the gentle man in front of her. They rose to their feet and Nicole graciously took his offered arm and was lead out of the waiting room, the small group following behind.

❖❖❖❖❖❖❖

Kris had been sitting in Franz' private room ever since he was returned from surgery to mend and set the compound fracture in his leg and his dislocated shoulder. Now, he sat in his bed with a full leg cast supported up off the bed and still slightly groggy from the anesthesia used on him.

"Kristina, I have something I need to ask of you," he finally said after thinking over the request.

Kris looked down at her brother and sat down carefully on the hospital bed, "Don't tell me you want your teddy bear," she said with a grin, happy to see that her brother hadn't suffered any life threatening injuries.

"No." He chuckled. "I need you to go back to the comp grounds and tell Hans that I need him to do my stunt for me tomorrow." The smile on his sister's face turned into a look of confusion.

"Franz, that explosion was no accident. We can't take the chance if whoever caused it decides to try again." Kris started to get up but was quickly held back by Franz' good arm.

"Kristina, we've been working a long time on this. You know how much the competition means not just to me but to Ludwig, Hans and the rest of the crew." An array of mixed emotions crossed his sister's face. "I know we have a good chance at winning this. We've never let anything stand in our way before. I'm not going to start now."

Kris studied the determined look on her brother's face. "You do know we'll be penalized for modifying the planned stunt, right?" she asked knowingly as the grin slowly snaked across her brother's handsome face. She brushed her hand through her dark hair, making sure to avoid her injury and sighed.

"Franz, do you really think Hans is qualified to do the stunt?" she asked, looking out the window as her mind spun. "He doesn't even know anything about the modifications we've made to the car..."

"I admit that he's not my first choice." His voice was soft.

Kris turned her head and focused on him. "What do you mean?"

"I mean I would much rather have the best stuntwoman in the world, but she isn't available."

Kris' jaw tightened as she stared at her brother. "What are you talking about?"

Franz looked very intently at the blanket lying across him. "I know in the past that a small injury like this wouldn't have kept you down. But now—"

Kris cut him off, anger flashing in her eyes. "What are you trying to say?" Her voice was menacing. "You think I don't have the guts to do it? Is that what you mean?"

Franz looked up and made eye contact. "It's more that I didn't want to encounter the wrath of my sister-in-law for asking you." Silence descended in the room as the siblings stared at each other for a moment. Then Kris burst out laughing, Franz joining her as the tension was broken.

She looked again at her brother who was smiling broadly now. *What am I getting myself into?* Kris thought as a smile of her own formed. "All right," she shook her head, "you've got yourself a stuntwoman."

Some time later, Kris walked out of Franz' room and found herself engulfed in a tight hug from Nicole. She returned the embrace adding a tender kiss. "I'm so glad to see you're all right," she said as they kissed again.

Nicole gently reached for the bandage on Kris' forehead and eyebrow. "I hear you gave the hospital staff a hard time." She smiled at the grin playing on her lover's face.

"I was just my usual self." Kris winked at her then looked up to see smiling faces. "Hey guys." She was glad to see that Kyle had come out of this whole fiasco relatively unscathed. She gave Nicole another hug then laid her right arm across the small woman's shoulders.

Marianne stood with Frida and Lars, looking relieved to see that her sister was all right. "I see they have a new dress code for the patients," Marianne joked, indicating her older sister's jeans and shirt.

"No hospital gowns for me. I'm not wasting any time, I'm outta here." Kris chuckled.

"And I'm sure Franz is tickled pink about having to stay here while you're walking out," Marianne teased. She knew that it would only be a matter of time before their brother drove the hospital staff nuts with his demands to be released from "his prison." It seemed to be an inherent trait in all the Von Deerings.

"I'm just glad that it's him staying and not me," Kris said and everyone around her snickered. A touch on her left arm made her turn to see the private investigator standing there. "Hey Klaus. What's going on?" she asked her friend, seeing the serious look on his face.

"I'd like to talk to you," the detective looked around them, "alone."

Kris nodded and pulled Nicole close to her. "We'll drive back to the competition grounds with you. We can talk then."

Marianne approached her sister and put her hand on her arm. "Kristina, are you sure this is wise?" she asked worriedly. "I know the hospital agreed to let you go but shouldn't you be resting?"

"I'm fine, Marianne. Besides, there's a lot of work to be done. We're going ahead with Franz' stunt. I'll be performing it in his place." Kris could feel Nicole stiffen beside her but to her surprise the younger woman didn't say anything. *Damn! Maybe I should've told her before I announced it like this.* She gave an apologetic look to Nicole. "I need to get the crew to work on the back up car as soon as possible."

"Well, I guess you're old enough to make your own decisions," Marianne said in resignation. "I just hope tomorrow's stunt won't knock you silly."

"Hey," Kris gently lifted her sister's chin to look at the face that resembled a younger version of herself, "I've had worse. Everything will be all right. This is important to Franz, I want to do it for him." Kris smiled as Marianne nodded silently. She then turned to Frida and Lars standing beside them. "And you guys still owe us a tour of Stockholm, ya got that?"

Lars smiled at his friend and fellow competitor. "Anytime you're ready. And Kris," he approached the tall stuntwoman, his hand extended, "good luck on tomorrow's performance."

She lifted her arm off Nicole's shoulders and warmly shook his hand. "Thanks." Kris then walked to the big American technician and poked him playfully in the stomach. "And thank you for taking care of Nicole," she whispered in his ear, giving him a quick kiss on the cheek, surprising the hell out of the bald man. Kris chuckled at the shocked look on Kyle's face as he struggled for words. Before going down the corridor with Nicole and Klaus, she shot Kyle a wink just to keep his mind reeling.

Kris waited until Klaus was some distance away before turning to Nicole. "Listen, I'm sorry that I didn't inform you of my plans before I—"

The young blonde put a finger to Kris' lips. "It's okay. Performing stunts is what you do. You don't have to tell me every single plan you make," she said with a smile. "If you feel you can do it, then I'll help you any way I can, you know that. Just be careful, huh?"

Kris kissed the finger still against her lips and nodded. "I will."

❖❖❖❖❖❖❖

Outside the city limits of Stockholm, the two other members of Klaus' investigating team continued their surveillance of the subject after she had climbed into a car driven by the same man she had met several times. Their target lead them through a wooded area and they noticed that the car slowed down as it turned onto a muddy road that led to an abandoned barn. Not wanting to risk being spotted, the investigators kept driving down the road further and eventually stopped, out of sight.

Grabbing the video camera, the female investigator opened the door and exited the vehicle. "I'll run around by the side and try to spot them. I'll call you on the cell phone if anything comes up. I'll have mine set on buzz," the sandy blonde haired woman said as she closed the door.

"Don't get too close, Trish," the driver warned. "I know how gung-ho you can get sometimes."

"Marius, you worry too much. What could possibly go wrong?" She gave a knowing smile and started towards the barn.

The henchman's car stopped in front of the dilapidated barn doors and he cut the engine. "You have the gun?" Martina asked. He slowly nodded as he pointed to the glove compartment.

The redhead opened the compartment and grabbed the handgun, checked to see how much ammunition it had then put it inside her jacket pocket.

The man got out of the vehicle, stepped into the muddy ground and walked towards the barn as squishing sounds followed him with every step. He carefully opened the barn door and entered, looking back to check on Martina who was having a hard time walking through the muck. He secretly smiled at seeing the woman struggle with her cane, trying to make her way without falling.

Once both were inside the barn, the man indicated a closed area with his chin. "The kid's in there. Where's my money? I want what's due me," he said. Facing the woman he saw, to his horror, that Martina held his gun and aimed it at him. "What are you doing?" He snorted nervously.

"What do you think?" she asked with a crazed look on her

face. "Let's just say that I'm not entirely satisfied with your work. I'm making a complaint." She smirked.

The man nervously stumbled backwards, desperately searching for a way out. "Listen to me, I'm sure we can work something out. Give me another chance." He tried to reason with the woman as she hobbled closer to him.

"Too late, my boy, you had your chance. Besides," she tilted her head and lifted the gun and cocked the hammer, aiming it at his chest, "you are the only one left who can connect me to this mess." She smiled maniacally. "You wanted what was due to you? Well, here it is. Enjoy!"

The investigator outside the barn had been making her way stealthily, until the sound of a gun blast rang through the air, making her jump in surprise. She quickly pulled out her cell phone and dialed her partner's number. "Marius, we've got some gun fire down here," Trish whispered into the cell phone. Spotting some movement by the barn's door, she quickly ducked to make herself inconspicuous.

"Stay where you are, Trish, don't move. What's going on now?" the driver asked, wanting to be with his partner.

Trish moved slightly from where she was hiding to get a better view with her camera. She started filming Martina, leaning on her cane, walking out of the barn towards the car. "She's coming out. I don't see the guy anywhere. Maybe he's still inside. Hang on...she's opening the car's door...what the hell is she doing? She can barely walk and she's sitting in the driver's seat."

Trish watched in surprise as the car spurted to life and drove off, its tires sending chunks of mud flying everywhere. "Marius. I don't know how but she's driving the damn car."

"Hang on, I'll come and get you," Marius said as he put his own car into gear.

"No. Follow her," Trish said quickly. "I'll go and check the barn. I have a weird feeling about this."

"Call Klaus if you find anything and Trish, be careful, okay?" Marius said as he spotted Martina heading back the way they had come. He shut off the cell phone, and kept a good distance between the two cars, trying to follow the woman unnoticed.

Trish turned her camera off and silently approached the abandoned building. She tried to peek through the cracked wooden planks to see if there was any movement inside.

❖❖❖❖❖❖❖

Klaus drove his car on one of the highways leading into Stockholm towards the competition grounds. He glanced into his rearview mirror at his two passengers sitting in the back seat. Kris was intently reviewing the video he had recorded this morning while Nicole sat quietly next to her, anxiously waiting for any news.

The dark haired stuntwoman slowly brought the video camera down and switched it off, the muscles in her jaw twitching. "Where is she now?" she growled through clenched teeth.

Seeing that Kris was about to lose her temper, Nicole gently leaned into the tall woman and glided her hand along the muscular thigh. The tense muscles relax slightly, but Nicole knew that her friend was close to her breaking point. Too much had happened so far for Kris to calm down.

Klaus' cell phone took this time to buzz insistently until the private investigator answered. "*Ja?*" he listened to the other voice then let a curse escape his lips. "Damn! Is Trish still there?"

"Yes, she is. I'm going back to pick her up," Marius said.

"All right, I'm calling her right now." Klaus ended the call then looked into the mirror back at Kris. "They lost sight of Martina. We'd better get some security around the camp. That woman's insane." He briefly looked down at his cell phone and dialed Trish's number then waited for the investigator to answer.

"You think she'd be foolish enough to show up?" Nicole asked Kris worriedly.

"From what I've seen on the tape, I know she's responsible for the explosion, but I doubt that she knows we're on to her," Kris said as she wrapped her arm around Nicole and pulled her closer. "We have to be prepared for anything." The tall woman lightly kissed her companion on the head. "Don't worry, I won't let that bitch get close to you."

"I'm more worried about you, Kris. I couldn't stand to lose you if anything happened," Nicole said as she tightened her hold on her partner.

"We'll have plenty of security, everything will be okay."

"What?" Klaus exclaimed into the phone then looked into the mirror at Kris. "She shot him."

Kris and Nicole looked at each other startled then Kris leaned forward to be closer to Klaus.

"I said she just shot the guy. I went in and saw his body lying on the ground. I thought that he was dead but I saw him move slightly," she explained, her voice shaking. "Before he died, he whispered Martina's name saying she's the one who shot him. What now Klaus?"

"Call the police, Trish, then wait for us. Marius is on his way and I'm close to the competition grounds. I'll be there shortly."

"All right. Damn this is starting to get too weird," Trish said mostly to herself as she closed the connection.

Klaus looked at Kris over his shoulder. "It looks like Martina shot the guy she was talking with after the explosion. We now have a murder suspect to look out for, my friend."

Kris sat back and Nicole leaned against her, tightening her arm around the small woman. Looking outside, she noticed that they were approaching the competition grounds and started thinking furiously about what to do next. "Hand me the cell phone, love?"

"Sure." Nicole reached into her jacket, pulled the phone out, and handed it to Kris.

Kris dialed Ludwig's number.

"*Ja?*" Ludwig answered.

"Lou, it's Kris. Listen we have a major problem. Get everybody back to the RV, we need to talk," Kris said as they entered the grounds, the three of them showing their passes. "Hang on, Lou. Klaus, we'll get off here. I want to talk to the security coordinator." Klaus maneuvered the car through the parking lot and stopped by the security trailer.

"Where are you now, Ludwig?" Kris asked as she got out of the car, keeping the door opened for Nicole to step out.

"Tiny and I are on our way to talk to Johan's wife. We're half way there," he replied. "Are you out of the hospital already?"

"I'm okay, just a few cuts and bruises," Kris reassured her brother. "Send somebody else to see Johan's wife. Go back to the RV and wait for me. I can't talk on the phone but this is serious, Lou."

Hearing the stress in his sister's voice, Ludwig stopped walking and grabbed Tiny's arm, stopping the big man. "Okay. I'll round up everybody."

"Thanks, Lou. We'll be there soon." Kris closed the connection and handed the phone back to Nicole. "I know that you need to get the tapes to the Stockholm police," she said to Klaus. "Come back as soon as possible, we're going to need all the help we can get."

Klaus smiled at his friend, gently patting her arm. "Marius and Trish will be with me. That'll take some pressure off the crew. See you later." He put the car in gear and drove off to meet his team members.

Taking a deep breath, Kris led Nicole towards the trailer to talk to the Security Coordinator and ask for some added patrolling around the Austrian camp.

Chapter 15

"So Kris and Franz are okay?" Hans asked Marianne as she climbed out of Ludwig's car.

She had just dropped off Kyle at the American area. "Kris had a few cuts and bruises. Franz will stay longer at the hospital but he's basically okay," she replied as they climbed the steps and entered the RV where most of the crew were already gathered.

Marianne looked around with a frown and spotted Ludwig. She carefully made her way to her brother and sat down beside him. "What's going on? I thought Kris said we were still doing the stunt tomorrow. Why is the crew not working to get the backup car ready?"

"I didn't know that," Ludwig said, confused. "When I talked to Kris on the phone a little while ago, all she said was that she wanted all of us here. She said that it was so serious she couldn't say what it was on the phone."

"I doubt very much it has anything to do with the competition," Marianne said as she spotted some movement outside the trailer and noticed Kris and Nicole getting out of a security car. "It won't be long now before we find out what this is all about, Kris is here."

As soon as the tall, dark haired stuntwoman entered the trailer, a chorus of whistles and applause welcomed her—the crew members glad to see her relatively unharmed.

Kris smiled at the warm reception and let them continue for a moment before she lifted a hand to quiet them down. Ludwig got up and offered his seat to Nicole, who accepted with a smile. Kris looked around at the waiting technicians and then turned to her brother who now stood beside her.

"Is everybody here?" she asked Ludwig.

"The only one missing is Martina. We couldn't find her anywhere," the stuntman said as he looked around for any other news.

Kris leaned her back on the wall, crossed her arms over her chest and took a deep breath. "Well, I don't think we'll see her anytime soon," she said as the group became silent.

"We have a serious situation here guys." Kris looked at each and every member of the Austrian crew. "Everybody knows that I never trusted Martina. Following the accident at the stunt school and after two of my best horses got killed, I asked a private investigator to follow her, thinking that maybe she had something to do with all of it." Kris paused. "To make a long story short, Klaus and his team followed Martina for some time before the explosion and taped her reacting violently when she saw some of us get up after the blast."

"You think she had something to do with this?" Ludwig asked.

"I heard that Johan might have done it, changing his mind at the last moment," Steve said as he looked at Ludwig.

"Nobody knows what Johan's role in all of this was yet," Kris replied. "According to Klaus, the only person Martina had contact with is an unidentified man and that's where the story becomes interesting." She accepted the offered water bottle from Marianne and took a sip.

"Ludwig and I were on our way to see Johan's wife. We'll have somebody talk to her. Maybe she knows something," Tiny said.

The tall woman nodded as she took another long sip and put the bottle back on the table. "That would be a good thing to do," Kris agreed. "As for Martina, once Klaus saw her reaction to the explosion, he sent his team to follow her and the man. They ended up outside Stockholm and saw the both of them enter a secluded barn, then heard a gun shot with only Martina coming out. One of the investigators found the man with a bullet in him, dead." Kris let the information sink in as she watched the different emotions play on everybody's faces.

Marianne and Tiny looked at each other with a shocked expression. Gunther stopped mid way with his can of Coke between the table and his lips and stared at Kris. Steve kept looking from one technician to the other, as they looked at each other also. Hans just sat there speechless.

The only one not showing any surprised emotions was Nicole who had already heard the news. Her eyes never left Kris' as her friend tried to silence everybody when the group started talking at once.

Ludwig shook his head and looked at his sister. "What's going to happen now?"

"Klaus and the other investigators are with the police as we speak, showing them the surveillance tapes," Kris said as she gently brushed her fingers through her hair then rubbed her tired eyes. "I guess they'll be looking for her now and search her hotel room." She slowly cracked her neck then stretched her battered muscles. "I also asked for added security around the camp site and gave a description of Martina for them to keep an eye out for her."

"Why don't you rest, Kris? You look dead tired," Ludwig stated as he put his hand on his sister's shoulder.

"There's no time for that. I talked to Franz at the hospital. He's got a broken leg and a dislocated shoulder by the way, but he's going to be all right," Kris said as sighs of relief were heard across the crowded room. "He asked me to go on with the stunt tomorrow. I'll be taking his place." She quickly lifted both hands as her brothers, Steve and Gunther disagreed loudly with her decision.

"Are you sure that's wise, Kristina?" Tiny asked. "You just got out of the hospital."

"My decision stands. We're doing the stunt," Kris said in a voice that bore no argument. "We'll have to work overnight to get the backup Malibu and the pipe ramp ready by tomorrow morning." She looked at everybody. "It's Franz' wish that we go on. Is everybody with me?"

For a fraction of a second, the room was silent then it exploded into cheers and whistles. "All right then, we have a lot of work to do. Let's get to it." Kris smiled as everybody got up and walked out of the RV towards a very long hard day of work.

❖❖❖❖❖❖❖

The crew worked furiously the whole day, in two teams. Hans and Tiny took care of building the pipe ramp along with three other technicians while Ludwig and Gunther helped Kris prepare the backup car. Marianne and Nicole took care of everybody, making sandwiches and offering coffees but more importantly by making sure that everybody rested once in a while.

As darkness fell upon them, the crew was forced to set spotlights to continue on with their work. As the exhaustion of the grueling day settled in, curses and small arguments erupted periodically. Marianne and Nicole were right there to calm everyone so that they could continue on with their work.

Around three o'clock in the morning, most of the work had been completed. Kris tiredly got out of the stunt car after welding the safety harnesses into place and making sure they would hold up to the test. She put the welding equipment into the semi-trailer that had been converted into a workshop and walked to the car and sat down in the seat to check the harnesses one last time. Satisfied that it was secure, she laid her head against the seat and closed her tired and burning eyes.

Nicole came out of the RV wrapped in a wool blanket to check on her lover, who had been for some time, the only one still up and working. As she approached the Malibu, she saw Kris fast asleep in the driver's seat. Nicole gently brushed her fingers on the soft cheek, causing Kris to stir slightly.

"Come on honey, let's go to bed," Nicole said as the dark haired woman lazily opened her eyes and looked at her smiling lover.

"What time is it?" Kris asked as she got out of the car and stretched her tired muscles.

"Almost three o'clock," Nicole replied, as her friend rubbed her tired eyes.

Kris felt her arm being gently pulled and opened her eyes as Nicole took her hand and led her towards the RV. She followed obediently with a smile.

The blonde opened the door and indicated that Kris should go in first. Nicole closed the door behind her, and saw that the sleeping crew already occupied most of the benches. She smiled to herself when she noticed that the crew had left one of the bunks available for them.

Kris slowly sat on the edge of the bed, stretching her sore muscles and looked down in surprise as Nicole unlaced her boots, took them off followed by her socks. "You don't need to..."

"Just relax. You look exhausted." Nicole smiled. As she sat down on the bed to take her own boots off, strong fingers scratched her back and she turned to see Kris wink at her.

"Thanks, Squirt. It's nice to be pampered every once in a while," she said as Nicole put her boots on the floor.

"How are you feeling?" the smaller woman whispered, lightly brushing Kris' thigh.

"Would you believe extremely tired?" Kris replied with a grin as she gave Nicole a long and gentle kiss. "Your skin is cold." She rubbed her hands softly on her partner's cheeks. "Come here." Kris lay down on the bed, opening her arms.

Nicole grabbed the blanket that she had brought in with her, pulled it over them and quickly took her favorite position cuddled against Kris' warm body. Her right arm curled around the taller woman's waist, holding her tightly as her head rested comfortably in the crook of her lover's neck.

"This is so much better," Nicole mumbled, giving Kris a light squeeze.

"Nick?" Kris asked softly as she brushed her fingers through the silky blonde hair.

"Hmm?"

"I love you," Kris said simply and Nicole's green eyes peered up at her.

"I love you too, Sprout," Nicole said smiling as she kissed

her lover, then went back to her comfortable position. In a matter of minutes, both women were fast asleep.

❖ ❖ ❖ ❖ ❖ ❖ ❖

Marianne climbed the steps of the RV and peeked inside, seeing that her older sister was still fast asleep with Nicole comfortably sprawled atop her. She smiled as she put two fairly large pieces of apple strudel in the small oven to warm them and poured two steaming cups of coffee. She carried the coffee to the women and placed the mugs on the small table then sat on the edge of the bed.

"Kris wake up." Marianne gently shook her sister awake. "It's time to get ready."

The tall woman woke up slowly, lost for a moment as she looked around at her surroundings then remembered where she was as the memories of the last day came back to her with vivid clarity. She stretched her bruised muscles, wincing slightly. Kris carefully disentangled herself from her sleeping lover making sure not to wake her. She took a quick glance around the trailer and noticed that the crew had already left. Kris then looked quizzically back at Marianne. "What time is it?" she asked as she sat on the edge of the bed.

Marianne took one of the coffee mugs and gave it to her sister who took a sip. "It's seven o'clock."

"What? Why didn't anybody wake me up before now?" Kris exclaimed as she quickly got up and went in the small bathroom to wash up.

"I'm the one who told them not to wake you, Kris," Marianne said. "You needed to get some sleep." She turned to look at Nicole who was slowly sitting up and rubbing the sleep from her eyes. "Good morning." Marianne greeted her friend as she grabbed the other mug, and handed it to Nicole.

"Good morning, thanks for the coffee." She smiled as she wrapped her small hands around the warm mug and took a sip.

"I know you were the last one to stop working last night," Marianne said in a louder voice so her sister could hear her over the sound of the shower. "Besides, you only slept one hour more than everyone else."

The oven's timer sounded and Marianne got up and took the sweet pastries out and put them on a plate that she hauled out of the cupboard above her. She then walked back to the bed and offered Nicole one. "Breakfast's ready, Kris," she called when the water was turned off and a wet Kris wrapped in a bath towel walked out.

Noticing the smile slowly creep on Nicole's lips and the hungry look she gave her lover, Marianne stood up and made a hasty retreat towards the RV's door. "Well, hmmm, I'll see you both later then."

"Thanks Marianne." Kris smiled at her departing sister as she turned her attention back to Nicole once the door was closed. "Good morning." She smiled at her lover and bent down to kiss her.

"Morning yourself, Tiger." Nicole smiled seductively as she wrapped her arms around the wet neck and pulled her gently back on the bed. The smell of fresh soap on her lover gently caressed Nicole's senses as she nibbled at the dark haired woman's ear.

"Love," Kris whispered as she tried to get her ragged breathing back under control. "Anybody could walk in." The bath towel slipped away from her body as small hands slowly glided over her back.

"What do you think this curtain is for?" Nicole grinned mischievously as she pulled it closed and was flipped around, landing on top of Kris' chest as she stared down into sparkling blue eyes.

"Now this is the way I like to start my mornings." Kris smiled as she brushed her fingers through Nicole's blonde hair and brought her lover's face down to her lips for a deep and passionate kiss.

❖❖❖❖❖❖❖

Some distance away, Ludwig did a last minute inspection of the backup stunt car. Verifying that the driver's seat had been securely welded in place and that all small pieces like the mirrors, door handles and radio antenna had been removed. Those items if left in place could easily become projectiles when ripped from the vehicle.

Crawling inside the Malibu, the stuntman turned technician inspected the interior of the car, noticing with satisfaction the removal of the passenger and back seats. The original gas tank had also been removed to be replaced by a smaller one, minimizing the amount of gasoline needed thus bringing down the risk of a fire in case the tank got ruptured somehow. Ludwig shook the small gas tank that had been welded where the back seat used to be, satisfied that it was secure and didn't move.

Stepping out of the car, he noticed his sister walking with a sure pace towards him carrying her safety equipment bag, already wearing Franz' red and white racing suit. Nicole walked quietly beside Kris, carrying the stuntwoman's helmet and the video camera. He smiled inwardly when he noticed the slightly short sleeves that didn't quite fit on Kris' long frame, but otherwise seemed okay.

"Good morning. Are you ready to rumble?" Ludwig asked as he leaned against the car, crossing his arms over his chest.

"As ready as I'll ever be." Kris smiled at her brother as she put the equipment bag on the grass beside the car. The Malibu had already been brought to the runway where the stunt was going to be performed. Kris noticed in the distance the area where the original car had blown up, the only visible sign that there had been an explosion was a blackened spot on the asphalt where the car had burned.

"I'll go check on the pipe ramp," Ludwig said as he left to join Hans and Tiny who were already waiting at the halfway mark down the runway.

Looking back at Nicole, Kris smiled as she saw her lover already filming her with the video camera. "You couldn't wait now, could you?" she teased.

"I would have started earlier back at the RV but then again, this is a family show." Nicole chuckled from behind the camera, as Kris raised an eyebrow and grinned.

Stretching herself to her full height, Kris did her warm-up exercises, making sure that her sore muscles were well stretched to avoid any further damage during the stunt.

Nicole was taping when she felt somebody close to her. She stopped the camera and looked at Marianne who stood beside her, both hands in her jeans' pockets.

"Hi." She smiled. "Thanks for the breakfast this morning."

"Ah, it wasn't much but I know Kris loves it. How is she?" Marianne asked as she watched her sister stretch her back.

"She's a little sore but I gave her a good massage, that should help her relax," Nicole said as she put her camera down beside Kris' helmet.

"Mmm hmm." Marianne smiled at her friend conspiratorially. "I'm sure it was a very good one at that," she teased, remembering the look Nicole gave Kris before she left.

Nicole blushed as Marianne wiggled her eyebrows. It was amazing to see how the young woman looked and acted exactly like Kris. Nicole opened her mouth to say something but quickly closed it, finding that what she wanted to say would only give Marianne another reason to tease her. She just shook her head and laughed.

"I hear the judges will be here in half an hour, Kris," Marianne said as they stepped closer to the car.

The stuntwoman cracked her neck one last time and sat on the Malibu's rear bumper and opened her equipment bag. "Thanks for the info, Sis." She smiled.

Kris dug through the bag, took out the pair of motorcross boots and slipped her feet into them, tightening the straps. She dug through her bag again and came out with her shin and kneepads, then fixed them firmly over the boots, making sure that nothing was loose.

After unzipping her racing suit and pulling it down to her waist, she took from the bag several different types of padding that would protect the rest of her body from the many violent shocks it was going to go through. She slipped on the hip pads and girdle that would protect her lower back first, the elbow pads were next as they were fixed into place. Kris then pulled the racing suit back up and zipped it closed.

Nicole silently watched her lover get dressed, feeling the well known nervousness take over her body. How many times had she watched her husband and friend prepare this way? As much as she hated the risks that Kris took, she knew it was such an important part of the dark haired stuntwoman's life. A gentle hand lightly brushed her shoulder and Nicole took her eyes off of Kris to look at Marianne who was smiling at her.

"I much prefer doing the stunt myself than having to watch somebody I love doing it," she stated as she squeezed Nicole's shoulder. "Don't let the impact of the stunt influence you, Nick. It looks a lot more catastrophic than it is. Kris has performed this stunt many times before."

"I know. I never could get used to this nerve-wracking emotion. I guess that will never stop, huh?" Nicole asked as she looked back at Kris who was speaking with Tiny and Ludwig, who had returned from checking the pipe ramp.

"Kris has been doing a lot of stunts this month, but it's not always this way. Sometimes she can go months without doing any," Marianne tried to reassure her companion. "It could be worse though," she added with a grin.

"What do you mean?" Nicole asked, confused.

"She could be working the daredevil circuit. Doing crazy stunts every weekend just for the crowd's enjoyment."

"I don't think Kris would go for the circus show." Nicole chuckled.

"All right, as soon as they're ready, let me know," Kris said over her shoulder as she turned to her lover, took the few steps to bridge the gap between them and gently wrapped her arms around the small waist. She felt the nervous tremors going through Nicole's body. "Hey, everything's going to be okay, I promise." Kris grinned, giving Nicole a light kiss on the lips.

Looking down at her left wrist, Kris took her silver bracelet off and handed it to Nicole, knowing that this would become a tradition every time Nicole attended a performance. "You'll hold this for me?" she asked with a smile.

Nicole silently nodded and took the gift she had given her lover. She suddenly threw her arms around Kris' neck and held her tight. "You be careful," she whispered in her ear. Pulling back slightly, she found herself held in place as she was engulfed in a passionate kiss.

"After this stunt, we'll take it easy for a while, okay?" Kris told her lover. "Just you and me. We'll even travel a little bit if you want. You'll be so sick of seeing me, you'll be begging me to go back to doing stunts again." Kris teased.

"I'll never be sick of being with you, Sprout," Nicole teased, giving the tall woman one last kiss before she stepped back, giving Kris her space to finish getting ready.

"Kristina!" a voice shouted from behind Nicole. Everybody turned to see Klaus make his way towards them, followed by a man and a woman. "Glad I caught you before show time."

"Hi Klaus, what's the latest news?" Kris asked as she took a harness and slipped her arms into it, wearing it like a vest. Two large rings were attached to the back of the suit, behind each shoulder.

"The police decided to have plain clothed officers patrolling the area to look for Martina. After hearing the whole story, they believe she'll show up and they want to be ready for her when she does." Klaus turned to introduce his team members. "This is Trish and Marius. With your permission, I'd like to have them stay with Nicole while you do your stunt."

Kris stopped tightening her harness' straps and looked at her friend. "You don't need to ask for my permission for that, Klaus. Marianne and Tiny already said that they would stay with her. To add your people to keep a watchful eye out is added protection that I don't mind at all. Thank you, my friend."

"I only wish we could do more. Be careful, Kris," he said as he shook her hand and walked back to stand with the two investigators turned bodyguards.

"It's time, Kristina," Ludwig said as he approached his sister.

"All right." Kris turned to Nicole once more and smiled. "I'll see you in a while." The blonde bent down and picked up her helmet then handed it to her.

"I'll be waiting at the other end for you," Nicole said as she stood on her tiptoes and kissed her. "I love you."

"I love you too," Kris replied as her lover walked away with Marianne, Tiny and the investigators. Taking a deep breath, she looked at her brother. "Let's rock 'n roll!"

The rest of the preparation was done in perfect timing. Kris sat in the driver's seat, while Ludwig passed a bungee cord through the two rings on her back, then up to the ceiling and connected it to the roll cage. This pulled some of Kris' weight up off the seat, holding her in place between the roof and driver's seat.

Kris reached for the five-point harness that was connected to the floor behind her, to each side of her and finally to two connecting points between her legs. She pulled herself down into the driver's seat as she locked everything, completely immobilizing her.

Lastly, she wrapped the big foam collar around her neck to avoid any risk of whiplash and slipped her full faced helmet on, tightening the strap under her chin. Looking at her brother, she finally gave him the thumbs up signal, indicating that she was ready to go.

Ludwig reached for his headset and spoke into the microphone. "We're ready to proceed," he told Hans who was standing with the judges halfway down the runway.

"You are cleared to start," Hans' voice replied through Ludwig's headphones. Reaching in the car to test the harnesses one last time, Ludwig winked at his sister. "It's a go. See you in a few minutes."

Kris stiffly nodded as she put her racing gloves on. She reached for her mouth guard and slipped it into place, playing with it in a nervous fashion before she bit into it to fix it in place so she wouldn't bite her tongue.

Starting the engine, Kris closed her eyes and took a deep breath. Images of Nicole flashed through her mind. She knew her lover was probably worried sick and doing a lot of nervous pacing. *I'll drive her crazy with all these gags. After this one, it'll be my last stunt for a while,* she promised herself, *for Nicole's sake.*

She slowly opened her eyes and shook herself into her harnesses, finding them holding her in place and then closed her helmet's visor. Even though she'd done this stunt many times before, she couldn't help her heart from pounding. She took a steadying breath as she willed her body to relax.

Nicole went with everybody else down the runway and stood at a safe distance away from any flying debris. As she looked around her, she noticed that the whole crew was there and waiting for Kris' performance to start. The only one missing was Ludwig who stood beside the car, making a last minute check. Nicole looked out at the crowd of spectators who were pushed up against the chain-link fence to get the best spot to watch the coming stunt. She caught several English words from the crowd behind her. It seemed that many of the spectators had heard of the accident and that the world famous stuntwoman would be taking her brother's place. They also wanted to show their support for the Austrian crew.

Nicole looked down at her video camera that was on the ground by her feet and wondered if her hands were steady enough to film Kris' performance. She knew that no matter what she did, her nervousness would not diminish. Taking a deep breath, she bent down and picked up the heavy camera and swung it expertly onto her shoulder, deciding that at least she'd have something to concentrate on instead of just worrying. She settled herself into a comfortable position and waited, along with everyone else, for Kris to start.

After leaving his two associates with Nicole, Klaus patrolled the competition grounds, searching the crowd for any signs of Martina. He knew she wasn't stupid enough to show up undisguised, so he concentrated his search on anyone walking with the aid of a cane or crutches. Those in a wheelchair didn't escape his vigilant eyes either.

Suddenly an engine revved to life, drawing everyone's attention to the end of the runway where they saw somebody walk away from the car and climb on a motorcycle and head back to the waiting crew.

Nicole started filming the car as it traveled down the road, gaining speed with every passing second. The hand that held the camera started shaking, her nervousness winning control of her body. Her breathing became ragged as panic gained ground. Nicole held her breath as she watched Kris' car thunder down the runway, heading straight for the pipe ramp that had been solidly affixed into the asphalt, ready to do its job.

Bringing the car up to the planned speed, Kris lined the Malibu dead center with the seven feet high pipe ramp, which ended up in a steep angled kicker. She prepared both her body and mind for the incredible shocks that would soon follow. Taking one last deep breath before she hit the ramp, Kris relaxed her muscles as best she could.

Nicole watched through the eyepiece of her video camera, her heart beating furiously as the stunt car approached at an incredible speed and climbed the ramp, lifting the Malibu up off the ground and sliding on top of the pipe ramp. The car had tilted down on the left caused by a last minute shift of the front wheels before the steep angled kicker threw the vehicle into a roll on its left side. Flying as it left the ramp, the car was at least forty feet high in the air, slowly turning upside down, as it dropped towards the ground.

Kris felt the first jarring shock as she went over, feeling the angled kicker push the car off the ramp and turn the Malibu into a side roll. A moment of weightlessness happened as the car floated in the air like a bird, slowly turning upside down. Kris knew that this was just the calm before the storm as she felt the Malibu make its descent towards the ground, nose first. Biting solidly into her mouth guard and closing her eyes, there was nothing the stuntwoman could do but ride it out.

The car headed down at a frightening speed and hit the ground with the screeching sound of tearing metal as it landed on its front right side. The shock of the collision made the Malibu bounce off the ground and spin sideways to land along the length of its left side and put the car rolling over and over so many times that people lost count.

Gasps were heard from the crowd over the deafening sound of the tearing metal as the car was pulled apart, sending shards of metal flying everywhere with every roll of the Malibu.

As the car rolled pass Nicole, the crew ran towards the twisted mass of metal. She kept her unsteady hands on the video camera, trying to follow the tumbling automobile and started off after the rest of the Austrian crew.

Kristina held on for dear life as the car rolled over for what seemed like an eternity. She was glad that she had worn her shin guards as her legs slammed up to smash again and again under the dashboard. She felt her side of the car being pushed inwards as another hit sent her crashing against the harnesses. Her hands kept their solid hold on the security straps for fear of losing her grip and risk having her arm injured by the buckling metal.

The car finally slowed down in its rolls, tumbling once more and then coming to rest upside down on its roof. Nicole ran, oblivious to the quality of the videotape that was still rolling. Solid arms stopped her from going any closer and she looked through tear filled eyes at Marianne who split her attention from the crew that checked on Kris to Nicole who looked like a nervous wreck.

Cheers could be heard from the spectators as everybody moved down along the fence to get a better view of the car and the working crew. The chain link fence toppled over from the sheer number of people pushing against it, opening up a path for the spectators to walk through and get a closer look at the stuntwoman still trapped in the car.

Seeing that a section of the fence had collapsed and the crowd heading towards the main competition grounds, Klaus changed directions and ran towards Nicole. It would be a lot more difficult to protect the young woman if Martina chose this moment to act.

Ludwig quickly went to the Malibu and worriedly crouched low to reach his sister. "Kris! Can you hear me?" Silence was his only answer. The sirens from the medic unit were soon heard as the ambulance stopped close by and the medics got out in a hurry to inquire about the stuntwoman. Ludwig leaned down on the ground and reached for Kris, gently lifting her visor and peered at her face. Kris was immobile, her eyes closed. Some movement on the other side showed Tiny carefully making his way inside the car from the passenger's side. With trembling fingers, Ludwig touched his sister's hand that still held the harness tightly and squeezed it.

One blue eye slowly cracked open and looked at him, fighting through the haze of dizziness as she tried to focus on the form that was close to her. She quickly shut her eyes again as the nausea assaulted her senses. "Tell the car it can stop rolling now," Kris mumbled as she spit the mouth guard out of her mouth.

A wave of relief washed over both men as they looked at each other with a grin. Moving aside to let the paramedic do his job, Ludwig watched as his sister moved both of her arms in response to the medic's questions.

Nicole could barely stand in place as the minutes seemed to stretch on into hours. She tried to see any signs, good or bad that would let her know about her lover's condition. She held her breath as Ludwig pressed on the five-point harness' release button and freed Kris from her restraints. Somebody supported her shoulders as her body slumped forward from its sudden release.

They gently pulled the stuntwoman out of the car and the crowd went wild as Kris stood on her own two feet, lightly held by the medic and Ludwig. She took her helmet off and the padded collar as she looked to try and spot her young lover.

Seeing that she was all right, Nicole gave the video camera to Marianne and ran to Kris, and wrapped her arms around the tall woman's neck. She was quickly lifted off the ground as Kris held the small woman in her arms.

"I'm so glad you're okay," Nicole said when she was put back to the ground. "How are you feeling?"

Kris grinned at the small woman. "Like I just came out of a blender," she joked, tweaking Nicole's nose gently. "I'm okay really, Nick. Just a little dizzy that's all. That's a normal reaction after a spin cycle like that." Kris looked at the medic who still stood beside her.

"That feeling will pass soon." He smiled, walked to the ambulance and left for another site where the competition was still going on.

Chapter 16

Klaus found it increasingly difficult to keep an eye out for their target as the crowd rushed excitedly around to get a closer look at the stuntwoman and congratulate her. Men, women and children walked the grounds freely. Even the older folks were thrilled by the performance they had just witnessed as they moved in to try and get Kris' attention. Even with all the added personnel, the security still had trouble trying to contain the crowd.

As the crowd grew rowdier, one old woman was rudely pushed by the fans, almost causing her to lose her balance. She tried to grip somebody's arm to stand upright and smiled at the young man who kindly helped her make her way to a calmer area.

The Austrian crew surrounded the stuntwoman, clapping her on the back and cheered as the judges announced a new world record for the number of rolls performed by a car on a flat surface. Unfortunately, a few points had been shaved off for the performance due to the change from the original stunt plan. Nonetheless, everybody was thrilled with the results and even though they had almost lost a few people caused by the explosion of the first car, everything had gone better than expected.

The security personnel tried their best to control the pushing crowd by backing them away from the celebrating Austrians. Klaus noticed a woman wearing sunglasses and a hat make her way towards the group, leaning heavily on a cane. He quickly went to intercept her and noticed from up close that this woman wasn't Martina. Frustrated, Klaus looked around and spotted two women in wheelchairs, an old woman holding on to a man's arm as well as a woman using crutches. Taking a second look at the woman with the crutches, he caught a glimpse of red hair sticking out under the wide brimmed hat she wore. Klaus decided to head towards her next.

"What if we move this party to the pub and celebrate properly!" Ludwig practically had to shout to be heard over the cheers of the crowd surrounding them.

Still holding Nicole tightly in her arms and laughing with the crew, Kris suddenly felt a chill run through her as the crowd pushed closer and closer. She glanced at the people around them, realizing that the situation was getting out of control. She was about to lead Nicole out of the crowd when a loud bang was heard and Nicole slumped in Kris' arms with a cry of pain.

"Nicole!" Kris screamed as she held on to the young woman and helped her down to the ground. Marianne and the two investigators quickly blocked with their bodies any access to the women.

The crowd parted in front of them, scared by the sudden sound of gunfire and someone hurt. Some people ran away, screaming and causing panic and confusion for everybody else. The only ones that hadn't bolted like rabbits were the women in wheelchairs, the two people on crutches and the old woman. The security personnel and the Austrian crew looked everywhere to find where that gunshot had come from.

Kris looked frantically for Nicole's wound and saw that a bullet had hit the back of her right thigh. The tall woman quickly covered the injury with her hand, putting pressure on the wound to stop the bleeding.

"Ludwig!" she yelled, trying to get his attention through all of the panic around them. She looked back down at Nicole who had her eyes closed in pain. "We're gonna get you out of here, love. Hang on." She looked up with fire in her eyes around them and screamed her frustration. "Where the hell are you, Martina?" she yelled into the crowd, feeling helpless as she looked out at all the people that were still near them.

Ludwig rushed to Kris' side and quickly replaced her bloody hand with a T-shirt one of the crew had taken off and offered.

Nicole clutched Kris' arm as pain shot down her leg. A laugh born out of insanity replied to the stuntwoman's call as Kris looked up to see an old woman standing several paces in front of them with her arms crossed over her chest. As the dark haired woman looked into the elder's eyes, recognition flashed through Kris'.

Additional security personnel quickly made their way towards the assembled group and stopped, looking around but seeing no apparent threat.

Knowing that Ludwig and Marianne would be taking care of Nicole, Kris got up and pushed her way past the investigators to stand between her lover and the woman.

"The game's over Martina," she spat. "Take off your disguise."

The old woman laughed as her right hand slipped out from under her arm, removed the gun she was hiding up her large sleeve and leveled it at Kris. With the left hand, she quickly reached under her chin and pulled at the latex mask that had been covering her face and took the movie make-up off as the gray wig fell to the ground at her feet.

Seeing that Martina had made her way through, Klaus got out his cell phone and dialed the number for the plain-clothes police officers that were looking out for her on the competition grounds.

"You're such an easy target, Kristina." Martina chuckled, then looked at the brothers and technicians from the corner of her eye as they slowly surrounded the gunwoman. "That's right, keep moving because my trigger finger is itching to shoot her," the redhead warned.

"Everybody, stay where you are," Kris calmly told the crew, but was directing her command especially at Trish who had slowly snuck in close to Martina from the left side. The investigator understood and stopped where she was. "You want me? Here I am, Martina, but let everyone else go." A sadistic laugh was her only reply.

"Do you honestly think I care about your little play thing?"

Martina spat as she looked at the blonde hiding behind Kris. "I don't think so. All I care about is making you suffer as much as possible." She aimed the gun over Kris' body from her head, snaking down to her torso and then slowly coming to aim at her left shoulder.

Kris watched the woman like a hawk, trying to guess her next move. As she saw the gun change directions, she focused on the trigger finger, knowing that Martina wouldn't bluff and prepared to avoid the bullet as best as she could. She watched apprehensively as the redhead squeezed the trigger. Kris twisted sideways, hoping that her reflexes would be fast enough, to no avail. The bullet crashed into her right shoulder just below where her collarbone and shoulder met.

"No!" Nicole cried out as she caught a glimpse between Marianne and Ludwig of her lover being shot. She tried to get up, but was held back by numerous hands and by the pain in her leg.

Kris fell down on her knee, bent over in pain, cradling her arm close to her. Her jaw tightened in rage as the look of near ecstasy brightened Martina's face. Slowly getting back on her feet, Kris kept her eyes on the insane woman as the redhead chuckled.

"How does it feel?" she asked. "How do you like the pain of torn muscles and flesh? After all, it's only fair that you start to experience what I went through since you were the cause of it." Martina indicated her artificial limbs. "Your pain is so delicious to me...and it's only begun."

"I had nothing to do with your accident," Kris said through clenched teeth, her shoulder throbbing painfully. "I wasn't even there when it happened."

"No, you weren't," Martina agreed, enjoying the look of suffering on the dark haired woman's face. "But you knew that by causing me to lose my focus, I would make a mistake. That's exactly what you did when you accused me of stealing those explosives." Martina became agitated as she relived the memories of her accident.

"Why would I want you to get into an accident? It doesn't make sense," Kris demanded as she noticed movement behind the gunwoman and saw men approaching silently with guns drawn.

She surmised they were plain clothed policemen. She hoped they were anyway, remembering Martina's late henchman.

"Why?" Martina tilted her head as she laughed, causing her to notice the new arrivals sneaking up behind her. "Why she asks. Because you wanted me out of your way. You didn't want any competition." She nearly screamed her frustration as she shifted on her artificial legs. "You tried everything to discredit me. Did everything so I couldn't find any work," she yelled, spit flying from her mouth. "Did you know that I couldn't find any work for two years because of all the lies you told about me?"

Watching from the corner of her eyes, Kris saw one of the men slowly walk closer to Martina aiming his gun at her legs.

"I wouldn't do that if I were you," Martina sang to the armed man behind her as her gun roamed over Kris' body, finally aiming at her legs. "I finally found some work and you managed to make it the last job I would ever have," the redhead continued, losing her smile as the rage shook her body. "With me in the hospital, you had to do the stunt yourself and get a new world record. That should have been mine!" she screamed, the hand holding the gun becoming unsteady. "I'll make you suffer the same way you did me."

As she was about to pull the trigger a second time, a shot rang out and a force rocked through one of Martina's artificial legs as a bullet tore through the plastic of her prosthetics. She was taken off balance by the gun shot but quickly recovered. In a moment of fury, Martina twisted to look at the surprised cop and sneered, "I warned you not to do that. That's Kris' gift to me." She pulled the trigger on the policeman, the bullet ripping through the man's leg. Quickly, she turned her attention back on Kris when movement from two more directions came at her.

Seeing that Martina's attention had been diverted, Kris launched herself in a tackle towards the gunwoman while Trish made her move at the same time.

The investigator had the advantage over Martina as she was in her blind spot. Her quick reflexes and close proximity gave Trish the jump over Kris at tackling the insane woman. She slammed her body into Martina sideways, sending the redhead sprawling to the ground as she lost her grip on the gun, causing it to skip across the pavement out of her reach.

Kristina pounced on top of both women, grabbing Martina by her throat with one hand in a vice like grip while she pulled back the other hand ready to slam her fist in the redhead's face. As she hauled back her right arm, her shoulder screamed out in pain. She winced, but otherwise ignored the shooting pain in favor of delivering her revenge.

All the policemen present rushed over to the women on the ground, and tried to pull Kris away from the gunwoman, with very little success.

"Kris, don't!" a voice yelled behind her.

The tall woman's fist halted half way down to its target, ready to strike at the sneering face as Nicole's voice broke through her fury and registered in her mind.

"It's over, Kris. Let the police handle her," Nicole said. "Please? It's the right thing to do." She could see the rage shaking her lover's body as Kris still held the woman on the ground by her throat.

Torn between wanting revenge for Nicole's and Franz's injuries, and doing what was right, Kris took a deep, shaky breath. The crazed eyes of her enemy stared back at her, sneering their resentment. *Just one hit,* she thought, but she knew Nicole was right. It was over. "Just be thankful that I listened to her," she said, as she painfully stood up and let the police officers handle Martina.

The police dragged Martina to her feet with minimal resistance as she started laughing. The policemen ignored her insane laughter and put her in handcuffs.

"Contrary to what you think, Kristina, this isn't over!" Martina screamed over her shoulder as she twisted in the cop's hands trying to look at Kris who had turned her back on her and headed to Nicole. "I'll get out you know. And when I do, I'm gonna finish the job I started!" The insanity flashed in Martina's eyes as she was led away by the police to a waiting car.

Ignoring the screams from Martina, Kris went back to Nicole. She fell to her knees and enveloped the small woman with her one good arm while a medic pushed his way through to care for Kris' injury.

"I'm so sorry," Kris whispered into Nicole's ear, ignoring everyone around them. She leaned her forehead tiredly against her lover's head and closed her eyes as silent tears rolled down her cheeks. "If it wasn't for me, none of this would have happened to you."

"You can't blame yourself for what happened, love," Nicole said as she hugged the older woman. "It wasn't your fault."

"Yes, it was," Kris said with defeat in her voice. "Your father went after you because of me." Her voice cracked with emotion. "Martina did the same just to hurt me. I wonder if being with me was the best thing for you to do," she finished in a whisper. She was pushed away by Nicole as flashing emerald eyes stared back at her.

"Don't you dare say anything like that," Nicole said in a tight voice. "Being with you is the best thing that ever happened to me." She grabbed Kris' racing suit and shook her slightly. "My father was unstable and anyone or anything would have eventually pushed him over the edge." Her voice gentled as she spotted tears falling freely from Kris' eyes. "And Martina, she was so jealous of you that it drove her mad. She couldn't accept the fact that everything that happened to her was her own fault. She may blame you for everything, but don't let her win by thinking she's right."

"But..."

"Now you listen to me, Kristina, being with you and being loved by you means more to me than anything." Nicole lifted the tall woman's chin to look into the watery blue eyes. "I'll never regret the first time we met or the second time around," she said with a gentle smile. "I love you and I want to spend the rest of my life with you." Nicole hugged her lover, as Kris' sobs shook the hard body under her.

Kris closed her eyes as she held on to Nicole. She knew this strong young woman she held in her arms was her life and that without her, her life would be meaningless. After all, how could one live without the other half of their soul? She buried her face in the silky blonde hair, breathing in Nicole's scent. "I love you, too."

The sounds surrounding them faded away as they completely melted into one another, oblivious to everything but the love that they shared.

Kris was faintly aware that the medic patched her up as best as he could and was trying to get her to come to the ambulance while somebody stood on her left side, a hand gently resting on her shoulder. She slowly opened her eyes to look into Marianne's, refusing to let Nicole go. Her sister's eyes were sympathetic to their plight. The dark haired woman glanced behind her friend and noticed for the first time that Ludwig hadn't left his post by her injured lover, even after the medics had taken over his task of patching up the younger woman.

Knowing that both women hadn't suffered life-threatening injuries and seeing the medics bring the stretchers to them, Marianne grinned. "Guess this means another trip to the hospital for you both." She watched as the injured police officer was put into an ambulance.

"I hate hospitals," Kris and Nicole said at the same time with chagrin. They looked at each other and laughed despite the pain they were in.

❖❖❖❖❖❖❖

Nicole looked around her private hospital room, completely bored out of her mind. Kris usually came by early in the mornings to keep her company, but it was nearly noon and oddly, no sign of her lover. The doctors had told her that her leg was doing much better now and she would soon be able to go home.

She reached over to a small table next to the bed and picked up the mystery book Marianne had brought her. She pressed the button on the bed to incline it so that she was in a sitting position to read more comfortably.

As she opened the book to the first page, her eyes read over it but her mind was elsewhere; namely back home with Kris in Austria. A warm summer's night, some champagne with only the light of the moon—a soft knock? Nicole broke out of her reverie as a beautiful face peeked in from behind the door.

"Good morning," Kris said with a grin as she strolled into the room, suspiciously hiding something behind her back as the door closed behind her. She walked up to the bed and gently kissed Nicole on the lips. "How are you feeling today?" She put the bag she held on the small table beside the bed.

"I'm doing better now that you're here." Nicole smiled as she put her book away, wincing slightly as she moved her leg uncomfortably.

Kris gave her friend a worried look. "Are you in pain? You want me to get the nurse?" she asked, fussing over the younger woman.

Nicole laughed, gently patting Kris' stomach. "No, I'm fine. I'm just bored." She tugged on Kris' shirt, bringing the tall woman closer to her for another kiss. "When can I get out of here?"

"Real soon, I'm working on it," Kris said with a grin as she sat on the edge of the bed.

"You mean you're terrorizing the staff," Nicole stated with a knowing grin and laughed as Kris shrugged her shoulders, trying to look very innocent.

"I just want you back with me, that's all," Kris said as she picked at the non-existing lint on the blanket.

"Oh, love, I know," Nicole said. "I can't wait to be back home with you too."

Kris smiled as she swung her legs onto the bed and leaned back, wrapping her left arm around Nicole's shoulders, bringing her young lover closer to her. They were just lying there, enjoying one another when a knock sounded and the door opened. Marianne slowly poked her head around the door.

"Am I interrupting?" she asked with a grin.

"Come in." Nicole smiled and twisted onto her back to see Marianne without straining her neck and still manage to keep a loving hold on Kris.

"I warn you, I'm not alone. Hope you don't mind?" she asked and opened the door before Nicole could answer.

Marianne walked into the room followed by Franz being pushed in his wheelchair by Ludwig. Hans strutted in with a huge smile then Klaus and Kyle brought up the rear.

"Hey guys," Nicole exclaimed with excitement at seeing all the familiar smiling faces, especially Franz since it was the first time she'd seen him since before the explosion. "What a great surprise." She looked at her grinning lover. "You knew about this?" She gave Kris a squeeze.

"That's why I was late today, sorry." She smiled sheepishly, kissing Nicole on the forehead. Another knock was heard on the door as it opened again and Gunther, Steve and Tiny walked in with bags of food.

"Thought you'd be sick of hospital food by now, so we took the liberty to stop for some burgers and fries. American food, Swedish style," Tiny said as they put the bags on the table.

"You guys are great." Nicole laughed as she hugged Kris before taking the offered burger from Gunther. "Hmmm, this sure beats that tasteless stuff they call food around here. And being woken up late in the evening to take a sleeping pill. Ugh. No wonder I hate hospitals," Nicole managed to say in-between mouthfuls of burger and fries.

"At least when I wake you up it's not for a pill," Kris whispered in Nicole's ear after swallowing her food. Nicole couldn't help the smile that spread onto her face as she chewed.

Looking about the small hospital room, Kris couldn't help but think how thankful she was to see her family and friends all together laughing and smiling once again. They had survived a near tragedy and everyone made it out alive—most of them anyway. They were going to miss Johan.

The competition was over now, with the Swedes having won by a few extra points over the Austrian team. The crew received a special commendation for their courage and perseverance to go on with the show even when faced with such adverse conditions.

Nicole snuggled comfortably against Kris' side as she and Marianne chatted away like long lost sisters. Her hand automatically settled itself onto Kris' muscular thigh and softly rubbed it, earning an unknowing smile from Kris. Marianne's eyes glimpsed the small gesture and smiled inwardly at the happy couple.

Everyone had been talking and laughing for quite a while when the door opened and Frida and Lars walked in, surprised at seeing so many people in the small room. The crew warmly greeted them as everyone clapped Lars on the back or shook his hand for a stunt well done, putting the Swedish team in first place. After saying hello to everyone, Frida headed towards Nicole and Kris who were still on the bed watching everyone with smiles on their faces.

"Nice party you have here." Frida smiled as she sat on the bed on the other side of Nicole. "How are you guys feeling?"

"Not too bad, but I'll feel much better once I'm out of here." Nicole chuckled as she looked at Kris who nodded vigorously.

The four women looked at the men when they broke out into laughter, teasing Hans about some new girlfriend of his. Hans simply stood there, smiling and shaking his head as a slight blush crept up his cheeks.

"She's just a friend," Hans said laughing as he playfully pushed Ludwig. "Unless she wants to come to Austria, I've had enough of Sweden." He looked around the room and remembered that Frida and Lars were there. "Nothing personal, you guys."

A few nods agreed with both statements. "I know I'm looking forward to being in my own bed again," Franz said as he made a face, trying to scratch under his cast. "And out of this damn thing." Everybody laughed knowing first hand how itchy a person could get with a cast on.

"I know Nicole and I will be taking a *long* vacation once things get back to normal. We've had enough excitement to last us a lifetime," Kris said and Nicole gave her a squeeze. She bent down to kiss the top of her head.

Ludwig nodded his approval to their plans. "I suppose a couple weeks of vacation will do you good."

"A couple of weeks? Nuh-uh, I mean a couple of months." She smiled down at the sparkling green eyes looking back at her. "We already talked about taking a trip somewhere." She looked at her lover with an amused twinkle in her eye. "I also have a few other things in mind, but that's a surprise." She grinned at Nicole who was now genuinely intrigued.

"A surprise?" she asked, her eyes lighting up like a child's at Christmas. "Come on, tell me."

"Nope."

"Please?" Nicole pleaded, giving Kris her sad puppy dog look as she batted her eyelashes. Her friend held firm so she decided to try a new approach. She put her hand under Kris' shirt and ran her fingertips lightly over her lover's taut stomach. "Please?" she tried again to no avail. Several snickers around the room sounded at Nicole's frustrated sigh.

"I'll tell you once everybody is gone," Kris promised, letting out a little chuckle to try and cover her suddenly labored breathing. She didn't need her family teasing her about the effect Nicole had on her even though she wanted nothing more than for her to continue her gentle exploration.

"All right then." Nicole turned to everybody. "All of you out, now," she ordered with a smile, only getting laughter in return. "Just kidding." She chuckled.

"Well, I know that I have to go soon. I have a flight back to Austria," Klaus said as he approached Kris. "I'm all done with the police here."

"How did it go?" Kris asked, knowing that his investigators' tapes would probably put Martina away in a prison or a psychiatric ward for quite some time by themselves.

"After the cops went to the barn, searching for more evidence, they came across an enclosed room that was well hidden and found a little girl," Klaus said. A few surprised exclamations came from those who weren't fully aware of everything that had gone on. "After talking with Johan's wife, we discovered Martina had kidnapped their daughter. One more charge to add to the list."

"Martina kidnapped a little girl?" Gunther exclaimed in disbelief, looking at the investigator.

"It seems that she wanted to make sure that Johan would follow her plan," Klaus said.

"How's the girl?" Kris asked.

"Physically, she's unharmed. However, when the police found her she was a little dehydrated, hungry, tired and very scared, but they say she'll be okay," Klaus said, to the relief of all present.

"I still can't figure out how Martina was able to drive that car away from the barn," Steve said. "It wasn't equipped for a handicapped driver, was it?"

The private investigator shook his head no. "This is the latest news I got. Apparently, Martina was able to move about better than we thought. The cane she always had with her was only used to get sympathy. She didn't really need it. But, she did use it to help her drive that car."

"I'm not following you," Steve said, confused.

"When the police inspected her car that was found at the competition grounds, they were looking for foot prints but found round dots on both the gas and brake pedals. It was later discovered that she was using her cane to push on them instead of her feet."

"She's full of surprises isn't she?" Gunther said, shaking his head.

"I'm sorry, Kris," Franz suddenly said, causing everybody to be silent.

"Sorry for what?" his sister asked as she looked at him. Franz had been quiet ever since the group had started talking about Martina.

"I should have listened to you. You were right about her all along," he said, refusing to look into her eyes. "I really thought she wasn't as bad as you said she was. Just a case of tough luck I guess."

"I could have been wrong just as easily," Kris said. "I'm just sorry that I was right, Franz." She hesitated until he looked up at her. "We often don't see eye to eye about lots of stuff, but that's what makes all of us stronger. We talk, discuss—"

"Scream and yell," Ludwig continued.

"Complain and bitch," Hans chipped in.

"We get the picture, guys," Kris quipped as everybody laughed, breaking the mounting tension. "What I'm trying to say is that by sharing our opinions, we get somewhere. Don't you start agreeing with everything I say."

"Or else we'll really be in trouble," Marianne added, not wanting to be left out. That earned her a playful nudge on her leg from Kris' foot.

"Well, I really do have to go," Klaus said as he shook Kris' hand and squeezed Nicole's shoulder. "See you back in Austria, my friend."

"Take care and thank you for everything," Kris said.

"Just wait until you get my bill," he said on his way out the door. "Take care everybody."

Kris turned her attention to Marianne and lifted an eyebrow, expecting something from her.

"Ah...yes, well we have to go too, right guys?" she asked the rest of the group.

She got a few quizzical looks from some of her brothers.

"You know, that 'thing' we discussed earlier?" she hinted with a stern stare and a raised eyebrow for them to leave Kris and Nicole alone now.

"Ah, yes. The 'thing,'" Ludwig agreed as he walked to Franz' wheelchair and rolled him towards the door. "You too, guys," he said to the Swedes who exchanged confused looks. "We'll explain later."

Nicole watched with a frown as everybody filed out of the room, one by one whispering amongst themselves. She noticed that a few smiles grew on the departing faces while Marianne flashed her a final grin and then disappeared behind the closing door.

"What was that all about?" she asked as Kris reached for the bag on the table beside the bed and put it on Nicole's lap. The young woman looked down at the bag with a growing grin of her own, amusement and excitement playing across her face. "Is that for me?"

Kris nodded. "I wanted to give this to you before we go back to Austria, but this isn't exactly the way that I had planned to do it." She smiled at the frown on Nicole's face. "Go ahead, look inside."

A smile tugged at Nicole's lips at the mirrored excitement on Kris' face. She brought the bag closer to her and took the colored paper out of it and peeked inside with a smile. "Oh, this is so cute," Nicole exclaimed as she pulled out a stuffed tiger and held it up in front of her. "Thanks, Tiger." She smiled as she brushed her fingers in the soft fur, only then noticing the small box that dangled from a ribbon hanging from its jaw. Nicole looked up at Kris who was watching her closely. Nicole took the box with a trembling hand and freed it from the ribbon, cradling the toy between Kris and herself.

The dark haired woman watched as Nicole slowly opened the box and held her breath as her young lover reached shaking fingers to touch the ring that was inside. As sparkling emerald eyes looked back at her, Kris took the ring out of the box and smiled nervously.

"I know this isn't the most romantic place I could do this, but I didn't want to wait any longer," Kris explained, her voice breaking from the emotion that tugged at her heart. "You mean so much to me Nicole, I'd be lost without you." She slid the ring onto Nicole's finger. "You're my reason for living." She looked at Nicole's face, seeing a lone tear making its way down her soft cheek.

Nicole's heart beat at a furious pace. She couldn't take her eyes off of the ring, hoping that this wasn't a dream. She brushed her finger on the intricate carving on the small jewel and looked at her smiling friend when she recognized where she had seen the carving before. It was the same pattern as Kris' silver bracelet.

"I want to spend the rest of my life with you. If you'll have me," she added with a grin, trying hard to keep her own tears from falling.

The petite blonde tried to speak but her lover's action had left her speechless and nodded with a smile. "Yes I do," she managed to say and wrapped her arms around Kris' waist, leaning her head on her uninjured shoulder. "It's beautiful Kris."

"Look in the bag again," Kris said, her voice close to breaking.

Nicole pulled the bag close to her and peered inside, then reached in to take another box out. She looked up at Kris who nodded for her to open it. Inside was a larger duplicate of her ring. She took it out as a fresh wave of tears streamed down her cheeks as she put her still trembling hand to her lips and took a ragged breath. Nicole gently held the larger hand in hers and slid the ring on Kris' finger.

"You're my first love, my best friend, my soulmate," Nicole said as she brushed the tears that fell freely down the older woman's cheeks.

Kris bent down to kiss not only her lover, but also the woman who held the other half of her soul for all eternity.

Also from
Yellow Rose Books
be sure to read

Lost Paradise: Book One
by Francine Quesnel

Kristina Von Deering is a young, wealthy Austrian stuntwoman working on an Austrian/Canadian film project in Montreal. On location, she meets and eventually falls in love with a young gopher and aspiring camerawoman named Nicole McGrail. Their friendship and love is threatened by Nicole's father who sees their relationship as deviant and unnatural. He does everything in his power to put an end to it.

Available at booksellers everywhere.
ISBN: 1-930928-12-2

Other titles to look for in the
coming months from
Yellow Rose Books

Prairie Fire
 By LJ Maas

Many Roads To Travel
 By Karen King and Nann Dunne

Second Chances
 By Lynne Norris

Innocent Hearts
 By Radclyffe

Strength of the Heart
 By Carrie Carr

Northern Peace and Perils
 By Francine Quesnel

Faith
 By Angela Chapman

Francine Quesnel has been living in Quebec for all of her life and presently resides in a suburb of Montreal Canada.

Aside from spending nearly all of her free time writing, she is the production supervisor for a mobile PC company. A retired military officer, Fran loves horses, ancient history, movies and music.

For years she has volunteered her time on numerous occasion in doing all kinds of charity work.

Printed in the United States
4091